The CITY *of* ICE

The GATES *of the* WORLD *Book Two*

K. M. McKINLEY

SOLARIS

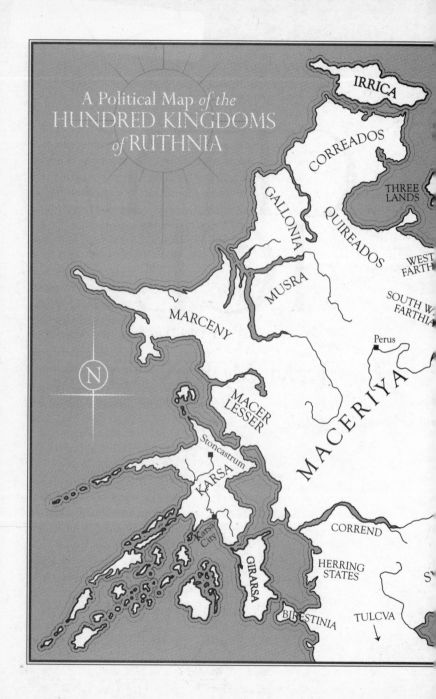

A Political Map *of the*
HUNDRED KINGDOMS
of RUTHNIA

IRRICA

CORREADOS

THREE
LANDS

GALLONIA

QUIREADOS

WEST
FARTH

MUSRA

SOUTH W.
FARTHIA

MARCENY

Perus

MACER
LESSER

MACERIYA

Stoncastrum

KARSA

CORREND

Karsy
City

HERRING
STATES

GIRARSA

S

BILESTINIA

TULCVA

THE CITY OF ICE

First published 2017 by Solaris
an imprint of Rebellion Publishing Ltd,
Riverside House, Osney Mead,
Oxford, OX2 0ES, UK

www.solarisbooks.com

ISBN: 978 1 78108 485-4

10 9 8 7 6 5 4 3 2 1

A CIP catalogue record for this book is available
from the British Library.

Designed & typeset by Rebellion Publishing

Printed and bound by Nørhaven, Denmark

PROLOGUE
The False Pantheon

ADAMANKA SHRANE KICKED her way through guano and dracon-bird skeletons. The ancient floor creaked under her weight. Hundreds of feet below the whispered devotions of Bishop Rousinteau hissed around giant columns of polished granite. Up there, in the forgotten lofts of the Pantheon Maximale there was no sign of the divine, only dust, and shit and dead vermin.

It amused her greatly that she, harbinger of the Iron Gods, should find sanctuary in the house of the false gods of Ruthnia, that the spokesman of the false gods should be the pawn that would usher in the return of the iron, and that she wove her schemes under Rousinteau's nose. Ironies within ironies.

The Pantheon Maximale had seen better days. Worship of the false gods had ceased to be fashionable once Res Iapetus had ejected them from the world. Until recently, and the spread of Rousinteau's apocalyptic cult, the pantheon had been left half-abandoned. The city councils had squabbled over what to do with the Pantheon, it had seen use as a venue for the arts, a school, even a barracks for a brief time. Gradually, it had fallen into decay, until Rousinteau and his mysterious backers had taken it off the city's hands and restored it as a place of worship.

She could think of no better place to hide.

She passed under huge beams holding up a lead-roofed turret, and into her lodgings. There was little in there: a bed, for even she needed to sleep, her holy book, a change of clothes, a flask of wine and one of water. Vessels for ablutions, all hidden away when she was absent. But it was clean, swept free of the choking dust of bird droppings, and safe.

She got down on her knees. Already last year's rejuvenation at the pool of the Iron Fane was fading. Next year, the one after at the latest, she would need to visit it again, if the world was not about to change.

She sketched a double circle on the floor, meticulously filling in the band with words she could read but could not speak. When done, she scrutinised it a few moments, then stepped carefully within, sat down, and placed her wooden staff across her knees.

She fell into a trance quickly. Her spirit left her body, and soared up over the many roofs of the Pantheon Maximale, up over Perus, past the so-called Godhome, and onward into the sky. Only a year ago she did not have this ability. As her masters grew in strength, so did she.

Ruthnia spread itself at her feet. She saw from the Tiriatic ocean in the west to the distance-faded mountains of the Appins.

Her destination was in neither of those places, or anywhere in between.

She flew higher, up into thin air, where the sky turned thin and purple, then beyond into the endless black, and toward the Twin. No other could pursue a sending so far, no other but her, for she was summoned by her masters, and they aided her where all others were sent away. Four times she had done this. Four times she had been to commune with the iron masters, and each time her power grew.

The Twin grew black and huge, the Earth blue and insignificant. Once more she was in its inimical atmosphere, and descended through black clouds to a landscape of bare rock and flame.

A palace awaited her. Its fabric offered no resistance, and she passed through it as a ghost and into the interior.

No building on the Earth was this big, for the palace was scaled for giants.

She arrived in a hall dominated by a giant throne. Upon it sat the king of the Iron Gods, his advisers at either arm. They too were gargantuan, but childlike in stature compared to their lord. Whereas she... What was she? A sparrow, a gnat, a nothing.

"I have come as commanded," she said.

The great lord stood, taller than a mountain.

"Ute-mene arbani kulleat…" it said in a voice as loud as the death of worlds.

A quieter voice, speaking Maceriyan, spoke over it.

"Servant of the Draathis, you are welcome. The time has come. You are able to come between the worlds, and so the wards of our enemy are weakened. Soon, we shall leave this place. Soon, we shall take our birthright."

"Kandan irrit makane arban…" went on the god's voice.

"Yet there is much for our servant to do. The last of our enemies must be destroyed. The first of the gates must be opened. You are not sufficient alone for this task."

Shrane lifted her head from the floor.

"My lord, I…"

The god ignored her interruption.

"Kandan mendene zeebar arbanak," it said.

"You shall be divided. You shall do the work of two in one."

Two of the Iron Gods came from the shadows, and set her on her feet with burning hands. How different they were compared to the last example of their kind upon the Earth. He was battered, hidden in the depths of the fane. The skin of these was still black and lustrous, free of the corrosion that crippled the other.

"Zeebar acckin arbani," said the god.

"The servant will take these staves," said the quieter voice.

Her hands flew out to her side. Two rods of red hot iron appeared in her hands. They burned her soul, and she screamed.

"Zeebar arbanak ute zeebar acckini," said the god king.

"From two staves, two servants."

The king himself rose from his throne. He held out his giant's hand. A blade of fire sprang up from his fist, and he smote her with it, splitting her spirit in two from the crown of her head to her crotch. She came apart, her being consumed with agony.

An unmeasurable time passed. The pain faded.

"Makanak," said the king.

"It is done," said the voice. "No longer Iron Priestess, but Iron Mages! Return to the Earth and serve us well."

Shrane had so much to ask, but no opportunity. The halves of her soul whirled away through the palace roof, back through the clouds and into the void between worlds, falling toward the Earth.

She slammed back into her flesh.

When Adamanka Shrane opened her eyes, she was staring at her own face. Eyes identical to hers looked back. Their movements mirroring each other perfectly, the two Adamanka Shranes sat up. In their hands were twinned iron staves, her original wooden staff was a line of black charcoal on the floor between, bisecting the magical circle.

"Truly," they said together, "the gods are mighty."

Winter was nearly over. In a few weeks time, Vardeuche Persin's ships would set out on their race to the pole and the city of ice there.

And one of her would be with him.

CHAPTER ONE
Rel Pursued

ARAMAZ SPED OVER the desert, head bobbing mechanically back and forth. After so long a gallop the dracon was tiring. His breath whistled in his nostrils. Foam sheathed his jaw.

The lights of the moons glittered off the Black Sands. A star field of infinite depth and intensity filled the sky horizon to horizon, the glittering of the sands made a second cosmos beneath the dracon's feet.

Cold, pure air burned Rel's nose and tore tears from his eyes. It seemed he rode in the void between the stars. He was at one with Aramaz, they were a single being made of two, flying like thought through the sky. His recalled his brother Aarin saying that the moment of purest clarity came before death. Rel had laughed, asking how anyone could possible know. Aarin had been so pompous when first invested, and Rel loved to rile him. Rel's laughter had died in his throat at the look in his brother's eyes. Aarin already knew so much about death, even then.

Silence fled. The hounds of the modalmen bayed upon the sands, coming ever closer. For hours the hounds had been chasing them. Soon it would all be over.

Finally, years later, Rel understood what Aarin meant.

Rel looked grimly ahead, the rhythm of his movement matched to his mount's, willing the reptile to find the strength to run until morning, though he could not conceive of why daylight would bring any reprieve. Deamathaani was far in front. In his blue robes the warlock was a pale ghost skimming the ground, his black dracon, Mordicar, virtually invisible underneath him. Deamaathani was a fine rider, Amaranth-born, raised on the savannahs bordering the Red Expanse, but none could outmatch a Khusiak in the saddle. Zorolotsev outpaced the warlock, so matched to the motions of his surging mount he appeared motionless. The two Karsans trailed, Rel ahead of Dramion who brought up the rear. Dramion swore loudly. If the exact content of his speech was lost, its sentiment was clear enough; terror had the trooper in its claws.

Rel risked a glimpse behind. Shapes moved over the dunes, starlight glinted from rippling flanks, and then cold fire ignited upon them. Ripples of colour spread over the hounds, showing their patterns. Ghostlight shone in their eyes and mouths. They no longer had need for stealth.

Dramion whipped at his dracon with his reins. His movements were out of synchronisation with his mount, and its bobbing run became a lurch. Rel rated Dramion a better rider than himself. Panic undid his expertise.

"Move damn you! Move!" screamed Dramion.

"Hurry!" shouted Rel.

The hounds sped across the desert. Rel got his first good look at them: grey skin, almost black, inset with whorled patterns of shifting gold, green and pink light. They were nothing like a man's dogs, more like dracons, larger than the biggest dray, six-legged, heads the shape of spearheads tipped with shear-edged beaks, high shoulders sloping steeply to stubby tails. Dramion screamed as the hounds closed. His mouth was wide, eyes terrified, reason fleeing the approach of death.

Face death calmly, Aarin had once said. *Show no fear. At the end, the loss of dignity is a teardrop away, as is the cessation of pain.*

Two hounds split around Dramion's dracon. It weaved from side to side in an attempt to throw its pursuers. Matching pace, the hounds snapped at the dracon's neck, forcing it to pull up. The dracon screeched. With a powerful bound it leapt over the snouts of the modalhounds, stumbling ahead. The hounds increased their speed, heavy feet thundering on the sand. They crossed in front, tripping the reptile. The dracon fell heavily, and rolled, springing back up, heedless of its rider. With a cry, Dramion tumbled from his saddle. He had his sword out before the hounds were on him.

"Come on you bastards!" he shouted.

Rel saw no blow land, and Dramion's defiant shouts became screams of agony as the hounds ripped him apart. The dracon fought hard. Modalhounds yelped as its sickle killing claws ripped into their flesh, but they were too many, and the dracon was dragged down. A hound caught the mount by the neck, twisted its beak violently, and sheared the dracon's head off.

Rel turned from the carnage and leaned further forward over Aramaz, crouching low. Wind roared in his ears, muffling the growling and snapping coming from behind. Zorolotsev had drawn far ahead. Deamaathani looked back at Rel, slowed his dracon and dropped back to ride alongside. Mordicar snorted.

"We will not survive this," said Rel. "If it comes to it, save yourself."

"Rel, I—" shouted the warlock.

"Get yourself away, by any means possible, Deamaathani. There is no need for you to die today. Get back to the fort. They will need you."

"I could," said Deamaathani. "Zorolotsev is going to get away, but we will only live if we fight."

"You can get away. Use your magic."

"It is too dangerous here, there is too much raw magic locked into the sands. I will not be able to control where I go, and my departure could set off the glimmer here for a mile around."

"I don't see a better alternative," said Rel.

"I do. We must attack." Deamaathani plucked a lance from its holder on the saddle, and turned back.

"Deamaathani!" said Rel. He swore furiously, grabbed one of his own lances, and followed.

They galloped at the hounds, scattering them. Rel counted a dozen, far too many to kill. Deamaaathani shouted out a warcry in his own language, and charged. He placed his lance exactly, skewering the hound through the heart, releasing the weapon as the hound flipped over and skidded some way on the sand, dead before it came to a halt. Mordicar snapped at a second hound coming for them, driving it away. Deamaathani wove between two more, and plucked his second lance free from its holster.

Rel drove at his own target. The monster was almost as tall as Aramaz's shoulder, and far stockier. It was difficult to miss, and Rel took it in the middle leg. It fell whining. He glanced back. It was alive but limping, out of the fight. Deamaathani hit a second, but his lance caught on the ribs, opening a long gash and broke in two before it penetrated deeply, enraging the creature. The warlock drew his sword. Rel urged Aramaz forward, digging his heels in to make it leap. Back legs extended, the dracon pounced onto a modalhound, raking its foot down its ribs and ripping it open. Aramaz jolted as he disengaged from the hound, a half-leap that turned to a sprinting stumble. Rel dropped his lance, barely keeping his seat. Aramaz levelled out and Rel drew his own sword. They jinked past a charging hound and Rel swept his sabre down. A yelp told him he hit.

Rel circled back to the warlock. Deamaathani was surrounded by hounds. Mordicar's claws and thrashing tail kept them at bay. Deamaathani slashed at them. The dracon was low to the ground in a threat display, hissing at the hounds with his mouth wide.

Another hound came at Rel. He slashed at it with his sword, opening a dark line across its glowing markings. It was unperturbed, and came at him again. A second joined it. A third came from behind. Aramaz slapped the first hard across the face with his tail, stunning it, but was forced to stop as the others crossed in front of him. The hounds stalked around Rel, snarling and clacking their beaks. Both sauraliers were surrounded.

"Deamaathani! Get away now! That is an order!"

Deamaathani looked helplessly back.

"I am sorry!" He closed his eyes. A hound leapt.

A bloom of lightning burst from the warlock, expanding rapidly into a sphere of energy, arresting the hound mid-leap. The front end was caught in the bubble. The rear fell away, trailing steaming guts.

The bubble imploded. Searing blue jags raced away over the desert. The glimmer trapped within the sands responded, liberating their load of magic in a titanic blast that lit up the desert for miles around. Rel was thrown clear of Aramaz in a tumbling chaos of flying hounds and grit. Somehow, he kept conscious. He got to his feet, ears ringing, sand in his mouth. The explosion echoed out over the desert endlessly, racing for every horizon. Lightning crackled in the sky. Zorolotsev was nowhere to be seen. Where Deamaathani had been, a circular depression of hot glass cooled to red. Hounds lay all around, three blasted to pieces. Those further away staggered round in shocked circles. Rel searched for Aramaz, catching sight of him heading over the crest of a dune. Five modalhounds remained, and they were recovering. He paused a moment, hefting his sword indecisively, then turned on his heels and ran after his dracon. The dune was steeper than he anticipated, and his feet slipped in the sand.

Moments later, the hounds followed.

The baying at his heels lent him speed. If Aramaz had halted on the far side, he may have a chance. Expecting to feel the hooked claws of the modalhounds ripping into his back at any moment, he made the dune's crest and looked out over a sea of black crowned by moonlit crescents that receded into the distance.

Aramaz' tracks led down the other side and away. Rel could not see him.

He could not outpace the hounds, not on foot. He would not escape even if he could run faster than a train.

The baying of the hounds came closer. Rel was done running.

"Come on!" he cried, spinning around. "Finish me!"

Rel felt a strange elation. Everything was beautiful, each mote of light, each pain, each breath.

The hounds had learnt caution. They bayed madly but came up the dune slowly, fanning out and prowling back and forwards thirty yards away. There they remained, and howled.

Rel and the hounds waited.

Reptilian howls answered away over the sand, many from behind Rel. The twelve he and Deamaathani had faced were but the vanguard.

"This is it. This is the end. Screwing the wrong girl," he muttered to himself. "I really wish I had listened to my mother." He laughed again. The hounds were stationary on the dune, awaiting reinforcement.

"What are you waiting for?" he yelled. "Get on with it!"

Three more hounds appeared. Two from the right, one from the bottom of the dune behind him. Strengthened in number, they advanced.

"I'm sorry," he said. "Veremond, Olb. I'm sorry. Too headstrong. Another thing I should have listened to. 'Our shortcomings are a long enough a rope to hang by', that's what father said. Well, damn him I say!" He brandished his sword, circling to keep all the hounds in sight.

Glittering sheets of sand ran behind the hounds down the dune. Their glowing mouths and eyes swept like lighthouse lanterns. Twenty yards, ten.

Rel raised his sword, marking the one he would kill first.

There was a flurry of noise. A monstrous lowing. A hoop of light opened in the night. Three modalmen sprang through a hole in the air atop giant, multi-limbed mounts, barbarously shouting. The hounds' masters had come. Rel's fear returned. At least death at the teeth of the hounds would have been quick.

There was a yelp, barking, snarling.

A modalman on his giant steed swept up the hill and charged into the hounds, transfixing one on a long spear. More hounds spilled down through the hoop of light after the modalmen and ran up the hill, slamming into the beasts closing on Rel. They snapped and reared, fighting insanely, their staccato snarling echoing over the desert. The modalmen galloped around the circle of hounds. Rel kept his eyes on them, they were the bigger threat. They were so huge, nothing he had been told prepared him for that. They did not attack, they were intent on the fighting hounds, slaying those that escaped their own beasts. Rel lowered his sword in confusion. The markings on the modalmen, their mounts, and their hounds were different in pattern and colour to those of the hounds that had chased him—a shifting red and blue rather than pink, gold and green.

A modalman drew his great bow and aimed an arrow long as a light spear at Rel. *So they mean to kill me anyway*, he thought.

The arrow sped towards him and past. A piercing yelp had Rel spinning around to find a rearing hound skewered by the arrow. It snapped its beak, and fell onto Rel, knocking him off his feet. He tried to shift the dead beast and could not. All he could think was how cold the sand was under his back.

The slaughter was done in moments. A giant hand gripped the hound's carcass and cast it aside, and Rel saw a modalman towering over him, its head lost in the stars. Whorls of red light played over its chest and four arms, slowly shifting to blue and back. In the upper pair of hands it held a spear. The shaft was eight feet long, but such was the modalman's stature it was a short weapon to him. Rel stared, mute, paralysed by anticipation of the worst. He could not fight this thing.

The modalman turned and called out to its comrades. The voice was profoundly, boneshakingly deep, its speech unlike any in the kingdoms.

The modalman sheathed its spear in a leather tube across its back and reached out its lower hands to Rel.

"If you wish to see the dawn," it said in rumbling, accented Maceriyan, "you will come with me."

Rel stared, unmoving.

The modalman's companions shouted at him. Horns sounded in the distance.

"We must ride. We cannot leap the light so soon. Now! The magecraft of your friend revealed your location. They are coming." The modalman's head was broad. His lips long and mobile, extending further round his head than on a man. His eyes gleamed with an inner light, like the hounds', but dimmer. He wore a leather harness which supported a metal breastplate and a sheet of mail for its stomach, short trousers and boots whose furry tops stopped short of the knee. All his life Rel had heard stories of the modalmen, though they scarcely held credibility in the far Isles of Karsa. The reality was different to the tales, far more human and more alien at the same time.

"Who is coming?" said Rel. He got to his feet. His sword was still in his hand. It was a useless weapon to fight the creature with, but he would not put it away.

"Those who wish to end you time on this Earth."

"Modalmen? Like you? You are killers, all of you!"

"And all the nations of your lands are the same?" The modalman blew out a disdainful raspberry, a curiously childish sound. "They are a different clan to mine. We do not kill the Forgetful, it is not our way. Forgive me, time runs swiftly, and we must go."

"F... find my mount, I will return to my company," Rel stammered.

"If you wish. Fifteen days hard ride to the west, through the worst parts of the sands. You can try. You will fail. We track those that you followed, before they chased you away. We fight the same battle. Come with us. If you will live, ride with me. If not, you may die here in a manner of your choosing."

Through his astonishment, Rel realised the modalman was asking his permission.

"Very well." He sheathed his sabre.

The giant plucked Rel from the ground in two hands, easy as a mother would pick up a baby from the floor. It ululated, and its mount thundered up to its side. This was enormous, big as the largest dracon cattle, though lacking the frill and horns of those beasts. Like a dracon, like its masters and the hounds, it had six limbs. The head was similarly shaped to the modalhounds, if blunter and lacking a toothed beak; instead it had a lipless mouth. In further contrast to the smaller animals, the glowing eyes seemed tiny, and it had a crest of stiff red fur that ran down the back and split to cover the upper parts of its limbs.

Still gripping Rel in its lower hands, the modalman pulled itself into the high saddle and deposited Rel before itself, enfolding him in its warmth and sharp scent, surprisingly like fresh human sweat. The two other modalmen cantered to flank him. One of them had found Aramaz, and led him on a long line held in one hand. The modalman said something to Rel, offering the leash. His ally, his captor, waved his follower away.

"Ha! HA! HA!" Rel's modalman roared. The markings on its body flared. It clapped its upper hands loudly and flicked the reins with the lower. The mount lowed and turned hard right. The Modalman dug in his heels, forcing the beast into a ponderous gallop.

They fled into the night, carrying Rel away from his pursuers.

CHAPTER TWO

The Temptation of Kyreen Asteria

THE GODHOME GLARED with the light of the White Moon. A canted plate thousand of yards across, forged of perishless Morfaan steel, the Godhome's silver underside acted as a gigantic mirror, doubling the moonlight and painting the rooftops it loomed over in reflected pewters and hard shadows black as coal. Atop the spires and ridges of Perus it was light enough to read. Down below was another matter. Perus had earned its other name of Umbra with reason; its labyrinthine, multi-layered streets and bottomless cavernas were thick with the dark.

Through this darkness Adamanka Shrane came, the Iron Mage, last member of the Iron Church, messiah to a forgotten people, herald to ancient gods.

A roseate hue seeped into the cold light of the White Moon as the Red Moon hurried up from the Earth, fleeing some celestial terror that mortals could only guess at. Though smaller, the Red Moon was brighter, and its ruddy light coloured the White Moon's illumination a deep pink in profound but brief influence. Only a few hours after emerging from the horizon, it would rush behind the high lip of the Godhome, taking its bloody tinge with it.

We of the Earth are the Red Moon, racing forever from the pursuit of death, thought Shrane. Death is tireless, it does not matter how fast we run. There is a night for us all when we dip below the horizon, and we never return.

Shrane had lived a long time. She had seen the Godhome when

it floated serenely over Perus. A city in the clouds, still home to the weakling Maceriyan gods, before Res Iapetus had driven them away, and ushered in the age of reason. Two hundred years had gone since then. She had watched them go. Thanks to the power of the Iron Fane, she returned to youth over and over, yet she had no illusions concerning her immortality. She had a little more time than others, that was all. Death's mastery was as great over her as it was over anyone else. She would die, perhaps soon. Already her latest flush of youth was leaving her, and it went faster every time. The magics she had wrought these last eleven months hurried her ageing, pushing a cruel decrepitude on her. The skin of her neck was loosening. Crowsfeet gathered at the corners of her eyes. The vertical wrinkles around her forehead and mouth faded slowly when she changed expression. Grey marred her lustrous hair. A pain had developed in her left hip that only magic might assuage, and that was a fool's road to travel. Expending magic to ease the pains of age would only quicken the ageing that brought them. She was locked upon a circular path. It was magic that sustained her, and magic that took its toll on her, body and soul.

The pain was worse since she had split, for two Adamanka Shranes walked the Earth, one in Perus, the other bound for the pole in the company of Vardeuche Persin. Each half was a diminished whole. This magic, she knew, would kill her.

Such things she did for the Iron Gods. She was glad to serve, despite the pain they brought. More, she was proud. To have a calling was worth more than a thousand meaningless lifetimes. Her death would come in service to mighty gods, iron in spirit and body, not like the banished fools evicted from their palace in the sky by a single man. Millennia her kind had waited, hundreds of priests and priestesses living out their days, praying for the call. At last, it had been made. So many worthy vehicles for the masters' return, but it was she who had been chosen, the last of the Iron Church. She was to be the instrument of return. She, the last of the last, had been chosen. The privilege lightened her spirit even as the pain of it wrapped tight steel fingers around her body.

The Iron Gods were coming home. No balm or magic could ease her hurts more than that thought.

Everything rested on her. There was no one else, not any longer. Her church had dwindled to one. If she failed, there would be none to take up her burden. Perhaps there were enough years left in her to train her successor, but in all probability she had left it too late to select an acolyte, train them in the magic of the masters and instruct them in the reading of the holy texts. Events had overtaken tradition. This was the last ministry of the Iron Church, she would not see it fail.

Shrane went down an alleyway, her tall, iron staff clicking softly on slick cobbles. Five-storey buildings leaned at each other belligerently from opposite sides of the street, scowling gables crowding out the mixed, pink moonlight. The road was quiet, the windows dark, only the thin lines of light coming round the shutters showed that people dwelt there. Muted laughter and the strains of a hurdy-gurdy drifted from one house as she passed. A door opened, framing a man in soft candlelight and allowing a gush of steam ripe with cooking smells to escape, quickly gone when the man shook out a cloth and went back inside. A scavenging draconbird croaked and flapped off a garbage tun. Small signs of life in the dark. Perus seemed as dead as the ruins of the Red Expanse.

She turned onto the Avenue Delforez, one of the few streets in the Scarlet Quarter wide and straight enough to permit the moon to light it properly, and everything changed.

Of all the cities of the Hundred Kingdoms—of which there were a great number—Perus was commonly reckoned the first, by the Maceriyans. National pride demanded that the title was contested by other kingdoms. The Mohaci claimed the title for Mohacs-Gravo, but their city was too young and too diminished in power to contend. The even more youthful Karsa City nipped at Perus's heels, the merchants there proclaiming their city's pre-eminence as foreign trade swelled its coffers and workers for the new industries swelled its population. One day that might be so, for Karsa City had grown in size three times over in a little over one hundred years, gorging itself on the countryside and its inhabitants, lately reaching abroad for ever more inhabitants. For the time being it was yet to overtake Perus in importance and splendour. None could oppose Perus in the matter of venerability; its age was great, its roots deep, founded on stacked histories stretching all the way back to Morfaan times.

Perus had not undergone the same drastic modernisation as Karsa City. The Maceriyan capital clung to its age pridefully, to its shambles and shanties, to the narrow streets laid down thousands of years ago, to all its deep wrinkles and sclerotic arterial ways.

The Avenue Delforez was one place where change was making itself known. Modernity crept in in the form of glimmer lighting and huffing, multi-limbed charabancs, impatient to overtake the dogcarts that rattled in front of them. Newly constructed, strong houses occupied half the avenue's length, haughty behind screens of shade-tolerant trees. But like every age before, the modern era was leaving the lightest touch. Only halfway along the street the mansions gave way to the high tenements in the Maceriyan central style; with steep roofs of scalloped tiles and draughty false turrets inhabited by starving romantics and draconbirds.

In two hours, the White Moon would follow its red brother past the Godhome. Moonlight would pass from the city. True Umbran darkness would fall, blacker than any in the Hundred, stars and sky blocked by the Godhome, and the choking output of factory chimneys. But not yet. For now the Godhome hung precariously in the sky, one edge buried in the hills of the Royal Park, the other lofted skyward in defiance of gravity. To the city it was a tipped lid on a cauldron. But though it threatened daily to descend, the sky never did fall in. "When the cauldron closes", they said in Maceriya, to mean something that would never happen. Perus was rich in ornaments from prior ages. The Godhome was its greatest.

No human being had set foot within the god's abode before Res Iapetus stormed it. None had since. The bones of those who had tried made mounds of shocking height around its base, so the stories went.

Shrane had no interest in the Godhome. It was a dead thing, lacking potency to her even as a symbol. Her gods would not be so easily defeated. She kept her eyes forward, walking slowly, weakened by her rushing age. Passersby recognised her for a mage and crossed the street. None dared approach her. Pickpockets gave her a wide berth. Hucksters directed their shouts elsewhere. Her bearing was proud, and her metal-sheened eyes brooked no other's gaze. Power clung to her as closely and brilliantly as the light of the moons did to the Godhome.

She halted before a tall building, brightly lit by oil and glimmerlamps, indifferent to the well-dressed Messires and Medames who spilled laughing down the steps. The club was called Marentant—"Now!" in the Perusan vernacular. A pretentious name, but the norm in a city in thrall as much to the vagaries of fashion as it was to the past. The uppermost floors contained apartments, the lower three comprised the club. The ground floor was fronted by a long run of tall casements, shop windows for vanity through which the fashionable and popular, dressed in the most expensive finery, could be viewed drinking their coffee and their wine.

The first and second floors had equally large windows, all curtained, concealing private rooms and halls for dining, business meetings, and more intimate assignations.

Kyreen Asteria had been frequenting Club Now with monotonous predictability for two months.

Shrane cast her hood back, revealing a curiously inhuman face whose beauty shone through the thin mask of age. Taking a tighter grip on her staff she mounted the steps leading up to ornate glass doors.

Liveried footmen in high, purple wigs immediately barred her way, gloved hands held up.

"No admittance to unaccompanied non-members." They did not ask her for her name, it was an establishment where the patrons were all known, and no manners were spared for the unwelcome.

"I am here to see a friend," said Shrane equably. "Kyreen Asteria."

The lefthand footman—his senior status denoted by the extravagant piping on his lapels—pulled a condescending face, cracking his pancake of make-up.

"We have not been informed, Medame, of any visitors for Medame Asteria. You are not permitted entrance. Good evening."

"Step aside," she said. Her eyes flared, her staff warmed in her hand, the contact between iron and magic needling her palm. The pain in her hip stabbed.

The footmen sagged in their costumes and blinked in confusion at one another. They looked at her anew, seeing her for the first time.

"Good... good evening Medame. Might we be of assistance?" said the senior.

"You will allow me within."

"Why certainly, Medame. Please." They bowed extravagantly and opened the door for her.

The beauty of an establishment as exclusive as Club Now was that if one could pass the doormen, then one would not be challenged again. Such places lived and died by the laws of discretion and servility.

At the cloakroom she handed her cloak to an attendant. No name was asked for, and she did not offer it. Her staff she kept. A uniformed waiter with bright rouge spots for cheeks and a moustache painted onto his smoothly shaved face came to her assistance.

"I am Hauvame, Medame. I see this is your first visit to our establishment. I bid you welcome, and enquire, how might I be of assistance?"

"I have an appointment with Medame Kyreen Asteria," she informed him.

The man frowned. "I was not informed."

"A surprise. We are old friends."

He paused. Shrane fanned the coal of magic that glowed in place of her heart, ready to cloud his mind. She did not need to. Hauvame bowed and led her through a wall of stained glass into the main hall of the club, a large space divided up cleverly into intimate booths by foldable screens. The lights were flatteringly low, a warm orange that smoothed out wrinkles and lent a maiden's youth to the haggard. A haze of narcotic smoke drifted over the patrons, all of whom were making a show of having a delightful time.

Hauvame led Shrane on a weaving path past a dozen tables to one against the wall. The lone occupant was Kyreen Asteria, a woman in her late twenties in finely tailored clothes. They were men's clothes, cut for the female shape and prettified with lace and rounded edges, finished in a delicate turquoise, but a daring outfit nonetheless, masculine enough to make a statement, feminine enough to titillate without bringing opprobrium down on the wearer. There was a trend for such outfits that year in Perus, inspired by the shocking antics of the Countess of Mogawn of Karsa.

Fashion or a desire for scandal had little to answer for Asteria's choice of daywear. Dresses were simply not suitable attire for a duellist.

Hauvame again bowed, a lesser version of the doormen's pompous display. With a flourish of his gloved hands, he indicated Kyreen Asteria and withdrew.

Asteria pointedly ignored him. She rocked a half-full wine bottle back and forth on its base with one finger, apathetically watching the liquid slosh around the bottom.

"Kyreen Asteria," stated Shrane. The quality of her voice ordinarily provoked a response. There was an imperative to it whether she drew on the power of her gods or not. The duellist was strong willed, and did not look up.

"Who wants to know?" said Asteria.

Weak. None who genuinely craved anonymity would ever use those words. It was the response of a tease who had grown bored with teasing.

Shrane sat. Now Asteria did look up as the chair scraped back.

"Who said I wanted company?" she said.

"You will want mine," said Shrane, resting her staff against wine-red wallpaper.

"How so?" said Asteria. She tilted the bottle off balance and let it go. It rocked musically, faster and faster, until the base settled with a hollow clonk.

"My name is Adamanka Shrane, I—"

"Ah yes," said Asteria. She knocked the bottle off the table with the back of her hand, snatching it just before it hit the floor and poured herself a generous measure. "The woman who has written to me so many times these last months. I replied once, didn't I? I believe I did. I try to reply to all who write to me. If I'm not mistaken I said that I did not wish to meet. I have no interest in dallying with admirers, no matter how much money they are offering. Playing companion was entertaining for a while, and gainful after that. Now that I have plenty of money, it is merely tedious, and it makes me feel like a whore. Like her." She nodded indiscreetly at an older woman sitting with a circle of bought friends, cackling loudly. Her make-up gathered in the wrinkles of her skin, her teeth were black from a surfeit of sugar. "She was a beauty once, her toadies behave as if she still is. She bore the attentions of the Infernal Duke for five years, and it made her rich. They are long separated—the duke prefers to bruise the youthful—but she still uses her association with the god to secure more money for herself. I am not that kind of woman."

"I am an admirer. Not of the kind you think."

"Oh, how lovely," said Asteria. "I have the other kind too, the ones that say they are special, who deserve my time, who respect me and wish to love me and lift me to the heights of physical ecstasy. I'm not interested in them either. If I want a lover I'll choose my own. Before you say that I am dismissing goods without inspection, I'm not particularly interested in women." She drained her goblet and slammed it onto the table. "To be frank, I don't care what you want. I'm leaving. Looks like I'll have to find myself another place to get some peace. Thanks for spoiling it for me. You know what? It was getting boring anyway." She raised a hand to summon the waiter. Her other she put on the table. Her strong, calloused fingers cradled thick gloves made for fighting.

Shrane leaned forward and grabbed her forearm.

"What are you doing?" said Asteria. "You best be glad I do not have my sword to hand." Asteria yanked back hard, meaning to free herself, but Shrane's grip was as hard as the iron that tainted her spirit.

"You will listen to me," Shrane said. Her voice took on a commanding growl. The air between them stirred with magic. "I do not have time to pursue you across the city. You will hear my request."

The magic did not hold. Asteria's brow creased, then smoothed out with delight. "Are you a magister?" Shrane did not respond. Asteria's eyes widened further and she grabbed something at her chest under her clothes. "Are you a mage?" She reached into her shirt and pulled out an ugly silver medallion. It vibrated in her hand, and she dropped it outside her jacket. "Hot! It works, and I thought the seller a charlatan. Genuine magecraft. Well, well, well."

Hauvame hurried over with a companion, a tall, squash-nosed man jammed into a ludicrous uniform a size too small for him.

"Medame Asteria, is there a problem? I am so sorry, this woman, she... There's no excuse, she told me she was a friend. I should never have brought her to your table. Say the word and I will have her ejected immediately."

"Hauvame," said Asteria. "I doubt you could."

"Medame?' He looked uncertainly at Shrane, his eyes straying to the hand gripping Asteria's forearm. "Shall I call the footmen?"

"Magic?" Asteria said to Shrane. "Is that how you got in?"

"Medame?" said Hauvame. The other man moved in closer.

"Never mind. I don't need you now, Hauvame."

Hauvame nodded, and shooed the larger man away, following him back into the restaurant.

Asteria glanced at Shrane's hand. She withdrew it. Asteria rubbed at her wrist. "Quite the grip you have there for one so frail. Hauvame!"

The hall master leaned back, his feet following his shoulders around as he changed direction again.

"Yes, Medame?"

"Fetch me another bottle of wine, and another glass. Medame..."

"Shrane," said Shrane.

"Medame Mage Shrane looks like she could use a drink."

Shrane waited while Asteria examined her face, taking in the microscopic changes to her expression as Asteria took in her high, feline eyes, the faint ridge running from the top of her nose up her forehead, the metallic glint to her pupils.

"You're a strange looking one. Is that the magic too?"

"I am not here to waste my time or yours, Medame Asteria. I have been watching you for a while."

Asteria's face dropped. "Ah, here we are. You *are* an admirer. How disappointing."

"You are bored," Shrane said, riding over the other woman's disinterest. "There is not a man or a woman alive who can hope to best you with a sword."

"True," said Asteria with a shrug. "I am feted for it. Since my duel with Zoltraras, this place and any other welcome me in with open arms for the custom I bring. I am pestered by the rich and the poor. I prefer the rich, naturally. They pay for my time, and smell less. It's good to be the best. Or it was, until I got bored. I liked it here. Here they keep people away from my table. Usually. You have spoiled my peace."

"You lie."

"Do I now?"

"Yes. I have been watching you for several weeks. You are restless, eager for action that will not come. You want to start a fight. You could start a fight, but you would finish it in seconds. I see you at your dinners and at your appointments, you no longer take care to hide your contempt."

"My, you have been watching me." Asteria grinned. "Yes, yes. I am lying. You are right, I am exceptionally, bone-achingly bored." She tapped at a deep pouch attached to her belt. "No one decent to fight since old Zoltraras. That was two years ago. I should never have killed him." She leaned in. "I need a challenge, you know? Something to test myself against."

"I do know. And that is what I bring you. A challenge."

Asteria pushed her wine glass back and forth. "That sounds ominous. I enjoy fighting, I enjoy the kill at the end, though lost gods know that it took me a time to come to terms with that," she said ruefully. "I thought I might be a monster, then I realised I was, and then I realised I didn't care."

Hauvame returned, he presented a bottle with a flourish.

"Just pour the damn thing," said Asteria.

Hauvame, piqued that the proper protocol had been interrupted, decanted the contents and left without a word.

"But I am not an assassin," said Asteria. "Any fight I have has to be straight. I'll not be involved in anything unseemly. It's hard enough being a woman in this game as it is. I have to be twice as good as the men, in every respect."

"I am not asking for an assassin. I came seeking the greatest duellist in the Hundred. What do I find, is it a sot or a swordswoman?"

"Oh, oh. Very good." Asteria gulped her wine. Shrane left hers untouched. "I could drink a crate of this and still beat anyone you care to name. You know, we are in the middle of a restaurant. Aren't you being a little candid? This is the heart of the Hundred! They say there are more spies in this city than in any other—a spy for every man, one for his servants, and a spy to spy on the spy."

"No one will remember me that does not need to remember me." Shrane lifted her chin. Her head grew heavy. She did not have long to conclude her business before the magic exhausted her. She must rest soon.

"More magic?"

Asteria's lips quirked when Shrane declined to answer. "Like that is it? Well. Saying I was interested, hypothetically, who is this man you wish me to duel? Hypothetically."

"I said nothing of a man."

"A woman? Little sport there," said Asteria scornfully.

"Nor a woman," said Shrane.

Asteria's eyebrow cocked. "Who then? A Fethrian either-or? Aren't they all pacifists? They have no tradition of swordcraft. Now I'm intrigued," she said sarcastically.

Shrane shook her head and smiled despite her weariness. "I do not propose you fight a human, Medame Asteria. I want you to fight a Morfaan, the Lord Josanad."

Asteria laughed loudly, startling nearby patrons from their social displays.

"I am deadly serious," said Shrane.

"Why?"

"I enjoy swordplay. I wish to witness the finest match in the world. As you see, I am old. My life runs out. I desire one last spectacle."

Asteria slapped her gloves on the table. "Now you lie," she said, but she was unsure. Shrane's odd face gave nothing away. "But do I care if you do lie?" She paused, looked away. When she looked back she was still suspicious, but interest was paramount. "A Morfaan—can it truly be arranged?"

"They will come soon, to preside over the selection of the new High Legate. The male is prideful and boastful. He has duelled men of the kingdoms before."

"Not for centuries. Not since before the driving of the gods."

"Nevertheless, it can be arranged."

"No one has ever beaten him," she said excitedly. "I have read the old accounts. They say he moves faster than the wind. Hyperbole, naturally, but maybe not by much."

"You might beat him."

Holding the table edge lightly, Asteria leaned back and beamed. "A Morfaan! Why, I might even die. There's no thrill, you see, without the possibility of defeat. Some might have it otherwise, taking pleasure in triumph over the weak, but not I. There is no joy in an easy victory."

"Then you will do it?"

"Fight a Morfaan?" Asteria lifted her glass high in salute and winked. "You know, I think I will."

CHAPTER THREE
The Iron Ship

THE *PRINCE ALFRA* laboured through a grey sea mounded up as high as hills. Paddles and screw chewed into the faces of watery slopes. Funnels belched luminous clouds of steam into the ominous skies.

The ship slowed at the top of a wave, paused upon the brink, then slid down the far side trailing a bright 'V' of foam. Away from the ship the wake widened, describing an arrowhead a mile across.

A shallow trough awaited the ship at the bottom, a moment of smoother sailing before the next wave. The engines growled, whistles blew, shrill and plaintive in the desert of salt water. The wave slouched at the prow, shocking a column of spume upward, and the ship began a fresh ascent.

Although the seas were high the tempers of the crew in the wheelhouse were even. Captain Heffira-nereaz-Hellishul vovo Balisatervo Chai Tse-ban stood at his station, watching his helmsman, Tolpoleznaen, guide the vessel onward. To a non-Ishamalani, Tolpol seemed statue still, doing nothing but holding the great spoked wheel steady. Heffi saw him twitch the wheel, making minute course adjustments that brought the vessel to the best possible position to climb each wave.

"This is a very fine ship that you have built, Goodfellow Kressind. A very fine ship indeed," said Heffi. "A floatstone vessel would never make any headway against this. Perhaps a well-built wooden ship, with the right wind, could last this sea out a while, but the *Prince Alfra* presses through it, swift and sharp and knife." He rubbed the brass railing around his station affectionately. It framed a sloping, three-faced desk full of gauges and dials; all the devices of the vessel, laid out for his perusal. "A shocking fine vessel."

Trassan Kressind had only half an ear for what the captain said. He stood at the bridge's windows and peered through the reinforced glass down the vessel's length to the forward funnel where a gang of men, roped securely to the ship, cleaned icicles from the rigging. They were unrecognisable, bundled up against the weather. Trassan had a piece of paper pressed against the sloping sill, and he consulted it, tutting and muttering to himself as he jotted down calculations, finished them, crossed them out, and started again.

"Damn it Heffi, the forward whistle is not sounding properly." He took out a watch from a pocket in his engineer's coat and checked it, winding it needlessly. "Four and a half hours ago it was clear, now look at it. It's the damn governors, the excess steam they vent onto the metal. Their exhaust should be hot enough to clear the ship without icing. Why doesn't it?"

Heffi's mood soured. Trassan's anxious need for perfection and the sometimes underhand way he went about achieving it taxed his patience. "You could not foresee every eventuality, goodfellow."

"Did you not hear?" said Tolpoleznaen, his attention fixed on the next wall of grey seawater. "Captain Heffira-nereaz-Hellishul called our ship a fine vessel. Rarely do Ishamalani give idle compliment." He did not look at Trassan. Very few of the Ishamalani ever spoke to him so directly.

"No, no," said Trassan. "I got it wrong. I miscalculated. This problem seems rather obvious, and it will get worse. How cold is it outside?"

First Mate Volozeranetz consulted the thermometer built into the wall, the quicksilver bulb exposed to the full force of the weather outside.

"Twelve degrees below frosting," said Volozeranetz.

"We can add three more for the temperature of the iron—the wind chills it." Trassan tapped his teeth with his pencil. "But that is colder than I expected, and we are not even into the Sotherwinter proper yet. The cold is the chief problem, compounded by unforeseen vortices around the structure." He glanced at his calculations again.

"What else have I missed?"

Heffi looked around at his mate and his bridge crew. The oiled, long top-knots they wore all differed, proclaiming their allegiance to the various sects of the One God, but they were all Ishamalani regardless.

"My fellows are not so easily upset by statements of that kind, Trassan," said Heffi quietly. "These men were born to the sea and will not panic, but only these men. I cannot speak for the non-Ishmalani. Have a care what you say. This is a difficult voyage, and we are doing well. This is unknown territory."

Trassan bit his bottom lip.

"Trust me," said Heffi. "Discretion is among a leader's many desirable qualities."

Trassan threw up his hand. "You're right, you're right. I worry, but with good reason. Persin is behind us..."

"If he made it past the Drowned King."

"Let's assume he has. I prefer to plan for the worst case scenario," said Trassan, more peevishly than he intended. He gathered himself before continuing. "Every moment we lose is a moment he gains. If the whistle ices now, what will happen when we are closer to our goal? The whole release assembly could get frozen, and then where would we be?"

Heffi adjusted his nose piercings with a heavily ringed hand, a habit of his when irked. "His engines are good, but not as good as yours. His ships are of stone. No floatstone can go as fast as this, not one! This ship, goodfellow, it is... it is a marvel! Take heart in that. It will not freeze."

"I will, I will," said Trassan distractedly. His eyes remained forward.

Heffi sighed. Trassan was paying no attention. He would not be satisfied until he had worked out his little problem. One day, his perfectionism might see them all dead.

"Sound the whistle Heffi, just the forward one," said Trassan.

"Sound the whistle," ordered Heffi. He tried to keep the weary tone from his voice, he really did.

Suqab, the Second Mate, pulled one of three chains by the chartdesk, where a large, mostly blank, map of the Sotherwinter was pasted down. Above it was a copy of the famous Morfaan map, discovered by Vand at the Three Sisters. More schematic than chart to human eyes, its use was limited for navigation.

The forward whistle blew a warbling note.

"See! That doesn't sound right," said Trassan. "Does that sound right to you?"

"No," admitted Heffi. "No, I suppose it does not."

"So then," said Trassan, enthused. He went to the door and took his oilskins down from their peg, donned them so hurriedly he tangled one arm up with the strap of his tool satchel. "I'm not going to stand around here when something requires my attention. Heffi, I've got an idea."

Heffi raised an eyebrow.

"Disengage the screw, bring number two boiler up to ninety hundredths full pressure." Trassan fished out a signal flag from a tall bucket. "When I wave this, blow the whistle until I stop waving. Do you have it?" Trassan had his hand on the handle. Heffi coughed into his fist meaningfully.

"Trassan?" said Heffi.

"Yes?"

"That flag is to signal that we have the yellow sickness aboard," said Heffi.

"No one can see to misunderstand. Does it matter?" said Trassan.

Heffi gave a strained smile. "Yes. Everything out here matters. There are rules. We obey them. It keeps us alive. Choose one less ill-starred."

"Right." Trassan slid the flag back and pointed at another.

"Anguillon breeding knot ahead," said Heffi. "Take the red, for the sake of the One."

"What's the red for?" asked Trassan.

"Depends how you wave it, but none of it is bad," Heffi said. "It is a standard semaphore pennant."

"That shall do," said Trassan. "Get ready."

The door flew backward and banged hard against the ship's modest superstructure. Trassan lunged out onto the deck, rope and clip in hand. Overbalanced by his heavy tool satchel, he had one chance to make the safety line. This was the moment of reckoning, a wrong move could send him skidding down the deck and overboard. He grinned in relief as the clip snapped closed. He grabbed the railing. Beneath him the sea heaved as if cheated.

The clip was another device he had invented for this adventure, completed after consultation with the polar explorer Eustache Antoninan. Lines of thin, strong rope ran along the ship port and starboard, passing through cleats attached to railing posts every forty paces. Two more were situated either side of amidships. The clips were springloaded, easy to open and close to allow men to unhook themselves and move between lines or over their supporting cleats. The system was, in its small way, revolutionary and would do much to safeguard the lives of his sailors in the tempestuous ocean of the Sotherwinter. Yet though his brothers often accused Trassan of being pleased with himself—unfairly in his estimation—when faced with even a minor failure Trassan took no satisfaction in his ingenuity. He was fixated on the ice growing around the funnel. Ice was already everywhere. Patches of it gleamed on the superstructure. Ice thickened the hawsers and rigging on the masts into heavy tubes. For reasons that he could not account for it was worse for the forward stack, and at the moment only the forward whistle was jamming. For the time being the deck itself was largely free of ice, kept clear by the tremendous heat of the glimmer engines working below. But already it encroached from the sides, making small inroads along decking planks. Small icicles grew from the railings. Layers gathered on the edges of bulwark drains, building the ice incrementally with each wave sluiced away. At twelve below freezing, Trassan was sufficiently warm in long oilskins and woollens, but the temperature would drop, affecting man and vessel. As they went further south, it would get colder and colder, and the ice would become a danger to the ship's stability. If one of the funnels could ice up, well...

It was a problem. Furthermore, it was a problem he had anticipated, miscalculated, and so failed to adequately engineer for.

Trassan swung forward with a reeling drunkard's walk, angry with himself. He passed the forward hold cover, tightly battened against the weather, and on past the tarpaulin covering the steam-winch, tied up with criss-crossed ropes as tight as a ham, all but the tall winding wheel unrecognisable under its swaddling. He made the funnel with a final stagger as the ship pitched down a wave, giving him a stomach-churning view of a long drop misted with spray.

The team of men were all clipped to the lines. Two were up on the staples welded to the funnel itself. The other two hacked at a runnel of ice running from the whistle assembly to the deck.

"Hey!" called Trassan as he approached. The wind was surprisingly light, the mountainous seas having been born in some more violent place, and Trassan did not have to shout loudly.

The team leader turned to face him.

"Bannord?" said Trassan. "What are you doing out here, lieutenant?" He unclipped himself from the starboard line and aimed for the line running right amidships. He stumbled and Bannord caught him.

"Thank you," said Trassan, snapping his clip home.

"You want to be careful out here," said the marine officer. "No place for a wrong step."

"You should be inside. This isn't your work."

"Nothing like a bit of fear to get the blood racing." He slapped Trassan's shoulder. "A life soldiering gets you hooked on the rush. I'd go cross-eyed with boredom without it. We're the Maritime Regiment, but some of my men are saltless lubbers, and need the practice. So I thought it best if we tackle the ice rather than the sailors."

"It is not a problem yet."

"Aye," said Bannord, that infuriating twinkle to his eye. "But it will be, won't it? That's why you're out here. Besides, I'm running out of money to lose to Redan up there, so I figured we should do something other than play cards." He pointed to the man fourteen feet up, hacking at the ice gathering round the whistle bell with a short-handled pick. "Mind you, I'm regretting my decision. It's fucking freezing out here. Best be bored than frozen, that's my new motto. I'll be sure to stick to it in future."

"Get him down," said Trassan.

"You're not going up there are you?" said Bannord. The lieutenant was a canny man, and unafraid to speak his mind. "If Redan falls in, big deal. As much as I love his cheeky little ways, he's only a marine, and I could blunt my mourning by reminding myself that I won't have to pay his contract out. But if you fall in, that would be bad news all around."

"Get him down, Bannord."

"No. What'd I tell your brother if you died in front of me?"

"I could tell someone else how to do this," said Trassan. "But it'd take twice as long. Now, I'm ordering you. Get him down."

"That's the spirit," said Bannord, slapping him on the shoulder again. "I wondered if you'd back down or not. Oi! Redan!" The marine looked down. "Yeah, you. Come on down, it's your lucky day."

Trassan grabbed his clip, fingering the release impatiently as he waited for Redan to descend, red-faced from the effort of holding himself steady against the motion of the ship while hacking at the ice. Despite the chill, Redan was sweating and his breath was short. He nodded at Trassan as he made the deck and clipped himself to the port line. Trassan handed his bag and pennant to Bannord, unclipped himself from the midline, and onto the safety rope running up the funnel. He motioned to Bannord to open the satchel, fished out an adjustable wrench, and took back the flag. He tucked both into his belt.

"Here we go," he said, and began to climb. It felt good to be working again.

Trassan was fit and strong for a monied man. Others of his class preferred to draw up the plans then sit back and shout at someone else to do the work, but Trassan liked to get his hands dirty. A matter of trust, a desire to see the job done himself, and a need to expend the generous amount of nervous energy that coursed ceaselessly around his system.

Climbing up the staples on the side of the funnel while the ship lurched from one extreme of inclination to another was among the hardest things he had ever attempted. The cold of the metal bit through his gloves, even though the staples stood a mere five inches from the skin of the funnel. Five inches, it turned out, was more than enough distance to chill the metal deeply. The swaying of the ship became pronounced as he climbed. *Obviously*, he scolded himself, *I'm climbing an inverse pendulum*. The wind grew in strength up there, unimpeded by the swell. Trassan's hood blew down. Spatters of sleety snow mixed with freezing sea water hit his face, burning it with cold. Fourteen feet was a height of no consequence under normal circumstances. On rough seas it felt far higher. When he looked down, he could see over the side of the ship to the churning paddle wheels, and that was significantly further still.

"Gods shit on me," he cursed. He reached the whistle. A braced steel arm jutted out from the stack there, with a ring rattling from the far end. With some difficulty he fished the attachment for his harness up and reclipped it to the ring. Now he could sit back, bracing himself on the ladder staples with his feet, freeing his hands to work. At least that was the idea. The *Prince Alfra* plunged down another twenty foot wave, and Trassan came loose, swinging from the arm. He flailed for the ladder with arms and feet, his heart dropping in his chest, heavy as a plumb bob. Panic ambushed him, and would not retreat for a minute after he had grabbed the ladder again.

"Are you alright up there, goodfellow Kressind?" said Bannord. He was laughing at him. Too familiar by half, but social convention demanded he put up with it. Bannord was a close friend of his eldest brother, Guis, and had known Trassan since he had been in child's dress. The Bannord family was dirt poor, but still aristocracy, and their title was older than the Kressind's. His ancestors had crossed the Neck with King Brannon, some even said the similarity of the name denoted kinship. Not for the first time Trassan wondered why his brother Guis had recommended Bannord and not his other friend, Qurion. Trassan found Qurion much less annoying.

"I'm just fine up here, thank you," shouted Trassan back. Gritting his teeth, he drew out his spanner.

There were steam whistles on each of the *Prince Alfra*'s stacks. Different bell sizes on each gave it a powerful, polyphonic voice, a fancy Trassan wondered now had not caused the problem. They were fed by subsidiary steam pipes coming off the boilers. Besides sounding the whistles, the vents allowed excess steam to be bled free at a steady rate to keep the pressure stable. The steam vent had a separate opening—a governor—that could be employed to blow steam without sounding the whistle, and that vent was currently clear, although a ring of ice caked the base of its tubing. Trassan poked at the vent hole with his finger, and the glove came away wet with warm water, so the problem was with the whistle.

He thought a moment. By being forced into the whistle bell, the steam had time to cool and condense. By the time it came from the sounding orifice and hit the cold air it was close to freezing. The water dribbled off the whistle and coated the governor vent. The cooler water froze the vent intermittently shut and prevented it from opening properly half the time. As the vent and the whistle were part of the same mechanism, some steam always went into the whistle bell, so simply not using the whistle was not an option.

"And so the vent water backs up, and also gets the chance to freeze," he said quietly to himself. "Blast Heffi and his Ishmalan insouciance, I was right to come up here." He forgot the swaying of the ship, the heaving water, and his precarious position. Invested in the problem, he became oblivious to the world around him.

He pushed back with his legs, tensing them alternately to deal with the swell, and leaned back to better look at the funnel. The smaller whistle bell size did not completely explain why the forward funnel was the worst affected. He had taken into account the sea spray it must bear, but there was more to it than that. The wind, most probably. The wind's power to snatch away heat outweighed its inhibition of the formation of ice. The other two funnels were sheltered by rest of the ship against headwinds if not from all sides. Could that be it?

Trassan narrowed his eyes. In an instance like this, there must be a short-term fix and a long-term solution.

After a moment's thought, he locked the spanner to the nut on the whistle assembly. His fingers were numb, and the tool felt unreal. The nut would not budge, and he had to smack the fist closed around the spanner handle with the palm of his other hand.

After four painful strikes, the nut shifted suddenly to the left. Trassan undid it quickly, removing the bell assembly. He took out the lead compression seal and washers, depositing them in his bag with the nut and bell, then descended the ladder.

"It's a problem with the steam," said Trassan to Bannord. "The exhaust is too cold. There are no gasses from combustion in the exhaust to keep the temperature up. If this were a coal-fired engine there would be."

"Right," said Bannord in a manner that set Trassan's teeth on edge. "So, can we fix it, and what do we do if we can't?"

Trassan would not be dissuaded. "I blame my own frugality." By which he meant genius in saving money. His crew were becoming used to such pronouncements. "The steam passes through three racks of condensing chambers to recycle the water through the boiler system. We draw a lot of residual heat from the water to heat the ship. By the time it leaves the funnel it's not very warm. The vapour may look impressive, but it's mostly down to the condensation of the moisture load as warm air hits freezing rather than actual steam. The venting you see from the stacks is pressure release, and glimmer residue disposal. By the time the steam leaves the vessel, it's barely above evaporation point. A few moments in the steam bell is all that it takes to condense half of it, this is dribbling out, freezing the overpressure valve shut."

"Right," said Bannord again. "The steam is too cold. You have cold steam."

"Bravo!" said Trassan. Now he clapped the soldier on the shoulder. Bannord pulled a face at him. "You are correct. The steam is, in effect, too cold."

Trassan retrieved his flag, looked to the bridge windows, and waved. The steam whistles hooted. The pipe Trassan had removed the whistle from sent up a giant plume of vapour.

"See," said Trassan. "It turns to ice the moment it leaves the ship." He continued waving the flag. The other two whistles moaned loudly, the spray of ice crystals sent out from the partially disassembled fore-whistle became a freezing fog that settled onto the ship's iron. He flourished the flag one more time, then let it drop and rolled it up. "That should have cleared the steam vent enough."

"You hear that Redan? You don't have to go back up now. Get up on the other side. Once we've cleared that, then we can all go indoors."

Trassan was energised by his success, eager to get to the root of the problem. "We are going to have to come up with a longer lasting solution."

"Are we now," said Bannord sceptically. "If you don't want something shooting, count me out. We're only doing this because it seemed like a good idea. It wasn't. Come on Redan!" he snapped. "I'm getting sick of the cold."

"Yes lieutenant," said Redan.

"Hey!" said one of Bannord's other marines. "Can you hear that? I can hear another whistle."

"What are you talking about, Drannan?" said Bannord. "There's not one ship within a thousand miles of this place."

"I heard it too, sir," said another.

"Well, that's just fine," said Bannord. "I can't hear a bloody thing."

"Shh!" said Trassan, grabbing his arm. "Listen!"

Through the moan of the wind and the singing of the ship's metal came a shrill cry.

"I hear it," said Bannord.

"That's not a whistle," said Trassan.

Bannord's attitude changed completely. "Leave the ice. Get inside. Fetch your ironlocks. Roust the others from the barrack," said Bannord to his men. Whatever Bannord's faults, Trassan admired his professionalism. "Redan, get me my gun."

The cry called again, nearer. A shriek similarly polyphonic to the ship's whistles, but rawer.

"Best fetch the magister and the mage too," said Bannord urgently. "Guns won't be enough."

"Yes sir," said Redan. The marines scrambled away down the deck.

"It came from the east," said Trassan. He and Bannord unclipped themselves and hurried to the port side of the ship as quickly as they could, ducking under the midship safety lines. Trassan gripped the rails, eyes sweeping the hillocks of dipping water.

"There!" he shouted, pointing at a spout of water several hundred yards away. A thin jet arced over the white caps of the swell, the top broken into spray by the wind.

Bannord reached inside his oilskin and pulled out a short eyeglass. He snapped it open and aimed where Trassan pointed.

"Hard to see," he said, steadying himself against the rail. Another spout lofted upward. "Hang on. Uh-oh."

Trassan saw nothing but the spout and a brief roil of seafoam at its base. "Uh-oh?" said Trassan. "What by the hells is 'uh-oh' supposed to mean?"

"Here." Bannord gave him the glass. Trassan set the cold metal against his eye. "Watch. Watch. There!"

"I don't see it," said Trassan. He lacked Bannord's experience at sea, and the telescope image bobbed sickeningly about between grey sky and grey sea. Bannord grasped the glass and steadied it for him. "Don't try to bring it to bear. Keep it steady. Follow the motion of the ship."

Trassan twisted the focusing ring, bringing a sleek, reptilian head into sharp focus. He got the briefest glimpse before it dived down, a long, frilled tail flicking after it.

"As I thought, sea dragon," said Bannord. Men shouted; Bannord's marines were spilling out of the doors of the superstructure, some still struggling oilskins over their woollens. All were carrying their long ironlock rifles.

"Five up on the tower!" shouted Bannord, pointing to the wheelhouse. "The rest of you range up on the rail." Redan came running, agile on the pitching deck, and tossed Bannord's gun to him.

Tullian Ardovani came after the marines down the midship safety lines, more cautiously perhaps but still nimble. All of them had had time to become used to the sea's constant motion. His strange weapon was slung over his shoulder. From afar it appeared as a bulky rifle, closer to it was clear the brass barrel was studded with crystal, and lacked an aperture.

By the time the magister reached Trassan and Bannord, all the marines were in place, clipped to the safety ropes, their rifles secured to their waists by chains running from a loop on the stock. They trained their weapons on the ocean.

Ardovani joined them. He was young for a man of his calling, little exerted by his walk down the rolling deck.

"Where's Vols?" asked Trassan. "We might need him."

"Ah," said Ardovani apologetically. "I am afraid our goodmage is indisposed. This sea is not to his liking."

"Typical," said Bannord. "He must be the only one left who's still puking his guts up. Scion of the God-driver! Useless piss-bucket."

"It is not easy for him," said Ardovani gently. "Mages are of a rare sort. The iron of the ship is difficult for him to bear, far more so than it is for me. The sea makes it worse."

"Can you banish a dragon?" asked Bannord.

"A dragon?" said Ardovani. "No, why, I have never seen one." He adjusted his parka hood thoughtfully. "I suppose I might given time, and the correct formulae, but—"

"Shut up then," said Bannord. "Dragon rising!" he shouted.

The face of the wave they approached broke apart near the crest. A short muzzle erupted from the sea, the head following, carried high on a long, serpentine neck. Brine streamed from its horns and the frills around its mouth. The dragon let out a hooting cry. Watery breath blasted from the nostrils atop its head. It dove beneath the water's surface, surfing below the wave face a little way as a rippled, flattened image of itself, before vanishing deeper into the water.

"Blast it," swore Bannord. "A male, and a big one."

"You have experience with these beasts?" said a fascinated Ardovani.

"None. Never been in this stretch of the ocean. Who has? Stories is all I have. The north was thick with them once, so they say, but they've been hunted out. Last I heard of one being seen up there was twenty years back, and a long way from the Isles. Down here, different matter. These are untamed seas. But I do know the males have the horns and the frills, and that they're the more dangerous. If we're lucky, it'll look us over then swim away. If we're not lucky, it'll take us for a rival, and attack."

"Very well," said Ardovani. He slipped the weapon off his shoulder, adjusted a number of switches near the stock, and began to speak swift words over it.

"Stand ready!" bellowed Bannord to his men. "Don't one of you wetboots open fire without my say so, we do not want to piss it off!"

"Any moment now," said Bannord to Trassan.

The sea parted, and the dragon speared up from the depths. It breached the surface and sailed over the crest of a wave. The full length of its body was revealed; eighty yards of glistening scale, blue on top, white beneath, the skin mottled where the two colours met. As it flew it twisted its six great flippers against its body. The dragon plunged back under the water and disappeared for several seconds. The ship rose over another wave, and then the dragon leapt from the ocean again, barrel rolling as it soared over the water's surface. Spray flew from its spiralling body, it dipped its head and vanished into the water, leaving a neat round 'o' of white foam.

"How marvellous!" said Ardovani.

"Yeah? Tell me how marvellous it is when it's biting your face off," said Bannord, sighting down his rifle.

The dragon surfaced vertically, rising from the water until its forelimbs were exposed. It blew out another long, song-like shriek and waited expectantly.

The ship churned the waves toward it. The dragon cocked its head, dipped down and swam alongside the boat. The marines followed it with their guns, but it made no move to attack. Instead it rolled onto its back, exposing the brilliant whiteness of its banded underbelly. A movement set up low down on its stomach; a pair of pointed tentacular organs, long and pink, squirmed out from two slits. The dragon screeched and slapped at the ship with a flipper, making the hull boom. Fully aroused, it rolled and pushed its organs against the metal.

"What's it doing?" said Trassan.

Bannord grunted. "Gods man, you're denser than your brother Guis when it comes to sex, eh? Look here, that boy dragon there thinks the *Prince Alfra* here is a lady dragon," he said patronisingly. "Do you see? Ha! Two cocks, lucky bastard."

His men put up their guns and laughed. Sailors left their work to come and goggle, while captain Heffi and the navigation watch came from the wheelhouse onto the balcony to look overboard.

"It's not going to attack us?" said Trassan. The dragon was keeping pace with the vessel, writhing against the side, thrashing at the water with its head.

"Not unless it intends to hump us to death, no," said Bannord drily.

They watched until the dragon's lovemaking stopped. The water around its stomach turned briefly cloudy.

It rolled under water, and popped its head up again, wide mouth screeching.

"Looks like we've hurt its feelings," said Bannord. He cupped his hands around his mouth. "That was lovely! We'll write to you, we promise."

The dragon was lifted up by the swell. From the crest it looked down on them curiously, head cocked. It let out a final shriek as it disappeared on the other side. When the water dipped again, the dragon had gone.

Bannord chuckled to himself. "Now I've seen everything. Alright, sea maggots, back to work, this ice isn't going to melt any time soon. You five, stay atop the bridge, in case old amorous there feels hard done by. No cuddles for him!" The marines laughed, and Bannord strode off among them.

"A fine sight," said Ardovani, his face alive with delight. "Goodmage Vols will be most upset he missed it." He too went back aft toward the warmth and safety of the interior.

Trassan stayed a while, watching the sliding of the seas. He was less awestruck. There could, he thought, be practically anything down there. He let the water hypnotise him a while and his imagination got the better of him, peopling the depths with mighty leviathans and the vengeful armies of the Drowned King. He walked away. There was still a problem with the icing, and it was going to get worse. What if it started to freeze in the funnel? He had to talk to Captain Heffi.

They were going to have to stop for a while.

CHAPTER FOUR
A Stowaway

TWENTY-FOUR DOGS accompanied the expedition, the finest drays in the western kingdoms, bred from pure Sorskian and Torosan stock. They displayed no mongrel tendencies to the small size, stupidity, congenital morbidities or physical weakness common to the northern breeds. All were majestic, prick-eared beasts, with high curled tails and thick double coats, princes and princesses of their kind.

High breeding afforded them little in the way of luxury. The dogs occupied narrow kennels of wood in a specially constructed hold aft of the superstructure. Though the dogs were naturally careful in their toileting, the kennels had become dirty as the journey progressed and the hold had taken on a rich, chemical stink.

The dogs lay in the gloom, their heads on their paws. Those wakeful stared over the heads of their fellows, sad brown eyes looking at nothing in particular. Most slept. Despite the ship's violent motion there was a sense of indolence to them. The dogs' movements were restricted to a flick of an ear, or a black-lipped yawn that briefly opened a cavernous mouth crowded with long teeth, snapping shut with a clack. The dogs lay in all attitudes, on their sides, on their fronts, two with their dirty white bellies uppermost, heads crooked at an angle uncomfortable for anything other than a dog.

Despite their poor lodging, the dogs were content. This was not their first voyage. They were patient by nature, a legacy of their hunting ancestry. But patience was not the only inherited gift these powerful animals had occasion to employ.

Tyn Rulsy scampered into the kennel, nervously looking over the dogs. She hated the teeth, the way they poked out over their lips sometimes when sleeping, as if to remind you they were three missed meals from turning wild.

Rulsy was delicate for a Greater Tyn. From a human point of view, she tended more to the agreeable proportions of a mortal child than the often ugly, large-headed form of her kind, although her face was just as wrinkled, her nose as large, and her hair as wiry as those of her fellows. Her small, slippered feet pattered on the decking of the dog kennel, her colourful skirts whispering over wooden slats. The floor was raised to allow the dogs' waste to be flushed away and out of the covered drainage holes set either side of the holds. This task was done three times a day by Antoninan's grooms but did nothing to alleviate the smell. Antoninan himself came often to talk with his animals, especially the big one, Valatrice, so Rulsy had to time her visits carefully.

Rulsy feared Valatrice the most. She hoped he would be asleep. She could tell the moment she entered he lay watchful in the dark. Rulsy hesitated, but could not turn back. It was one of the few times of the day no human was present, and she had no choice but to continue.

Valatrice's cage was bigger than those of his pack, as befitted his status and size. Nevertheless it was a mean lodging for so mighty a being.

Valatrice stood as Tyn Rulsy came toward his cage. He stretched majestically, thrusting his forequarters toward her and his hindquarters up in a rigid, canine bow. He extended first one hind limb then the other in a long, quivering stretch. When finished he stood straight. He was a huge dray, high as a man at the withers. To Tyn Rulsy he was as solid and imposing as a mill wall.

"Well well, little sister," said Valatrice. No dog living spoke so well as he, his voice was clear of canine growlings; strong, clean and more often than not dripping irony. "Where are you going? Have you come to continue our discourse, or do you have alternative business there, in the aft hold? Is that soup in the bowl you have?" he said, his square black nose snuffling. "Is it for me? I thank you for it."

"Not wanting to speak to you," Rulsy said, shifting from foot to foot. "Soup not for you. Soup's for me! I wanting a moment's peace is all, eat my lunch, no 'Rulsy, Rulsy!', for a moment." The ship lurched over a wave, and Rulsy clapped her hands over the bowl lid, her eyes narrowed suspiciously at Valatrice.

"Well then, stay and talk awhile while you eat. Our lives are not so distant in character, we both serve men against our desires. We might be friends, you and I."

"No! Not friends," said Tyn Rulsy. She lowered her eyes; Valatrice's were a dark yellow, cold and ancient as amber.

Some Tyn liked dogs, feeling a kinship with them. Not her, they were animals, yes, and all Tyn had affinity with animals, but these were creatures moulded so much by humanity it was impossible to picture their original form. There was nothing like them in the wildernesses of the Earth, save where tame dogs had gone feral. They were not natural, as foreign to the world as the men that had brought them there.

"You are man's creatures, coming with man. Tyn are not. We are free in our hearts."

"You do not think a dog is free in his heart? How interesting," Valatrice stepped closer to the bars of his cage. He peered down at the Tyn. She shrank back from his warm, moist breath.

"Let me be!" she shrilled. "Just want a little peace!"

Valatrice smacked his mouth wetly. "A shame. I could do with diversion. On your way then, on your way." He sank back down and curled up on himself. His eyes glittered with amusement as she went by. "Be aware, I smell more than soup, more than Tyn!" he said slyly.

Rulsy hurried away.

"Your secret is safe with me!" he said.

The other dogs stirred but little as she passed them.

There was a narrow gate between two of the cages to the rear of the kennels. She opened it, passed through, bolting it after her. Behind the kennels a store took up the remainder of the hold, stacked with the tools of a drayman—rakes, brushes, and bales of straw. The guttering for the drains came to a raised, tapered end there, and there was taps for fabric hoses, these neatly coiled onto their spools. Heating pipes ran right around the walls of the hull. At the back wall, they rose up in an artful square to bracket a door leading into the hold behind the dogs', the last large open space toward the aft of the *Prince Alfra*. Rulsy hurried to it. She put the soup down and spun the lockwheel open, grunting with the effort of turning something meant for a being twice her height, her hands and temples tingling painfully at the touch of solid iron.

She looked behind to make sure she was not followed, and slipped through.

A canyon of crates greeted her. Stacks of wooden boxes and trunks held equipment for the expedition onto the ice that was not required during the voyage. Thin light leaked around the cargo hatch high overhead, steady drips of freezing water glinting in it as they fell. The sharp fronts of three giant dog sleds poked out from behind a mountainous tarpaulin. Boxes long as coffins, full of tools and surveying equipment, occupied shelving racks that went the full way to the ceiling in two rows either side of a central aisle. The very centre was less cluttered than the spaces behind the shelving, but only slightly. Four massive pallets covered with oilcloths and bound about tightly with ropes and chains loomed over her. She pressed on to the back, down the narrow clearway between shelves and pallets. Everything was lashed down against the sea. There were none of the heating pipes here to stave off the cold, and her breath gathered in clouds.

An infrequent inspection by the boatswain was all the hold received. That was all that recommended it as accommodation. Rulsy felt sorry for its lone occupant.

At the back someone had hollowed out a small den in a pile of crates, but it was empty. Rulsy desultorily turned over the furs lining the space. There was no one there.

"Goodmiss!" she hissed. "Where've you got to?"

"I'm here," said a woeful voice, loud in the quiet. Rulsy went out from the musty hideyhole and looked about. Behind another stack, the girl had made a tent from a tarpaulin and a rack of skis. Rulsy waddled over to it and ducked inside.

"What you doing in here Goodmiss Ilona?"

Ilona Kressinda-Hamafara sat up, her pale face resolving from the dark like the White Moon rising. She had straw in her hair, and was thoroughly dishevelled. Rulsy wrinkled her nose at her smell.

"What was all that banging and rasping?" Ilona asked.

"Randy sea dragon," said Rulsy matter-of-factly.

"A dragon?" said Ilona in a small voice.

Rulsy waved her hand in front of her nose. "You stink," she said. She turned the lid of the bowl a quarter and lifted it off. The savoury steam of broth filled the tent.

Ilona put up her hand and pulled a face. "Take it away. I can't keep anything down. When will this rocking stop?"

"You must, you must!" said the Tyn, thrusting it at Ilona. "Take it!"

Ilona took the bowl in her hands and sniffed at it. Her eyes were underlined with misery, dark circles painted in by sleepless nights and seasickness. She pulled a face and put the bowl aside. "I really can't." She drew her legs up under her and rested her head on her knees.

Rulsy knelt beside her and shook her shoulder. "You think you are in bad place? Think how it is for me, in this iron box all the while," Rulsy looked around at the dark hold theatrically. "If this seems like a prison, you be Tyn surrounded by iron. See how you like that! Headaches, all day!"

Ilona frowned. "Don't turn me into a Tyn," she said.

Rulsy scowled. "Don't be stupid, little goodmiss. I no do that. I can't do that. I no mage. I not say that either. Just imagine!" She dropped her hand. "I just look for a little fellow feeling. I find none, only stupid rich girl." She stood up. "Maybe big dog right, maybe he and I have more in common than you and me."

Rulsy lifted her skirts over her shoes and turned away.

"I'm sorry," said Ilona. "Please don't go." She took the Tyn's small leathery hand in her own. "I meant no offence."

"No. I go now. I have to make sickness brew for the Goddriver's kin. He very ill with the sea. I can make you some now too, make extra."

Ilona nodded meekly. "Thank you."

"Now, eat! You don't eat, you get sicker. You might even go die. Yes," she said solemnly. "How you like that?"

"Maybe I should come out now?" said Ilona hopefully.

"No!" said Rulsy. "You one girl? Two hundred men on this boat.

What you think they do, eh?" She squinted out of one eye, and rammed a finger in and out of her clenched fist lasciviously. "You get very sore. You stay put, goodmissy."

"I have to come out sometime! I can't stay here forever. Trassan will protect me."

"No! You stay!" Rulsy insisted. "You come out, you big trouble for Tyn Rulsy. You big trouble anyway! You sad you come, it stupid girl's own fault, not Tyn Rulsy's."

"I'll be found sooner or later."

"Not now!" snapped Rulsy. She backed out of the tent. "Rulsy think about it. I come back with sickness draught, maybe in morning. Go sleep."

"But—"

"Sleep!" said the Tyn, her voice strangely resonant. She made a fluttering pass with her hand.

Ilona fell to the furs with a thump, dead asleep. She would just have to eat her soup cold. Serve her right. Rulsy left, shaking her head. What to do, what to do?

CHAPTER FIVE

Aarin Waits

SURF ROARED UPON the uppermost shore of the Final Isle. The surge of it withdrawing over the stone pavement was a thousand frightened shushes. Pasquanty slowed as he rounded the fifteenth turn of the dismal spiral stair. The close confines of the tower amplified the ocean, like the curl within a shell. He had yet to grow accustomed to the sound. Pasquanty was a Correndian, born far inland and away from the Cos, that land's great tidal river. Seven years in Karsa had done nothing to quell his unease at the sea. He was no islesman, and nor would he ever be.

Upon the Final Isle, there was no hiding from the sea. The sound of the ocean permeated every corner of the monastery. In those rooms above ground the booming of the waves was constant, for all the lack of outward windows, whether the tide gripped the island's greensward tight, or sulked at the bottom of the infrequently bared cliffs. In the deepest chambers carved into the rock it was worse. There the sea could not be heard, but it could be felt, a crushing presence made up of faint impact tremors, malevolent seeming. The sea was jealous of this tiny nugget of stone, the most remote of the Karsan Isles.

Only one building occupied this desolate speck. The monastery was a triangular block enclosing a bleak courtyard, a solitary tower rising from one corner, made of the same, grey stone as the rest. The tower was not in itself tall, but its position on the shoulder of the steep mount lent it height. Pasquanty could not stop thinking of the precipitous drop on the other side of the wall. Not being able to see worsened his vertigo. So he avoided putting his hand on the outer wall, and kept closely by the central pillar of the stair. The wedge steps were narrowest there, but he felt safer away from the wall.

Cold air blew down at him, making the few bird-fat lamps it did not blow out gutter in their alcoves. Upward, daylight filtered in, and the stairway took on the hard grey of sea skies. He paused, nearly at the top. He had no desire to complete his climb, but less to return below to the silent monks, so he hitched his robes, and continued up the slippery steps.

He emerged into a round chamber. Four windows were set around its circumference, the only ones that faced the ocean anywhere in the monastery. When monks spoke on the sole hour a week they were permitted, they often complained about the weather, and had told him the winter gales there were murderous, bringing up waves as high as the building itself if the tides were right. Pasquanty really wanted to go home before that happened. The longer they waited at the monastery, the more likely the chance became that he would see out the year trapped within the walls, freezing and damp, surrounded by monks who resented his very existence.

There was a pair of stone benches in the middle of the room, set back to back and sharing a common rest. One faced out to the trackless ocean of the south. The other faced the north. From there it was possible to look down into the monastery's struggling vegetable garden and the grim walls enclosing it. The northern wing, forbidden to the Guiders, loomed over the yard. Pasquanty had only had the courage to look down once. The sight of vertical grey stone streaked with tears of dissolving mortar had made him ill.

Upon the southern bench sat the Guider Aarin Kressind, Pasquanty's master. Already rangy before they had come, Aarin had lost weight. He had put aside his rich Guider's garb and jewellery, replacing it with the grey robe of a novice monk. The shaved back part of Aarin's Guider's haircut was growing out. He, like Pasquanty, looked permanently damp, chilled, and miserable. The relationship between the Guider and his deacon was strained at best, but Aarin appeared so glum that Pasquanty took an involuntary step toward him out of concern. The waiting here was hard on both of them. The slap of Pasquanty's sandal on the wet stone made Aarin stir.

"What does the sea fear, Pasquanty?" asked Aarin. He went back to looking at the southern view, the direction Aarin's brother had taken his monstrous iron ship on his fool's errand.

"Guider?" asked Pasquanty.

"The sound of the ocean rushing back and forth. It seems afraid."

Pasquanty gave a hunted grin. He hated Aarin's abstruse questions, each one was a small trap. "I suppose it does, Guider."

Aarin sighed. "You have no imagination Pasquanty."

Pasquanty looked out over the sea. The green mound the monastery occupied was the only part of the Final Isle permanently free of the water. At the lower tides, a wide margin of pockmarked rock framed it. Then the rock seemed like a yoke, hung around a condemned man's neck. When the sea was in and the island surrounded by boiling foam, he felt like the same condemned man chained to the Drowning Rocks waiting to join the legions of the Drowned King. Beyond the spume the limitless, rolling sea merged with the grey of the rain and clouds so that it appeared the monastery were pinned under a bowl lost underwater, and that great beasts might come upon him at any time, flip over the bowl and devour him. Or else he would drown, or suffocate, or simply forget who he was.

Guider Aarin was wrong, Pasquanty had a surfeit of imagination.

"No, Guider," he said.

"Are they ready?"

"Guider Kressind?"

Aarin rolled his eyes. "I am hoping that you have come up here to tell me that the Abbot Uguin has relented and that today, after three weeks of sitting around and being told this is forbidden and that is forbidden and that the time is not right, that the time finally is right and we may consult the oracle."

Pasquanty slumped. "No, Guider Kressind. He has not relented. I have not seen Abbot Uguin for days, and the brothers will not speak with me. I have come to inform you that our evening meal is ready. The monks go to the refectory. Did you not hear the gong? If we wish to eat, we must hurry."

"We have a little time," said Aarin. He moved up a few inches on the bench and patted the stone. "Come sit with me and look at the ocean, there's precious little else to do here. Even so late in spring, the days are short. Join me, and enjoy the remainder of the day before we are plunged once more into night."

"Yes, Guider," said Pasquanty. The carved bench was cold under his backside, the wind blowing steadily through the unglazed window was wet. The two men were so close they were touching elbows. Pasquanty's world filled with Aarin—of his smell, the slight staleness of his breath, the heavy scent of damp wool, the heat from his body. An unwelcome intimacy he dare not shuffle sideways to avoid for fear of acknowledging it.

"Being here is, I imagine, very much what it is like to be dead," said Aarin. "You have seen into the next world, during our guidings," said Aarin. "Everyone sees something different. What do you see?"

Pasquanty was surprised by Aarin's question. He rarely spoke with him about such things. *Get this Pasquanty, carry that, do stop snivelling.* That was the most Pasquanty heard from him. Pasquanty relaxed cautiously, his posture losing some of his defensive stiffness.

"Not much," said Pasquanty. "My sight is worse than yours," he gave a chuckle, an embarrassed recognition of his own inferiority. "My family is not so rich as yours in mageblood. I see glimpses, sometimes glorious, sometimes dark, always terrifying. They are difficult to frame in words."

"And when we fought the Drowned King, and the mage Vols Iapetus amplified my guiding?"

Pasquanty shuddered at the memory. He had been cowering in a doorway when the drowned attacked, crippled by fear. At the combined magic of Aarin and Iapetus, the sky had opened onto a vista of darkness, green faces roaring across it. Their expressions had been anything but kindly or serene.

"Quite," said Aarin when Pasquanty did not answer. "Rarely have I seen the veil torn so fully back." His face was heavy and lined.

"You are not well, Guider. You should rest. It is this place, it is joyless, dark. My dreams are bad, my sleep broken."

"The boundary between life and death is thin here, that is why," said Aarin. "If I look unwell it is not for sleeplessness. I can't stop thinking," he turned from the sea to look at Pasquanty. "What is it exactly we are guiding the dead towards?"

Pasquanty blinked rapidly, he could feel his larynx bobbing up and down in that way that so infuriated his master, but he was worried. Aarin had aged since they had departed Karsa.

Aarin gave a rare smile and gripped Pasquanty's hand. The Guider's own hand was freezing. "Being here has given me much time for thought, too much perhaps. I have become introspective, and a Guider should ever look outwards. Enough of the melancholy of the ocean. Let us go the miserable monks now, and find somewhere warm to eat."

CHAPTER SIX

An Unexpected Gift

LIKE MOST OF his siblings, Garten Kressind had shown his father's aptitude for making money. Unlike his brothers, he also had the knack of keeping hold of it.

Consequently, he had a large house of his own. Not so grand as the family manse in the Spires, but solid, fashionable, and situated in the best of the growing Karsa City's new districts.

In its selection he had given his wife Charramay her head, save in one regard. He insisted upon a practice salle, properly equipped with a bouting circle of hard clay. His wife had agreed only reluctantly, but knowing fencing was how Garten spent most of his free time, she conceded that he might as well do it at home.

"I tell you, Sothel, I'll not permit you to get that close again," said Garten. He tapped Sothel's blade with the flat of his own, making them both ring. They wore padded clothes to fence, but not full masks. Garten could never countenance that. At his wife's urging, he and Sothel fought with blunted blades and wore heavy leather goggles, beaked over the nose, the eyes protected by a mesh of stout wires. He would have done without them if he thought he could get away with it.

Sothel teasingly answered the tap with three of his own. "You're getting slower, Gart. Where would you rank now if you still competed?"

"Getting slower am I?" Garten pushed forward, feet spread perfectly. He drove two downward cuts towards Sothel's cheek. His opponent parried them with minimal effort, his guard never drawn to expose himself.

"You'll have to do better than that," said Sothel.

"I shall!" shouted Garten. He launched a blurring series of attacks that drove Sothel back across the bouting circle. Sothel parried each one with economy, but was hard pressed. He essayed only two ripostes, both dealt neatly with by Garten.

"Very well, you are not slowing down." Sothel was close to the edge of the circle. With a quick twist he disengaged, ducking under Garten's sword to avoid a rap across the back of the head. He danced back toward the centre.

"I've got plenty of fight in me," said Garten, levelling his sword point at his friend. "I may spend much of my time behind a desk, but I have not ceased improving, despite what my brother Rel might say."

"Yes, he did say that to me, last time I saw him."

"Well, we all know where his cockiness got him," said Garten. "He's going to have to be good where he's gone."

"He is a good swordsman," said Sothel.

"Just because you can't beat him does not mean he is better than me," said Garten.

"I can beat neither of you."

"Exactly."

They stepped carefully, both looking for an opening, circling in true warrior style. Garten preferred the older schools of defence.

Upstairs, the front door bell rang.

"Expecting anyone?" asked Sothel.

"No," said Garten.

"Aren't you going to answer? That could be the duke's man."

"I don't give a damn," said Garten, executing a flawless attack from the second position. Sothel parried it with difficulty. "Whoever it is can wait a few more moments."

The door boomed unnaturally loudly.

Garten and Sothel paused. "What the hells...?" said Garten.

"Perhaps we should finish for the day?" said Sothel. "You must have a lot to do."

Garten swept his sword around. "Perhaps you should shut up

and defend yourself. Besides, I can't have that pissant little brother coming home from his military adventures a better warrior than me. Say I affectionately. He's always bragging that I'm past my prime, and that he'll best me one day. I'll give him a shock when he gets back."

"I don't doubt it. You are getting better. You should be teaching me."

"You've been a good coach, Sothel. It's not your proficiency that I value, but your advice, your ability to break down each attack and to analyse it. I am a better swordsman than you, but you are a fencing master, I merely a skilled practitioner. I bow before your superior knowledge, if not your skill."

Sothel laughed. "So modest."

"Goodfellow, excuse me."

Garten put up his hand, Sothel lowered his sword. Garten pulled free his goggles. One of his maids waited at the foot of the stairs into the salle.

"Gods return, Hellonay, I told you no disturbances. I shall not get to give Sothel here a beating for several months!"

Hellonay curtseyed. Garten was jocular, vitalised by adrenaline. Ordinarily he was far more reserved. "Begging your pardon, goodfellow, there's a goodman here to see you. He has a delivery. And a, and a... Well..."

"Come on girl, I haven't got all day."

"Well he has a Tyn with him. Dortian says one of the Mandelway band from the Weave. I think it's a woman, but I can't be sure. I'd have the kitchen take the package for you but he says you have to sign for it—the young man is very insistent. Shall I tell them to return later?"

Garten left the ring, put his sword back into a rack and took up a towel. "No, no, I'll deal with it. Sothel, you wait here. I'm sorry. I'll be back in a moment, I won't be long, you're too damned expensive to pay to hang about."

"I shall come up, if I may. I could do with a drink."

"If you wish. Hellonay, see to the goodfellow would you? There's a good girl."

Hellonay curtseyed again, and Garten bounded up the stairs past her, two steps at a time, mopping sweat from his face as he went. He thrust his towel at a footman and jogged the length of his hall to the front door. It didn't do to be running about in front of the servants, but protocol be damned. His spirits were high from the bout. Warm, late spring air wafted in from the street, pleasant on his sweaty skin. In a few days he would be leaving on the most important assignment of his life; in his current mood he saw only the joy of the challenge, and none of the possible pitfalls. His butler Dortian manned the door, looking sidelong at the man in a drayman's long coat topped by a short cloak waiting outside. By the man's side was a trollish Greater Tyn. Hellonay had it wrong, it was certainly not a female. In the street, dog carts clattered by through bright sunshine, but the creature on his doorstep threw the day out of sorts. His skin tingled with its magic.

"Well then, you've dragged me up here. What is it?" asked Garten, his good humour replaced by forced cheer.

"A delivery, goodfellow," said his butler, eyeing the Tyn disdainfully. The young man did not seem bothered by the creature in the slightest.

"Yes, yes Dortian, thank you."

His butler bowed and withdrew.

"I recognise you," said Garten to the man.

The drayman was young, but not callow. He had poise. Behind his legs was a leather-bound box, two feet in all dimensions. A pair of clasps a third of the way down the front held shut a foldaway lid, and there was a carrying handle upon the top. "We work for Arkadian Vand, and the goodfellow's brother, Goodfellow Trassan Kressind. Perhaps the goodfellow has seen me at the shipyard, or at his brother's home?"

"We have a note," said the Tyn. It held out a bulging envelope.

"That's a treatise, not a note!" said Garten. "What the hells is it?"

"I am sorry. It is quite a list," said the man.

"Our little cousins are so very particular, goodfellow," said the Tyn. Its smile was insinuating.

"List?"

The drayman picked up the box carefully. "Of geas. Your brother told me to bring her here."

"Her, who? What? Oh gods, he hasn't has he?" said Garten. "Not that Tyn he had in the cage. Whizzy, or something. Why?"

"I am afraid you must accept her care," said the Tyn. "You are the chosen inheritor. We cannot take her elsewhere. You are bound by the nomination."

"Geas," said Garten wearily. He tapped the envelope on his thumb. It was well stuffed.

The drayman nodded, still proffering the box.

Garten took it and held it out at arm's length. "Dortian!" he called. "Take this through to the dining room. Be careful with it." The butler reappeared and took the box. "I have been told you require a signature."

"In a manner of speaking, goodfellow," said the Tyn. It held out a pin and a piece of paper.

"Blood? In seriousness?"

"I am sorry, goodfellow," said the man, and gave the Tyn an admonishing look.

Garten groaned, took the pin, pricked his thumb and pressed it to the paper. Glimmer laced ink impregnating the paper glittered and writing appeared around his print. The Tyn took it and hid it away inside its garish, filthy clothes.

"Marvellous, now I am enchanted to boot," said Garten.

"I doubt it, goodfellow," said the man.

"I don't," said the Tyn. The man nudged it with his boot, bringing an evil look to the Tyn's face.

"I am sorry. Your brother's wishes," said the man.

"Yes, very well. Good day," said Garten. He made to close the door. The Tyn stuck its foot in it. Garten looked down at it with a frown, and opened the door again.

"What is it?"

"Now begging your pardon, goodfellow," wheedled the Tyn. "What with work and bringing this over, I've been off my home ground too long. Feeling it now, goodfellow. Feeling cold even on so warm a day as this. Get the terrible aches in me shins when I've been out from me home ground too long. Take days to die, those pains do. It doesn't do to take a bound Tyn away from his home ground for long, oh no goodfellow." It looked up at Garten expectantly with big, brown eyes.

The drayman had the decency to look mortified. "I am so incredibly sorry, goodfellow. Ludloss!"

The Tyn Ludloss kept his hopeful face pointed at Garten. "Ever so painful, goodfellow."

"No matter," Garten grumbled. He fished a coin from his pocket. The Tyn took it in a filthy brown hand and bobbed and bowed its way back down the steps into the street. Garten pulled out a second and handed it to the man.

"For your manners, and your forbearance of the lack thereof on the Tyn's part," he said. The drayman nodded in gratitude.

Garten shut the door and stalked off into the dining room, his mood quite blackened. The case had been set upon a cloth on his table so as not to mar the wood. Sothel lounged against the jamb of the door leading back to the kitchens, a large tankard in one hand.

"Is that my best porter?"

"Naturally," said Sothel. He raised his tankard in salute. "Fighting you is thirsty work, and you'll be gone soon. Better I have it than the servants, eh?"

Garten approached the box. He weighed the envelope in his hands. His blood stained the corner.

"What's in the box?" asked Sothel.

"I shall show you," said Garten. He tore open the envelope, and found within a long list of handwritten instructions, wrapped in a letter penned in Trassan's untidy hand.

"A letter from my brother Trassan," said Garten. "One moment."

Brother,

Please accept this small gift, if gift it can be named. She is a delightful companion. A little demanding (I apologise for the list, a necessary evil), but useful nonetheless. I could not take her with me upon the ship, despite my future father-in-law's intentions. On the first count, although she has proved herself a fine friend, she is bound to report upon my activities to Goodman Vand, and to be frank with you I could do without the additional pressures this would bring upon me in this most vital and demanding of ventures. As you are aware...

"What does he say?" said Sothel.

"He is laying it on thick. Trassan never speaks so well in person, and only does so in writing when he feels he has gone too far," murmured Garten, scanning further down the letter. He turned the page over. "Not that that ever stops him from going too far. That man plucks favours as if I were an orchard of apples and he a starving man."

"What is in the box?"

"Wait a moment," said Garten. "Doing this hurriedly may be dangerous."

"Really? How exciting!" said Sothel.

Garten read on.

My most hearty of wishes that she... Blah blah, get to the point Trassan, thought Garten. *I did think that she might be of use to you in your embassy to Perus and that...* Hm, yes, I wager that you did not! thought Garten. *You are the most likely of us all to take good care of her...* Indeed, and now I have no choice, thought Garten. He scanned further down, scowling at Trassan's unctuous turn of phrase.

"Aha, at last we come to the bloody point," he said.

Shortly before my departure, I imposed upon the foreman of my Greater Tyn, Gelven, to procure for me a certain mixture of herbs and liquids, appropriately enchanted, to render a Lesser Tyn asleep for several weeks, long enough for Vand to assume I had taken her with me, no matter what occurs. Today is the date, according to Tyn Gelven, that she will awaken, and so I entrust her to your care. Thanks again for your aid in securing me the License Unconditional, and further humble thanks and apologies for this imposition. I promise I will make both up to you some day.

Your affectionate brother,

Trassan.

PS Do pay attention to the geas. They are rather important for your safety, I am afraid to say, rather than for hers.

"Little…" breathed Garten, crumpling the letter. "Typical Trassan, always pushing it just a little too far, wanting a little too much." He sighed. "Nothing to do. Let's get a look at you then."

He reached out to the double clasps on the front of the box.

"Are you sure this is a good idea?" said Sothel.

"No," said Garten, and snapped the clasps open.

The top half of the box front and top folded neatly away at the back of the box. The bottom half folded down, revealing that the box was a cage, with solid sides and back, and a ceiling and front of bronze bars. The interior was set out like a doll's house with two floors, a tiny staircase between the two. It was well appointed, with small chairs and tables, a bed, a miniature bookcase for tiny books, and a press to hold drinking vessels and the like. Some attempt had been made to secure the house's inventory, but all had been upset during transit, and piles of delicate crockery, books and furnishings cluttered the rumpled carpets.

On the upper floor, in the middle of this miniature disaster, sat a tiny, perfectly formed woman in a rocking chair, her arms and legs crossed. She was as finely featured as any goodlady, and dressed in a red velvet gown that would draw much positive comment at any ball, were she not three inches tall. Her expression would also have provoked discussion for entirely different reasons; a glower thunderous enough to crack mirrors. Garten drew back from her fierce regard.

"You are not Trassan Kressind," said the Tyn.

"I am not," said Garten.

"It is good you are not. I am very displeased with Trassan Kressind," she said in a way that chilled Garten's bones. She sniffed at him, like an animal. "You related. You have his family scent."

"I am his brother, Garten Kressind," said Garten. He bowed slightly, half-convinced that this was not a Lesser Tyn in front of him, but an aristocrat shrunk by wicked magic. The Tyn smiled, exposing a mouth full of horribly pointed, perfectly white, teeth, and that dispelled Garten's notion.

"I am Tyn Iseldrin, Garten Kressind," she said. "And provided you treat me better than your thoughtless brother, I am sure we shall be the very best of friends."

"I am sure we will," said Garten. He recovered his manners and his wits. "I am sorry, you have been in that box a long time. Can I get you some refreshment, Tyn Iseldrin?"

"Tyn Issy," said Tyn Iseldrin firmly. "Call me Issy, then fetch me tea. Tea made of hazel bark, with goat's milk and three grains of crystallised honey. Stir it three ways sunwards, four turns to evening."

"That's... very particular," said Garten.

She smiled wickedly again. "I assume you have a list of my geas."

Garten held it up. "I do." It felt fatter than ever in his hand.

"Then I refer you to article fourteen," she said. "Run along now."

"I think I'll let my servants take care of it, if it's all the same to you." He called Dortian and relayed the Tyn's request. "No news from the sea?" he said in a low voice to the Tyn.

"None goodfellow. How would I take it? I can do no sending. Once, treading the immaterial layers of this world were as easy as breathing to me. But now, I am not able." She tapped her iron collar. "You should ask your brother's master, Arkadian Vand, although I advise against that. He will be most displeased that his humble servant, by which I mean myself, is in your undeserving hands."

Garten sighed. "Very well."

"Cheer up," she said. "It could be worse. I could be free and collarless, and then you would all be dead." A different smile curved her lips, all sweetness. This one was worse somehow. "Instead we shall have tea. Yes?"

Garten nodded unsurely. Sothel laughed into his beer.

"Tea all round," Garten said with a brightness he did not feel. "And maybe cake?"

"That," said Tyn Issy, "will do for a start."

CHAPTER SEVEN

Into the Sotherwinter

IN THOSE DAYS when the gods dwelt there, the Godhome was in its glory. It sat levelly below the clouds, and consequently the teeming people of Perus laboured in shadow more then than now. Although direct sunlight was theirs for but a few hours of the day, they were happy in the knowledge that their gods lived above, and took pride that theirs was the holiest of cities. There were many churches then, and the Pantheon Maximale had been full of the devoted. From lofty towers bells rang and hymns were sung, each church in competition with the others to attract the attention of the divinities floating in their city of silver.

Vols Iapetus remembered, though he had never seen the Godhome with his own eyes. Not as it had been two centuries gone, nor as it had become in his day. Vols Iapetus had never been to Perus, or set foot in Maceriya. It was through the eyes of his ancestor, Res Iapetus, Driver of the Gods, that he saw, and he did so every single night.

The vision began as it always began, a smeary view of gold and light, a sense of woozy formlessness. Vols came to himself—or to Res, it made no difference, the two were indivisible in the dream— striding down a high hall aglow with all the splendours of heaven. Giant statues lined walls that shone with an inner light, gifts of gold and silver from worshippers desperate for favour heaped carelessly in the alcoves between. Beyond half-closed doors there were rooms piled with items of inestimable value. Platinum treasures from the days of the Maceriyan Empire, strange devices of ageless steel saved from the death of the Morfaan. There were chambers filled with the light of stolen stars that shone pitifully under curtains, burning out ignored, never to be looked upon. There were rooms crowded with captive souls sacrificed in other, less civilised times hung on copper pegs. Their howls for release went unheard. Res Iapetus walked by them all. From the mundane to the esoteric, there was not a treasure the gods did not possess, and they possessed them all in selfish abundance. Res had no interest in any of them.

A few, a very few, members of the human race had been aboard the Godhome during the rule of the gods. Res Iapetus was the last, the greatest of the mages, the peak of that breed reached as the evening of their kind fell. A last great hurrah before their ways slid into decline and the colleges opened their doors, and the magisters took their place as the world's foremost practitioners of magic.

How Res Iapetus gained ingress to the home of the gods was not known to Vols. That part of their shared memory had been burned clean, leaving a hole as raw and hot as a gouged eye. Vols shied from it fearfully. As a child he had poked and pried around Res's head, and that void had hurt him horribly. His curiosity vanished in that instant, taking with it a large portion of his confidence. Dread anticipation and a desperate desire to have the experience over and done with were his ruling emotions while he dreamed. These emotions seeped poisonously into his waking life.

Vols moaned in his sleep. Res approached the great throne room, straight-backed and determined at what he must do. He exhibited no terror, nor did he experience the tedium of familiarity, for unlike Vols, Res would do this only once. The greatest mage had been wrathful, he had been excited. Now the moment of his triumph was at hand, he was cool inside, detached. Today he would wear the fires of his rage on the outside, but within all was still. He was watching his own actions at one remove. Almost like Vols. The two mages, kin separated by centuries, shared the royal box in the theatre of Res Iapetus's mind.

First to suffer Res's wrath was Andrade, the tutelary spirit of the Earth. Under her protection came all living things. She had a throne within the god's great hall of the Yotan with the rest, but her station was outside the gates. Andrade was strange and beautiful, a blue glass titaness with the lower body of a snake. Her face's loveliness was surpassed only by her sister Alcmeny's. Unlike Alcmeny, beauty was the least of Andrade's talents. She was first and foremost a warrior. As befitted her kingdom, she was crowned with a high helm, and wore wondrous, supple mail that clung to her from the neck to the tip of her tail. Her stone was white sapphire, her month was Frozmer, when men needed more protection than most from the terrors of the universe. Her star was the bright Andrabus. She had been hatched, legend had it, from a dragon egg her father Tallimastus had swallowed whole and shat out in great pain, thus giving birth to her. Her armour and trident were forged by her brother Gudricun, lord of smiths. With the trident, she had slain lords of hell. Such legends surrounded her. Bright stories, beloved stories. Mankind regarded her favourably.

None of the stories mattered to Rel. He would write the last of her legends.

She performed her role as she was intended, raising her weapon and shield, singing her challenge with music that made Vols claw at his head in his sleep. She thrust her trident forward. Blazing lightning leapt from it.

Six inches from Res's nose, the lightning went awry, curling away like burning hair to blast apart the marble facings of the walls. Her song went unfinished. Stellar fire blazed from Res's eyes, ears, and mouth, from his anus and his penis, setting his clothes alight. He raised his hands and howled; a wordless, terrible sound that no human throat should make. A dim sensation of what that power felt like was as much as Vols shared. A fraction, and it was too much. When the moment of Andrade's destruction came, Vols convulsed in his sleep. He slept with a wooden bit in his mouth to stop him biting off his tongue.

Res's body shook from bone marrow to hair tip, and he wished Andrade away.

Having experienced their destruction several times a month since infancy, Vols knew more about gods than most. When they had occupied the Godhome they had been mysterious, ineffable beings. Since their banishment what was known of them had become more unreliable, the stories apocryphal at best, most from books of stories told by the gods themselves. None knew whence they had come, or to where they had gone. Sharing the memory of the God Driver, there were many things Vols knew that no other did. This was the hardest to know, more than frightening.

Not all the driven gods were banished. Some Res had killed.

Vols told no one but his animals this truth. He had a habit of telling them things he could tell no one else. Imagine, he told them, what that knowledge could do to a child? Sometimes Goodwife Meb found him weeping by the hen coop, unable to speak. Only her chicken soup made him feel better on days like that, and then he always felt worse for his hypocrisy—Vols loved his chickens.

For the thousandth time, Vols watched the immortal confront mortality. Andrade's features went through a swift succession of expressions: her premature cry of triumph gave way to shock, fury, defiance, and lastly a look of absolute horror.

Andrade vanished. Her form blurred at the edges and collapsed, shattering into uncountable pieces of blue glass. Her scream was pitiful. Vols' kindly heart ached at the sound.

Res's clothes burned from his body, whirled away in a flock of sparks. With an outpouring of white hot thought, Res Iapetus slammed open the ivory gates of the Yotan. They cracked, sagging from their mounts. Hundreds of perfect figures carved from dracon teeth depicting the deeds of the gods clattered to the floor, and burst into flame. Cold fury building, Res Iapetus marched into the hall.

Res found the gods variously seated or standing by their individual thrones around the wall of the circular hall, arrested in a tableau of amazement fit for a painting. They recovered their wits soon enough, when Res sent a looping curl of starfire towards their chieftain, Omnus.

Omnus banished the fire with a flare of his eyes. His father, Tallimastus, blinded and chained to his throne by his usurper of a son, laughed and laughed. Gudricun came at Res with his hammer, the god-goddess Caesoniopon with her sword. Both were thrown backwards for their trouble by a wild blast of power that charred their flesh. Tiriton cowered behind a rolling wave of water. Hespereona nodded sagely, as if she had expected this all along. Shunatrix bowed her milk-white head, hiding her red eyes. Alcmeny wept decorously.

Two were absent—Eliturion, who would survive this expulsion and dwelt in Karsa in Vols' day, and the Dark Lady, whose name was never spoken. She was permitted no entrance to the Godhome, and yet was honoured with a throne there; black where the others were white, festooned with carvings of the worst atrocities.

Omnus rose from his gold-chased seat, his staff of office shining in his hands, his brow heavy with wrath.

Res waved his hand. A ripple in the fabric of reality pulsed across Alcmeny and her throne, twisting the goddess of love and perfection into a mewling exercise in teratology. The wall splintered, and was sucked inwards. Behind the marble a whirling vortex opened. Young stars danced there.

"Out, out, out!" shouted Res. The mage's madness was upon him, his mind warring with the world to make it be as he demanded.

"Stop!" bellowed the king of the gods, and his voice was awful. In his youth, Vols had wet the bed at the instance. "This trespass—"

Res waved a hand. The lord of the gods of Ruthnia shrank to something little larger than a draconbird. Screaming shrilly, it whirled away into the vortex. A brief flash marked Omnus's ignominious passage from the Earth.

Some force exerted itself upon the bodies of the gods from the vortex of stars, ripping at their robes and hair. They became dishevelled, the weaker of them scrabbling for a handhold on the slippery marble of their thrones, the stronger shouting at Res for him to cease. Gudricun came at Res again. Res punched out a fist, a shockwave distorted space, lofting the smith god backwards into the vortex. Caesoniopon transmuted to her female aspect and called for peace. For her troubles she was blasted to glinting shards of clay that fell halfway to the floor before they were sucked away. Res strode on through the maelstrom.

One after another, Res removed the gods from their mastery of the Earth. Tiriton's veiling wave was snatched back, the sea god hurled at the vortex. Shunatrix and Hespereona went of their own accord, walking with what dignity they could through the gale of magic, picking up the warped Alcmeny between them on the way, and stepped out from the world voluntarily.

Tallimastus remained, held in place by his chains. "At last, at last!" he cackled. Res approached, sending the chains to pieces with a grunt. Tallimastus stood unsteadily, the wounds of his crucifixion raw in his wrists and ankles.

"At the beginning, so at the end. From nothing you came and to nothing you go," said Res.

Tallimastus grinned moronically in agreement, then without warning, he reared back and became a sheet of darkness that plunged toward the mage. Res twisted aside, his hands circling one another. The god of death and creation was sucked through the ring of Res's fingers, and sent speeding on his way into the vortex.

Res snapped his fingers. The vortex responded with a crack of its own, slamming shut. Behind the marble facing of Yotan, the metal fabric of the Godhome glowed red where the vortex had been. Abruptly the light pouring from Res Iapetus shut out. Exhausted, he collapsed to his knees in the centre of the room. He hung his head, unable to lift it.

Thunder boomed. The whole of the Godhome shuddered gently. Cracks appeared in the domed crystal roof. The luminescence emitted by the walls flickered and went out, blue daylight taking its place. Squares of sunlight fell hot on the flagstones, but a perishing chill took hold of the grey shadows. A rippling series of cracks sounded from somewhere deep within the structure. Very slowly, the Godhome slid sideways.

Vols' connection with his ancestor weakened, and he floated free of his body. Res Iapetus raised his head to watch him go. Blood ran from the corners of his eyes and his mouth. He smiled a bloody smile. Vols knew that Res saw him.

A tremendous shattering came from above. Cold, rarefied air rushed in. The Godhome lurched, pitch steepening.

As always Vols awoke before the crystal shards of the dome slammed into Res's back. Clutching at his sheets, gasping in fear, it took him a moment to realise that the vision had ended.

WEAK LIGHT ENGENDERED a sudden rush of nausea. Vols shut his eyes tightly again until it passed. Not only did the mass of iron around him upset his delicate abilities, but he had discovered a susceptibility to seasickness in all but the flattest seas. The Ishmalani promised him sealegs. They had yet to come.

Gripping the high edge of his bed, Vols emerged blearily from the dregs of sleep. The steam horns of the *Prince Alfra* hooted sadly, and he shuddered. He reached for the leather flask of water he kept by his bunk. His mouth was dry and his head hurt. He could thank the stars that the bucket by his bed was empty. The Tyn woman had been in while he suffered, leaving him some more of her foul-tasting remedy. He begrudgingly owned that it worked.

"The symptoms of revelry without the cause," he said glumly. Shivering, he slipped his legs from out under his blankets, and took a long draught of water. He ran his tongue around his teeth. They were blessedly smooth, free of post-vomit furriness. He considered his medicine, then seized the bowl and drank it down in three, spluttering gulps.

He wiped his mouth on his nightshirt. The medicine made his stomach flip, but once that had passed he felt better.

Vols rose carefully so as not to bang his head on Ardovani's bunk. On the opposite side of the room the Tyn foreman's small hammock swung. He was alone, his cabinmates having risen without disturbing him. That was no surprise. When he was in the throes of Res's past he never woke until it was done, no matter how others might try to rouse him.

The ship pitched slightly. For the benefit of the mageborn and the Tyn, wooden slats lined their quarters and though cold, they were not as cold as bare iron. Three steps took him across the small cabin. He tugged his clothes from the heating pipes running along wall. He gasped in pleasure at the warmth as he slipped them on. More light flooded in as he retrieved his jerkin, uncovering a brass framed porthole looking out to sea. The cabin was fuggy, but the porthole stayed closed. He doubted it could be opened now. Frost and salt rimed the glass. Green ice clinging to the bottom made an effective weld.

Vols peered outside, looking past his own reflection. Buck toothed, balding, his red hair untameably wild. Res had been handsome. Vols had inherited neither his power nor his looks.

An angular swell, almost too sharp to be water, slashed the ocean all the way to the horizon. The sea was a startling green draped with laces of foam. A mountain broke the divide between sea and sky, hard to discern against the bland grey cloud cover, but impossible to miss once seen. Not land but, as Captain Heffi had explained, but ice, floating free in the ocean. The ship surged on, spreading a boiling road from its wheels. The ice mountain seemed to sail in the opposite direction, cutting up the horizon. Vols watched it silently for a time.

Two sharp raps on the door, delivered for propriety's sake. Magister Ardovani waited for no reply, but pushed into the cabin, bringing with him a cloud of freezing air and the smell of outside on his clothes.

"Ah, you are up, friend Vols!" said Ardovani. "I came to check on you."

"That I am," said Vols, pulling his over trouser up over his longjohns. They were made of dog felt, a little tickly but warm. "I have felt better."

"You have also felt worse," said Ardovani, handing him his boots.

"These storms do nothing for my constitution."

"Do not be ashamed for that. During the high seas I am as afflicted as you. Even the Ishmalani find this ocean hard, and they are born to the sea."

"*Were* afflicted. You have adapted. I have not. If only we could moderate the water's heaving but a little."

"We both try, my friend. These seas are beyond our magic."

Vols gave Ardovani a little frown. His own powers might be a little erratic, but he was a mage, not a mere magister like the Cullosantan. Ardovani responded with a good-natured smile. Vols had been determined to keep Ardovani at arm's length, he coming from the rival school, but it was immensely hard to dislike him, and Vols was too kind to sustain petty rivalry for long. It had seemed to Vols he was being rude because he felt he should, and so he had given up trying.

"Yes, well. Perhaps we shall be better prepared for the next storm," said Vols.

"Perhaps we shall finally grow used to them and not be vomiting into buckets!" said Ardovani. "That would be a help."

"I do hope so. Captain Heffi repeatedly tells me, unnecessarily gleefully I might add, that the seas become wilder once one crosses into the Sotherwinter," said Vols a touch woefully.

"We have some high times ahead of us!"

Ardovani relished adventure. Vols did not, but Ardovani was of that type whose moods are infectious, and he found himself returning the magister's smile.

"So, Goodmage Iapetus. Would you care for some breakfast? Hot from the galley." Ardovani pushed a warm paper package, done up with string, at the mage.

Vols took it reluctantly. He had intended to let his stomach rest. Ardovani saw it in his face.

"You need to eat, goodmage."

"Thank you," said Vols. "But I believe what I really need is to get some air."

"Very well. You might eat on deck. I shall join you." Ardovani stepped neatly round him, and retrieved their parkas from their hooks.

Vols did not protest. He was too timid to raise his need for solitude, and Tullian Ardovani was a very difficult man to put off.

On deck it was bone-achingly cold, the sort of cold that Vols had no idea existed. It burned the nose and shocked the throat when inhaled. Upon exhalation their breath turned to sparkling clouds of ice crystals. The ship's complement went about its business as best it could though they all drowned in their outdoor clothing. Oilskins had given way to fur parkas. Over knitted gloves huge mittens engulfed their arms to the elbow, though they folded the mittens back for finer work, they never removed the gloves. To touch the skin of the ship was to leave one's own attached to the iron, as more than one crew member had painfully discovered.

Save for one wet patch, roughly square, over the centre of the vessel where the boilers worked, the ship was now frozen stem to stern. The deck sparkled with frost and had to be gritted with ash from the cooking fires. Rippled icicles hung from the ship's railings, rigging and superstructure, sea spray joining them into solid sheets if left too long. The rhythm of axe heads thocking into ice was a constant of ship life, broken by the occasional clang of steel on steel, and followed always by the musical shattering of ice on the deck. Ice clearing was a neverending task that occupied a large part of the vessel's crew. By midday they would have cleared those parts that needed clearing, but in a day or two the ice would be back, and thicker than ever.

"It gets colder every day!' exclaimed Ardovani as they emerged onto the deck. "And we are but three quarters of the way there. Can you imagine how cold it must be at our destination? I admit that I am freezing now, and I wear all my clothes." He laughed. "It is true!" he protested, although Vols had said nothing to deny it. "What I shall do when we draw further south, I do not know."

Vols made a noncommittal noise. Ardovani was voluble. Vols had determined some time ago that his input was not strictly required, so he let the Cullosantan talk. Ardovani's habit was to comment enthusiastically at every new thing and talk about it at length. Vols could not object, he shared the magister's wonder, and letting Ardovani do the talking for both of them was by far the easiest option. As Ardovani chattered, remarking upon this thing or that, Vols attempted a little magic to warm himself, reaching deep inside himself to find that place of perfect calm a mage—of Vols' modest talents at least—needed to work his magic. Putting Ardovani's commentary from his mind, he attempted to convince himself that he was in fact perfectly comfortable. Through his magic, reality would fall into line with his opinion.

It didn't work. The actuality of the cold was absolute, far too immediate. It would not be swayed.

So Vols hunkered into his parka and retrieved his breakfast. Deep in his pocket, the package had retained some of its heat. He did not have his mittens on, and chanced his fingers against the cold, pulling the gloves off with his teeth so that he could open the paper. Inside was a small meat pie, surprisingly hot. The heat of it against the cold of his fingers was a pleasing contrast. Vols bit into it, letting the steam flood into his mouth along with the savour. Both were pleasurable. He ate it quickly to save the heat from the cold, suddenly ravenous.

"Good, is it not? These Ishmalani know how to cook!' said Ardovani. "Is it—"

Vols balled up the paper and held up his hand. "Look over

there," he said with alarm. A group of three marines hung from ropes, battering at the thick flow of ice that had accumulated around the rigging close by the middle funnel. Although Trassan had temporarily solved the issue of the overpressure valves, it had become so cold that even the heat of the main exhaust did little to discourage freezing as the steam hit the air, and a large portion of it ended up whirling around to cling to the ship. Most alarmingly, in this ice were trapped motes of part-exhausted magical solids, visible as a faint mage shine beneath the surface.

"Lieutenant, lieutenant!" called Vols.

Bannord, looked down from the ice cascade. His face, sweaty with work, was framed by the dog fur of his parka.

"What little I know of glimmer engines aside, I doubt lambasting that ice with a steel axe is a good idea," said Vols.

Bannord looked down at him questioningly.

Vols spread his fingers. "Bang!" he said. "The interaction between iron and magic is volatile."

Bannord shrugged. "There's not much danger, Kressind says. Blunts the axes quick though." He held up his hatchet. The edge was eroded by contact with the ice's glimmer load. "No sooner has he solved one problem, we get another. I don't envy the boy Trassan."

"May I be of assistance?" Vols said. *What are you doing?* he rebuked himself internally.

"Magic?" said Bannord. He and his men shared a look. Vols had his great-grandfather's reputation to live up to. That one incident with the Drowned King aside, he had singularly failed to do so. "By all means, goodmage," said the marine.

The insolence in the man's manner tugged at a rusty lever deep in Vols. He turned to the funnel purposefully and held out his hand toward it.

Vols saw reality as it was—ice caked the upper parts of the funnel, thick icicles joined it to the rigging. The mage's trick was to see it as he wished it to be, and convince the world its version of fact was in error. *I cannot do it*, he thought. *Why am I trying?*

But something was happening. The magic came more easily than it had for a long time, taking him by surprise.

It helped Vols that the ice was laced with glimmer. The fabric of things as they are was thinner because of it. Furthermore this cold, unlike that he had failed to push from his bones, was affecting something other than himself, and thus abstract. Abstracts were easier to deal with than absolutes. For a fleeting moment, Vols saw both states of reality. A moment was all it took.

"Melt," he whispered.

The ice ceased to be ice. All at once it became water that slooshed down to the deck with a wet slap, soaking Bannord's arm in the process. Everyone on deck turned at his cursing.

"I'd get out of those wet clothes, Lieutenant," said Vols. He wished his words did not whistle through his teeth, and that his voice were deeper. They were satisfying to say nevertheless, and there was a good deal of merriment at his quip.

Ardovani slapped his mittened hands together in delight. "The working of magic in your school is miraculous, friend Vols. The imposition of a shift in basal reality by will alone! I am thankful for the modern age, I should not be able to work magic at all the old way, without formulae or device. You are a marvel."

Vols bowed slightly. Privately, he wished what Ardovani said of him was true.

Taking care not to slip on the water refreezing to the deck, Vols went back inside with his head held high.

CHAPTER EIGHT
The Train to Perus

GARTEN'S HOUSE WAS in uproar. Men in the admiralty's livery came in and out of the open front door, weaving past each other, threatening collision but always somehow avoiding it. On the way out they bore crates of light wood. Packing straw littered the floor. The weather had taken a turn for the worse. Rain fell through a miserable fog, and it had become cold again.

Garten pushed his way irritably through the press of men. Charramay stood in the doorway to the dining room trying to catch his attention. Garten was aware she wanted to speak with him. Her need irritated him. Could she not see how busy he was?

"Garten dear," she began timorously.

"Careful with that!" shouted Garten to one man. "You have it upside down!"

The man stopped, causing the one following to bump into his back.

"The arrows man, the arrows!" Garten tapped his hand on the stencilled marks on the side. "Can't you understand something that plain, eh? Eh? That's a fine china set for the Ambassadress of Pris. If it gets broken I'll take it out of your wages!"

The ingoing and outgoing streams of men tangled themselves into a knot around Garten.

"Yes Goodfellow Kressind, sorry Goodfellow Kressind," mumbled the man. Garten winced as he recklessly righted the box. The men resumed their hurried procession. Outside a dray barked impatiently.

"Garten, if I might, may I have a moment with you?"

"Look at the state of the floor," Garten said. Muddy prints covered the tiles. Charramay sniffled and tried to stifle a cough. "Darling, get in out of this draught! You'll catch your death."

"It's just a cold, dear," she said. Garten smiled at her. She opened her mouth to speak. Garten's smile turned to a frown.

"Have you seen the post?" Garten said. "Dortian! Dortian! Damn him, where is that man?"

"Goodfellow!" Dortian came into the hall, his smart suit covered with an apron and sleeve protectors. Somehow he maintained his poise when all around him lost theirs.

"Where the hells have you been?"

"Overseeing the devastation of your study, goodfellow," he said drily.

Garten managed a smile.

"Surely they must have a very good library at the embassy?" ventured Charramay.

"They're my books! All packed?"

"Almost," said Dortian. "We have made good time. You leave in two hours. Most articles are ready to be taken to the station and loaded upon the ministerial train."

"Do you have the post?"

"I do, goodfellow." Dortian went into the first of the house's reception rooms. He came back out with a sheaf of papers.

"Has she replied?" asked Garten.

Dortian handed the most important letters to Garten, and passed the rest on to a maid. "I believe so, goodfellow."

Garten riffled through his post, coming to a neatly folded letter sealed with a slab of wax bearing a three-towered mark. He smiled as he tore it open. The smile grew as he read.

"Finally! A relief! Such a relief. She replied, and will be coming."

"Very good, goodfellow," Dortian nodded and went back to his duties.

Charramay tugged at his arm. Garten turned to her. She was a foot shorter than he. Some said she was plain and that she lacked wit. It was true it took her a while to understand certain things. But she was refined, considered in her actions, kind and sweet. Garten loved her for those qualities, and there was a cunning to her that others overlooked. She looked so earnest his anger was doused. He grasped her gently and steered her into the relative quiet of the dining room.

"I am sorry, husband to take you from this hubbub, but we have had so little time together of late," she said.

"It is I who should be sorry my sweet. My temper has been short for too long. I am afraid you have borne the brunt of it."

She nodded, her eyes downcast.

He placed a hand under her chin and tilted her face back up to look at him. "You understand. This is such an opportunity! Trassan has his ship, Katriona her factory, Aarin his Guidership—this is my chance to make my mark, to make father proud! It is no little thing I do, accompanying Duke Abing to the election of a new High Legate. I will have a chance to meet and talk with the highest lords of all Ruthnia, and effect real decisions. If I am careful, and not a little lucky, then the world will be our bauble, my love. A minister's coat awaits me, and then, in a few years, who knows? Chancellor, prime minister?" he smiled at her. He meant to tease himself, but it was a thin veneer to his ambition.

Charramay dabbed at her running nose. "I understand."

"Then, once my position is secure, perhaps you may pursue your dreams?"

She hugged him close, but did not speak. She had heard his promises too many times before to put much currency in them.

He stood back. "Be safe. Dortian will look after you. If you need additional help, or become lonely, go to Katriona. Give my love to the children."

"We should have brought them home from school," she said.

Garten smiled. His purpose was to reassure, any other woman but Charramay would have found it condescending. "We cannot coddle them. Too much indulgence is bad for their mental constitution. We cannot interrupt their studies, even for such an important day as this. I will write to them, tell them of my new position. They can take pride in that."

"Be careful Garten. The fog is all over the isles. It is always so when the Morfaan come into this world."

"It is the weather, my love. Such fogs are nothing unusual this time of the year."

Charramay's round face pulled inwards, like a pudding on the verge of collapse. "It is the mists of the Morfaans' own land that cloak them from the sun. The gate to our world from their land of exile is open. Noises have been heard on coasts, the things from their realm!"

Garten gave her a sympathetic hug.

"Enough folktales," he said. "There are monsters enough in this world without imagining those of another." He embraced her again. "Now go and rest. If you insist on standing here in this cold you will only become more ill. I will come to you before I leave. We shall sit a while and talk of pleasant things before I go."

"Promise?"

"I promise."

She took his hand. He squeezed it. She went to her room, her maid following.

"She's right you know," said Tyn Issy, who had been watching their conversation from her travelling case upon the dining table. She sniffed ferally, a contrast to her ladylike appearance Garten still found disturbing. "This is Morfaan mist. They will make the crossing soon."

"Yes, well," said Garten. "It is about time."

"HERE IS THE state coach, Goodfellow Kressind. Duke Abing will be with you in a moment." Abing's man pushed the door of polished red wood back into its housing. Everything on the train rattled and banged. Truckles jostled on the rails, beating out a frantic march tune as they hurtled down the line. Decanters on the tables chimed against each other. The pulls on blinds slapped against windows. Unsecured doors slid back and forward as the train crawled looping lines up Karsa's many hills and sped down the other side.

The man held out an immaculate white-gloved hand as invitation to proceed. Garten tugged the brim of his high secretary's hat and passed from one carriage to the other. The door slid shut behind him, small hidden wheels rolling on fine rails. The catch clacking into place echoed the gentle bangs of rail joints passing under the train. Sounds nested in sounds, endlessly recursive, so that Garten felt like a ballbearing rolling down the track of some novelty machine, himself ticking and clicking as thunderous clockworks unwound all about him.

The train slalomed from side to side. Garten's fencing had trained his poise, and he remained steady. He did, however, swing out his arm to balance himself, momentarily forgetting the small rosewood box in his hand and knocking it against the wall.

"Ow," said Issy's steely voice from inside.

"Sorry," said Garten. A couch tempted him to sit, but he did not wish to appear too comfortable when Abing arrived. Taking a seat at the meeting table dominating the end of the carriage would be presumptuous. There was a small half oval table bolted to the wall a third of the way down the carriage, furnished by two padded leather chairs. Judging that a fair compromise, Garten took a place there and set the box upon it. The box was tall and narrow, not unlike a lantern in shape but lacking panes. Carefully, he opened the front.

Behind a delicate barred inner door, Tyn Issy sat inside on a cushioned bench, her ordinarily immaculate hair askew.

"Ow, I say again," she said. "Ow and ow and ow! Be more careful. Your brother was never such an oaf."

"Is there a geas against smacking you into a wall?" said Garten, attempting to make light of his error.

Issy sniffed. "It is a common courtesy not to. I thought you a goodfellow! And this box! The one that scoundrel Trassan packed me off to you is small, but this... It is intolerable!"

"The other is in my quarters. You see how this train clatters about. I cannot carry you in it."

Issy stuck her nose up at him. "So," she said, and just that.

"If you are with me, you are with me. You are supposed to be useful, so I shall make use of you. Unless you wish to sit out your days in your toy palace?" She ignored him, which Garten took to mean she did not. Garten adjusted his clothes, hitching his trousers to prevent creasing, unbuttoning a few of the lower buttons on his long Admiralty coat so that he might move his legs more comfortably, and settled a little better into his chair.

"It's too hot in here," he said. There was a small iron stove in the corner of the room. The belly of it was stamped all over with a magister's warding sigils against conflagration, helping to contain the fire inside and lessening the need to tend it. The stove belted out a deal of warmth. Garten loosened his collar.

He yanked on the blind pull, and it went shooting up to the roller. The revealed glass of the window radiated a deep chill. Fog blotted out the night, a luminous gloom lit by unseen moons. From Karsa City the train had climbed up and out over the moors. Avoiding the deep valleys of the Lemio and Var's many gushing tributaries, the railway headed instead across the spine of the plateau of the Hardenweld. The most direct route to the Neck was through the high wastes of the country.

Garten sighed. Even were the fog to lift, the view up there was dismal, endless rolling hilltops of heather and yellow grasses fractured by peaty gullies, bogs and mean, dark little valleys whose brown waters raced to be off somewhere better.

"So desolate a place," he said.

"There are worse," said Issy. "I have seen them."

"I'd thank you not to tell me," said Garten. "I have burden enough on my mind without you adding nightmare to the load."

Issy grinned. She enjoyed working on his nerves.

"You don't have to ride in the box at all. What if I were to let you out?" he said to the Tyn. "You could ride on my shoulder. Such a situation would be gentler on you. My brother Guis has a Lesser Tyn that sat on his shoulder. That was bound to him by a tiny chain, thin as two twists of hair."

"Of what kind?" asked Issy.

"Bronze, I think," said Garten.

"Cretin! The Tyn, not the chain! What race was the Tyn?"

"A Lesser Tyn," repeated Garten.

"And I am sure we look all alike to you." Issy snorted at his ignorance. "It is a kind offer, but you cannot let me out."

"I could. All I must do is open the inner cage door, and you are free."

She narrowed her eyes in consideration, but she slowly shook her head. "There are geas against that, and for good reason. I like you Garten. Do not release me, for your own sake. I would not like to kill you."

Garten laughed; he did not believe the stories many did of the Tyn's magic arts, and Issy seemed too ladylike. "You are tall as my thumb. If you pose me peril, I can stuff you back into the cage. You tease me."

"I do not," she insisted. "I am deadly."

Garten sat back. The rocking of the train and its attendant percussion was less jarring now he sat. "It is strange that Guis has his Tyn, then you came to Trassan and now you are with me."

"There is nothing strange about it at all, dear Garten. Magic is in the blood of certain families. We Lesser Tyn are drawn to it, guided by the rivers unseen."

"Ah," he said gravely. "Rivers."

"Do not mock me! You are dismissive for one whose brother is a Guider, another is a mage, and a third tinkers with engines powered by the universal spirit. Yes, *rivers*. Those of time and fate. You cannot see them, they are nevertheless there."

"I see."

"You do not see. Think. You cannot see your heart," she said. "I am sure you have one."

"Well." He tapped his fingers on the desk. "I maintain your coming to me was coincidental, the result of my brother, not unseen fate."

She shrugged. "How very human of you to think so."

Garten looked to her for further explanation.

She widened her eyes and stared at him. "It appears you are somewhat dim," she said slowly.

"Because I don't believe in child's stories, and I know that Tyn are liars?"

"Children learn stories for very good reasons. Tyn truth is different to human truth, that is all. You have much to learn, goodfellow. It appears I am forced to play your tutor." She stuck her minuscule pink tongue out at him. "Get some tea," she said. "I'm thirsty. Your stupidity bores me."

"I am not your servant," said Garten. "You are the one in a cage."

"But you are the one getting the tea," said Issy wickedly. "So who is the servant?"

Garten gave her a hard look and pulled on a bell cord. A few moments later a man in admiralty livery appeared. Garten requested tea and cakes. The servant returned quickly, and they ate the cakes while they waited for Abing. By unspoken, mutual agreement they made small talk on matters of fashion and the weather.

Duke Abing's approach was like that of thunder. Nothing stirs in the sky, and then all is tumult. Yet it does not come unexpectedly. As surely as barometric pressure builds before the lightning, Garten's anticipation of the duke's arrival crested at the precise moment Abing shoved the door back with a bang. Several men accompanied him, waving papers over his shoulder and shouting for his attention.

"Later goodmen, later!" bellowed the duke. He hurled the door closed, almost taking a petitioner's hand off at the wrist. The shouting persisted, albeit muffled.

"Damned fools, makes one feel pursued all the while!" shouted the duke. He straightened his tie as he came toward them, mighty as a thunderhead. Everything about the duke was solid, larger than life. He put Garten in mind of Eliturion, a notion he had harboured for some time but which he had never shared; Abing despised the god, and thought him a liability. But the chief reason Garten held his tongue was that Abing was one of those men who had an excellent sense of humour, until the joke was on them.

Abing's gut was large with rich living, his shoulders broad with muscles, his cheek marked with a scar won in war against the Oczerks. Deep into his fifties, his hair was still thick and black, and he wore it swept dramatically to the side in a younger man's style. Thicketed brows dragged down his forehead into permanent glower. Deep, well-oiled muttonchops and a small triangle of beard at the tip of his chin completed the framing of his face. He wore britches and fine stockings, a thigh-length coat the same as Garten's, but parti-coloured, one half Foreign Ministry green, the other the blue of the Admiralty, to denote his double posts. At Prince Alfra's request, Abing was both Minister for the Admiralty and Minister of Karsa-of-the Hundred. Tall heels added to his already considerable height. His cloth was expensive, his uniform idiosyncratically adapted. A thick stack of the day's broadsheets were wedged under one elbow.

"Never a moment's peace!" Duke Abing said everything forcefully, his voice complementing his nature as the booming of surf complements the tempest. "Damn!" he said. He went back to the door and opened it again. The men were still there, waving their papers. He reached into the scrum, and yanked out a thick folder bound with the green ribbon. Hands withdrew sharply as he slammed the door shut again.

"Read this," he said, coming to Garten's table. "Correspondence from the Fifteen Preeminences, our chief embassies in the leading realms of the Hundred." He dropped into the chair opposite Garten, shaking the table. "Damn continent's dropping into the first hell as we speak, and the gates of the other ninety-nine yawn wide."

The duke put his newspapers on his knee and looked them over.

Garten picked up the folder.

"Not now man!" barked the duke. "I have—" he fished out a watch from his waistcoat pocket. Garten had laughed at Trassan's watch when he got it, but it was quite astounding how quickly the devices had caught on. He had to get one for himself.

"—four minutes for you," finished Abing. He slid the watch back into its pocket and plucked up a cake. "You shall familiarise yourself with that when I am done here, not before."

Garten put the folder down, the duke slapped the papers on the top. He had been waiting to see the duke in private since the embassy train departed Karsa City that lunchtime, and had spent much of the time paring down his questions to the bare essentials.

"Is there anything I should know about the situation I do not already, your grace?" asked Garten.

"You tell me," said Abing. "You're the secretary."

"Your general impression will suffice, please goodfellow, if you would."

"Dire," said Abing, spraying crumbs. "The Maceriyans have not yet chosen their candidate, and that is unprecedented, and bloody bad form to boot. There's some sort of tussle going on between the Three Comtes. The one thing they do agree on is their adamance that their candidate be elected High Legate, no matter who he is. The Khusiaks disagree with the Maceriyans, but also disagree with us. They are pushing their own man. For once the Mohaci have put aside their differences with the northeast, and look likely to back the Khushashian candidate. Between them they have got the eastern kingdoms behind them. Maceriya can rely on the Maceriyan blok, as per bloody usual, but if the east can sway the middle kingdoms into line then the Maceriyans will lose and we absolutely cannot have that either. Khushashia has been getting too big for its boots recently, and if they and Mohaci throw in their lots together, it will not take a skilled demagogue to whip up imperial sentiments. Again. Damn thing's a mess. It all depends on who the Maceriyans pick for their candidate. They're being bloody tardy about it, let me tell you."

Abing kicked back and laced his fingers on his gut. Despite his girth, the muscles of his legs were clearly defined beneath his stockings and britches. "None of this would matter but for the Twin's apsis, idiots agitating in the capital, talking of the return of the gods and suchlike called up by the perigee. It's millenarianism, pure and simple. But simple ideas appeal to simple folk no matter the idiocy of the notion."

"I have been keeping note of the Church of the Return."

Abing sighed. "That's a fart been brewing for a while, and riper for its gestation. The Church of the Return! Until now, they have not had much traction, but people are scared. All this balderdash in the archaeological journals has been snapped up, blasted out by the papers and that has given the church's claims some momentum. Word has it they have the ear of Raganse, the second of the Three Comtes of Perus. He might only be second, but he's a slippery bastard, and has built up quite the power base. What he whispers tends to come out the mouth of the Parliament in Perus very loudly. Perhaps a few months ago the Maceriyans would have conceded the vote to the Khusiaks. In those circumstances we could have isolated them from the Mohaci, but now? Raganse is pushing for a church nominee, and will fight to get him in the big chair. They need each other to fight this out. Damn legate died at the wrong time, a year before the Twin's closest approach for four millennia. Inconsiderate bastard. Too much pride in Perus. Damn Godhome hanging over their heads day in day out, gives them a terrible case of the religious rectitudes. Gods and politics, never mixes! Never! Mark my words young man, that's why we keep that blasted sot Eliturion in a glass box. They've never forgiven Karsa for Res Iapetus and the driving of the gods. He acted of his own accord, but..." He quirked his eyebrows. "They don't see it like that, naturally. I'm just damn glad our pet deity is amenable to staying sozzled and staying quiet."

The torrent of "damns" ceased. Abing helped himself to a biscuit.

"Please do not eat all my cakes, Duke Abing," said Issy.

The duke's head snapped round. His bushy eyebrows shot up.

"What the hells is this? I thought it a vanity case, which, by the way Kressind you were due a drubbing for. But a cage, with a... a Tyn! Listening in? Far worse than powdering yourself like a Perusian. Have you gone mad, Kressind?" blustered the duke.

"She's a gift of my brother's, though I'd say an imposition. Vand gave her to him, he gave her to me."

"Can't trust the damn things. Get rid of it. Immediately!"

"I cannot, goodfellow. It is bound to me now, thanks to Trassan."

"Ah yes, your brother and his damn ship. Another fine dray's mess he's dropped in my lap too with his bloody expedition." Abing rubbed his face and gasped. "On top of everything else, the drowned are displeased at his crossing of the Drowning Sea. I should never have agreed with Alfra and taken the foreign ministry in as well. Too much work, bloody thankless it is. Karsa-in-the-Hundred! A hundred pains in the arse, more like."

"You are the best man for the job," said Issy. "For a man, and a human." She curtseyed demurely. Somehow, her hair was perfect again.

"Damned impertinence of the thing," complained Abing. He turned to Issy. "Listen, imp. The correct phrasing is your grace, or goodfellow at the very least. I have my position by birth, but I earned the right to enjoy it by bloody hard work!"

"I know the terms, Duke Abing," said Issy mildly. "It is you whose etiquette is mistaken. I am of higher degree than you, a princess among my people."

"What sort of princess lives in a box?" scoffed the duke.

Issy looked around the frame of the lantern door. "I do live in a box. I like boxes. So who put me here—you humans, so sure of your power. Or did I?"

"I do not enjoy riddles, goodlady," growled the duke.

"It is not a riddle," insisted Issy. "It is a question. Riddles have no foil against ignorance, they tantalise but contain all that is required to answer them within themselves. Questions do not. This is a factual matter. You either know the answer, or you do not. "

"What is the answer then, damn it all?" The duke banged the table with his fist, making the teacups jump in their saucers.

"If you do not know, you will have to suffer in ignorance, and I shall remain an enigma."

"An irritation. Get rid of it," Abing said to Garten.

"She is harmless," said Garten. He cursed Trassan inwardly for passing this curse on to him. Abing would be within his rights to replace him as secretary.

"I am not," said Issy.

"Then she is useful," said Garten.

She grinned widely. "Now that I am."

The train swayed from side to side, shaking the contents violently.

"The rails on the moors are warped with frost," said Garten, keen to change the subject.

"The ride gets easier once we come to lower altitudes," grumbled Abing.

"My father once bid for the contract. He did not win it."

"Your family has enough power, Kressind. The refusal was a deliberate check," said Abing bluntly.

"Were the priorities right in that refusal?"

Abing gave him a hard look. "Do you question the cabinet's judgement?"

"If my father's companies had made and laid the rails, they would not have warped. One must ensure that the correct priorities are taken into account." Garten laid a hand on Issy's case.

"Damn you Garten, you are a sly one. Very well! The imp stays, but only if she proves herself. If she doesn't, well, we'll get a mage in and get your geas cut, and then I'll sit on her myself." Abing stood. "You better have something for me Garten. I need mollifying."

"But I do have something."

"You little dog! Waiting to the end. You do? What? Spit it out man!"

"Who."

"Who then?"

"Lucinia Vertisa, the Countess of Mogawn."

Duke Abing swayed with the carriage. A look of calculation crossed his face.

"Why her? Isn't she a risk?"

"The Maceriyans admire her."

"The Maceriyans, the Perusans in particular, they're all bloody perverts," said Abing dismissively. "There had better be a better reason."

"The Twin. She has calculations. Scientific calculations. She presented to the Royal Institute in Karsa earlier this year, and was received favourably."

"I heard."

"Her expertise is outrunning her reputation for licentiousness. We can use both to our advantage."

"What? Have her do her presentation again, undermine the god-talkers? Scandalise the dracon eaters of Perus a bit? Is that your play Kressind? Sow some doubt, unseat Raganse and reap a candidate more to our liking? Then we could side with the Maceriyans, and stick it to the bloody Khusiaks!"

Garten made a modest moue. "And more. That she is a woman will play well with the Queendom. The Queendom, along with the Duchy of Daiserich, hold the keys to the votes of the petty princes of the Olberlands. If she performs either duty well, then we have great advantage. If both, then the legate can be ours for the choosing."

"Alright, alright, don't overstate your promise. But still, very good, Garten, very good." Abing pointed a square-ended finger at him. "When you do this sort of thing, it reminds me why I promoted you to secretary. When is the Hag joining us?"

"Please, your grace. Not that name. We must try not to offend her."

Abing grunted. "I hear she looks like a man and ruts like a bitch."

"What of it? She has the finest mind of this generation."

"A woman?" said Abing doubtfully.

"She awaits us at Vieyve-su-nare, at the edge of the Neck," said Garten. "I wrote to her sometime ago, and received her letter of acceptance this morning before I left."

"In the nick of time! Fine, fine. Don't let her upset anyone. But good work, good work all the same." He jabbed his blunt finger at Garten several times. "Now all we have to decide is who we're going to back for High Legate!" He barked out a mirthless laugh. "Back into the fray."

"Duke Abing?" said Issy. Her voice was so high and fine it could cut glass. "If you have finished with your periodicals, might I have them?"

"You read, your highness?" said Abing sarcastically.

"Yes I do," said Issy. "Avidly. I desire to consume the agricultural sections. You have eaten my biscuits, and I am still hungry."

CHAPTER NINE

A Careful Purchase

MADELYNE FORS WAS the fourth in a line of seven girls, all made up for display. A footman dressed in the garish costume of the Jhaydue House of Pleasure took the girls from the back hall, into a plain corridor and down a set of worn stone steps. A small door awaited, opened solemnly by the footman, as if it were the way into a glorious palace, and not a dirty little cellar. The lintel brushed the top of Madelyne's hood, smearing the velvet with rotten lime. Beyond was a vaulted cellar. Four anguillon oil lamps burned on hooks in the wall. Otherwise it was bare of any adornment, the walls unplastered. The rough cut stone bled moisture.

Medame Verralt, owner of the brothel and, it was said, most of the city block it occupied, awaited them. Her hair was tied in a neat but unattractive bun atop her head. Her dress covered her almost completely, from the base of her age-wattled chin to her ankles. The cuffs covering half her hands, leaving only her fingers and face exposed. Despite its coverage, the dress was immodestly clingy.

Madelyne had met Verralt once before, on her visit to the debtors' prison where she had selected Madelyne for the sale. She had seemed severe then, now her pinched face was angrily set. She held a cane of the kind employed in schools.

"Quickly now, you little sluts," she barked. "Into line, or I shall not spare the whip on you."

All seven were beautiful, all young, all desperately poor, on the cusp of attaining full womanhood and thereafter losing their looks to the ravages of poverty. Madelyne wore her best gown, the only one she could save from the tax gatherers: threadbare, but still elegant. Most of the rest of them wore clothes borrowed from Medame Verralt's girls. All of them had had their faces heavily painted. They had been bathed, perfumed. Under their dresses they wore nothing as they had been instructed, and the cellar chilled them.

Medame Verralt fussed over the row of girls, adjusting their hair gently, rearranging their postures less so, pinching their cheeks to make them redder, shoving up their chins, forcing their bottoms and breasts out so that their spines creaked. "Smile damn you!" she snapped, tapping at the sixth girl in the row with her cane.

The girl began to cry, her head sinking to her chest.

"Oh my dear, are you sad?" said Verralt with mock sympathy. She struck the girl's arm, and the girl snatched her hand behind her back. "Pull yourself together, the Infernal Duke will be here in a moment. He cannot abide misery, and you look appalling when you weep! Look at you, like an anguillon sprat, all pouty and wet. Stand straight!"

The girl shook her head. "I don't want to," she gulped out. "I've changed my mind. I want to go."

Medame Verralt raised her cane for a hard blow, and the girl's tears dissolved into chesty sobs.

"Pathetic," said Verralt. She lowered her cane. "Get her out of here. Take her upstairs. If she won't earn her debt out with the duke, she can do it on her back. You'll regret your choice soon enough," said Verralt.

"Medame," said the footmen, and led the girl from the room with a sight more kindness than Medame Verralt exhibited. Verralt chivvied the remaining girls along to close the gap, smacking at Madelyne's thighs with her cane when she fell an inch out of place. Through her skirt the blow was an annoyance rather than painful, but Madelyne glared at her. Verralt looked back, unimpressed. "Quickly now, quickly. He is coming."

"He's a little premature," said one of the other girls slyly. The others smirked.

Verralt rounded on her, finger out to scold. "Less of that, you speak of a goodfellow of the most refined tastes and manners. He cannot abide coquettishness."

"Makes me wonder what I'm doing here then," said the girl. Verralt cracked her on the wrist.

"Ouch," said the girl sarcastically. "Now you're getting me excited."

"If there is more of your insolence, there is more of that to answer it," Verralt said. She struck the girl with a heavy, snake-swift blow and this time she gasped. "Is there any more insolence?"

"No Medame," said the girl. She narrowed her eyes and rubbed at the red weal on her arm.

"Cover that up, you are to be perfect for him! Perfect. No mark on you," she smiled lasciviously. "He will want to put those on you himself. Now hold your positions, and wait."

Madelyne fixed her eyes on a line of mortar in the wall. She was nervous, conflicted at what she was doing. The cellar was well hidden from prying eyes. Madelyne could disappear, and no one would know. Those women who had been in the duke's service were highly visible in society, but for all anyone knew, the duke had associated with more girls than advertised. There was no sign the cellar was used for anything else, no scrapes on the floor to show that items had been removed, no scraps of wood or straw or sacking. The Medame must make plenty of money selling girls to the duke to keep this valuable space bare, and she must do it often.

Any movement or sound, be it the slightest sigh, was met by a sharp look from Verralt.

They waited, stiff and posed as soldiers at attention. The cellar trembled with nervous breathing. From hushed, snatched conversations upstairs Madelyne had discovered that three of the girls had been bought from the poorhouse and the debtors' gaol. Verralt had given them all a choice whether to present themselves to the duke before buying out their debts. Although choosing between the Infernal Duke and the gaol was not much choice at all, if they were not picked long years of working in the Medame's brothel awaited. The other three girls were there voluntarily, of that rare sort genuinely excited by the duke's proclivities. Their faces were flushed under their make-up. Verralt had no need to pinch them.

A loud knock at the outer door made them all jump. Madelyne's heart hammered. She had lived her entire life in the city of Perus, but she had never seen its god. Muted voices spoke at the end of the hall.

One which surely belonged to the god rumbled and purred, so deep and assured she shivered. She forced herself to focus, to concentrate on why she was there.

Not for him, she thought, not because I have to. Because I choose to. Because Harafan knows what he is doing.

Slow steps came down the hall accompanied by the rap of a cane. The footman returned, opened the door, and stood back.

The god stepped into the room, bending almost double to pass the tiny door. He dusted his shoulders off as he stood.

Madelyne's eyes disobeyed her and strayed to the duke. He filled the room, as tall as a Torosan, but without their lumpishness. His horns brushed the ceiling, his shoulders kissed the walls. Despite his outlandish appearance he was well formed. His exquisitely tailored clothes were tight on large muscles, elements of a physique so perfect as to be almost a caricature—wide shoulders, small hips, and fine, tapering legs. His face was imperious, proud, possessed of a broad, bullish nose wrinkled with a pattern of curved clefts. A pair of modest fangs protruded from his lower jaw, leaving delicate indentations in his top lip. He was shaven-headed but for a long queue of bronze hair running down his back. He was copper-skinned. His curled horns, black and smooth as onyx, were polished to a high shine.

Verralt's demeanour changed utterly at the appearance of the duke. Her face smoothed, losing some of its hard angles and a measure of its age. For the first time, Madelyne saw that she must have been beautiful once. Verralt clucked and bobbed, smiling wide enough to show off every one of her shining secondhand teeth. Clutching her cane tightly, she went before the duke and curtseyed low, her silks and laces rustling decorously. Fearing Verralt's wrath, Madelyne returned her attention to the wall.

"Your grace, the Duke Infernal, we have been expecting you."

"Gisellia, my sweet," said the duke. His voice was so deep Madelyne's skin prickled. "Please, get up."

Verralt looked up at him with adoring eyes. She shone in his presence. The duke cupped her face in his hand and wiped away a tear, smearing powder onto his giant thumb. "You were one of my favourites."

Verralt smiled at him.

"You served me so well in the past, and continue to do so today."
He cast his eyes over the women. "Tell me what we have."

"A fine selection, your grace."

"Ah, but only six?"

Gone to girlishness, Medame Verralt nevertheless retained her
acumen. "Six of the very best, your grace."

The Duke Infernal curled a lip in amusement.

"You were ever quick witted, my dear. A little *too* quick witted."

For all her admonishments against coquettishness, Medame
Verralt laughed and flapped at her face. The duke brought such a
transformation of spirit upon her. "All personally selected. I bought
their debts."

"All from the gaol, none from the poor houses?" asked the duke.

"Just one from the poor house. Most are hags by twenty in there
these days, your grace."

Madelyne stifled a twitch in her neck. She had come from the gaol,
but was far too familiar with the poorhouse also.

"Times are not what they were, I remember many a sweet poorhouse
girl. Never mind, six will do. This is a rare collection. I sense you have
exactly what I require, right here in this room. Well done, well done!"

"I certainly hope so, your grace."

The duke walked down the line, shoulders hunched against the
curve of the vaulting. "Such pretty butterflies, enjoy your moment
in the sun, beauty is fleeting," he said to the girls. "Tell me of this
one," said the duke, pointing a heavy finger at the girl next to
Madelyne, a brunette in a yellow dress. Madelyne struggled to keep
her eyes forward as she had been ordered, and could not resist a
glance at his hand. His nails were finely manicured. She felt obscurely
disappointed.

He turned to Madelyne suddenly, and she flinched. "Expecting
talons?" he said genially. There was a challenge to his smile. Expensive
scent wafted from him, but it could not quite mask his own odour: a
mix of hot stone and a healthy, animal sweat.

Caught off guard, Madelyne stammered. "N... no your grace."

The Duke Infernal returned his attention to the girl in the yellow
dress.

"A farmer's daughter," explained Verralt. "She was arrested for licentiousness, and could not pay her fine for working without papers, nor afford a permit."

The girl trembled. Madelyne could guess her story; off to seek a bright future in a dark city, finding no mercy and no money, forced to part her legs to eat. How could she pay the fine?

"A whore?"

"Unfortunately, yes," said Medame Verralt so gravely one would have thought she regarded brothels as the world's most singular evil. "Not a very good one, or she would not have been caught. Does her sullying disappoint or excite you?" said Verralt. Her lips and eyes glistened in the lamp light.

The Duke Infernal waved his hand dismissively. "I care nothing for your petty human morality. It changes quicker than the wind. What is abominable to one generation is practised with enthusiasm by the next."

"I do not wish to second guess your desire, your grace. I merely thought you would enjoy the drama of her fall, from ingénue of the forests, to night walker."

"I do, I do!" said the duke. "You know me so well, my dear. It is all in the context. I may not care personally for human mores, but how they affect you, how you feel, how you suffer and thrill when you transgress, well." He chuckled. "That is sweet wine, exquisite to sample, and the pleasure it brings you when your misgivings are overcome... How old are you girl?"

"Fifteen," said the girl in a small voice.

"Did you run from home, from your boring life?"

The girl nodded miserably.

"Naiveté! A frequent road to disaster." The duke lifted a tress from the farmer's daughter's head and sniffed at it. "Exquisite. Alas, this one is bound for more tawdry assignations. She is not for me. This is a story I have enjoyed too many times. Novelty, novelty, bring me novelty!" The Medame gestured to the footman, and the girl in yellow was led away, her head low with misery. There she was passed to a second man waiting outside, and went forever out of Madelyne's knowledge.

"The next then, if you please, your grace. A very interesting story of betrayal and privation. The brown-skinned beauty, at the end."

The Duke Infernal gestured with his cane top. "This one? A very pretty jewel, yes." He walked over to stand in front of her.

"A fine lady. Once," said Medame Verralt, "a noble of Ferrok where the sun is hot. She was abandoned by her husband here. With no money of her own and no way to send for more, she fell on hard times and was taken to the gaol. Too much high living, my dear, that you cannot afford!"

"I am a goodlady. In my land," said the woman with cold dignity, "I am of important family."

"Eyes forward! You are not to speak!" Verralt raised her cane. The Duke Infernal caught her wrist softly in his massive hand, swallowing her arm to the elbow.

"That is not necessary, my dear Gisellia, let her speak," said the duke. "Your family cannot have held you in any regard my dear, if they leave you here to fall into debt." The woman shook with anger. "I am sure you shall earn the Medame here much money, but you are not for me."

The woman was removed. Four were left. So it went on, the duke chuckling good naturedly at Verralt's barbed comments. He took his time, his joy in the selection evident. Two more were examined, humiliated by Verralt's crowing, and dismissed until only two— Madelyne and one other—remained. For a long while, the duke asked nothing of them, but looked them over like a farmer appraising cattle dracon. He rested his chin in his hand. "Both debtors you say?"

"Yes," said the Medame. "Pretty girls, and unspoilt."

"I really can't decide. I might be tempted to take both. If only I could!"

"Why not?" said the Medame eagerly, scenting double profits. "It would be something new for you, something exciting!"

The duke shook his mighty head. "Nothing is new to me, Medame. No, one it must be. Two together become unruly, hard to train. Disaster is the most frequent outcome." He sighed and gestured at the girls. "I need to see more. Could you?"

"Strip them," said Verralt harshly.

The footman came forward, and tore the dress from Madelyne's back. The last vestige of her old life fell away, ruined. Madelyne did not fight, she kept her eyes forward, put her arms back at her side once the footman had finished. Her breasts tightened in the cold, bringing an appreciative noise from the duke.

The footman went to the other girl and tore the dress from her also. The girl's head sank with shame. She covered her mound with one hand, her breasts with the other.

"Arms down!" snapped Verralt. This time the duke did not stop Verralt, and she lashed at the girl's buttocks with her cane. The girl dropped her arms, arched her back to get away. She knew she should not move, but could not help herself and took a step from the stinging crop. The footman grabbed her biceps and held her in place as Verralt lashed her. The Medame did not stop until the girl was screaming, covered in livid red slashes. The footman let her go and she crumpled to the floor in the scraps of her dress, her arms protecting her head.

The duke licked his lips at the display, exposing the whole row of teeth. They were all sharp. He touched the tip of each with his tongue. "Modesty will be a great hindrance to my plans. I will take that one. She displays herself properly in the face of her shame."

He pointed his cane at Madelyne. "She is fine featured, her body is superlative, she shows self-control, she has the will to do as she is told, and yet," he strode over to her, passing his hands over her body without touching her. The unnatural heat from his hands brought forth goosebumps on her skin. "I sense an edge to her. Defiance, and... Yes, something else." He laughed again. His breath was hot as fire.

"Markos will pay you, Verralt." He bowed low, took her hand and kissed it. "A pleasure, as always." He bowed to Madelyne. "I will see you soon, girl."

He stooped under the door, and was gone. Madelyne let out a long shuddering breath, still keeping her eyes on the wall. She would suffer the duke's attentions if she must, but she had no desire to taste Verralt's sadism.

A pallid, unkempt man came in from outside. His suit and tall hat were dirty and tattered. Over one arm he carried a fur-lined cloak, in his free hand he had a large purse, which he passed to the Medame.

"For your continued service and discretion," rasped the man. He came to Madelyne. His skin was unhealthy looking, very dry. She shook at the thought of those fingers touching her, but as he draped the cloak over her nakedness he was careful not to handle her. "I am Markos, the duke's servant," he said. Around his eye sockets the skin was deeply lined, his eyelids red, puffy and flaking, but his eyes were such a pale blue, clearer than the sky, and the whites brilliant as fresh snow.

Verralt watched all this, running her eyes over Madelyne's nakedness with relish, excited by the duke's purchase of her.

"You are very fine. I am sure he will enjoy you," said Verralt to her lasciviously. "If you fail, I will buy you back and enjoy you myself."

"Hush now, Medame," rebuked Markos. "She is no longer yours."

Markos guided her through the door. So small, how could the duke pass through it, Madelyne wondered. She was dazed. Success brought its own problems.

"Pay no heed to the Medame," said Markos softly. "You belong to the duke now. He is a fair master, if you please him."

Markos took her outside into the fog. A carriage awaited her, drawn by four jet-black drays. She half expected slavering jaws and glowing red eyes, and laughed nervously when they put out their pink tongues and wagged their tails in greeting.

Markos helped her gently into the carriage and took her to her new home.

Once there, she did not see the duke until three days later.

CHAPTER TEN

The Tower and the Hag

DESPITE ITS NAME, in appearance the Neck was more akin to a dragon's backbone. A long sinuous ridge that ran from Great Karsa to the shore of Macer Lesser, it cut the Karsan sea in two except at the very highest tides, when the gap at the Neck's centre was inundated, and the two halves of the sea joined into one. At those times it was a magnificent sight, a razor of cliffs surrounded by surging waves, the whirlpools of Gorgoantha and Sryman churning either side.

Most of the time it was a bleak ridge in a world of mud. Only the hardiest of plants made their homes upon it. The windblasted sandstones were grey with exposure, the nodules of quartz studding the grit scrubbed dull. Giant colonies of seabirds and draconbirds occupied the sides, constructing their higgledypiggledy nests more or less in peace. Their droppings streaked the rocks white and gathered in caves. This guano was harvested for its chemical content, providing a modest living for those who went to collect it. Otherwise there was precious little profit there. The stone of the neck was so friable and riven with cracks it had never been quarried. The seabirds nested in such inaccessible places and were so aggressive they were rarely troubled for their eggs or hunted for their meat. The neck's flora was also undisturbed, for there were richer, easier pickings to be had on the landward cliffs. Nothing edible would grow in its thin soil, the sea was impossible to access from the clifftop, and so no sane man would live upon it. What rubbish swirled out from the cities either end rested only a while before being sucked out into the wider ocean.

The railway necessitated viaducts and causeways of packed stone, but they had been artfully built, incorporating the elegant piers of the fallen Morfaan bridge over the Gap, and were regarded as an adornment to nature's art. Therefore the Neck remained defiantly unspoiled, unformed by human hand despite being trapped between two populous lands, a band of wilderness throttled by mud.

Vieyve-su-nare's roots were Morfaan, set down in times no chronicle remembered. Atop ancient foundations were the lesser efforts of the High Maceriyans, and the inhabitants spoke a queer bastardised dialect of that language still. The flimsy buildings of the dark age following the Maceriyan Resplendency had not survived well, and so the progression of the town's architecture took a giant leap across aeons. In places ancient walls, none higher than a woman's waist, had been unearthed from the peaty earth and left on display. Bronze plaques spoke boastfully of secrets dragged out of time's depths. But the true pride of the town was far more impressive, and it was no ruin.

At the heart of Vieyve-su-nare was a slender tower many thousands of years old. It had outlived all else built around it by men or Morfaan. Vieyve-su-nare had undergone a spate of rapid building over recent decades. New hotels, a domed town hall and a train station designed by Per Allian himself early in his career rose over the crooked streets. The tower had yet to be eclipsed, and was more than twice as high as the tallest modern building. A tapering construction of surpassing beauty, three hundred feet around at the base, one hundred at its truncated top. The original crown had fallen away, the floors of the interior long gone. Still it stood, a reminder to the Karsans that greater beings than they had trodden these lands.

Garten and Duke Abing toiled up a stair winding around the exposed walls of the interior. Stone was used in the construction of the tower, not the Morfaan building glass. The masonry was so finely fitted that even after eight millennia the joins were hard to see. Garten trailed his hand along the wall. Except where wind and rain had chewed at the windows, the stones were smooth, and in places maintained a marble's lustre.

"Damn delays!" grumbled Abing.

"Your grace could demand the train press on. It is the ministry's own train. We rush to meet the Morfaan, and their own mists blockade us. The train's lamps will suffice to light the way. Why will they not move?"

"The fog is up too thickly in Maceriya. The drivers insist we cannot cross at night," said Abing.

"For fear of creatures in the mist that do not exist. You are not afraid of old wives' tales, your grace?"

"I certainly am not. But the drivers will not drive. Every train that has tried to pass the Neck on nights of Morfaan mist, they say, has suffered some misfortune. Let us leave aside the fact that the Morfaan have come to Ruthnia three times in the eight decades since the railway was built, and that the misfortunes were nothing more serious than a scalding from an upset tea kettle. Goodmen and their superstitions! Still, they will not be moved, and we should not force them or we will have no driving crew to take us to Perus. We must wait."

"There is one consolation," said Garten. "I have always wished to climb the tower."

"Your pet hag made it quite clear we were to meet her here. We have no choice in this either, your desire to clamber up these wet stones be damned." Abing huffed up the stairs, his face red with the effort. Garten found the going easier physically, but less so psychologically. The drop down the hollow tower stump was dizzying. He put it to the back of his mind, determined not to let fear overrule his interest in the tower.

Clouds of water vapour swirled around the open top. A thick mizzle beaded the velvet of their coats with shiny dewdrops. By the time they reached the summit, they were quite damp, though not yet soaked.

The mayor of Vieyve-su-nare had installed a viewing platform at the top. Slippery green beams rested on ancient corbels. The stairs carried on through a cut-out in this new floor, ascended another ten feet, and stopped their ascent. The last step was a hopeless block against the white skies. The wall had been sheared off diagonally, as if by a sword cut. The wall to the east was higher than the wall to the west, which dropped so low a cast-iron guard rail had been installed to safeguard visitors. By this stood a slender figure, a woman in man's clothing, wearing a long waxed drayman's coat with short cape, a wide brimmed hat with a spray of dracon feathers in its band.

"Countess! Countess Lucinia Vertisa?" called out Garten.

The figure turned to them. She raised a gloved hand in greeting.

"Garten Kressind?"

"You are here!" said Garten. She came across the slick wood to meet with him halfway. They shook hands, like men. "Might I introduce his grace the goodfellow Duke Abing of the Vestral, Minister of the Admiralty and Minister of Karsa-of-the-Hundred to his highness Prince Alfra?"

"Gods protect his soul," said the countess with a quirked smile. She held out her hand. Abing looked at it disbelievingly.

"Go on then man, take it, I don't bite. Well, not under these circumstances," she said.

That pierced Abing's distrust. Sensing a character of similar will, he let out a cloud of steaming breath and smiled back. Garten looked on in disbelief as all the lines Abing's face had accrued in saying hag this and hag that melted away. He grabbed her hand firmly, pumped her arm and said, "A pleasure, goodlady. I am glad to have some real blue blood with me. These new money fellows are all well and good but..." He cast a meaningful look at Garten. The countess let out a light, feminine laugh that belied both her reputation and her mannish look. Garten studied her face surreptitiously. She was no beauty, but nor was she the monster popular gossip had her to be.

"Our fathers were acquainted rather well, so I understand, during their time in cabinet," she said. "It is well to maintain the links between families such as ours."

"Indeed." Abing kissed her hand. Garten was amazed at Abing's fickleness, and not for the first time. On matters of import the duke was resolute, but on occasion what appeared to be deeply ingrained ways melted away like ice in the sun. He had thought this a weakness of character for a man with the duke's duties, but he was beginning to think it was, in fact, not.

"I believe you know my brother and sister, Guis and Katriona," said Garten. His attempt to claw back the initiative proved clumsy. Her face clouded at Guis's name.

"Katriona is a fine goodlady. I know her but little, but I feel she and I could be dear friends, given a little time in one another's company," she said sincerely. She held Garten's eyes and his hand a little too long. He cleared his throat and gestured to the railing. The three of them returned to where the countess had been standing.

"Tell us why you chose to meet us here, goodlady," Garten said. "I suspect it is not only because of the opportunity to visit such a historical building."

"You are right. I suppose I am being a little theatrical. I have many vices. Melodrama is but a small one. I am sure you can forgive me, but I arranged to see you here because I wished to make a point."

"About the Morfaan," said Abing. They looked out over the view. The edges of Vieyve-su-nare at the tower's feet were softened by the fog, the bustle of the town damped to nothing. Only the Neck and the tower seemed to have any solidity.

"In part, but not only," said the countess. "This tower demonstrates the power of the Morfaan, and it is a mighty edifice by the standards of this lesser era. Did you know, when he built his station, Per Allian spent more time drawing reconstructions of this building? The Prince's father grew quite angry at the delays. The drawings are exquisite, beautiful studies in pen and ink. Some of them are a little fantastical, but the least extrapolation puts the original height of this tower—based on its proportions and the masonry Allian uncovered built into the later town—at double this height. Double! One could see clearly into Macer Lesser from the summit. And this is not their finest surviving work. It is a fragment, nothing compared to the city being uncovered by Arkadian Vand in the ash of the Three Sisters, or the indestructible fortress at the Gates of the World."

"My brother Rel is stationed at the Glass Fort," said Garten.

"He is lucky. The Glass Fort is one of the wonders of Ruthnia. I long to see it one day."

Garten's mind went to Rel, sitting out his banishment in a drafty glass castle. Rel's early letters had been optimistic, but Garten supposed whatever awe Rel had felt at the power of the ancients had worn off long since. Although far north, the gates were cold in winter.

"The Morfaan were a truly remarkable people. Their dominion of the Earth persisted for untold ages," the countess went on. "And yet their civilisation collapsed in little under a century. The why is what I have devoted my career to uncovering."

"They did not fall. They ruled and later advised the Maceriyans through their resplendency," said Abing. "A matter of historical record."

"If you can call the legends that have survived to the present day 'history', then what you say is true. But the most generous reading of such ancient myths suggests those who oversaw the building of Old Maceriya were much diminished in number and power from those who came before. Do you know, the first signs of man's habitation are found in layers of the ground only a little lower than the final rubble of the Morfaan's world? This begs a number of questions in addition to why they fell."

"Nations fall all the time," said Abing.

"They do. But when one discerns a pattern to the rising and collapse of empires, should we not dig deeper?" said the Countess. "Goodfellows, I have performed a thorough investigation. My research these last months has taken me all over the near continent. I have read many volumes of the most obscure and venerable sort. The trip was not pleasurable. You can imagine how I, as a woman, fared in some of the less liberal kingdoms. But I had to do it, and I did it to put into context my calculations regarding the movement of the heavenly bodies, to whit the Twin and the two moons, Red and White. This is my hypothesis. Eight thousand years ago, the Morfaan's empire sank into ruin after centuries, if not millennia. They were masters of this world, and yet they barely survived. A little while after, along come the Maceriyans."

"Their world, the Classical World, lasted five thousand years," said Garten. He nodded at the duke encouragingly.

"I am sure you are well educated enough to know it is not so simplistic, Goodfellow Kressind. There was the period of the Maceriyan Resplendency. The Turmoil finished it, seemingly at the empire's height, afterwards followed by the period of Maceriya the Shadow. Finally, the Age of Ignorance, the curtain of which we ourselves only lifted some six hundred years ago, and which marks the beginning of our own civilisation. There is a pattern."

She slapped her hands together impatiently. "A cycle running over periods a little over four thousand years in length. Look into the ground burying the ruins of the Morfaan, and there is a band of charcoal one foot deep. Above it there is little new building. Dig down to the close of the Resplendency, and there are similar signs of upheaval. The civilisation that followed was much debased, and withered. The Maceriyan empire followed a similar track to that of the Morfaan—ascendancy, abrupt upheaval, slight recovery, then decline."

"And what has this to do with our current problems?" asked Abing.

"She has a theory, Duke Abing," said Garten. "This is why I wanted to bring her. Hear her out."

"It is the Twin, goodfellows. It is not the gods as the old scriptures tell. I do not proclaim this without basis. I have spent much time with Eliturion. He is evasive, but I am persistent. I have inferred that he is no more than five thousand years old."

Abing frowned at Garten.

"You mean to say, the gods are younger than the Morfaan?"

"Much younger," said the countess. "It has not been discovered yet simply because no one else knew what to ask, or how to interpret Eliturion's blather. He openly says the gods were made. The remnants of the church have always dismissed this." She made a derisive noise. "The words of their last god! The gods are young, the Twin is eternal. The Twin, I have mathematically proven, comes closest to the Earth on a repeating period of four thousand, one hundred and twenty two years, fourteen days. I have rolled my calculations backward into the past—"

"And the fall of the Morfaan and the end of Maceriya's Resplendency coincide with this celestial event," said Garten.

"Don't interrupt the countess, Kressind," rumbled Abing. "I will not have you treating her as anything but an equal. She might be a woman but she talks sense and is still a degree of class above you. Show some respect to the goodlady."

Garten nearly choked. "I am sorry, your grace."

"Do not be. I enjoy it when people grasp what I am saying, to have them leap to the chase with me. Hunting alone is tedious. Having to spell everything out becomes mightily dull. One shouldn't douse the flames of another's epiphany. You are correct, Goodfellow Kressind. What I do not know is how the catastrophe occurs, only that is has done so twice before, and that the third befalling is predictable. It will happen on the 33rd of Gannever, year 461 of the current era. A little over one year from this date."

"Hmmm," rumbled Abing. "As long as you can convince the Three Comtes of Perus to stop listening to the damned pantheon revivalists, that's all I care about. There's a whiff of war. Gods and politics don't mix; I've said it before and I'll say it again until somebody bloody listens to me. You are, I trust willing to do this for Karsa and the Isles?"

"I hear they write plays about me in Perus, and copy my clothes. It would be amusing to see them. Yes, I will do it."

"Good," said Abing. "A fat duke, a new-money ladder climber and the most scandalous libertine in all the isles." The countess bowed ironically. "A fine company to save the kingdoms."

"I doubt we can save it," said Lucinia. "Whatever happened was cataclysmic enough in scope to destroy two civilisations far in advance of ours. We will be quite helpless before it."

"Then what by the hundred hells are you doing here?" murmured Abing. The fog was parting over the neck, exposing the lumpen black spine of its ridge.

The countess smiled. It lit up her face. For all her manliness, at that moment Garten understood why men pursued her.

"Your grace, I merely want the satisfaction of being right."

"You spoke of several questions, goodlady," said Garten. "I believe you have addressed the most pressing. What were the others?"

"Ah, yes. There are two. The first is one asked many times over—where did we, our race of humanity, come from? I find the placing of the first human archaeological remains intriguing. If the gods did not create us, and I am certain now they did not, then who did? The third question is a trifle in comparison to the other two, but it troubles my nights the most." She leaned out and looked down the curve of the tower. "One fascinating thing Per Allian determined with his reconstructions was that this fortification was built to defend the Neck."

"Self-evidently," said Abing.

"What is not so self evident, your grace, is having completed his construction, Allian determined that its defences face *into* Karsa. This tower is the first line of a defence to protect the mainland *from the isles*."

"Is that so?" said Abing. "Well."

"So one has to ask," she said. "What once dwelt in our land that the Morfaan were so afraid of?"

A long, haunting bellow sounded out in the low clouds hiding the mudflats.

"The Morfaan's creatures," said Garten.

"Old wives' tales," said Abing, and shook his head. He flipped aside the front of his coat, took out his watch and glanced at its face. "Damn these delays," he said, snapping it shut. "My magisters calculate the Morfaan will reenter the world in the evening, five day's hence. We must be in Perus by then, or we'll lose the advantage of their favours to the others. They're damn picky for a nigh extinct race."

CHAPTER ELEVEN
Beyond the Mists

WARM DEATH BECAME cold life, and Josan the Watcher awoke. The last Morfaan woman floated upward, only to bump her nose against hard glass. Her newly started heart fluttered. Her cot was still closed. The lid should be open. Darting blue lights chased themselves around the angular lines graven into the glass over her face. Through vision blurred by the liquid immersing her, she watched for the lights to stop. Had the machines failed, bringing her to life only to drown her?

The cot lid's lights ran away down their angular grooves. No more came to chase them. Cot, lid and water blinked red, and the lid lifted upward, and slid away.

Josan's instinct to sit quickly went unfulfilled, she had no strength. Weak fingers, slippery with alchemical fluids, scrabbled at the edge of the glass cot. She half turned to bring her head out of the bath and struggling it up to rest on the side. Viscous liquid slipped off her skin in sheets, draping itself over her mouth as she coughed, clogging her eyes as soon as she blinked them clear.

She rested there with her face on the edge of the cot, unable to move. The warm fluid chilled rapidly. She needed to get out. Difficult movements brought her leg clear of the liquid, more brought her knee over the side. By employing her vestigial middle limbs to grip the edge, she dragged herself out, her head never coming fully vertical as she swung first one leg then the other down to the floor. Pain skittered up her calves and thighs as her feet touched marble. She paused again, holding onto the edge of the cot for several minutes, trying not to retch. For her, the most unpleasant aspect of awakening was the purging and she put it off as long as she could Finally she gave in to her body's demands and allowed herself to vomit. Long threads of the fluid rushed out of her stomach. She coughed. Her lungs burned as they struggled to clear the remainder of the liquid pooled in them. The coughs' violence surged so she thought they would never end.

When they did she was shaking with shock and cold. Groaning, she stood upright. Her head spun. Black spots swirled across her vision, threatening a return to unconsciousness. She gripped the cot until they abated, then released the edge of her resting place. As she did not fall, she took an experimental step. Her mind was dull with the deathless sleep. Much of this fuzziness would retreat, but not all. The mental fog worsened with every waking. With a scientist's detachment she wondered how much she had lost of herself this time.

Cot was a kind word for her bed, for it really was nothing but a tomb, a glass box moulded to fit her prone body, set upon a marble plinth. Tracks for its sustaining magics covered all surfaces. More angular circuitries were incised into the plinth. All were dark, the darting energies quiescent now their task was done. There were dozens of such devices in the Hall of the Deathless Sleep. She no longer recalled why, and as far as she remembered they had never been used. There had only ever been the two of them sleeping there—Josan and Josanad the Watchers, last of the Morfaan.

A foot-long mechanical beetle emerged from its lair in the walls, shook its wing cases free of dust and went to her bed. Implements unfolded from its head, like bizarre mouthparts, to clean away the mess with fussy movements. It was none the worse for its own long deactivation. She wished she woke as easily as it did.

Her twin brother was not yet awake, but lay peacefully asleep in his own cot. She went to check on him. She knew only enough of the device to see that it functioned correctly. Perhaps she had once comprehended its workings fully. She could not remember remembering if she had, but that was no surprise. Josan watched her brother awhile in worry. The transition affected him more than her, and she deferred waking him in part because she feared what she would find.

His naked physique seemed mightier magnified by the thick alchemical fluid. His upper pair of arms were cleanly muscled. Being a male, his midlimbs were larger than hers. They were crossed on the lower part of his chest, carefully manicured claws interlocking. His double penises floated above the light banding of his stomach.

In his repose Josanad appeared as noble as the first day they had been laid to rest. While they had walked among the living he had been perfection in mind and body, one of the paragons of their race—kind, just, and passionate. Sadly she recalled that man, lost forever. Last time they had been recalled he had emerged petulant and childish, quick to anger, impetuous in his decisions and unkind in his lovemaking. Fighting back sorrow, she decided to put off his waking as long as possible and went to prepare herself for the Marble Council.

The Hall of the Deathless Sleep was a lozenge shape taller than it was long. Lofty ribbed vaulting arched high over the machines it harboured. Doors were set at opposing points of the diamond. One led to the inner body of the Castle of Mists, the other to the robing rooms. There were no spiders to weave cobwebs in the pocket realm, nor any dust or leaves to blow in through gaps to coat the floor. Devices kept the marble that constituted the majority of the building spotlessly clean, and yet there was a sense of neglect to the castle, of air unbreathed, of spaces undisturbed by the passage of living bodies. No one would have entered the robing rooms since she had shut them up, however long ago their last waking had been. No one could, she knew, but the desolation of quiet chambers too long unfrequented upset her nonetheless.

A bath waited for her. She pulled a face at its stale-smelling steam. A thought drained the water and ran it again. The second filling lacked the odour, and she was relieved that the water purifiers had not failed.

She lingered in the bath, letting the heat of it seep into her body and quicken her sluggish heart. The perfumes she favoured had lost their potency. She would have to make more before she bathed again.

The warm towels that awaited her as she got out of the bath

had the same sense of neglect that suffused the rooms, as did her clothes, stored in one of many sealed wardrobes grown from the castle's translucent stone. They had been scrupulously cleaned, and sealed away. Even so, they smelled musty and felt damp. And yet by these simple actions of waking, bathing, dressing, she felt her life reinvigorate the castle. The glow of the walls shone brighter, sounds told of mechanisms activating elsewhere in the building. She donned the three layers of her underwear quickly, binding up her secondary arms—no bigger than those of a human infant—along with her breasts. She spent her time choosing her outerwear. After deliberation, she selected a fine, close fitting gown of iridescent dracon feathers. Her primary arms went into gloriously embroidered sleeves that she attached to the gown with laced points. After inspecting the dress, and smoothing individual feathers down, she began to feel alive.

From her wardrobe she went to her preparation room, an oval space filled with her cosmetics and jewellery. Aside from a table curling around the circumference of the room and a solitary window, the room was featureless. As she entered the blank walls swirled, becoming a flawless mirror, and glimmer light ignited softly behind it. She examined herself from every angle. She was middling height for a Morfaan, which meant taller than most human men. Her face was longer and thinner than a human's, the septum of her nose went further toward the mouth, shortening her deep philtrum. Her lips were full. Her teeth not unlike a human woman's, but were fewer in number. Like all her people, her torso front was subtly banded by soft creases. The folds in the skin came to the bottom of her neck, so faint there as to be barely noticeable. Her spine was more pronounced than a human's, but lacked the horny spikes the males of her race possessed. Her jet black hair followed a hairline that would look odd on a non-Morfaan, but in her case accentuated her beauty. Despite her physiological differences, or perhaps because of them, humans found her attractive, although unlike some of her friends she had never given in to curiosity and lain with a member of the younger species. She wondered if the attraction would remain, or if the aesthetics of beauty had changed so much in her absence from the world that she would be regarded as an abomination.

She turned her attention to her hair. It was listless with long sleep, but it did not seem to be falling out this time. She set about it with a brush, dragging out the tangles. When it shone, she dressed it up with combs of dragon bone and carnelian. Then she reached for her brushes and began to paint in her culture's ideals of perfection. Calmness settled over her as she became absorbed.

A roaring screech jolted her. The creatures in the mist never came that close. She looked to the window. Beyond its panes fog swirled in complicated arabesques. Individual droplets glittered in the light streaming out from the room.

She set her brush down and frowned in concern.

The window was cracked.

The roar sounded again, drawing away from the castle. Another screech answered it, then the terrified screaming of a smaller animal caught and devoured. She went to the window. The land outside of the castle was never visible, and she had never glimpsed the beasts that roamed the mists. She ran her hand over the cracks in the glass. The creatures had been here while she slept and they had damaged the castle.

It was only a crack, but it had never happened before, they had never come that close.

Her hand traced the damage. Nothing but pressure from the building held a rhombus of broken glass in place. It had not repaired itself. A memory of a man came to her. He had once been important to her, but she could not recall why.

Very clearly, she saw him in that very room, before the castle had been folded into this nowhere place and the poison sun still shone upon the walls.

"Never!" he laughed. "This castle could never fall, Josan. You will be safe here, safer than the rest of us." This fragment played in her head in perfect clarity, but she could bring no more of the encounter to mind. It was gone, along with everything else.

The castle will never fall.

She returned to her cosmetics and completed her face, but the pleasure had gone from the task. When she was done she examined herself a moment. She was pleased with the effect, but the truth was she did it for him.

Josan went to see her brother.

Josan was concerned that Josanad had not begun awakening when she returned, so she started the process manually with the appropriate incantation. The lights flickered and the cot chimed out the sounds of small silver bells. She stood back and watched in trepidation, fearing the machine had failed and that life had finally fled him.

Lights shone and turned about the plinth, blinked, and the whole shone red as her own had done. His lid slid up and back before he awoke. Eyes the colour of spring leaves opened in the medium, his white hair stirred into a halo about his head as he jolted awake. Josan made for the cot to help him up, but Josanad had preserved his impressive strength throughout their many deathless sleeps, and sat up smoothly. He hung his head until the alchemist's fluid had ceased drooling from his face. When he looked about himself, his expression was guarded, the skin around his eyes wrinkled in puzzlement.

"My love? Brother?" she said.

An emotional blank looked at her. She balked, fearing violence from him, but the lines on his brow smoothed, and he blinked. He commenced coughing, spewing up the fluid from stomach and lungs back into the cot, streaking the clarity of the liquid with his bile. He was done purging quicker than she had been. When their eyes met again, she saw the man she loved looking at her.

"Josan? What is happening, where are we?" he croaked.

She went to his side, and rested her hands on his slippery skin. "The Hall of the Deathless Sleep. We have been woken. The Marble Council calls to us." She heard the desperation in her own voice. He must remember their purpose, she could not face the coming centuries on her own.

He cocked his head. "The council?" His face rumpled as if he tasted something unpalatable. "Yes, the council." he smiled at her reassuringly. "How long has it been?"

"I do not know."

"Help me," he said.

"There is no rush, my love."

He would not wait but clambered from the fluid. He was taller than her. Overall he was heavier, and his shape more different to a human man's than a female Morfaan's were to a human woman's.

His shoulders were broad, upper arms well muscled. The elongated proportions of his limbs gave him the illusion of being willowy, but he was powerful.

"You should wait a moment, gather your strength," she said.

"There is always a need for haste when the council calls," he said. A boyish glint came to his eye. She loved this and despaired at it. That expression had been on his face often as a younger man, until the hardships and pain of war had driven it out. She welcomed its return, but feared the loss of the wisdom that had replaced it.

"We can make love first." He took her arms gently. She sank into them and shut her eyes, heedless of the slime coating her fine clothes. His double penis stirred against her skirts.

"As you wish," she said. She could have stayed enfolded by him for much longer, but he was insistent.

They made love in the Hall of the Deathless Sleep, with her lying across one of the unused machines. It was uncomfortable, but she welcomed their intimacy. To do something as vital as make love in that place of death invigorated them both. He was gentler than he had been during their last waking. The impossible hope that he had returned to himself rose sourly in her heart, and towards the end she wept through her brief ecstasy.

After he was done, he pulled her up again, wiped at her tears and held her tightly with all four arms. When he asked her what was wrong, she could not say, only wanting this echo of the old Josanad to last, whole and undamaged by their cycle of death and waking.

They went to the dressing rooms. While he bathed, she told him of her own slow revival. This concerned him. The news of the broken window worried him more. He was about to say something on the matter, but became confused, and sat with his mouth hanging open. His lapse hurt her, and she had to turn away. She sponged him carefully, looking to the flawless brass beetles working around them. They were eternal, they still functioned, so could she and her brother. Then she pictured the last of the devices fastidiously cleaning the corner of a tumbled ruin, clambering over the Morfaan's bones, and the reassurance she had gained from their industry disappeared.

She spoke her wardrobe to life again, and thought a curtain of golden light into being across the entrance. When she stepped through, the magic restored her clothes to their pristine state. Josanad selected a tunic, soft tight trousers and high boots for his garb. Unlike hers, his secondary arms were left unbound, given freedom through embroidered slits in his tunic, although they would be covered by his outerwear as was only proper. Josan chose a jacket whose collar spread in a fringed fan to finish her brother's outfit. Between moments of confusion, he looked like the lord he had been. She showed him the crack in the window in the preparation room, then helped him finish his dressing.

"Come," she said when his face was painted and hair coiled. "The council awaits."

CHAPTER TWELVE
The Council of Marble

FROM THE HALL of Deathless Sleep Josan and Josanad went into the main body of the castle. Once out of their sanctuary, voices intruded into the minds of the twins, bypassing the ears and making them both nervous, though they had heard them a thousand times before.

Far back in time, the voices of the council had been measured. Millennia of close proximity had eroded their learned debate to bickering. The council never slept, not through the long ages of the world. They could not move. They were forever in each other's presence, cellmates in an inhumane prison. That they were as sane as they were was a triumph.

The Castle of Mists comprised seven diamond-shaped wings—of which the Hall of Deathless Sleep was one—arrayed like petals around a central, hollow tower several hundred feet tall. This keep was encompassed by a tall, backward curving curtain wall bolstered by seven towers, one to mirror each wing. The design was deceptively compact. Its simple geometry held huge spaces crushed by higher dimensional magics into tiny corners. The castle was a warren whose parts were attached by unconventional means to unexpected places. One could depart the north wing and arrive in the southeast petal.

In the Hall of Gates there were dozens of semi-transparent doors of glass, each leading to another world or plane. When watched for a while, one could see vile shapes moving beyond; linger longer and the shapes watched back. There were chambers no person could enter, spaces that should be vast halls but were tiny compartments.

Oubliettes that could be accessed only once; storerooms full of things Josan no longer recognised. The windows outside did not match the number inside. Josan had tried to count them early in their vigil, and never got the same number twice. From underground the noise of machines growled. Occasionally they might receive visitors, wanderers stumbling into the Place of Mists, for though hidden it could be found. The beetle constructs and warding spells dealt ruthlessly with those that survived the creatures outside the walls; there was a courtyard for the bodies, full of tangled grey bones and broken devices from a hundred different realities. During their periods of waking Josan forced herself to go there to see the remains of new unfortunates. Their fate was a reminder that no matter how awful immortality was, it was better than the alternative.

Every wall, vault and floor in the castle was of seamless, glowing marble. Ribs in the coign of floor and wall hinted at its organic provenance; like many of the things made at the height of the Morfaan's power, the castle had been coaxed into life from the earth by magic, not built one stone atop another. Only outside, in the empty stable blocks and storehouses of the ward, were more commonplace methods of construction seen, glorious buildings by any measure but that of the castle. Compared to it, the outhouses were crude shacks.

Within the tower a central courtyard contained the Council of Marble. The twins came to it via a door carved from a single emerald of stupendous size. There were seven other doors of differing gemstones, each pointing back to one of the wings. The twins were permitted only the emerald door. Though they could see through the silk-thin minerals, they had never dared the others.

Beyond the emerald, mind-voices raged at one another, thrusting deeper into Josan's thoughts with all the subtlety of a dagger. She bore the pain with a dim understanding that hearing the voices had been easier once, in a time when she had grasped her duties better. She was no longer sure if this were actual knowledge, or an awareness of knowledge that had faded, or a fancy conjured from the mist.

Josanad's face flickered with fear. "I don't want to go inside there. It hurts, sister." He spoke a child's words with his hero's voice.

"We must," she soothed him. "We always must."

Josanad licked his pale lips and cowered. Irritation threatened the purity of Josan's affection. "Come now, it will not be long."

He nodded reluctantly. Before he could change his mind, Josan opened the emerald door, and the voices rang louder still. The twins went into the Court of Marble.

The court was open to the sky. Grey strands of mist scudded overhead, promising faithlessly to part. A tree of green stone spread branches perfect in every detail save life. Gold and silver fruit depended from delicate twigs, leaves of thin foil rustled around them. Ringing the tree were five large statues, sculpted in poses of heroic endeavour, their lips stoppered with silver. Pale green veined the cream stone, putting Josan in the mind of cheese. She stifled a giggle. She was alarmed; inappropriate humour was the first sign of Josanad's deterioration, and she replaced the thought with something more respectful. The twins bowed as they entered the court and went to kneel before the statue of Lord Mathanad; the leader of the five, as much as any could claim to lead the sorry rump of the Morfaan race.

The statues did not cease their arguing at the arrival of the twins. Their voices echoed angrily in the twins' minds.

"The time is due, I say," said Mathanad. "We at last have a chance. We must lay our strategy out carefully."

"You are a fool!" said Lorinan, her hatred of him electric.

Were it not for the echoing mind-voices of the council, the Court of Marble would have been a serene place. Josan hated it.

Her mind wandered. Eternity stretched ahead, thousands of years blurred into each other. She was light-headed with relief that they would soon leave the castle for a while. Journeys to the world of their ancestors were undertaken far too rarely, and provided the only diversion to their purgatory.

There had been five elders in the Council of Marble. Four remained. Qurunad had fled his duty two thousand years into the long vigil. His statue's mouth was broken, revealing the cavity inside that had held his spirit. The stone of his face was black and streaked with melted silver. Bereft of spirit, the statue was inert and no longer spoke. The others never mentioned his betrayal.

Of the remaining four, proud Mathanad took the most care

over their duties. He would never cease talking of it. Over time his soliloquies on their terrible task had become increasingly impassioned, until they had taken on an edge of hysteria. Josan was convinced he went on so to convince himself of the council's importance, and that suggested to her that he too had lost faith. Then there was quiet Helesin. She remained wise, and though she hardly ever spoke Josan prized her rare advice. Next was Solophonad, who had become senile in his stone cage, and lastly Lorinan. Lorinan had been the most garrulous and brightest-humoured of the council, and for centuries her wit lightened the weight of the years. Sure enough, time's merciless drag had introduced a morbidity to her mind no less deadly than that afflicting Solophonad's. Her gaiety gone, she had at first turned sullen, then uncooperative. Lately Josan had come to fear her temper.

Solophonad's ramblings intruded into her mind, gabbling of flowers and the sun. Josan disliked to hear him, for Josanad sounded the same, when he was at his worst. Lorinan was no better to hearken to, she did not care to shield her poisonous ruminations on the loss of the eras of glory, and tainted them all with her despair.

"We are doomed!" she said, an echo of her lost cheer in her bitter glee. "There is nothing that can be done. Let it be over, fin—"

"We are not!" Mathanad's mind voice rode over Lorinan's. Sometimes he managed to convince Josan that his sense of obligation was an unbendable rod of steel. She was glad of it, only his commitment kept them all close to sane, but it was failing. The edge to his pronouncements was shrill. His own boredom moved sluggishly behind his words, worsened by the pain of abandonment, of dreams of honourable endeavour chafed away by the reality of an eternity in stone. He could not hide these feelings behind ceremony. They leaked out.

"Mathanad, do shut up," Lorinan's laughter bubbled into the twins' thoughts. Once so light and cheerful, now it conveyed only spite. "The enemy shall never be defeated. We cannot outwait them. What are we doing? When shall we concede their victory? Our vigil was never meant to last so long. There can be no return. We are defeated, done. Have the twins open our mouths and let us all depart into death. The Morfaan are no more."

Mathanad's weariness came to bear on Lorinan as a crushing weight, grinding against Josan's consciousness in the process. "It is not so. The successors regain their prior knowledge. A new era of machines dawns. The Long Vigil plays out as predicted."

"It does not!" said Lorinan. "Humanity has no sophistication, no understanding of the relationship to will or form. They draw too heavily on the world spirit, driving the Earth further from will towards form. The wards on the gates weaken because of it. Humanity cannot save us, they doom us all. If the enemy lives, they shall have easy ingress to the World of Will. What is the point in continuing?"

"The enemy did not require the gates last time," said Mathanad. "They came from the sky, and still the humans drove the enemy back."

"The only reason the humans were victorious was that the gates remained closed and the Draathis mustered such small numbers," countered Lorinan. "The enemy's trespass ended the last of the great ages. This current world is weaker still. When the enemy come again, it will be in full strength. This era is impure, they have become weak, and will be destroyed. We have waited for nothing."

"And if the enemy are extinct? Perished in exile?" said Mathanad. "The enemy's last attack smacked of desperation."

"You hang everything on optimism," said Lorinan. "Reality is crueller. We have failed. You are fools, rotten in soul and mind. Why are we still here when we should go! Set our spirits free to find new form and engagement. The Morfaan type has outlasted its time."

"Lorinan!" said Mathanad. "Silence!"

"Release me!" she whined. "Let me go into the mist with the rest. This is torment, we are done!"

"No!"

Josan shuddered as Mathanad and Lorinan argued, their shouting crashing agonisingly into the secret spaces of her soul.

"Whether the enemy returns or not, these two must go forth into the world." Helesin's quiet voice cut through the bickering of the others. They ceased speaking. Solophonad's inanities murmured in the sudden silence. "The people of the Earth call to us. A new High Legate must be selected. Our agreement is to aid them, and I fear it is no coincidence that it occurs a year before the nearing of the

World of Form. It is likely we come to the end of their time, and of ours," said Helesin. "Whether at the hand of the enemy, or because the Draathis have dwindled and died upon the World of Form. Only then we might finally return. Why do you argue? Despair calls you to inaction, Lorinan. The chances of our success lessen every year, but however slender they are, they remain chances. To flee into the mist is to take certain death over an opportunity at life."

"The enemy will inflict upon us a fate worse than death," said Lorinan fearfully. She had too long to think on Draathis cruelty. Memories of atrocity had come to obsess her.

"In which case, you will be free, as is your desire, you must only take a little pain before the end," said Helesin. "This is my decision— the two will be sent again into the World of Will. More, this time they must stay. If the enemy come, we should be there to help."

"The humans are degenerate," complained Lorinan. "Not one of the strains have proved sufficient in our defence in the past, and they have mixed freely. Our design is lost. How can they triumph?"

"They persist still, we do not. What does that say for their endurance?" said Helesin. Never once losing her temper, her voice remained calm and quiet. When she turned her attention to the twins, her serenity soothed them both. "You shall go into the World of Will. Return from exile to our lost home, as is your privilege and your peril. May the light of the sun never kiss your skin, my children, until its rays burn clean again. I second Mathanad."

"You are outvoted," said Mathanad smugly.

"There are four here," said Lorinan. "What does Solophonad have to say?"

For the first time they listened to the mumbling of the fourth councillor.

"Round and around, back and away," he said. "They'll come again and again, what to do, what to do? Oh to see the sea, oh to see the sun! Was it yesterday it went down, or before?"

"Solophonad!" boomed Mathanad.

"Who calls to me? Who disturbs sweet woe with their demands?" he laughed, a sickly sound.

"We vote upon the sending of the twins out from this fortress, to our old holdings upon the World of Will. What say you?"

"Go? Go? Go?" he echoed himself, each repetition more bewildered than the last. "We are here, we are here to... Why are we here? I have not finished wringing my hands, and then I will paint."

"You have no hands, Solophonad!" said Mathanad. "Concentrate!"

"I judge his maundering a no," said Lorinan. "A tie. We wait it out then, as decided. If the enemy returns, then we shall flee, or destroy ourselves. An end to torment, one way or another."

"No? Did I say no? I did not!" said Solophonad. "Always you steal my words, putting new ones cold as pebbles in my mouth. No? I said no such thing! Always go, if you do not, you only stay. A motion from repose to action is always welcome. Why is it so cold? Where are my hands?"

"He said go," said Mathanad. "That is a vote for yes."

"Go, yes go!" shouted Solophonad, and began wailing.

"It is a waste of effort," said Lorinan. "We should escape while we have our chance."

"Who then will return our people to existence, if we are gone?" said Mathanad. "This is the correct course. The way is open," he said portentously. "You leave this castle as ambassadors of our kind to those who succeeded us. Guide them. Impart our wisdom upon them. Love them." Josan had heard the words before so many times they were engraved upon her soul. What Mathanad said next, he had never said before. "I speak to you now with greater earnestness than ever before. Our time here approaches its end. Four thousand years have passed since the last approach of the World of Form, the dark world, the Twin. Our enemies may still live, they may not. You must be alert for them, for any sign. A time of peril is on us, but fear not, for there is hope, the greatest hope of all. If the enemy do not come, they will not come again, and the vigil shall be done. Now prepare! Already mists of this place spill out of the final gate to shield you from the sun of the World of Will. The time is now, depart!"

"You sent the mists without our consent?" said Lorinan indignantly. "What use this debate then?"

Mathanad ignored her. "You venture into the world of men."

CHAPTER THIRTEEN
At the Home of the Duke

OF ALL THE awful thoughts flitting through Madelyne's mind as they had driven through the fog to the duke's residence, being left to her own devices was not among them. Markos took her to a pleasant room and left her to sleep. She awoke the next day alone and unmolested, clothes laid out for her on a wooden valet stand in the corner. After waiting a while, she washed, dressed and ventured out of her room. No one stopped her.

The Duke Infernal's home was anything but hellish. Imposing, and somewhat sombre from the outside, with tall, thin pavilions at either end of the house. They looked like the folded wings of a scavenger bird, if one were really looking for something sinister. She supposed the lamplight gave the tall windows an ominous air in the unseasonable mists. Viewed from the garden during the day, the duke's house appeared like any other mansion of the outdated Musran style.

The mansion had a fine situation on the edge of the Place Macer, the cobbled square right at the top of the Palatine Hill which rang night and day to iron wheel rims and the noises of drays. There was a neat public garden in the centre, delineated by boxtrees so carefully trimmed they could have been cut from cardboard. An ancient statue of Omnus dominated the centre. Madelyne had always found it telling that he faced away from Res Iapetus, who in clearer weather could be seen gleaming goldly atop his empty mausoleum several blocks away. The square was edged all round with enormous buildings as many of the more important government ministries were there.

Directly opposite the duke's house was the palace of the Three Comtes of Perus, who ruled the city—and effectively the country—together. Next to it was the palace of the king, smaller than the Three Comte's home in proportion to their relative power. On the duke's side of the square were other grand mansions, the homes of other dukes and earls and comtes and every other rank of nobility, though none of them were as exalted as her host.

People went to and fro in great throngs. Very few of them paid the house any attention whatsoever. Those that did were sightseers. The locals were accustomed to the devil in their midst and had ceased to see him as anything but a man.

The interior was similarly undiabolical. The duke had impeccable taste, and plenty of money. Every room was beautifully furnished. The sole disquieting note was that her own room was decorated *exactly* to her preferences. She could not have designed a room to suit her better herself. From the room's decoration she divined that the duke had known she would return with him from the very start. She almost left there and then. Although she did not, her misgivings persisted as a faint sense of unease.

All through the days and nights after her selection the mist pressed hard up against the windows. At its thickest, the city seemed to retreat, so that the house was an island in an ocean of cloying vapour. This added further to her sense of isolation. Madelyne was a calculating person, not given to letting her emotions run away with her, but yearned for sunny weather.

Every day her bed was made for her, her clothes laundered and fresh outfits provided. Food waited for her in the dining room at every meal, always steaming hot, a place for one set at the head of a table as long as the river Olb. Who did all this she did not know. She saw nor heard any life in the building. The only other human beings she had dealings with were Markos, who was apt to come and go at the oddest of times, and the gardener, Gaffne, who did not set foot within the house.

She made her plans and rested; despite care and her innately rational mind, emotion took her on its ride. In time, fear gave way to curiosity, then to boredom. She opened every door that was not locked. The luxury grew tawdry in her eyes, and she longed to walk the streets of the tatty districts she knew so well, to see the life of Perus and be surrounded by beings who lacked such wealth, but she feared that to leave even for a short time was forbidden, and that she would lose her place.

Instead she whiled away the time walking the perimeter of the mansion's extensive grounds. A large formal garden fronted the mansion. Behind the duke's house lay the edge of the Royal Park. The back garden, a small park in its own right, was bounded by high walls topped with a barrier of spiked iron wheels.

The front garden was divided from the street only by a wrought iron fence, and she lingered there as long as she dared, watching the coaches and the wagons clatter past and the pedestrians hurry along, coat collars turned up against the chilly mist. She felt cold herself, but only returned indoors when she could stand it no more. While indoors she read in the duke's library. She slept too much. She spent time dressing up in the glorious clothes laid out for her. Every second lasted an age, ticked out leadenly into the moist air by solemn clocks.

All that changed on the morning of the third day. She awoke to another chill dawn to see the duke by the dresser close to her door. He leaned casually against the wall, rolling a porcelain figurine of a female goatherd back and forth in his enormous hands. She let out a small yelp when she saw him and shuffled back into the bed, the sheets clutched to her chest. The night gowns provided her were variously lacy, sheer, or clingy. All of them accentuated more than concealed. That morning she was dressed in a chiffon nightgown. Despite covering her modesty, it did not conceal it.

"I did not mean to startle you," he said mildly.

"I think you did," she said. "You are smiling. You enjoy my reaction."

"You know what I am." The duke shrugged. "I am sorry I have not been to see you. I have been away on business, and it is my custom to allow my companions to acclimatise themselves to the house. How do you like your new home?"

"Very well, thank you," she said. She was strangely embarrassed, as if caught up to no good.

"But?" said the duke. He toyed with the porcelain goatherd. Looking at it she felt his hands on her own body, as if it were representative of herself. She tore her eyes away and looked at his face.

"I have no reason for complaint," she insisted.

He raised his eyebrows and set the figurine down onto the light wood of her dresser, then turned his full attention back on her. She drew the covers further up her neck, ashamed, and feeling faintly ridiculous for being so.

"If we are to explore each other properly, Medame, we must be truly honest with one another, do you not think?"

She nodded mutely.

"You are not being honest," said the duke. "We shall strike our first bargain. I shall offer you the same courtesy that I offer any of my lady guests—you may ask me what you will, and I will answer as truthfully as I am able."

"Anything?"

"Anything at all." He chuckled. Away from Verralt's hideous cellar his laugh lacked its darkness, and seemed avuncular. "I have seen that look before. I am afraid I am no oracle. In return I expect absolute honesty from you. Absolute." His horns shadowed his face, stern with quiet authority. "Now. We shall begin again. How are you enjoying your stay?"

Madelyne rested one hand palm up in her lap and looked down at her fingers. The fog leached the colour from her skin, everything was grey. "Your house is glorious, but it is like a cage," she said. "This splendour chokes me. To escape I walk the gardens, but they are fenced. I wish to go beyond, and see the city again." She paused. "Might I, your grace?"

The duke's eyebrows rose in surprise. "You may leave whenever you wish," said the duke.

"I do not wish to. I made up my mind to come here. What would I be if I failed you at the first test?"

The duke smiled, pleased by her anguish. "I meant that you are free to come and go as you will. You are not a prisoner. If you were to go out to shop or to take afternoon tea I would not take it as a rejection."

"Truly?"

"Are you surprised? As long as you inform Markos where you are going, and you return at the appointed time, all will be fine. And I ask only that you tell him of a time so that we might know should something amiss occur, not to control you. Not yet. You must treat this house as your own." He paused. "Does the mist bother you?"

"Yes," she replied honestly.

"You are in the company of the entire city in your discomfort then," said he. "These are the mists of the Morfaan. They fall before they come to this sphere. They are not natural. I assure you the house is of an altogether more pleasant aspect when the sun shines. The Godhome catches the light just so. From my turrets there are views across all the city, right over the Foirree. It is quite beautiful, although we cannot see it today. I apologise for the timing, this is a most unusual confluence of events. Wait, and you shall see. After their arrival the mist gathers about the Morfaan and follows them closely, freeing us of the murk. We shall be spared its dreariness soon enough."

"It is not only the mist."

"Oh?"

She said nothing.

"Madelyne?" he said.

"The room!" she blurted.

"The room is not to your liking?"

"It is exactly to my liking, and that is the problem. It is too perfect, a precise recreation of the room I would have in my own home if I..."

"If you had the money?" he finished for her. "No need to worry about money now, not while you are here."

"I feel that you knew that I was coming, that you are toying with me."

The duke laughed. "I am toying with you, but only a little. I will toy with you a lot, should matters proceed to our liking. Those shall be games we shall both enjoy, and I wish you no discomfort now. Come with me, dear Medame." He unhooked a dressing gown from the back of the door and held it out for her. She stared at him until he looked aside. He found this amusing. Flushing scarlet, she covered her breasts. Her blush went deeper as her nipples stiffened against the touch of the nightdress. Madelyne slid out from the sheets and crossed the room to put on the gown.

"Come with me," he said, when she was done. He offered his hand. She took it, her fingers not closing around two of his. She was reminded of holding the hand of her father as a small girl. "I will not hurt you," he said.

"I... I know it," she said, bemused. She did know it.

"Here in this corridor are many rooms," he said, leading her down the landing. "Have you looked within?"

"They are locked," she said.

"Ah, you have the freedom of this house, but it has not yet got the measure of you. It will open all its doors soon. Personally, I have nothing to hide save a few rooms, and one of those you will see soon enough. Do you have anything to hide my dear?" His gaze accused her. "Each of these rooms was outfitted to exactly match the tastes of the women at the Jhaydue who were with you that night." The duke opened each door in turn. "Evanderane's this would have been." A childishly decorated place, full of rag dolls. He crossed the landing. "And this would have been Ankalueia's." Madelyne looked into an outlandish room, decorated to the tastes of a distant nation. She assumed he meant the others, she had never learned their names.

"So you see, I did toy with you, but only a little. I knew in advance the particulars of each woman Medame Verralt was to present to me, although I had not seen them before. I like to keep some of the game fresh for myself."

"You did not know you would pick me?" she said.

"No!" he laughed. "I have no powers of foresight. Did you think I did?"

"You are a god," she said weakly.

"I am not that kind of god, Medame. I am of a modest order." He took both her hands, his swallowing hers completely. "Go and get dressed. My servants lay out your clothes for you, but if you look in the room next to yours you will find it full of dresses of every sort. It will be unlocked from today. I hope they please you."

"I thought I was to dress to please *you*," she said.

"It will come to that, if you stay. But not now. The clothes left for you were suggestions, and a test. One you passed well."

She had no idea what the nature of the test she had passed was. He lifted her hands up to his lips. She had to stretch so he could kiss them. His lips were hot, almost scalding.

"We will talk after breakfast," he said. "Now you have had a few days to think on your decision, it is time to hear the fullness of my offer, and to determine if you wish to remain here."

Madelyne went into the wardrobe. Too much choice was presented her, so she dressed in the clothes left out in her room When she came into the dining room, mountains of food were waiting. Unlike every mealtime before, she had company. The duke sat at the head of the table, halfway through an enormous meal, absorbed by broadsheets in half a dozen languages spread out on the table in front of him. Dirty plates and the other debris of breakfasting dotted his reading matter. As he munched on a piece of toast, hunched over a paper he seemed charmingly human. This window of vulnerability closed as soon as he noticed her. He became large again, standing when she entered, and pulled out a chair for her. "I apologise for starting without you," he said. "I do not eat upon my trips, and returned famished."

"Where did you go?" she asked.

"Go?" He pulled an odd sort of face. "The gods are gone, I remain. I have duties still. I promised honesty, but these tasks I can speak of with no mortal. You may see me, sometimes, heading to the tower at the tip of the north wing. It is there I do much of my work. You are not to follow me there," he said sternly. He apologised as soon as he had said it. "I do not mean to be brusque. I had intended to discuss that with you afterwards. I preempt myself. You have not even agreed to remain! It shows, my dear, that I have a good feeling about our arrangement."

"There is no need to apologise, your grace," she said.

"Please, eat. I shall finish my papers. When you are replete, we shall talk."

She did as he asked. Having company was agreeable. She found herself watching the duke while he read. He was in his way very handsome, and exuded a confident masculinity that put the character of every man she had ever known to shame. His horns aside, he was not so bizarre in appearance. The Hundred was full of men of all kinds, sizes and colours, and other creatures besides. She considered if it would be possible for a mortal woman to love such a being, not simply be besotted with him, or be worshipful of him, but to honestly love. She cut the line of thought dead. She was not here for that.

When she finished, Markos appeared, his grubbiness all the more obvious for the richness of their surroundings, and cleared the crockery away onto a trolley. He gave her a friendly wink as he vanished out of the door. The clink of plates receded down the corridor and they were alone.

"You will be aware that I seek a companion. A permanent companion."

"Yes," she said.

"And that she must be of particular tastes and manner. Very particular."

"I am aware of them," she said. "All of Perus is."

"I abhor secrecy," said the duke. "There is no shame in what I am. But some do not know me, or choose not to believe. Some women come here with entirely the wrong impression. They expect something from a tale, a handsome prince cursed and made whole with a kiss. I am as you see me here. I cannot be changed any more than any other man, though that never stops women from trying. It is a mistake to try, do you understand? You must accept me as I am."

"I understand," she said.

"Others are repulsed by what they know, believing me a sadist."

"Are you not?" she said.

He paused before answering. "No. I am not. I will hurt you, but not solely for the pleasure of it."

"You choose your women, your grace, including those who are ill-informed. Surely the fault in their selection lies with you?"

Again he smiled at her boldness. "I am not infallible," he said. "I have not yet been right, after all."

"If not a sadist, what are you?"

"A caller of passion," he said sincerely. "I see the world from a sensuous perspective. To awaken all parts of your body will enable you to glimpse what I see. Sensuality opens the mortal mind to the possibilities of the numinous. How else can we share a life?" He clutched at a napkin. "And I admit, I enjoy it. I enjoy forcing a woman over boundaries her time and place and being have set up around her. Most of all, I enjoy her shame and pleasure at those boundaries crumbling."

Madelyne bit her lip.

"So," he said. "Now you are aware. It does not worry you?"

She shrugged slightly. "A little."

"You will also know that should I find the right woman, who can endure my attentions and learn to find ecstasy in them, and who is also perfect in demeanour, intellect, obedience, independence... then I shall bind myself to her, and she shall be raised up by me, to live forever by my side. I have found many women who enjoy the... activity I offer. It is not an uncommon trait." He smiled a smile halfway between shy and sly. "But they have not possessed all the other characteristics I desire."

"Medame Verralt?"

"She was among them. Those that fail enjoy their stay, however long it lasts, and they are well compensated when they go."

"I am no whore."

"Any money I give you is a gift, not payment," he insisted. "We contract between two free souls."

This was a surprise to her. For all the talk of the lovelorn Duke Infernal, she had not expected complexity to the arrangement, only a brutish lust fulfilled by scandalous women. Having steeled herself to masquerade as one, she found herself wrong-footed. "Is companionship so important to you?"

"Another surprise for you? First no claws, and now a heart?" He waggled his fingers. Three of them bore rings the size of pocket watches. "All men must find a wife, one that suits their temperament. A mortal might compromise a little, but for those who live forever, perfection is essential. Any flaw can fracture under the weight of eternity."

"But you are not a man."

"I am not truly a god either," he said. "Though they all say I am. I was messenger to the Dark Lady, not a god in my own right. I am a functionary, my dear! Who really knows who or what he is? Not I. We all wear masks—some for others, some for ourselves. Some are placed upon us without our knowing."

"You were worshipped."

"I was, wasn't I?" He grinned. "I am a lowly sort. But even were I of a higher order of being, I should still be a man, and still crave a companion. Even gods desire love, else what is the point?"

"Children," said Madelyne firmly. "They are the point for a mortal, and children are the product of love. Children are our immortality, so what does an immortal need love for?"

"Very well put Medame!" he said delightedly. "The current breed of philosoph, and I have been unfortunate enough to see many schools of thought bud out from the tree of knowledge and wither again, have it that love is the body's way of securing children, a manner of passing on characteristics of the parent down through time. A trick, as it were, of the flesh on the soul. They are wrong, to a degree. There is a drive to heredity in all living things, but children are not only born of love, they are vehicles of love. They carry love with them into your life. There are easier ways of ensuring the perpetuation of a bloodline. Besides," he said, "nothing is immortal, not even an immortal." He paused and regarded her gravely. "This is a particular role. There are many things I will ask you to do I expect you will not like, and there are things I will make you do that I know you will not, not at first."

"I understand. As I said, your appetites are well known."

"Rumour of an appetite and the sating of it are very different things," he said.

"Do I have a choice?"

"Choice?" He sat back. "You can go free. Your debts are paid, neither Verralt or the state have any hold on you. You will leave with nothing, but that is more than you had. There is a choice. Here is another—stay. But know this now, all of this, everything we are to embark on, it is and must be of your own volition. The moment it ceases to be so, the contract will end."

"My options are loaded in your favour. Where would I go?"

"It is still your choice." He leaned close and took her hands in one of his. "There is always a choice Madelyne!" he said urgently. "How else did you come to be here? When Verralt offered to buy your debt, you could have remained in the Debtor's Gaol. When you first saw me, you could have chosen to stay in her house."

"I was desperate."

"There was still a choice."

"You are making me a whore."

He shrugged. "You would have been had you remained in that brothel. You will be well treated here, well fed. You will suffer no disease and experience only sensual violence, nothing that will kill or permanently harm you."

"I would have made the money eventually to be free."

"You would have sickened. Here you might live forever."

"An eternity of servitude," she countered, "rather than three or four years on my back?"

"An eternity of love, as opposed to the whore's early death."

"A brutal love."

"I am enjoying this already," exclaimed the Duke Infernal. "Let us cease these verbal feints. You have an idea of what I expect. Do you accept? Will you know the rest of my terms? I am impatient, eager to begin."

"Tell me, before I decide. Have you been searching long?"

"Forever," he whispered.

"Have any ever come close to success?"

Sombrely, the duke reached around his neck and pulled out a necklace of blue beads and laid it on the front of his shirt. Spaced evenly between the beads at the front were seven skulls of jade, exquisitely carved with the highest degree of realism, each unique as real skulls are unique. They were so realistic Madelyne could imagine the faces that had once clothed them.

"Seven. I wear these to remember them. They were all dear to me." He touched them tenderly.

"And did you love them?"

"Every one." Profound pain dimmed the light in his eyes.

"What happened to them?"

"They dissolved our contract, and left me without their companionship," he said.

She took a deep breath. "As you wish, I am ready. Tell me the details of your terms."

"You may read them."

He went to a sideboard and took out a document folder from a drawer, bound up with blue ribbons and sealed with the stamp of a prominent legal firm.

"My terms," he said, handing them to her.

She cracked the seal and unwrapped the ribbons.

"Take your time." He went to look out at the fog.

There were four pages of closely printed paper. The first page was innocuous enough, a general set of terms and payments. The longer she remained, the more generous the duke would be when she departed, if she were to go. She flipped the page and her breath caught in her throat. The page coldly listed, in fine print, a series of sexual practises outlawed in many kingdoms. Madelyne was no stranger to a number of them, and had enjoyed the majority she had tried, but seeing them printed there in black and white embarrassed her. There was no way to opt out of them. They were all to be accepted, or none were. She flipped the page over, revealing the next. There was a further list, she was to consent to being whipped, restrained, caged, chained, cut, branded... The list went on. Magic was mentioned. A statement at the bottom, signed by the duke, insisted all were to be performed for their mutual pleasure. It did not blunt the savageness of it.

The final leaf held details on how she was to behave and to dress.

"Why?" she breathed.

"They are my terms," said the duke, still staring at the mist. Outside a dray howled. The sound of traffic echoed in the mist. The noise so mundane, it seemed surreal. "Accept them, or do not. You knew what to expect."

She nodded.

"Yet you are shaken," he said disappointedly. "Very well, you can leave."

Again Madelyne almost went. But she could not. She found it hard to hate the duke. Some would call his list depravity, but she had known men and women who exercised their lusts the same way. He seemed kind, and she had not expected that. She felt almost guilty to accept. She was the one being dishonest, not he. The duke was not the only one with plans.

"I will stay," she said in a small voice.

The duke's russet face broke into a broad smile. "Excellent! This list is comprehensive, brutally so. But I will not inflict it upon you all at once." He knelt before her. Once again his massive hand enfolded hers. A flinch betrayed her feeling of entrapment. "The ultimate aim is to open your body to all forms of pleasure," he said. "It is not barbarity." His excitement unnerved her.

"But the pain..."

"All this is a route to pleasure," assured the duke. "Nothing more. If your body is open, your heart will open, then your mind, and finally your soul. If your soul opens itself, then you will have succeeded. If you, at any time, decide enough is enough, then you may go. But I warn you, there is only one refusal. Once the words are past your lips you shall be sent from here, and the doors will forever be locked against your return."

"I accept," she said quietly.

"So quickly?"

"Do not question me, your grace!" she begged. "Take my acceptance."

"Then you must sign here." He produced an ink pencil. Her signature was ragged.

"I also must place my mark," he said.

"There is nowhere for you to sign," she said, looking at the document.

"Not the document. Bend your head forward."

She stared at him.

"Do it now," he said firmly.

Hesitantly, she bowed her head.

"Part your hair. Expose your neck."

Her skin bared, the duke pushed his thumb against her nape. An intense cold burned her. Just as it became unbearable he removed his thumb. Hotness flooded the mark, so intently she felt every bump of it. She reached up to explore the change in her skin. She expected a thumbprint, but there was a pattern like upon a seal. Her fingers tingled as she brushed it.

"Your neck carries my mark. You will keep it until you decide not to. If you leave, it shall fade."

"It will go away?"

"If you wish, yes."

"I do not wish it," she said.

He looked triumphant. "Then we shall begin tonight."

"And what am I to call you, if we are to experience intimacy?"

"Your grace."

"Do you not have a name?" she asked. The mark throbbed on her neck, sending shivers down her spine that were not unpleasant. To her dismay, it triggered sympathetic responses from her sex. She became flustered.

"I do."

"You will not tell me?"

"No Madelyne, I will not," said the duke.

"I see," she lowered her eyes from his smile; it had a predatory look. "If it is your pleasure to keep me at a distance and have me refer to you as your grace, then so be it."

The duke laughed. "It is, it is! I would tell you my name, if only to have you enjoy the exquisite discomfort of knowing me familiarly yet being forced to address me formally."

"Then why not tell me?" she asked.

"Because if I did tell you my name, my child, it would kill you."

CHAPTER FOURTEEN
The Sea People

THE *PRINCE ALFRA* stood off a white island upon a flat sea crowded with plates of ice. Ice, ship and island moved together upon the Southern Gyre, a circular current that rushed around the Sotherwinter Sea and which marked the beginning of the end for Ruthnian knowledge of the south.

The largest piece of floatstone Trassan had seen outside of Mogawn made the centre of the island, rising some hundred feet over the water. A snow cap covered its domed summit, scoured from the windward side of the higher, hanging in a rounded sheet over the leading edge of the lower. The surface of the rock below was exposed, too steep for snow to cling to, although the hollows and bubbles that gave floatstone its buoyancy were packed out, marking the beige rock with hundreds of pure white circles. A shelf of ice fringed the stone at the waterline. With its crest of sculpted drifts and brim of ice, the island had the likeness of an extravagant, misshapen hat.

Antoninan, Heffi, Bannord and Trassan watched from the top of the superstructure. Four more days they had sailed south, and the ice had become ever worse. Icicles hung from the rails, filling the gaps between with an undulating sheet. They looked down from an iron fortress, ramparted with ice.

Quiet reigned, of that imperturbable sort found only in the coldest, stillest places. The men had paused their work at Antoninan's insistence. The island was inhabited. From somewhere behind the crown, a thin line of smoke drifted upward, stretching itself into lateral lines in the cold air. A score of canoes lay like basking sea beasts on the false beach of ice. Short upright dashes of black on the white were people. The iron ship was being watched.

"That is a fortune in floatstone," said Trassan appreciatively.

"A Sorskian sea village," said Heffi. "I have heard of them, never seen one. A fine adventure you have brought me on, goodfellow. These stories will buy my tavern dinners for some years to come." He clapped Trassan upon the back.

Trassan extended his telescope glass and scanned the island. What he took to be natural humps were in fact small domed huts of snow with windows of clear ice. The people were gathering on the ice where the white gave way to the grey sea, faces shadowed by the wells of their parka hoods. The garments were identical to the ones Antoninan had designed for the expedition. They were gathered around a canoe much larger than the others, with space upon its benches for a score of people. It was all of white, and the prow, carved in the image of a roaring monster, was taller than a man. A number of the figures were attending to this boat, attaching ropes to its sides and working around the hull.

"They are nearly ready to meet us," said Antoninan, careful not to point. "If we are careful, they will allow us to remain here while you proceed with the modifications. If we are careful." For much of the voyage Antoninan had kept himself to himself, and Trassan, initially excited by the explorer's presence, had become disappointed by his standoffishness.

On 17th Sunbright they had passed the eighty-sixth parallel that marked the beginning of True Sotherwinter. Isolated for much of the voyage, Antoninan had emerged from his kennels and started to exert his authority.

More people emerged from the strange huts. They wriggling up from the ground a little way out from the walls so that they looked like they were popping out of the snow. The crowd of them became substantial. The men and women were identically dressed, and impossible to tell apart, but there were many children.

"They live in burrows," joked Trassan.

Antoninan grasped the field glass and lowered it gently. He was in his forties, his brown hair shot through with white strands, his eyes were cold and piercing, his face was craggy from long exposure to the polar sun. He had spent so much time in the chill south it had entered into him. Trassan still did not know him well. They had met when Trassan had recruited him; they had discussed the expedition in depth, they had spent weeks together on the ship, but Antoninan preferred the company of his dogs to that of his fellow men. Trassan expected to be disappointed by Antoninan again, because Antoninan was turning out to be an arrogant arse.

"They do not, goodfellow," said Antoninan. "Be respectful of them. They can teach us much. As you see, these coats and britches we wear are of their design. I owe my life twice over to the Sorskian sea clans. If you offend them, we will gain nothing."

"Touchy, are they?" asked Trassan, closing his glass. He played the ignoramus to annoy Antoninan. "They look a little primitive." Without magnification the huts became humps again, the people on the shore dark smudges on the white.

"Comments like that is why Antoninan will be handling the negotiations, Trassan," said Heffi. "He has spent a lot of time among these tribes."

"Not so much time with the people of the floating ice. I will do what I can, Captain Heffishul," cautioned Antoninan. "The sea-peoples are distant from the land clans of the Sorskian peninsula. Their dialects vary greatly. We may refer to them as Sorskian, but most of them do not think of themselves so, and unlike those of Sorskia proper none are subjects of the Hundred Kingdoms. They are proud and free. I admire them. Anyone who can survive in this place deserves our respect." He went quiet, eyes narrowing. "I have not encountered this band before. The sea-peoples can be dangerous. I will meet them."

"The boat is almost ready," said Heffi.

"Take a couple of Bannord's marines," said Trassan.

"It'll be a pleasure to go myself," said Bannord.

"Unarmed men only," said Antoninan. "You must leave this to me. It is their way to greet strangers on the neutral ground of the ocean. We must go out first, as indication of our good intent. Then they will come out to meet us."

A team of six Ishamalani sailors had undone the tarpaulin from the jolly boat aft of the superstructure, and were attaching it to the short booms of the winch there, ready to swing it out over the side of the ship. Two of them stood at either end of the little boat, the other four went to the windlass that powered the crane, unwrapping it and inserting the turning beams into their sockets. The winch chains rattled, the boom was pulled upwards, and the boat swung out over the gunwale, guided by sailors at its prow and stern.

"Does it always proceed in that way?" asked Heffi. "They are launching many boats."

Antoninan squinted back at the island. "Hold!" he said urgently. The sailors stopped, looking to Heffi for instruction.

Trassan extended his telescope again; Antoninan shot him a warning look, but Trassan ignored it.

"They're coming," said Trassan. "All of them."

The crowd onshore had become active. Without a glass they seemed small and agitated as baccillae on a magister's microscope plate. People climbed into the canoes, four to each. They were shoved into the sea, and with quick dabs of their paddles struck out from the shore. When they were twenty yards out from the ice they rested their paddles across their boats and waited. Meanwhile ten men boarded the great canoe. More stood around the side, ready to push it into the water.

A horn blew, reedy in the expanse. From the largest hut emerged their chief. He was clad in white fur, and when free of the ground he paused so that his fellows could put beads about his neck, a staff hung with many ivory carvings into his hand, and a headdress mounted with spreading antlers upon his head. Thus adorned, the chief was helped into the white canoe.

Shouting rhythmically, the men at the sides heaved and ran the great canoe off the ice. The sea water parted smoothly before its prow, turning over like ploughed, silver earth. Momentum carried the great canoe several yards out from the shore, and there it stopped.

"They have no paddles," said Trassan.

"Wait, and watch," said Antoninan.

The horn blew again, a long rising-falling wail that went on without stopping for a minute. Two men leaned out over the front of the canoe, gripping handles set into the side of the carved beast.

They held lines in their other hands, and watched the water's surface intently.

A churning set up at the prow. Things rolled in the water. Leaning down so far their noses skimmed the sea, the men darted their hands under the surface where they looped their lines over something, and leaned back. The horn blew a third time. The lines went taut, and the canoe came skimming toward the *Prince Alfra*, drawn by its strange aquatic drays at such speed it knocked aside platelets of ice and sent them spinning. Once the canoe was clear of the flotilla round the island, the people in the smaller canoes dipped their paddles into the water and, letting out a shrill ululation, followed their leader.

"What do we do now?" said Heffi nervously. "They can't be so foolish as to attack us."

Antoninan watched the Sorskians carefully. "They have little metal, primitive weapons by modern standards, but their magic can be strong. Don't underestimate them. Lieutenant, draw your men back from the rails. Have them put up their guns."

"Trassan?" asked Bannord.

"Do what he says," said Trassan.

Bannord whistled and waved his men back to the starboard side of ship. He lowered both hands twice, and his men dipped their guns.

The water at the bow of the great canoe rippled with the sinuous movements of its beasts. It cut a strong wake, clean as polished glass and jewelled with amber by the low southern sun—it was late evening, but the summer nights there were short.

The white canoe was made of dracon skins stretched tightly over a frame of bone. The gunwales were carved from the same material, while the prow and stern were single pieces of sea dragon ivory, each a massive tooth.

The boat slowed, the creatures pulling it bobbed to the surface, showing bodies insulated by sleek black feathers and short, whiskery faces ending in beaks.

The chief handed his headdress to one of the others in the boat. Throwing back his hood, revealing that he was, in fact, a woman. A lined, snow-pale face looked across the water, broad with black eyes narrowed to slits by folds of skin. As outlandish as the chief appeared to the men of the Hundred, her gender was unmistakable.

"A woman?" said Trassan.

"The sea-peoples and southern Sorskians make little distinction between the station of the genders," said Antoninan. Bannord and Trassan shared a sidelong glance; Antoninan answered every question as if its asker were an idiot.

Antoninan called out to the woman in a clipped tongue, full of clicks and abrupt stops.

The woman regarded them impassively.

Antoninan tried another dialect, then another. The woman waited for him to finish, then responded. Her voice carried clearly over the glassy sea.

"Your coming is written by the sky and the wind."

"Ha! She speaks good Maceriyan," said Trassan. He smiled at the others. "That makes life easier."

She passed her hand over her head at the sky, then below at the water. "The ocean whispers of you. You bring war. You bring pain. You are outrider canoes of destruction."

"Ah," said Heffi.

"But you may stay, though I cannot welcome it!" said the chief. "It is the wish of the Unshe, and I cannot go against them."

Antoninan did not appear discouraged. "Greetings to you and yours under the stars and sky, woman of the waters," he said.

"You speak the greeting well. You are known to us," replied the chief. "The northerner who buys dogs. You are Antoninan, the far-wanderer."

"I am he. How do you know of me?" he asked, very pompously, thought Trassan. Antoninan's face was glowing at the chief's recognition.

"The wind, the waves. We have heard of you from our kin in the north."

"Your fame precedes you," said Trassan quietly.

"Not an advantage. The more they know, the harder they will deal. I must have their blessing, or we are at risk while we are here," replied Antoninan under his breath. "This sort of display is normal. She will be seeking favourable trading terms." He raised his voice again to the chief. "Do we have your blessing?"

The woman shook her head emphatically. "No blessing can be

given. The Unshe wishes your presence, not I. Tell me your purpose, and perhaps the blessing shall be given despite the portents. Speak truthfully, I have the small gift of divination."

"We are explorers," said Antoninan. "We require a haven to effect repairs to our ship."

The chief closed her eyes a moment. When she opened them again she smiled. "You speak the truth," said the chief with satisfaction. "That is good. One condition I can impose, you must trade."

"He got that right," said Bannord to Trassan quietly.

"Of course," said Antoninan.

"We don't have much to give away," said Trassan. Antoninan silenced him with a hand.

"You have dogs? Your dogs are fine creatures, all upon the frozen seas know this," said the chief.

"Yes," said Antoninan guardedly. "We have dogs."

"Then we will trade with you for them."

Antoninan's face hardened. "It cannot be done."

"Then you may visit the Unshe, but then you must be gone," said the chief.

"Antoninan, we need to modify the funnels, or they'll freeze solid further south," said Trassan. "We will not get a better opportunity than this. Without the modifications, we will have to turn back."

"I will not give up my dogs," said Antoninan.

"Negotiate then," said Trassan, throwing up his hand in exasperation. Antoninan glared. What little warmth he had in his manner had chilled quite away.

"No one takes my dogs."

"Listen, friend Antoninan," said Heffi soothingly. He placed his hands palm to palm. "Let's agree in principle, talk them down later. It will be well. You look like you know what you're doing."

Antoninan was not swayed. "They will ask for Valatrice, that is the only reason she asks at all. If she knows of me, she knows of him. Their breeds are purer than our northern stocks, but none is so fine as Valatrice. Such is his fame, they covet him. We should never have come here."

"We shall make sure it doesn't come to that," said Heffi.

"I'll recompense you for any that you might lose," said Trassan.

Antoninan swung his head angrily, about to rebuke the others. With visible effort he mastered himself, and shouted down to the chief. "We come ashore to negotiate."

"Be not wrathful. Nothing can be freely given. There is always a price," said the chief. "There is a message for the others among you." She spoke again, in a new language.

The effect on the Ishmalani was incredible. They stared at the chief and each other.

"Is that... Croshashian?" guessed Trassan.

Captain Heffi tugged at the rings in his nose, troubled by what he heard. "Not quite, goodfellow. That is the secret tongue of my people. We teach it to no one."

"Then how does she know it?" said Trassan.

"It appears more than I have something to lose here," gloated Antoninan. "Now are your feelings different? Shall we leave?"

"Definitely not. I intend to find out how they know it," said Heffi. "Get that boat over!" He yelled at his crew. "We're going ashore."

THE SHIP'S BOAT crunched into the ice and lurched to a halt. The Ishamalani put up their oars. Heffi tossed a painter to the Sorskians from the prow, Trassan from the stern. The sea people hauled on the lines, bringing the boat alongside the ice.

The ice around the island proved to be more expansive than they had guessed. The jutting ridges of an iceberg lurked beneath the jolly boat's keel, its convoluted surface stark blue in the midnight water. Sea-sculpted shelves and razor thin edges projected out into the ocean, a deadly, underwater cliff that no doubt did a great deal to keep sea dragons away. Trassan and his shipmates were grabbed by red, calloused hands and hauled over the abyss onto the ice.

The rock embedded in the ice was truly impressive. Trassan could see little evidence of the faulting that could ruin a floatstone piece, and the cavities were perfectly formed; a good, uniform roundness. Trassan knew a fine raw rock when he saw one. A vessel made from the island would be enormous.

The ice shelf extended some fifty yards out from the core of floatstone, and there they were greeted. Villagers crowded round

Trassan and his companions They patted at him, sang out greetings in their language, faces all smiles as they clustered around the travellers. They were shorter by a head than the majority of the northerners, with bright blonde hair and broad faces, dark blue eyes peaking out from their strange folded eyelids. Their chubby appearance made them seem soft-fleshed, but when their fingers touched him they were strong and hard.

The rounded lumps of the huts clustered all along the rim where rock and ice were wedded together. From these more people emerged, and others came around the shelf in the ice from around the island. Trassan was buffeted by their attention. Heffi flinched at their touching.

"They are over exuberant," said Heffi. "Can you get them to stop?"

"Let them greet us in their own way," said Antoninan. "The sea-peoples are hospitable, but easy to anger. Do not dismiss them as savages. Their culture is complex. We are the foreigners here. To touch a stranger is to show their care for them and their acceptance of you. Let them have their way."

To Trassan they did seem savage. They had little metal on them, most of their decoration, from the beads of their necklaces to the toggles fastening bags and clothing, was carved squares of sea ivory.

The press of fur clad bodies slackened just as it was becoming unbearable. The chief's canoe arrived back at the shore and was hauled back up onto the ice, passengers and all. The chief was reverently helped from the side. The crowd parted to allow her to approach the expedition. Villagers that lingered overly long or continued to pat and stroke were sent away by rattles of the chief's staff.

"I am Chichiweh Akuna," she said. The k was pronounced hard, back in the throat as a hard click. Trassan dared not try it.

"I am Trassan Kressind, of the Isles of Karsa." He bowed as graciously as if she were a debutante and not a savage.

"Captain Heffi," said Heffi, not troubling the woman with his full name. The rest of them introduced themselves—Bannord, Ardovani, and the four oarsmen.

Antoninan repeated her name, and added something further. Chichiweh nodded, pleased with his efforts.

"You speak the language of the Hanweri well."

"I thank you," said Antoninan.

"But we are the Tatama Awa-Ata, People of the Dragon's Tooth."

"Perhaps you might teach me a little of your language?" said Antoninan.

There was a game going on there, deft as a fencing match, though Trassan could only guess at its meaning. The woman wore an exaggerated expression; Antoninan underscored his words with small movements of his fingers. Trassan looked at the other Tatama, now drawn back from the expedition, but still chattering away and laughing. Much of what they said was accompanied by meaningful gestures.

"Perhaps I might," said Chichiweh. She rattled her staff. The crowd fell silent. She pointed it toward the floatstone hill. "First, we shall trade, then the blessing might be given. Or it may not."

"The fairness of our trade will decide," said Antoninan.

"No," she said. "The gods."

She led them from the ice, round the corner of the hill. At the top of four tall steps a cavity had been hollowed from the stone. She removed her headdress, climbed the short stair and ducked within. Trassan followed first.

He expected a reeking darkness lit by guttering oil lamps that smelled of burned fat. He expected a small space, full of the unpleasant heat of unwashed bodies. He expected something primitive.

He was instead taken into a domed cavern with polished walls. The cavities of the floatstone were plugged with flat panels of sea ivory, each one marvellously carved with scenes in strong relief, so that he was presented by an astounding display. In the few cavities left open there were bright, modern glimmer lamps traded from the north. A couple of others contained carefully arrayed objects. A large fire burned in the centre of the room, its smoke captured by a chimney of floatstone left free when the cavern was hollowed out. In the chimney the rock's characteristic holes had been plugged with more ivory, and so the smoke was drawn cleanly away through the dome's apex. Back from the chimney five thick panes of clear ice were set into holes cut into the ceiling, each swept free of snow.

The chamber was bright, clean, and fresh.

"They do not appear so primitive now, eh?" said Antoninan.

"Indeed not," said Trassan. "It is a marvel. Ask them if we might have the expedition artist draw a sketch."

"Later," said Antoninan. "We will be lucky to be allowed to remain at all."

Twelve people rose from stools around the fire. Their parkas were piled at the side of the room, and they wore closely fitting garments of dog velvet, brightly embroidered about the cuffs.

"The council of the Tatama Awa-Ata," said Chichiweh. She went to them one at a time to grasp their elbows and touch foreheads.

"Is this Unshe here?" said Heffi. His expression remained pleasant but Trassan heard the strain in his voice. The business with his language bothered him.

"This is not their place," said Chichiweh. "They live apart, close to the spirits. They will call you when they will speak with you. That is their way." The woman made a warding gesture and frowned. "We will speak of this no further, it is bad to speak spirit business in the Hall of Life." She gestured to stools stored at the edge of the room, also carved of floatstone. "Please, sit with us."

Trassan and his comrades took up the stools. They were lighter than wood.

"You see we are successful in our trading." She pointed out the glimmer lamps. "We have sea ivory and ambergris, much to offer the northmen. What do you bring?"

A man rolled out a blanket containing a fortune in ivory. Slotted neatly into loops within were three dozen dagger-sized sea dragon teeth. A second presented a ball of waxy sea-dragon ambergris, another piled up two mounds of skins, one furred, one feathered.

"What we need is time, and a place to rest," Trassan said.

"And the blessing must be given," said Antoninan flintily.

"We shall see." Chichiweh stretched her lips alarmingly wide and smacked them. The council clapped hands. Chichiweh sat. "The goods are presented. We shall begin exchange."

CHAPTER FIFTEEN

A Foreigner's Impressions of Umbra

GARTEN HAD BEEN to Umbra twice before, but he had never seen it like this, shrouded in fog so dense that the city might well not be there. The fog had grown thicker the closer they had come, slowing their passage across the continent. When they crossed the canyon of the river Marceuil that divided Macer Lesser from Maceriya proper, the fog was so thick Garten thought he might step from the great railway viaduct and walk upon it.

Perus's characteristics worsened the fog. Though it lagged behind Karsa City in the new industries, many factories had sprung up there, and the fog thickened to a chemical brume choking as the worst Karsa City had to offer. The taste stuck in the back of the throat and stung at the nose. Many times Garten resorted to his sleeve to dab at his streaming eyes.

The shadow of the Godhome further darkened the streets. Their ride by cab from the station was a lurching stop-start as the driver braked to avoid running into the back of other vehicles they could neither see or hear. Lamps burned everywhere, though it was late afternoon when they arrived.

They had scarcely been shown their lodgings at the Karsan embassy on the Avenue of Peace when trumpets rang out all over the capital, announcing the imminent arrival of the Morfaan.

"The Basilica! They come to the Basilica!" called a reedy voice from outside, amplified by glimmer horn. Most diplomatic missions were housed on the avenue, and his cry was passed on down the row of mighty buildings by a dozen voices until it became inaudible and went beyond the ambassadorial district.

Garten's hopes of a restorative nap and a change of clothes were dashed. Food was brought to him, then they were forced back out of their rooms and into a coach. Grand on the outside, it was no more comfortable than the taxicab in which they had arrived.

Abing was already aboard with the ambassador, a portly man with thick white whiskers that could not hide his lack of chin.

"Garten Kressind, Gelbion Mandofar," said Abing.

"Gelbion is my father's name," said Garten. He shook hands as he climbed in.

"You don't say," said Mandofar sniffily. "Is that a lantern?" he asked, staring at the box in Garten's hand.

"Personal effects. An unusual valise, I admit. It was a gift from my brother," he said.

Abing raised an eyebrow at him and cleared his throat. "Bloody Morfaan might have given us a rest, eh? Never mind, our stay here will be hectic throughout. No point in being lulled into torpidity by an easy first day."

Garten took a seat opposite the ambassador and put Tyn Izzy's case between his leg and the coach's side. "You are related to the Mandofars of the Green Reach?" Garten asked. "A fine family."

"Yes," said the ambassador with such condescension it told Garten all he needed to know about the man's opinion of him. His greeting of the countess when she arrived shortly after was no more cordial but far more servile. He made it clear he disapproved of Lucinia Vertisa's antics, but she was of old, high blood. He clearly disapproved of Garten's fresh-minted aristocracy far more than the countess's lewdness.

The countess had changed into another of her man's outfits, a suit of clothes wholly masculine except for its bright turquoise colour and the yellow piping. She sat down next to Garten and gave him an encouraging smile. He nodded back. He covered the surreptitious rasp of Tyn Izzy's vision slit being drawn back with a cough.

"Terrible fog, excuse me," he said, prompting a scowl from Mandofar. Taking pity on the creature, he balanced the case on his knee, and angled the front out through the window so that she might see. "That's better, more room."

Mandofar sniffed loudly and looked away. "Drive on!" he said. The carriage pulled away from the embassy, down its drive and out of guarded gates onto the avenue.

The city, long subdued beneath its grey blanket, had erupted with life. Hundreds of people were pouring onto the avenue, most of them servants from the embassies, excitedly chattering. The coaches of the ambassadors pushed through, their drivers and coachmen screaming at the throngs to get out of the way. The servants were not alone. From every district bells rang, steam whistles blew, and the chimes of magically amplified instruments clashed discordantly with one another. Overhead, a hundred voices bellowed from notice-towers, hollowed out by the fog and the glimmer horns they were projected by.

"The Morfaan return! The Morfaan return! To the Basilica, the Basilica of the Lost Gods!" they shouted to mismatched rhythms.

"The Church will be pleased," Mandofar said sarcastically. "You are aware that they have been preaching from street corners that the Morfaan are the heralds of the gods? The Church of the Return is becoming something of a problem here."

"Another little problem to resolve," said Abing gravely.

Work stopped. Shops closed. Houses emptied. The silence the fog brought was torn to shreds by the movement of the entire city in one direction. Thousands of people clogged the roads. Their shouting and the clattering wheels on the cobbles chased off the fog's gloominess, and the city assumed the atmosphere of a chilly party, where the obscuring mist was the city's carnival mask. Summoned by the noise, street hawkers appeared from nowhere, their cries spearing through fog and hubbub alike to announce hot nuts, warmed beer, candies, fruit, hats, glimmer-fed pocket warmers and a myriad other things that might be of use to the crowds.

The carriage rumbled off the Avenue of Peace, and out of the wide spaces of the ambassadorial quarter into one of Perus's labyrinthine assignatures. Tenements tottered through the murk like drunken giants. Walls pressed in on both sides. The coach slowed, unable to move faster than the flow of foot traffic. Their coachman swore in the thick Perusian dialect, his whip flicked out, cracking over the heads of the throng, the dogs bayed at those blocking the way. There was nowhere for them to go, and the coach was forced to a crawl. Passing a tight sidestreet, the coachman took it upon himself to try a different route. With a snap of the reins, the dogs spilled down the street, dragging the coach sharply around. The walls and windows of the apartments were close enough to touch. Low-hung washing slapped against the decorations on the roof.

Abing clicked open his watch and hummed at it impatiently. "I hope this fellow knows where he is going."

"Shelluse is one of the best," Mandofar assured them.

"One could live one's whole life here and lose one's way on a night like this," said the countess.

On one side the buildings disappeared, giving out to a pavement bordered by a sheer drop. There was not room for two lanes of traffic, and a generous pedestrian pavement took up the remainder of the street. This allowed those on foot to squeeze out of the coach's way. The carriage lurched as it picked up speed.

"As you see, Shelluse is a fine driver," said Mandofar. "He was born to these streets. If a way can be found, he will find it. We go now past the Callanches Caverna. A clever shortcut."

Garten craned his neck to see over the heads of the people on the pavement. A stone balustrade delineating the edge flicked past like a zoetrope. On the other side were the pan-tiled rooftops of a row of houses clinging to the cliff. These cavities, the cavernas, were particular to Perus. There was Foirree, which Perus had long ago claimed both sides of. Although unusual there in the west, being built both sides of one of Ruthnia's great canyons was a trait Perus held in common with many eastern cities, most notably Mohacs-Gravo, Kuz and Astermung. But the cavernas were unique. Throughout the city there were many unanticipated cavities, collapsed caverns open to the sky whose bases were crammed with the toppled stones of ancient metropolises. Through a gap, Garten saw the hazy shapes of buildings marching down the steep cliffs to the bottom of the pit, their lamps lighting the fog from within. Hundreds of feet below their road, the blurred shape of a bridge crossed the gap, disappearing into a circular tunnel mouth. These parts of Perus were rich with history, but were amongst the very poorest.

"Once matters have calmed, would it be possible to visit the cavernas?" Garten asked.

"What on Earth for?" asked Mandofar.

"My sister is most interested in redressing the problems of poverty brought about by the changes wrought by this modern age," said Garten, somewhat pompously, but blast Mandofar, he thought. "It would do her cause, and our own national prestige, no end of good if we could demonstrate that Karsa is ahead of its old rival, Maceriya, in the betterment of the conditions of the poor."

"I am sure it is quite impossible," said Mandofar. "They are poor, you are right, and consequently dangerous. Why do you want to go poking your nose into the business of the common herd? Those forced to live in the cavernas are undeserving, idle. Save your pity for those who wish to work."

"There is the history, the—"

"Not now, Garten," said Abing firmly.

"Of course, your grace," said Garten. He returned his attention to the caverna, resolved upon a visit nevertheless.

The fissure closed suddenly, and the road was captured again between towering apartment blocks.

By this shortcut, the coach managed to clear a space between itself and the crowds surging toward the Basilica, but there were many other vehicles on the streets, and Perus's hellish traffic was thickened by the cavalcade.

No sooner had the coach picked up speed, it was forced to slow again. Floating orbs in the fog were glimmer lamps marking an intersection. All four roads leading into it were jammed with vehicles.

The coachman forced his way through a tangle of drays and wagons. At the edge of the mess two drivers rebuked each other loudly. Shelluse joined in with gusto. The dogs snarled at other teams as he forced his way through.

"Good grief!" said the duke.

"The traffic here is appalling, your grace," said Mandofar drily.

They pushed past, only to stop again. A great procession of hooded men walked by, each carrying a tall candle. They sang sadly as they walked. Many of the people on the pavements made signs of devotion, others shouted curses. The hooded men paid attention to neither.

"Ah, the Church. I said they would be out in force. I was not wrong!" said Mandofar, pleased with himself.

Abing opened the door and thrust his generous body out into the fog, setting the carriage rocking. "Kressind"" said the duke. "Look at that! Thousands of them." The procession trudged past slowly. Bells rang frantically still everywhere, but around the church members a silence settled, deeper than the fogs. Not reverence, but an anticipation, an imminence.

Garten craned his neck, barely able to see past the duke's ample backside. There were men and women in the procession. Armed men with hard faces flanked them, hoods down, shoving at those who hurled curses. Intimidation was the cause of the silence, not religious feeling.

The last of the faithful filed past, their column of candles and lamps swallowed up by the fog. Ordinary citizens came behind in a disorganised and knotty mob. Shelluse took his chance, a crack of the whip sent the dogs barking through the stream of people. Shocked faces flashed past the window, and they were through.

Another warren of tenements approached. More and more people were about. A babble suffused everything, a voice as indistinct and all pervasive as a brook at night. Garten was entranced by the crowd. Men and women of all stations and all nations moved together with common purpose.

"Come on, come one!" growled Abing. "If we are not there to greet the Morfaan we shall lose a great deal of face."

"Does it really matter, good Tomas?" asked the countess. She too was fascinated by the surging mass of humanity outside the coach, smiling with genuine pleasure at the things that caught her eye.

"To the Morfaan, our presence is irrelevant, to them it is the crowd that counts, not who is in it," said Abing. "But being late or absent will give our rivals ammunition I would rather they did not have!" Abing banged the ceiling with his cane. "On driver!"

"He is doing his best," said the ambassador.

No sooner had he said this than a horn wailed over the Maceriyan capital, coming up from the direction the group was headed in. Voices went up from unseen towers. More horns joined in, rocking the sky with their sorrowful blaring.

"Place di Azamund!" the town speakers wailed, their voices pitched deliberately high to cut through the unnatural night. "Place di Azamund! The Morfaan will come to Azamund!"

"Damn it!" shouted the duke. "The place of manifestation has altered!"

"It is not abnormal," said Mandofar. "I was undersecretary to the secretary when the last visitation came. On that day it changed seven times before they finally pierced the skin of the world and came through. He said they were cautious, personally I suspect they are paranoid."

"And this fog, was that the same?" asked the countess.

"Always, countess," said Mandofar, who in spite of himself was warming to Lucinia. She was plain and not ugly, Garten decided, and open, engaging, and sharp. "It is said they can no longer abide the light of our sun."

"So it remains foggy for their entire stay?"

"Around them, yes. But only for the space of a few hundred yards. Once they have made the crossing from their domain, the weather returns to normal. We are in their murk when attending upon them or at the business of the parliament, but we have respite when the day's business is concluded. At least, so it once was. I must give advisement that like our own dear Karsa City, Perus is prone to choking on the exhalations of its industry. There is always a taste of sulphur on the air, I'm afraid, and they lack the good strong coastal winds we have at home to blow it all away."

"He's not turning. Damn him! You said this man knew his business! Driver!" Abing banged on the ceiling hard, scuffing the velvet upholstery with his cane. "To the Place di Azamund! Azamund man!"

The coach wheeled around sharply again. The duke flung out his arm to steady himself, pinning the older Mandofar against his seat, discomposing him. The countess slid into Garten's thigh. She glanced down, squeezed his leg and gave him a saucy look.

Pedestrians hollered angrily after them. Theirs was not the only carriage turning around. People milled about as the news filtered through the crowd. Furious shouts were everywhere.

Twice more the location changed.

"Marmore district, the Place of Heroism!"

"The Foirree, Adomas Bridge!"

It was by now late. The last of the summer evening slipped away into grey obscurity unnoticed by mankind. The omnipresent light of lanterns, candles, glimmer lamps and torches carried by the crowds supplanted the sun completely. All the world was aglow. It reminded Garten of his father's foundries.

The crowds became frenzied with anticipation and exhaustion, every new announcement was greeted with groans and shouts. Men and women who should have known better ran along streets like beggars in pursuit of an over-generous passerby. The Maceriyans were an unruly lot to Karsan eyes—sexually licentious, often drunk, haughty and prone to riot at the slightest provocation, and what shreds of decorum the Maceriyans did possess took leave of Perus that night. Matters became tense. High born men brawled with factory workers over perceived slights. Well bred women drank and caroused with the lower orders, singing bawdy songs to welcome in the Morfaan. For the well-mannered Garten, it was all a little too much, and his fascination turned to disgust.

Mandofar noted Garten's change of heart with satisfaction. "I am sure your sister would approve," he said.

And then another location was called, "Royal Park, Royal Park, at the Meadow!"

By the time the Royal Park was announced as the destination, it was well past midnight. The carriage had jogged from one side of the city centre to the other, up and down and back up Perus's nine hills. Garten's curiosity was blunted by tiredness and he had become oddly nervous. Abing was irascible. They had spent days travelling and no opportunity to rest. Mandofar, insulated from high expectation by local knowledge and a certain amount of affected disinterest, drew pleasure from their discomfort.

Again the coach pulled ahead of the crowds. Again they accelerated, their driver racing against others to be the first to the Meadow. Coaches thundered on the cobbled streets. The mist thickened and became darker as they left the crowd. Behind them the city appeared to be aflame.

A wide road brought them to the bounds of the Royal Park. The famously high walls rose over them, no nonsense constructions of deeply rusticated stone topped with silver-chased iron. "Against Wild Tyn?" asked Garten.

"Allegedly so, although I have never seen one," said Mandofar. "And nor has any man I have spoken to."

"Nonsense," said a small voice.

Mandofar looked around himself. "Did someone say something?"

"It must have come from outside," said Garten.

"Really Kressind, you are the most unconvincing liar," shouted Abing. "Come clean. Tell him what's in that blasted box."

Garten grinned placatingly. "A trifle, nothing more, a—"

"Get on with it!"

Garten undid the box door, displaying Tyn Issy clutching at her bars with two dainty hands.

"I'm not a trifle," she said. "I'm a menace." She showed her teeth to the ambassador.

"Driven gods!" he gasped. "You new money people are beyond belief! A Tyn as a pet?"

"Not a pet, a geas, I'm afraid," said Garten. "I assure you it is not my choice to accompany her."

"Even worse!" choked Mandofar, his face reddening. "My father warned the old prince that elevating a bunch of factory men and farmers to the ranks of the peerage would end in disaster, that they'd drag up all their uncouth fancies and abnormal practices with them. He was bloody right!"

"I am a princess of my kind," said Issy loftily. "High magics bind me to humanity's path, and I am exceptionally expensive. I come from a family far finer and high than even yours, so do not cast aspersions upon the breeding of the Goodfellow Kressind."

"By all the gods, it speaks, it speaks!"

"Of course I can speak! You manage it, and you are a fool. Why should not I?"

"What did you say?"

"You heard me before, you buffoon." She grinned again.

"Mandofar, calm down, there's a good fellow," said Abing. "Anyone would think you have never seen a Tyn before."

"Calm down? I will not calm down! I will not! This is most irregular! Do you know how the Maceriyans will react to this? This is not Karsa City! They do not take kindly to creatures of... that sort," he flapped a hand at the Tyn, "in their midst. Why do you think they go to all the bother of the park wall over half-believed folktales?"

"They shall never see her," said Abing.

"I make a very fine spy," said Issy.

Garten glanced at her box questioningly.

"My great uncle died because of a Tyn's curse," said Mandofar. "I will not have it in the embassy."

"What did he do to offend?" said Issy. "I shall guess! Pomposity. Being pompous is not enough to draw our ire."

"Nothing! He was struck down for nothing. Tyn are untrustworthy, dangerous, deadly."

"All of that, and in your carriage," said Issy.

"Do you threaten me? How dare you!" shrieked Mandofar.

"That's it! All of you, quiet!" bellowed Abing. "You must swallow it, Mandofar, no matter how it sticks. The Tyn stays. Now be quiet. A man can barely hear himself think!" He tapped the head of his cane against his chin. "Best keep her under wraps, eh Garten?"

"Your grace." He made to close the box.

"No, no, don't shut the poor thing away. Let her see the arrival. Be sporting, eh?"

The countess smiled at Abing. Tyn Issy curtsied. Garten obliged.

CHAPTER SIXTEEN
The Church of the Return

THE MOTION OF the carriage set the wall into rolling animation. Fine coping stones took the place of iron spikes, and it rose and fell in stone waves to meet thick pillars, upon which were mounted massive stone spheres carved all over with angular designs. When the walls bent inward toward the Meadow Gate, they seemed to leap backward like acrobats. Scores of coaches were rushing into the park, spraying orange stone chippings onto the dark grass. The Karsan carriage smoothly joined the line, and the dogs bayed for the joy of running with their own kind. Tall trees sped by. The industrial burned grease and old wool reek of the fog was supplanted by the scent of damp greenery. The road headed downwards through open woodland, before splitting to run all the way around a broad area of landscaped grassland. There the coaches drew up, depositing their passengers into a chattering crowd of Perus's well-to-do. Their excitement dispelled the gloom of the weather.

The crunching rattle of carriage wheels on gravel abruptly ceased as the Karsans' coach went onto the grass and stopped. The driver and coachman jumped down and opened the doors.

"The Meadow!" said Mandofar. "A good place for the arrival."

"Everyone out!" boomed Abing, and left the coach rocking as he sprang out.

Garten had the presence of mind to shut Issy's door before she was seen, and stepped out into the Royal Park. Moisture from the grass soaked his shoes and stockings. Fog drifted in murky swags through the forest surrounding the meadow. It was unseasonably cold and dreary and altogether sinister.

Languages from all over the Hundred drifted over the gathering as a stream of wealthy men and women walked out onto the Meadow following the bobbing will o' the wisps of lantern bearers. The Karsans' driver remained to water the dogs but the coachman joined Garten, the countess and the rest, carrying a lantern in one hand and a stout stave in the other. Abing took the lead. Walking side by side with the coachman, he pushed on to the front of the swelling crowd as if he, and not Mandofar, were the old hand in Perus. Bursts of music filtered through the damp air. Food vendors proclaimed their wares. The hawkers seemed to anticipate every move of the crowds, and the rest of Perus was coming. Toward the gates gathering torchlight lit up the eaves of the park woods.

"It looks like this will be it. The mob will be here soon," said Abing, waving his cane at the pursuing glow. "We shall to the Meadow Mound. Come!"

The crowd of well-to-do Perusians were headed to a small hillock fronted by a crag that looked out over the flat of the Meadow. Abing's muscular walk pulled him ahead once more. Mandofar tried his damnedest not to pant as he kept up. Garten took his time, threading past knots of laughing women and men of serious countenance in exotic costumes. The countess stuck by him, a private grin on her face.

"Do you find all this amusing?" asked Garten.

"That's a loaded question, Kressind," she said, gently mocking Abing's manner. "I am trying not to laugh. Not from devilment, but from delight. Such a gathering! I am a connoisseur of parties, goodfellow, but this is quite extraordinary."

"And crowded. Where has Abing got to?" said Garten. They had reached the crag. A line of the well-to-do were winding round the side towards the back.

"Does it matter? You can protect me, can't you? I hear you are quite the swordsman," she said with a wink. "We shall stand there. Let the rest jockey for position on the summit." She pointed out a shelf of rock jutting out from the base of the crag that would afford them a good view over the heads of the crowd. For the time being, it was vacant.

"Look how carefully this has been prepared," she said, knocking a knuckle against the rock. What Garten had taken to be natural had in fact been carved to resemble weathered stone.

"None of it appears to be real," he said. "The boulders have been mortared in place."

"The irony of the Maceriyans! A rock crafted by the elements is not wild enough for them. Such aesthetes," said the countess. "They say nothing is as it seems in Perus, apparently they are right. Whoever they are!" She laughed, and bounded up the stone in a most unladylike manner, turned and reached out a hand to Garten. He shook his head, and she withdrew it. He wished he'd taken it, the rock was slippery.

"Ah," she said as he struggled up beside her. "A man of action who requires no help. So much better than these popinjays and dilettantes. I look at this display and I see falsehood as rank as this stone." The people around them glanced up disapprovingly. The countess set her hands on her hips, bold as a young blade, and enjoyed their opprobrium. "Let them goggle, we can see right over their empty heads," she said. She spied a trio of young women whispering about her behind their hands. She waved, and they waved back, smiling.

"You are famous, goodlady," said Garten.

"I think I am," she said. "How fucking marvellous!"

Garten cringed to hear a woman speak so. She grinned widely at him. Issy tittered.

Besides the richer denizens of the city, many other diplomats had gathered around the stone. There were no constables keeping the crowds away from the crag. Convention alone made a sufficient barrier to the lower orders entering the park and spreading out across the field. The poor kept away.

So many finely dressed men, and a few women, so much power in one place. The emissaries of dozens of the Hundred's kingdoms, standing in the soaking grass.

"There is something bizarre about this gathering," said Garten. "It is as if they are all ensorcelled."

The countess laughed.

The flood of people filled the Meadow side to side. Though the crowd thickened uncomfortably, no one ventured into the woods.

The Meadow was well tended, with lit pavilions, drinking fountains, a large bandstand, elaborately planted centrepieces and smooth gravelled paths. Garten looked about for the city's famed duelling grounds, but he could not see their entrance, to his disappointment.

"I cannot credit the stories I have heard about this place," the countess said. "It seems so peaceful, so pleasant."

"Do not believe that it is so, countess," said Issy very quietly. "There is a great deal of danger here, not only from my kin. This city is old, older than the Maceriyans, older than the Morfaan. The present you dwell in is as thick as the skin on warm milk."

The countess peered into the box. "What is it with you and your family and Tyn?" she said.

"My brother Guis?"

She nodded dismissively. Again, Garten caught that flicker of annoyance at his eldest brother's name. What had he done to her?

"My brother's is a medical necessity. This one was... I should say *gifted* to my brother Trassan, but she was more of an imposition on the part of his master Arkadian Vand. He in turn passed her to me. Now I find myself, well, rather stuck with her. Apparently something horrible will happen if I put her aside."

"Imposition?" said Issy. "Once a goodfellow would never have said such a thing, not even to one such as I. And something horrible would happen. You would be without me. That would be terrible. So don't."

"She's a little feistier than your brother's creature," said the countess.

"I am almost certainly better bred," said Issy.

"I knew that you are acquainted with my sister, Katriona. Do you know my brother well?" asked Garten.

"You might say that," she said, but the jaunty expression she affected hid pain. "Now what's this?"

A chanting came from the entrance to the Meadow, and a concentration of light. Heads turned, the crowd parted.

"The Church has caught us up," said Garten.

"Is it me, or are there more of them?" said the countess.

There were, a long snaking line of thousands of them. This time, they saw the head of the procession. A tall, cowled man went at the front, followed by others in ancient priestly attire carrying icons of the Ten. A figure in black marched alone behind the ten, carrying an eleventh icon covered in black damask.

"And even the Dark Lady is represented," said the countess, pointing out the lonely priestess.

Behind her three dozen other priests and priestesses came flanked by two lines of shave-headed, armed acolytes. The procession made its way around the Meadow. Reaction to their presence was mixed; some jeered, others knelt. Whatever the individual response, the crowds parted. Whether from fear or reverence, the effect was the same. Conversation from the crowd was excited but hushed, and the priest's singing was clear across the field.

"Fear and wonder," their leader sang. "The gods will return. Exile is done, the gods will return. Fear and wonder." The others sang in rounds divided by pitch, so that the song was layered, sweet as a cake. The majority present did not find it palatable.

"The gods can suck my cock!" shouted someone from the crowd.

"What did they ever do for us?" called someone else.

"That pisshead in Karsa bought me a pint once," said another. Scattered laughter greeted his comment. The glaring acolytes shoved their way roughly into the crowd. There followed signs of a scuffle.

"I can only agree with the detractors," said the countess. "Although I have no cock to suck, although I sometimes wish I did."

More insults and catcalls competed with the chant, but could not silence it. Arguments broke out. Patches of the crowd eddied with the beginnings of more tussles. The procession turned. A clod of earth torn from the ground described a graceful arc, slapping hard into the shoulder of a priestess. A devotee of Andrade, thought Garten. He was a little rusty on the costumes of the sub-denominations. She was steadied by her fellows, and they walked, completing a circuit of the field and beginning another. After ten more minutes had passed, they began another circuit. They drew nearer to the crag with each pass. He and the countess watched them for nigh on an hour, as they came closer and closer to the crag while the crowd grew denser and became noisier. The smells of cooking food joined that of unwashed bodies, music began in earnest from several sources. The little violences they had witnessed before were swallowed up by the chaos of the Perusians at play.

The Church approached the crag, their ruffian priests pushing their way through those groups of diplomats and worthies that did not step voluntarily aside. The distaste of those manhandled was clear, but no one made a move to stop the priests. Again, Garten wondered where the authorities were. The procession passed right by the shelf Garten and the countess occupied, so closely their icons wobbled by their noses.

He leaned in close to the countess. "Bishop Rousinteau, Primate of Omnus," he said. "He is their leader."

"I always imagined a bishop to be grander," said the countess. "His costume is very drab. I suppose his church no longer has the money. Although looking at this display, perhaps it is simply an affectation."

People melted from the path of the bishop as he ascended the crag. He disappeared from view a moment, then reappeared at the brink of the artificial cliff, a dozen feet above Garten and the countess's position.

The priests kept up the circular refrain of their song. Rousinteau began to shout in time to the music. His words were amplified by magical means, and the crowd fell quieter, although not silent. The cries of tradesmen and entertainers would cease for no man or god, if a profit could be turned.

"Fear and wonder!" declaimed Bishop Rousinteau. "The Twin approaches. Fires on the Twin! The gods will return! Now is the time to state your devotion! Those who do not display respect shall burn in the wrath of the pantheon. They will come with flame and sword. Oh my brothers, oh my sisters, hearken to our ministry! Join us in our prayers, or forfeit your souls to the anger of the gods! They return, they return!"

"It's the Morfaan coming tonight, dickhead!" someone jeered.

The bishop reacted directly to the insult. He hunted out the heckler, and held out his hands beseechingly.

"Yes, yes! The Morfaan!" he said, as if the man had apprehended some aspect of the ultimate truth and should be congratulated for it. "They are the messengers of the gods, they herald their return. Do you think it coincidence that the High Legate dies so close to the Drawing of the Twin? Do you think it coincidence that the old masters of this world return?"

"Pfft!" said Issy. "Nonsense."

"The Twin has nothing to do with the gods, my goodfellow," the countess shouted.

The priest ignored her or didn't hear her, and continued his sermon from the rock.

More voices called back at the bishop, hurling insults and refutations. But there were others, many more, who heeded the priest, and listened raptly, alternating their attention between the bishop and the sky, where they imagined the Twin to loom, fires on the black surface. The priests' foot soldiers moved through the gathering, intimidating those that dared shout. Like hunting dracons passing through long grass, one saw the disturbance rather than the agitator.

Issy's box jiggled in Garten's hand. He opened the doors, to find Issy leaning right up against the bars, shaking them hard.

"Lift me high!" she said loudly

"Quiet! You'll be seen."

"Never mind that! There is something unwholesome here," she said. When she turned her head, her eyes flashed a luminous blue. "Something not right."

"I will have to close the door," Garten said nervously. "The Maceriyans do not like your kind, and the priests of old declared you anathema. I doubt they have changed their minds. I cannot hold off a hundred ruffians, certainly not in this press.

"I must see!"

"Then look through the vision slit, and be careful!"

"I am well aware!" she snapped. "Quickly!"

Garten shut the door again. Issy's eyes glowed behind the vision slit. "Up, up!" she said. "Turn about, point me upwards, at the priest." She made a cat-like growl. "Back, back. Get off the stone. Go up and round. There is magic on the summit."

The countess had her masculine face tilted up at the priest ten feet above, undisguised scorn large on her features. "What a lot of perfect rot," she said as his sermon grew more excitable. "Fucking fool."

"Excuse me a moment," said Garten.

She nodded at him distractedly.

Garten dropped from the shelf. The crowd had grown thicker, and he had to utter many an excuse me and sorry to make his way through. Issy wisely stayed quiet, and he kept his free hand protectively over the vision slit.

A grassy slope bordered the fake crag. Around the front it was too steep and slippery to stand on, and so was free of onlookers. As it offered the quickest route, he scrambled up.

Garten came out on a flat-topped earth mound big enough to accommodate several hundred people. From this new vantage the hill's constructed nature was obvious. Steps lined by an elegant stone rail allowed access from behind, opening onto a paved area which occupied a large part of the top. There the highest diplomats gathered, the richest men, the mightiest lords. In their midst Garten got his first sight of organised Maceriyan power in the form of a square of soldiers in garish uniforms, their faces painted like dolls beneath brocaded mitre caps. Armed with heavy ironlocks, they formed a barrier to a further group of ostentatious lords. If those around the hill represented the great and good of Perusian society, and those on top the mightiest present from the rest of the Hundred, then these men and women at the epicentre of the gathering were the real powers of Maceriya. They were heavily made up, faces white and red and blue, dressed in elaborate clothes stiffened with jewels and embroidery to the point of impracticality. They were raised up over their guardians on boxes, so that they appeared like a party of bizarre giants awaiting some grim ceremony. All of them listened politely to the bishop, although he had his back to them. Such a lack of deference to the powers of the land sent a chill through Garten.

At the very centre of the nobles, raised up over them all, were the Three Comtes of Perus arrayed in height according to their order of seniority. From sketches and lithographs Garten recognised Arvons, Comte of Low Perus, the only one of them that appeared discomfited by the bishop's oratory. Raganse, Comte of Outer Perus, was the most painted and ornately attired of all three. He listened to the bishop most avidly, conferring often and animatedly about this thing or that the bishop said to a pair of ladies whose lesser podiums brought them only to his chest. Lastly was Juliense, Comte of High Perus, senior of the three, his expression blank.

As Rousinteau spoke, the priests sang their song joyously. A further ring of the armed men, these the church's own, protected them. There was a clear gap of three yards between priests and potentates. Painted soldiers faced warrior priests garbed in sackcloth. The priests glared at the soldiers, the soldiers looked over the priests' heads. Garten hung back from this, amazed that such a display of might would be permitted by the government.

"Things are worse than we thought," he said to Issy.

"If I am right, they are far worse than you can imagine, let alone think of," said Issy. "Further forward!"

"I'll expose you," said Garten.

"A risk we must take. I cannot see, therefore I cannot expose this thing that is here. Forward!"

Reluctantly, Garten moved to the very edge of the space between the soldiers and the priests. He stood behind one ludicrously uniformed man—although his ironlock seemed serviceable enough—and cradled Issy on his hands at chest height, unwilling to brandish her box like an unlit lantern. The bishop's voice resounded unnaturally around the whole Meadow, too loud for comfort so close in.

"Left, left, left," she said on the edge of hearing. Garten rotated on the spot like the mechanism of a lighthouse. The box swung in his hand as Issy jumped inside. "Stop! There! The woman behind the bishop."

There was someone behind the bishop, hooded and garbed in long robes without decoration, so Garten could not tell if it were male or female, even if Issy could. In their hand was a staff that appeared unremarkable, but as Garten tried to discern what possible threat this person might possess, his perception lurched. The staff remained the same, but was also somehow different. He saw it now for what it was, no simple stave, but the tool of high magic.

"A mage?" he said. "I thought there none in Maceriya currently. I do not recognise the costume. And why would a mage have anything to do with the priests?"

"You know them all?" said Issy.

"There are currently fifty-two, none resident in Maceriya. There is a list, you know."

"She will not be on your list of mages. She is something else, something worse that I have not encountered for a long time," said Tyn Issy. "There is more than one church here tonight."

Sensing eyes upon her, the mage turned around abruptly and fixed Garten directly with her gaze. She was indeed a woman, and a strange looking one at that. He nodded to her respectfully and made to leave. To his dismay, he found he could not move. A pressure grew in his eyes. His sinuses throbbed.

"She has seen you!" said Issy. "Get out of her sight."

"I can't!" choked Garten. Something burst in his nose. He tasted blood at the back of his throat.

The bishop's words reached a crescendo, and he held his hands aloft. "The Morfaan! They come!" he bellowed. A crackling rent the sky, stirring the fog. The mage looked away, out into the field, and her grip fell away from Garten. He ducked back into the crowd on shaking legs, thence back to the top of the slope where he stopped and spat blood.

"She tried to kill me!" he said.

"I perhaps should have said that she might," said Issy.

Before Garten could reply, the sky over the Meadow split.

CHAPTER SEVENTEEN
The Morfaan on Earth

A FLASH OF blue sheet lightning carved through the fog some fifty feet up, then another. Three more strobed the crowd. A bone-chilling cry rolled out of the forest, spooking the crowd. They drew back from the middle of the Meadow stumblingly, then in quick panic.

"They come," said Issy. "The world gates open."

An invisible explosion accompanied by a deafening boom burst in the centre of the Meadow, flattening the grass and agitating the mist, driving the crowd back further. There were more flashes in the fog, a crackling like fireworks. A rattling noise approached, metal drumming on stone. A thrumming discordancy blared out of nowhere. A scattering of screams outdid the crowd's collective gasp. Another blue flash, and a banging. The mist parted, revealing a grey-lined tunnel reaching far back, as if the fog had gained substance, and spun itself into walls. The trees were gone, the meadow was gone, some other place was revealed, foggier even than Perus's night. A damp chill blasted down the swirling, vaporous throat. The sound of the rattling metal grew louder.

The fog of the faraway world parted like a torn flag. A mellow golden light spilt down the tunnel, and the carriage of the Morfaan appeared.

No drays pulled the carriage. Its motive power was provided by mechanical legs similar to those of a charabanc, but this was no lumbering, hooting contraption. The legs were articulated to the smooth cab by uncertain means and moved too quickly to be counted, their metal tips clattering loudly on an unseen stone surface.

The carriage ran silently as it cantered out of the tunnel onto the wet ground. Purple lightning and smoke burst around its feet as they hit Earthly soil. Behind, the tunnel pulsed, and collapsed with a clap of thunder, sending the mist rushing away at ground level in waves. The crowd scattered before the machine as it galloped across the turf. Magic discharged from it, wreathing it in foxfire, until all the excess was gone into the ground and the carriage took on a less otherworldly appearance. Still the tell-tale blue glow of glimmer light shone around the joints in the legs, but it was brighter and cleaner than the luminance emitted by human machines. The upper surfaces were dark, reflecting the torches and lamps of the crowd from its surfaces.

The cab was the shape of a seed, the tapering end pointing to the rear. There were no windows. Garten suspected it to be a direct-glimmer device, but no human had succeeded in getting such a high power output from raw magic. He saw none of the odd effects associated with the manifestation of a mage's art, nor any of the sigil marks that indicated the craftsmanship of a magister. The carriage gave off no exhaust, and ran nearly silently.

The crowd parted smoothly to let the Morfaan through to the foot of the crag. Panick eased, but there was no sign of jubilation. Humanity had been struck dumb.

The carriage decelerated. Now they were slowing, the legs became clear and appeared even more strange—four groups of four, mounted on sideways wheels that turned as the legs ran. Garten was put in mind of agricultural mechanisms used for turning hay, though the resemblance was superficial.

Light burst all around as the carriage stopped, bright as if the sun had punched its way through the fog and the night to illuminate this one patch of the earth. Seams appeared in the side. A door popped open and drew itself back along the body of the coach. Steps unfolded with a mechanical ticking.

Down the steps came a woman and a man. A collective sigh rippled through the crowd. Few there had seen the Morfaan. Garten had been a boy last time a High Legate had been elected, far away in Karsa. His knowledge of Earth's ancient masters was restricted to archaeological artefacts and drawn reconstructions. Neither captured the reality. The Morfaan's own art had been highly stylised, while this era's imagining of them was woefully inaccurate.

What he saw were of a similar shape to a man, but they were as unlike men as a raindrop is unlike a snowflake. They were taller, thinner, and moved oddly as they walked, their heads bobbing a little like those of a strutting dracon. Their heavy multilayered costumes and make-up were more sophisticated versions of those worn by the aristocracy of Perus, rendering them further alien. The Morfaan numbered only two, always the same pair that came back to the world, and they brought no servants with them.

"We are Josan and Josanad, emissaries of the Morfaan," pronounced the male. "We have come by ancient agreement to vote in the choosing and witness investiture of the new High Legate of the province of Ruthnia."

A number of people nearby fell to their knees. The male smiled widely as he beckoned to them to rise.

"The Morfaan have come!" shouted the bishop. He held up his hands to the heavens. "Where they go, soon the gods will follow!"

The male's smile faltered. The woman stepped forward. "I am sorry?" said the male.

"You are emissaries of the gods!" shouted the bishop in ecstasy. "You herald the dawning of a new age!"

The male Morfaan burst out laughing. The female put her hand on his arm to restrain him, but the male did not stop.

"Where are the Three Comtes? It is they who have greeted us on our past fifty-six visits," she asked.

The bishop's voice was thick with anger and humiliation. "Juliense, Comte of High Perus, asked us to greet you, as was proper, as it was in the old times before the driving of the gods."

"We are not the emissaries of your gods nor have we ever been," said the female. "As long as there have been comtes, it is they who have greeted us, not the priesthood. They attended us, welcomed us in the name of those Y Dvar who had taken residence in the Parrui." She gestured to the sky, in the direction of the fallen Godhome. "A politeness, nothing more."

The Morfaan conferred with each other. They were not so alien or so far away that Garten could not see their concern.

"The Three Comtes were accompanied by the Primate of Omnus," said the bishop, losing his composure. "We seek to honour the gods in the proper way. It is written in our histories that the primate was present, that it was his role to relay the substance of the meetings to the lord of the eleven, that—"

"Where is Juliense?" interrupted the female. "He was first of the Comtes upon our last visit. He was not old by the measure of your race. Is he still the First?"

The crowd's sense of awe was slipping. Confusion took its place. If the priests had been invited by Juliense, then the Church's influence had grown great indeed. Garten knew nothing of the rituals involved in welcoming the Morfaan two hundred years ago, but it was not so far in the past. Why did the bishop's version run counter to that of the Morfaan?

"Well, this is awkward," said Issy.

Trumpets broke the tension. A troop of soldiers jogged around the base of the crag, surrounding the Three Comtes who were brought down in pulpits upon palanquins. The group stopped before the Morfaan. The soldiers parted, and the palanquins were carried forward by matched pairs of tall, pale brown Fethrians, beautiful in their androgyny.

"Welcome to the World of Will," said Juliense in archaic High Maceriyan.

"Your welcome gladdens our hearts," said the male, stifling his laughter.

"What is the meaning of this, these priests?" said the female in bewilderment.

The Comte of High Perus made no attempt to lower his voice.

"A theological error," Juliense said. "This is a time of omens, the bishop assured me that this was the correct etiquette before the Driving." He held up a powdered hand at the bishop, a questioning look on his face. "I am sorry, he must be mistaken. Forgive us for our mistake. We shall note it in the chronicles." He regarded the bishop directly. "So that it might be remembered."

Josan and her companion bowed.

A hand clapped Garten on the shoulder.

"There you are, Garten. All this business with the Church, eh?" said Abing.

"Not a good sign, your grace."

"No, indeed not. There is more to all this than meets the eye. I'm going to need you tonight. We have to formulate a plan. I had not expected the Church to wield so much influence that they could appear here, of all places, to make fools of themselves in front of the Morfaan."

"Maybe that was the intention," said Garten. "Maybe Raganse put pressure on Juliense to allow the priests to greet these 'heralds of the gods'. He might have agreed in order to undermine them, knowing full well that they would appear foolish."

"Well read," said Abing. "Mandofar has been filling me in. The Church have the total support of Raganse and half of the Perusian nobility. I doubt any of them are believers, but the Maceriyans do so love to bet both ways," he said. "However, if Juliense was forced to play such a risky game as to humiliate the bishop in front of the crowd it does not speak well to his current position. The Lord Comte has the power of veto over the other two. Why get drawn into such a dangerous play?"

The Morfaan returned to their coach. The soldiers came down from guarding their lords and were pushing the crowd back for the carriages of the Perusian lords. Now the greeting was done, the mob was looking forward to the more serious business of getting drunk. Celebration reasserted itself. Music started up again, fireworks joined the noise. More traders with handcarts and wagons were arriving, most carrying barrels.

"Because the people are beginning to believe," said Garten. "Did you see the support they had from the crowd? What was notable about all that was how many of them were quiet. How much stronger is that going to get as the Twin comes closer? If we are troubled by major earthquakes and aberrant weather as we often are around the greatest of tides during the Twin's regular perigees, then it would exacerbate the situation. The election summit starts in two days, once the Morfaan have had time to rest. Juliense needs to silence Raganse now."

Abing nodded. "Could be, could be." He slapped Garten hard on the back. "This is not the place for this discussion. Too public. Attend me in my rooms after dinner. Steel yourself, my boy, you have a long night ahead. Not least because of that fellow Mandofar, not the sort of decisive chap we need in a situation like this. I've wrung what little use out of him I am going to find, and it's barely enough to wet my hands. He knows the scene, but he's a damn ditherer." He spat "ditherer" as if it were a curse. "I've had nothing else but objections from him all evening. A good choice for a diplomat in ordinary days, but he is hardly dynamic."

"Thank you for drawing him away from myself and the countess. Without him, I think we have been able to look more objectively."

"Hah! Noticed that did you? Good chap. I knew I made the right choice for you as secretary." Abing was behaving so much like a pleased uncle in that moment Garten half-expected him to pinch his cheek there and then, or pull a half-thaler coin from behind his ear. "Excellent. Now, best we get back to our own carriage, make sure we're far up the procession back to the Avenue of Peace, don't want us trailing at the back like some sleepy Olberlander! Come come, work to do, there is work to do!" Brandishing his cane, he plunged into the crowd. Abing was one man who did not require the way cleared for him.

CHAPTER EIGHTEEN
The Room of Dawning

"BEGINNING TONIGHT" PROVED to be less than Madelyne expected. By the end of it she almost wished for what she feared instead of what she got.

Madelyne had an early dinner of chops, alone as usual. After finishing, she went to read in the library. There was plenty to occupy her in there, though one bookshelf she avoided; it had heavy doors studded with square-headed iron nails, and gave off a malign feeling. Otherwise the library was as one would expect—tall and open, a gallery railed with gold curlicued metalwork at the midpoint; quiet, pregnant with knowledge pressed between pages, scented with paper and old leather.

Madelyne had educated herself. Although she felt like reading something light, she decided to advertise the fact and chose *Fourteen Dragons*, a novel from the Maceriyan Resplendency. Supposedly based on fact, it had only recently been unearthed and reprinted. She found it diverting enough. Though the period's bewildering host of unfamiliar terms and its strange social conventions was made even more difficult by the edition's extensive footnotes, Madelyne lost herself in it.

The Infernal Duke came for her at the fourteenth hour, not long after sunset, although the fog made the position of the sun moot. The day was pale grey, the night dark grey. A knock on the door made her jump and sent her scrambling up from her sprawled position on the reading couch, dropping the book in the process. The duke walked in.

"You are comfortable."

"I... Yes," she said.

He recovered the book. He snapped it shut with one hand and nodded his approval at the title. "You read High Maceriyan."

"Yes," she said. "But I expect you knew that anyway, your grace."

"Naturally." He laid the book down and held out his hand. "If you will, it is time to begin."

"Do I have a choice?" she said, affecting lightness. Her stomach tightened. She had been through worse. She had done worse, she reminded herself.

The duke bowed his horned head. "I said there is always a choice, my dear, but if you wish to remain here, you must come with me now."

"Then I am ready." She took his hand, curling all her fingers around two of his. He led her out of the room, down the long transverse corridor leading from the central hall and its staircase to the tower at the end of the north wing. Artworks and artefacts from dizzyingly ancient eras lined the panelling. Suits of antique armour, battered from use, were mounted upon lacquered blocks at regular intervals. Doors led off to either side, most of which she had been through. Drawing rooms and sitting rooms to the front on this side of the house. Toward the back there was a huge ballroom that occupied much of the length of the north wing, the chandeliers covered with sheets and dusty with disuse.

Their feet whispered over the runner that stretched the full length of the wing's hall. All was deathly silent. The city's noise was muffled by thick walls and thick fog. Madelyne was gripped by the vertiginous feeling that she was trapped in a fog-bound mansion from which there was no escape. There was a story that the Morfaan lived in such a place. It was a dreadful thought, and the presence of the duke reassured her.

What the hells am I doing? she thought. Too late for that. She kept her mind on her prize.

They came to the north tower. An open staircase occupied the bulge of a turret set in the outer rear edge. It curled away into darkness.

"This tower contains my personal rooms," he said to her. "The room on the ground floor, which I am to take you into, you may frequent when you wish, though I doubt you will want to. That on the first floor you will come to know soon enough. Until I have taken you in there, it remains locked. After that it will stay open. The second floor has a chamber you will also be introduced to, but you are only ever to go in there with me, never alone. Upon the third floor is my chamber, to which you may come and go as you please. On the fourth, at the top of the tower, there is a room that you are never to go into under any circumstances. Do you understand? Please say that you do, and mean it."

"Yes your grace," she said.

"Say that you understand."

"I understand, your grace."

He was relieved by her reply. "Very good. Now we shall begin."

He placed a hand upon the handles of the double door of the ground floor room, and opened first one, then the other. With a smile, he gestured her within. "This is the Room of Dawning," he said.

A fire burned in the grate. Despite the chill of the mist on everything, the room was too hot. The ceilings were too high for the room. It threw the proportions off, and made her feel small. A tall plaster freeze ran around the top of the wall depicting dozens of figures—human, animal, Morfaan and other less identifiable creatures. They cavorted lewdly with one another. Their limbs were posed in postures of delight, but despair was on the faces of all. Flickering firelight made the plaster mouldings dance nauseatingly, and she looked away.

The duke went to a high, wing-backed chair by the fire and sat within. Elsewhere in the house there was a mix of differently sized furniture for the duke and his guests. The few pieces in there—couch, large table, occasional table and the chair—were proportioned for his inhuman frame alone, intensifying her feelings of helplessness. She made to follow him.

"No," he said. He took off his jacket and draped it on the chair. "Stand. There." He pointed to the centre of the rug. She did as she was told. "Now then. When we are engaged in these activities, you are to behave demurely. You are not to look me in the eye. You are to obey my commands without dissent and immediately.

When addressed, you are to respond but only so that I know you understand. You are to say 'yes, your grace,' and nothing more."

"Yes, your grace," she said. She looked at the rug. It did not extend as far as the walls, and the marble tiles there were uncovered. The centre was occupied by a stylised depiction of a rose. She concentrated on the patterns, and withdrew into herself. This trick had saved her before, when she had sold herself, staring at cracks in old plaster as men grunted on top of her. She had spent a lot of time convincing Harafan this would be the same, although now she realised she was convincing herself. It was not the same. Terror made its oily way up from her stomach, threatening to block her throat. Her legs shook.

"Good. Now strip."

"Yes, your grace."

She slipped her arms from her dress, pulled down the top and began to unlace the bodice. An unexpected feeling of shame hit her. Before, the few times, she had not known the men, and that had made it easier. But this god she had conversed with pleasantly. It was more difficult to divorce herself from what her body was doing. She panicked and fumbled the clasps of her corset.

"Slowly!" he growled. "I wish to enjoy this." He lifted an oversized decanter from the small table by his side and poured a bottle's worth of wine into a glass as big as a vase.

She did as she was bid, slipping from her clothes carefully and silently. The duke made a noise of approval as her petticoats and underwear slid to the floor, revealing her nakedness.

"I cannot abide mess," he said, his voice thickening. "Pick up your clothes, fold them, and place them on the table."

"Yes, your grace." She took care not to rush, stacking the clothes into a pile at her side, then carried them to the table.

"Do not slouch!" he rumbled.

She stood straighter.

"No, no, no!" he said. "This will not do. You must display yourself!" The glass clinked down. He came to her. Placing one hand on her lower back and the other just below her breasts he adjusted her posture. "Stick you backside and your tits out," he said. Madelyne was surprised to hear him utter so mild a crudity. He had not used language like that before in her presence. "Did not Verralt inform you of how to stand?"

"Yes, your grace."

His hands, so large they met around her midriff, clenched slightly. They were so hot. "Then do it."

She forced herself into the uncomfortable position, bending her spine into a shallow 's'.

"Place your legs more widely apart. How am I to get to the crux of the matter if you do not?"

Horns sounded from outside, dozens of them. The duke looked up as voices rang out from the rooftops.

"The Morfaan come into the World of Will," he said. "That is not our concern."

His hands dropped away and he retrieved something from his pocket.

"Look at this," he said.

"Yes, your grace."

Draped over one finger was a leather collar pierced with metal eyelets, a worn buckle at the back. A large ring hung from a plate riveted to the front. He lifted it up to her neck. It was old, the leather rough and flaked, and it was musty with the perfume and sweat of other women.

"Bow your head, move your hair, aside" he said.

"Yes, your grace," she said.

"Good, you are a fast learner," he said. He fastened the collar about her throat. It pressed into her skin, not so tightly that she could not breathe, but tightly enough that she was aware of it.

"This is in addition to your mark," he explained. "You will wear this when I deem fit, and only remove it when I say." He took a small silver lock studded with emeralds. It clicked into something at the nape of her neck. "I have the key, just in case." He revelled in telling her this. The touch of his unnaturally hot breath on her cheek sent shivers of treacherous pleasure crawling along her limbs. "Should you prove satisfactory, I will present you with a new collar. For now, this one will suffice. If you wish something prettier, you must earn it."

She was so busy trying to maintain her posture she never expected the stinging crack of his hand across her face. She gasped with the pain and the rush of hot blood to her cheeks. He grabbed her with rough fingers, forcing her eyes up to meet his and crushing her cheeks into her teeth; the left throbbed with the blow.

"No so fast a learner, then. Respond when you are spoken to, else how will I know that you understand? You do understand, don't you, dear Madelyne?"

"Yes, your grace," she said.

"Good." He let her go. Twice more he walked around her, admiring her. The heat radiating off him and the fire made her sweat. "Now," he said, standing before her. "When in this position, you must keep your hands on your head."

She immediately complied, remembering just in time to say, "Yes, your grace."

"Often I will ask you to kneel. Kneel now, maintain your posture."

She did so, leaving her hands on her head.

"Very good. You are a woman that thinks ahead. Whenever you wear the collar, you are my property. You must be prepared to please me in whichever manner I demand, no matter how distasteful you find it. If I ask you to wait, it must be in this position, unless I specify otherwise. Remember, all this is for our mutual pleasure and your ultimate gain."

She did not see how it could be so. In that moment, she hated him. "Yes, your grace," she said.

"Very good." He fetched a rope from a small chest at the end of the larger table in the room. He told her to place her hands in her lap, and he bound her wrists together, then her ankles. Then he had her lift her arms and he bound her stomach with a tight belt of rope, and tied her hands and her feet to this, so that she was forced to remain kneeling.

He took a thick, velvet blanket from the cupboard and spread it on the marble off to one side of the fireplace, then he bent and picked her up as if she weighed nothing, and placed her upon it. There was a ring set into the wall, and he ran a length of chain from this to the collar at her neck, locking it at both ends.

"There," he said. Then he sat, looking away from her, thinking unreadable thoughts and drinking the whole carafe of wine slowly. He said nothing more to her. She was uncomfortable, thirsty. Crowds of people flooded the streets, she could hear their excited voices. Half an hour passed, and they receded. Her arms and legs throbbed with holding the posture. The duke did nothing. Fear gave way to boredom. Oddly she felt in no danger.

The crowds passed on. Over the course of the next two hours the horns sounded several more times, the voices shouting out new locations in the city. These too ceased.

The duke finished the last of his wine, set down the glass, and stood.

"You will wait here upon my pleasure," he said while he buttoned his jacket again. "I may return to use you. I may not. You can only wait and see." His voice purred with pleasure. He put a hot hand under her chin and tilted her head up. "What do you say?"

Fearing a trap, she did not meet his eyes. "Yes, your grace. At your pleasure, you grace."

He considered a moment. "Very good," he said. "I am pleased."

A single peal of thunder cracked from behind the house, far on the other side of the park. And then he left.

Madelyne spent hours kneeling naked upon the velvet, trembling in anticipation. Sleep would not come. At any moment she expected the door to creak open and for him to come in. How would he take her? Would he coax her? Would he force her? He had shown her every kindness, but underlining everything he did was the reason she was there—she was his toy. At some point, he would bed her, she doubted she could achieve her aims without avoiding that. She was not sure how she felt about it. Before her heart had hardened, in the past she had given her virtue to less worthy suitors without a fee, though often they had made themselves appear otherwise. In some ways, the prospect of sleeping with the duke excited her, for how many women could claim to have lain with a god? In others, she was terrified. There was his size, for one thing. He could crush her in his embrace, and if he was sized proportionally all over he might split her in two. Again the worrisome question of how many girls had passed through his doors and been with him arose. He could have the pick of Perusian society, yet he chose from the poor. He always had. The obvious explanation was because they were easier to dispose of should they displease him.

The fire died, and she became cold. The noise passed away from the house.

The quiet of the city was eerie. Although she was far from prying eyes she felt exposed there, in front of uncurtained windows. She was ashamed of her nakedness. This fear of unseen eyes combined with the chill of the room to arouse her senses. She was aware of every inch of skin. When she moved, her nipples brushed against her bound arms and stiffened in response.

The night wore on. The questions whirled around and around her head in a parade of anxiety and doubt. She determined that he would not come, and needed to cover herself. By that time, the thought of him looking at her like this made her feel sick. There was the blanket beneath her, she could cover herself with that. She could barely move. She shuffled about. Getting off the blanket was easy enough, and she regretted it. Cold marble chilled her and she began to shiver. Now she would have to arrange the blanket so that she could sleep on it, fold it over and cover herself with the other half. She despaired at the task. Manoeuvring it into position was frustrating. Her hands were next to useless. She was forced to grovel, balanced on her forehead and knees, tugging the blanket this way and that like a dog with her teeth. All the while, the chain running from the collar on her neck to the wall rattled so loudly in the quiet that she became certain the duke would hear her and return and beat her, or worse. She sobbed with the fear, the cold, her shame and her frustration. What was she doing? Nothing was worth this humiliation.

Finally, exhausted, trembling with effort and with cold, she managed to stretch the blanket out so that she might lie on it. Another interminable half hour of flicking her hands and biting with her teeth, and she had most of her body covered, though her feet remained outside the warmth all night.

She fell asleep as the sky outside lightened, to the frenzied ringing of bells and blowing of horns all over the city.

SUNLIGHT STREAMED IN through the high windows. Madelyne's head emerged from under the blanket, squinting at bright light. The fog had gone, and blue sky roofed the city where the Godhome did not.

Madelyne tried to sit, forgetting she was tied. She groaned at the binding, and lay there. By day the room's exaggerated proportions were more pronounced, but the lascivious frieze of figures had gone, replaced by a repeated pattern of twisted roses armed with giant thorns.

She scratched her nose with difficulty on her shoulder and yawned. She was warm again, but had no feeling in her hands and feet. She needed to piss.

As she was wondering how long she must wait, the door opened silently and Markos came in. She had the sickening sensation that the duke meant to share her with his filthy servant. Had he not called her his property? An involuntary moan escaped her.

Markos did not harm her or look at her. He averted his eyes as he unlocked the chain from her neck and slid an inwardly curved knife between her flesh and the ropes by touch. She flinched as his cold fingers brushed her.

"Lie still, Medame," he said softly.

The rope fibres parted with a near silent rasp. She gasped as the blood rushed back into her fingers with the stab of a thousand tiny pins. She turned her head so that Markos could not see her blink back tears.

He cut the rope around her midriff and her feet, then rearranged the blanket to cover her. Not once did she feel his eyes on her. He straightened the room, going about his business as if he did this all time, like he was in the kennels grooming the dogs. She stared resolutely into the wall, unable to look at him. His footsteps stopped beside her head.

"The duke told me to inform you that you are released. Breakfast is ready," he said. "Clothes have been arranged for you in your room. You are to take your leisure today. You will accompany his grace to the Grand Ball this evening."

"Thank you," she said, her voice muffled by the blanket. "What time is it? When did the fog lift?"

"It is not long until noon, Medame," he said, staring fixedly at a point above her head. "The fog went early this morning, save for a patch about the Place di Regime. The Morfaan are in the city, and are at the Palace of Nations now."

He did not remove her collar.

Later, dressed and fed, Madelyne headed outside to enjoy the sunlight. Now the fog was gone she was eager to be out. She stopped in the porch, arrested by the view. It was as the duke had promised. The palaces of the king and the comtes blocked her view to the east, but to the north and south she saw right across Perus, all the way down to the canyon of the Foirree. From the back of the building she had a fine view of the Godhome, shining like burnished bronze in the early day. She used the pretext of seeing it closer to go around into the rear gardens, toward the wall separating the house grounds from the Royal Park. The grounds there were given over entirely to roses arranged in geometric beds between paths of perfectly round gravel. Not one piece of stone was on the close cropped grass, not one weed grew out of place.

Stopping to examine this bloom or that, she slowly made her way to the border around the foot of the wall as if she were aimlessly wandering. The collar at her throat felt like a betrayal, although of what she was not sure; of the duke, or of Harafan?

She headed for the rear of the duke's kennels, at the southwestern corner of the garden. The wall rose up over her, fifteen feet of weathered brick topped with spiked iron chased in silver. Where the kennel joined the boundary wall was a water butt. Looking about her nervously, she peered behind. Half a clay flask, green with age, lay belly up out of sight. She turned it over and scraped away a layer of soil. Beneath was a waxed paper envelope which she quickly took.

"Fancy a bit of gardening, Medame?"

Madelyne whirled around. "Gaffne!" she said, one hand flying to her chest while the other hid the letter behind her back. The gardener had silently emerged from the back door to the kennels, and was carrying a hoe and a spade.

"Now you don't want to be getting too close to that wall, Medame. Wild Tyn are in those woods." Gaffne looked up at the ancient trees towering over the wall.

"Is that really the case?" she said. Gaffne came toward her; he was old, deeply tanned and heavily lined, but moved with a youthful lightness. She shifted to keep her back away from him. Only the danger of the letter kept her from being acutely aware of the collar around her neck, but Gaffne was used to such adornments on the duke's women.

"I know they say it's all rubbish," said the gardener. "But I've heard some strange things over that wall working here, especially in the winter when my work goes on after dark, or early in the mornings in summer, when no one's about and the light's clear as water." He looked higher, to the lip of Godhome hanging there. "They're in there alright. On account of the Godhome, so they say. And they're at their worst where it comes to ground."

"The Godhome touches the ground three miles from here, in the Park Hills," said Madelyne. "I have been on the other side of this wall. It is well frequented. Children play there."

"Not at night," said Gaffne. "Best not linger too close to the wall, in any case. The uncanny attracts the uncanny, and there aren't none so uncanny as the Infernal Duke in all Maceriya, and I'm saying that with them Morfaan sitting pretty in their cloud of mist."

"Thank you Gaffne," said Madelyne, "for your concern."

"Don't you mention it," said the gardener. He tugged the brim of his cap, and sauntered away back into the stable block. She waited, until she heard him banging about and whistling.

When he had gone, Madelyne unfolded the wax paper and took out the letter inside. It was a simple note, penned in Harafan's untidy hand.

The fog has gone! Meet me today, half past noon.

She crumpled it in her fist. Checking no one had seen her, she hurried to the house to tell Markos she was going out. She was already late.

CHAPTER NINETEEN
A Bad Trade

"I AM REALLY not terribly sure about this," said Vols. Antoninan's assistant groom led him down the ship's central corridor to the holds at the rear. From below and behind came the vibration of the ship's engines, throbbing powerfully even while the ship was stationary. Above a hammer rang and men shouted. All the doors and hatches were open. Sections of the deck around the funnels were being taken up. Consequently it was freezing cold in the ship. Vols didn't care. The *Prince Alfra* had stopped moving, for which he was immensely grateful. The clanging of dropped metal echoed down the main corridor. Vols stepped aside as sailors pushed past bearing parts and equipment, losing the groom. The boy did not slow for the mage, and he had to trot to catch him up.

"Dogs are not among the animals which I care for ordinarily to tell you the truth," he said weakly.

Antoninan's groom must have been all of about seventeen, but had an air of forcefulness about him. He paid no attention to Vols' protestations. "You work a lot with animals," he said.

"Well, yes, I ah, er. Yes. I do. They are gifted with will, but weakly. It makes them susceptible to alterations of the fund—"

"Dogs are animals." The boy ploughed on through the crowded corridor. Sailors moved aside for him, but most did not see the mage, and he had to duck and apologise the full length, all the way to the main aft hold door. "In here," he said gruffly. He spoke High Maceriyan with a thick vernacular accent that he made no attempt to moderate.

The boy opened the door. The smell of dogs kept in close confinement hit Vols. It was harsh and pervasive, stinging his nostrils, filling his mouth. Urine, faeces, soiled fur—a stink worse than the dirtiest hen coop.

Three dogs were out of their kennels. A young dog, a bitch and the most enormous dog Vols had ever seen.

"Valatrice," he breathed. He could not fail to be awed by such a beast. During his two months aboard the ship, he had avoided the kennels. He felt vaguely ashamed of himself for doing so, like he should go over and apologise to the kingly dog on bended knee.

One of the indigenes was looking the two smaller dogs over. Antoninan stood by grim-faced.

Valatrice saw him first. "The mage comes," he said.

"Hello, hello," said Vols, forcing cheer. "I am here as requested. I do not know how much help I will be."

"You are a mage. You are not engaged at the moment," said Antoninan.

"Well, no," said Vols, taken aback at Antoninan's brusqueness. "The er, the Sorskians' shaman will not allow me upon their island." He smiled weakly. "Something about upsetting their gods. So, yes. Well, I am rather at a loose end."

"So make yourself useful." Antoninan was surly. "The Sorskians have secured a heavy price for our stay. Two of my best dogs," he said venomously. "And they want verification of the dogs' health from their shaman. I do not want to rely on their opinion alone, however. The last we want is accusations of cheating."

Vols approached the dogs gingerly. "I will do as you say, it may be hard. Although, ah, I have some experience of animals, I leave the care of my dogs to my grooms." He did not mention the unreliability of his powers. He reached out a hand toward the young dog. He looked at Vols with yellow eyes so piercing Vols drew his hand back. "In truth, I am not overly fond of them," said Vols. "They kill my hens."

"I find chickens very fine to eat," said Valatrice.

Vols took a step sideways away from him. The human-like way in which the dog spoke was unnerving. "Ah, yes. Um, exactly."

"Get on with it!" said Antoninan.

"Yes, very good. I shall," said Vols. He pushed his fingers into the dog's coat. Fur enveloped his hand to the wrist. A powerful heart pounded beneath his palm.

The native watched him carefully. Vols shut his eyes. He let his heart slow, then allowed it to quicken again, picking up the rhythm of the dog's. The outer world was not always responsive to his will but his own body was his kingdom, altering its rhythms to his whim.

The next part was harder, pushing his mind into the dog's, so that they ran in a synchronicity as close as their heartbeats. As the pounding beats became one, Vols jolted as their minds touched. Never had it been so easy. The dog startled in response. Vols lost contact for a moment, then, with increased confidence, slipped into the dog's world.

"Woah, woah, Jolatrice," said Antoninan, but Vols heard from far away.

Vols ran with the dog along a beach at morning during the lowest tide, the sun cresting the mudflats, the wind cold on the dog's nose. Birds and draconbirds whirled skyward in alarm. A world mediated by different senses overlaid Vols' perceptions, colour drained, greens dominated. A thousand smells filled his thoughts. Vols began to pant lightly. He pushed past the dog's memories, into his emotion and thought. The dog was strong-willed. He was sorrowful at the coming parting, but proud he had been chosen. A desire to run dominated his thought. Vols raced by, water gushing down into deep caverns. He was into the part of the mind closed to the thinking creature, that segment that moderated the alchemy of the living being, the interface between meat and soul.

A picture of the dog's body pulsed in his mind, each beat of the heart a magic-lantern show of its internal workings.

Run, run, run!

Vols pulled back with a gasp. He pulled out a handkerchief from his parka sleeve and mopped his high forehead. "This one is fine, very fine. Such will!"

"What about Miralka, the bitch?" said Valatrice, raising one eyebrow. Vols wasn't aware dogs could even do that. He shook a little under Valatrice's scrutiny. The touch of Jolatrice's soul faded slowly, and he had the urge to submit to Valatrice, rolling on his back and exposing his neck. "Will she be to your liking?"

"I am sure she will, um, gooddog," said Vols.

Valatrice's froideur evaporated and he laughed in the deep, rumbling manner of talking drays. "Gooddog! Such an honour. Better than being a good dog, eh Antoninan?" The edge returned to Valatrice when he spoke to his master. Antoninan stared with hostility at the Sorskian.

Vols pressed his hand to the female, and declared her hale also. Without a word, the man of the Tatama nodded his approval and waved to Antoninan, gesturing that he was satisfied.

"Go," he told his grooms. "Take them."

The grooms—the boy and a man not much younger than Antoninan—moved in to place halters around their shaggy necks. But Valatrice growled, and they backed off.

Valatrice went to the dogs and sniffed at their faces and anuses. They returned the farewell. Then the two males pressed their necks together, side to side, tawny eyes closed. Only then did Valatrice allow the dogs to be haltered. With backward glances, the dogs followed the Sorskian from the hold. Antoninan ran his hands down the flanks of the dogs as they left, head bowed.

One by one, the dogs left in the kennel began to howl.

The atmosphere became oppressive. Vols felt the sorrow of the dogs and the anger of the man. He had to get out. "If you won't be—" he shouted over the howling chorus.

"They wanted to take Valatrice," said Antoninan fiercely. "His fame is so great, they know of him even here! But I would not let them." He looked jealously at his lead dog. "He is the finest, biggest, strongest. The bravest and the most intelligent."

"He certainly speaks Maceriyan well," said Vols.

"He speaks Karsarin and the lesser Sorskian also. There is not a dog anywhere in the Hundred like my Valatrice!"

He grabbed at a handful of Valatrice's fur. The dog growled and shied back.

"Get off me, Antoninan," said Valatrice. "I am no mood to be petted like some spoiled turnspit hound."

Antoninan clenched his hand into a fist.

"It is not only your loss," he said. "I loved them too."

Vols was extremely embarrassed, Antoninan was close to tears.

To his immense relief, Antoninan turned on his heel and departed without further word, leaving Vols alone with Valatrice.

"The dog, he was your son," said Vols quietly.

Valatrice closed his eyes.

"My heir, a Sorskian pack leader. He had not yet come into his voice, but he will. Antoninan was sure he would one day take my place as so-called king of the dogs," he growled contemptuously. "A hollow title for a slave. The sea-people must have bargained hard to take him. Love my kind he might, but it does not stop Antoninan from treating us as chattels. That was not the first child I have sniffed farewell, and he will not be the last."

"The female, was she close to you?"

"She was a bitch of no consequence. I bear her loss lightly, but she was part of my pack even so."

Vols shuffled awkwardly, feeling that he should ask this noble animal for leave to go, but not being able to bring himself to do it.

"Will you do me a service?" asked Valatrice.

"Of course, gooddog," said Vols in surprise.

Valatrice shook out his fur with pleasure. "I do like that. I like that very much. Come. This way, she is in here."

Valatrice led the mage to a kennel with a door secured by a pin. Inside a dog lay, breathing heavily. Vols could tell she was sick as soon as he saw her. Valatrice plucked the pin out with mobile black lips. He motioned his head for Vols to hold out his hand, and dropped the pin into it.

"This bitch is my favoured. She is injured. Can you calm her hurts?" asked the dog.

Vols went into the cage and knelt beside the dog. Her chest heaved unevenly in her sleep. Vols put his hand on her and felt blood in the fur.

"What happened to her?" said Vols.

"I bit her," said Valatrice.

Vols looked up sharply.

"If I had not, Antoninan would have bargained her away. She has borne only a few litters, and has in her lineage many pack leaders. She is very valuable, but she is worth less than my son, and he would have traded her to keep him."

"You must love her very much to sacrifice her for your son," said Vols quietly.

"Perhaps I do, for we know love as well as man. But my actions were born of love for my son, not her. My boy would have gone to make his own pack one day, or been sold by Antoninan anyway. His leaving was inevitable. By biting this bitch, I have determined the circumstances of his departure. Here he can live as our ancestors did, among the ice, in a world we were born to. He will enjoy a freedom here that I experience rarely, and I will continue to enjoy this female." The great dog sat down on his haunches. It only made him seem bigger, his head higher than a man's. "Only I bit her too deeply, and now I will lose both."

Vols sighed and sucked at his protruding front teeth. "I will see what I can do. Fortunately, I have some talent in the field of healing magics." He smiled to calm the dog. Valatrice stared at him in that enigmatic manner unique to dogs.

"Aha, yes," said Vols, uncomfortable. "Very well. Here goes." He shoved his hands deep into her fur. She was delightfully warm. Pleasant sensations helped his magic. Vols let himself enjoy the touch of the creature. The bitch shifted under him uncertainly as he attempted to bond with her. Now he must match her erratic heart with his own, to lend her his strength.

Come in, come in, he thought.

Again the magic was easier than at any time before. Her consciousness entered into his, shy and halting. He saw her as she should be, proud, eyes alive with the deep wisdom of animals.

He gained access to her dreams, strange things full of frustrating, phantom scents. He visualised the wound. He must convince the dog itself that the wound could close, or it would not work. Some lingering sense of betrayal stymied him a moment; she was not of the same degree as Valatrice, and did not understand why he had bitten her. But she wished to be unhurt, and that was something he could use.

Vols whispered his focusing phrases under his breath. A mage's chants were meaningless cantrips if spoken by anyone else, even another mage. The magisters used the employment of this technique by some mages as validation of their own complex rituals and machines. But whereas they used learnt ritual to channel change of a measured, predictable, but limited nature, what Vols did was something far purer, and far more potent. His words were not a spell, but a tool to focus a mind. Only a mage could see through the veils of reality to the fundamental structure beneath, and overwrite it wholesale by will alone. There were no limitations on a mage, except those coming from within.

"She is not so badly hurt," said Vols. "I can heal her."

The dog's breathing steadied. He shared the itchy sensation of the wound closing up. He coaxed the dog's body to do in minutes what should take days. When he was done, shiny pink skin showed through the bitch's hairs, the rest of the wound was crusted with scabs.

Vols sat back on his heels, shaking slightly with the effort. "There. It is not completely repaired, but will be within a day or two. Best let the body's nature take care of it."

"I have no money. I suppose a vigorous lick to the face would not be sufficient thanks for your work?"

Vols looked horrified. "Verbal gratitude will do!"

Valatrice laughed. "I tease you, mage. Thank you."

Vols laughed along with him, mostly from nerves, for the thought of coming closer to Valatrice's lengthy teeth was disconcerting. He stood and slapped the fur and straw from his palms. "You certainly speak very well, better than any dog I have ever heard."

"Many of the other talking dogs could speak so well as I, if they chose to," said Valatrice.

"Then why do they not speak as you, if they possess the facility to do so?"

Valatrice growled darkly. "Because, Goodmage Vols, it hurts."

LATER, VALATRICE JOINED his wounded consort. She smelled healthy, and that was good. Before he slept, he licked her wound clean of its crust of blood. She opened her eyes at the disturbance, panted lightly, and stretched into a more comfortable position.

"Rest, my sweet," Valatrice said. She looked back at him with dimly intelligent eyes. Valatrice nuzzled her, and laid himself down beside her.

As he rested his great head in the straw and closed his eyes, he pretended he could neither hear nor smell Ilona creeping around at the back of the kennels.

CHAPTER TWENTY

An Important Meeting

HARAFAN WAS WAITING for Madelyne in the House of Small Delights, a coffee shop that proclaimed a fine line in confectionary. The name carried an air of exclusivity the shop lacked, it being situated in a less salubrious part of town. The cakes, however were as good as advertised.

Madelyne paused before she went in. The old windows of small warped panes of glass, had been replaced recently by a single flat sheet of modern Karsan manufacture. The old windows had been thick and green; the new let in far too much light, robbing the place of its privacy. The proprietor, a certain Messire Lamain, was hoping to take the shop upmarket. Maybe it was working, his face certainly lit up when he saw Madelyne's fine clothes. But this recent alteration to the shop front upset her, as if her life had changed forever and she visited old haunts now denied her. She threaded her way to their usual table at the back as if in a dream.

"You're an hour late," Harafan said. "I was about to leave."

"You gods' damned bastard!" said Madelyne. "Late? You've no idea what I've been through."

"Alright, alright, keep your voice down," he said. There were several other customers in there, most in pairs, conspirators like they from their cautious manner and quiet conversation. She had known Harafan since they were children. He had grown into a foppish man, thinly moustached, his hair curled back in a bouffant. He wore the clothes of a rake and the attitude of a scoundrel. Madelyne was greatly relieved to see him, though she was in no mood to say it.

She gripped the chair rest and leaned in. "Let me be. I'll not be able to shout very loudly anywhere soon, my friend. Every bastard in Perus will recognise me." She yanked the chair out and sat down hard. "He's only taking me to the bloody ball." She felt like crying.

"The ball? The big ball with the bigwigs and the Morfaan and all the ambassadors from the Hundred. That ball? *The* ball?" Harafan whistled. "Holy mothers of the driven gods."

"Yes you moron, the gods' damned ball!"

"I certainly hope you don't speak like that around him."

"I only speak like this around you. You bring out the worst in me."

"Don't I know it," he grinned, and reached for her hand. She snatched it away.

"Don't touch me."

He held up his hands to say sorry.

Lamain sidled over, fawning in the way of waiters from higher class places than his.

"Medame, what is your delight, in the House of Small Delights?"

"What have you done to your hair, Lamain?" said Madelyne.

He narrowed his eyes, squinting over his spectacles. "Madelyne? Madelyne? Is that you?"

"Don't you start. Yes it's me. And you recognised me as soon as I came in, so stop the act."

"You look marvellous!" he leaned closer. "Hit good times eh? I always knew you would, a bright girl like you. What's that on your neck?"

She adjusted the scarf covering her collar. Of course the damned thing was still locked on, she could cut it off, but that would be that, and she'd have to leave the house for good. "Nothing," she said. "Stop hovering over me, Messire. Fetch me what I always have."

"Immediately," said Lamain. "A plate of pastries and a coffee for the fine goodlady. Harafan?"

"Usual for me too, Messire, thank you."

Lamain nodded and busied himself behind his small counter.

"What is that around your neck?" Harafan asked.

"Nothing!" said Madelyne. Her cheeks burned under her powder.

"Alright, alright! Seriously, are you well? Has he hurt you?"

She shook her head. "Not yet. But the things he has planned..."

"He told you?"

"I had to sign a document," she said quietly. She looked up, defiant. "I spent all last night tied up and chained to a wall like a dog!"

"He is a dirty devil, isn't he?" Harafan said. He came close to asking if she enjoyed it; it was a failure and strength of his to make light of all things. Her expression stopped him dead. "Is it true what we heard, that you can leave if it gets too much?"

"That part is true. I can go at any time."

"Are you going to?" he asked. "We've put a lot of time into this. You've worked hard to drop it so close to the end. But if you're not—"

"I'll not go, if that's what you're worried about!" she snapped. "Gods, Harafan, it's not as if I have much choice. I'm not going back to any gaol or pleasure house. I'm done."

"Hey, Mads?" he said. This time she let him take her hand.

She drew in a shaking breath. "I'm sorry. I'm sorry. This isn't what I expected. I feel... strange."

"How so?"

"He is different. Very different. It is not so simple as I thought, whoring myself out for a few nights in return for riches like all those other women. He is not so straightforward as I expected. He was cruel yesterday, intentionally so, but he did not hurt me, only shamed me. The rest of the time he has been very kind, and honest, charming even. There is no subterfuge to what he does."

"Now it sounds like he is getting to you." Lamain returned with their drinks and cake. When she stirred sugar into her coffee, the spoon rattled against the side.

"Madelyne," said Harafan. "Hey, Madelyne, look at me."

She looked up from under lashes thick with mascara.

"We can stop. We've had a good run you and I, a lot of successes. We can turn away, go back to the small stuff. You've cleared our debts, we've a clean slate. We can make lives for ourselves. There's none so good as us. Perhaps we've overreached ourselves this time. You've had some big ideas, but this is the biggest yet."

The stirring of her spoon slowed. She tapped it on the cup and laid it carefully on the plate of cakes. "No. Not now. It's not like I need to endure it for years like those other women, just a few weeks. He'll talk soon. He's surprisingly voluble."

"If he doesn't talk, you could always stick it out. He rewards his mistresses well."

She glowered at him. "Don't."

"Just saying," Harafan shrugged. "Leave, stay. There's always choice."

"He says the same thing." She sipped her coffee. Her lipstick stained the rim. She was not in the habit of painting herself so. She felt like a fraud, a doxy pretending to be a lady. Ordinarily she regarded herself as neither—she was only herself, it was her strength. Now she had no idea who she was. She was in danger of losing herself.

"So? What'll it be?" asked Harafan.

"I'll go back," she said. "Don't use the water butt for messages again. I can leave whenever I wish. Pay a messenger boy to deliver me notes, that would be safer. I can be outside at noon every day."

"Fine," said Harafan. "It was hellish work getting up that wall anyway."

"You have the easier role."

"I know." He squeezed her hand and let go. "Just a few more weeks, like you say, and the job will make us rich! Get him to talk." He drank from his own coffee, black and unsweetened. "As soon as you have discovered how to get into the Godhome, then you can leave, and we'll be rich forever."

CHAPTER TWENTY-ONE
A Matter of Justice

A MAN AND a boy approached the gates of the Lemio Cloth and Shoddy Company. Neither of them were anything exceptional, coming as they did with a throng of workers arriving for their shift. They looked like any other members of the urban workforce—heavy clothes, baggy trousers, clogs, thick jackets, all worn and patched but with crisp starched shirts underneath, dazzling white and immaculate in that way of the proud poor.

They were not as they appeared. The man was not a man, but a woman. The boy was not even human. Katriona Kressinda-Morthrocksa and the Tyn Lydar of the Mothrocksey band wore faces not their own.

Katriona forced herself to hunch and walk with her head down. Nourished well throughout her life, she was bigger than the tallest men. This workforce were muted, cowed almost. Such a swell of people were around her, quietly talking, jostling one another. There was a modicum of relief in their voices, they talked of little but the arrival of the Morfaan in Perus and, more importantly, the final dissipation of the awful fogs. Some of them laughed and made light of things, but as they came closer to the factory gates their chat tailed away into silence. The click of hobnailed clogs striking sparks from the setts was louder than their voices. Katriona was fascinated by them. She had never walked with her own workforce. The scent of carbolic soap and sweat came off their bodies, along with the smell of stew from washed clothes drying in cramped kitchens. No perfumes or other scents, they were too expensive. She peered into faces, wondered at their lives. They were pinched, tired. Did her own people look so glum when she was not about? Did she treat them so badly? She hoped not. They were at the Clothing and Shoddy because the mill had one of the worst reputations in that part of town.

"Hsst!" said the boy who was not a boy. "Be wary, good Kat! This is not so thorough an enchantment as that on Goodfellow Demion's thrice-damned cousin, it is but a glamour. Do not gaze into the eyes of another, or they will see through it. Speak to no one, look at no one. If you do, we will be noticed. If we are noticed, more likely than not they will see us as we are and not as we wish to be seen."

Katriona shuddered slightly at the disturbing sound of the reedy, whispering voice of Tyn Lydar coming from a child's mouth, and she hunched lower.

They allowed themselves to be carried along through the factory gates. The Lemio Clothing and Shoddy factory was a small concern, high up one of the steep valleys that creased the land around the twin bowls of Karsa City. It was not actually on the small stream that carried the Lemio name, but one of dozens of others that flowed one into the other, together conjuring the sizable Lemio river rapidly from the boggy sponges of the highlands. A river not unlike the Mothrocksey, thought Katriona guiltily. The stream was bounded in a tight, jacket of stone. The bed had been levelled and straightened. There might once have been a Tyn band dwelling near its waters, if so they were long gone.

Still, this nameless brook retained a modicum of wildness and ran along its artificial course with silent vigour. Like so many others, this factory had been water powered. The remains of its wheel sagged in rusty exhaustion from the original mill building. That was built of stone, the rest, bigger, were of brick. From the mill's engine houses chimneys fountained magically polluted steam into the sky. They were but a few among hundreds of similar stacks all across the city. The day was cloudless and the blue sky was streaked with browns and whites spewing from Karsa's ten thousand chimneys like the brush strokes of a careless artist.

The progress of the crowd slowed to queue outside one of the building's double doors, high enough to admit a wagon, the glossy mid-green paint flaking off to show blue beneath.

Such was the factory's position that Katriona could look through the main gates down the hill into the basin of the Lemio. A brown haze was gathering there to replace the departed fog. On the far side, she could see the fantastical carved stone mansions of the Spires, set out like models on a general's campaign map. Her own family manse was there somewhere, hidden by the elaborate turrets and gables of others. There was a gap between the Spires and the highlands where the Lemio flowed toward the Var. The Var's valley was too low to see from her position, but past the river basin the hills rose up again, stepped with streets leading to the high cliffs north of the city. The broad seaward aspect of Var-side Karsa was reduced to a small chink in the wall of hills by her situation. Somewhere to the south and out of sight the rivers fed into the docklands, then into the locks of the Slot leading down to the ocean. She was afforded a glimpse of the glistening endless mudflats, trimmed by the bright, silver line of the distant sea.

The factory whistle went and the doors of all the buildings, save the original mill, opened wide. The night shift poured out. A few muted greetings passed between the night workers and the day crew, and the occasional embrace as husbands and wives encountered one another. The whistle sounded again. Katriona followed the line of people into the factory.

They passed a group of foremen marking names on personnel sheets as the workers shuffled through. Katriona's name was not in the book. Her stomach curdled as they approached the desk. She kept her face low, following Tyn Lydar's commands. Thanks to the Tyn's glamour the foremen did not even notice them. To the workers and their overseers, the odd pair were unremarkable in every sense. "This magic I work, it is a fooling of perception, nothing else," the Tyn had explained. "It is effective, but we must be very careful."

The workers trooped down a corridor and into a machine hall lit badly by grimy skylights. The sun outside made the day warm, inside it was cold. Drive shafts rumbled above the rows of machines, leather drive belts slapping and whirring. The workers headed down iron steps to their lathes and presses, but Katriona and Tyn Lydar left the line, heading not down to the production lines, but carrying along the raised path running the length of the hall, and toward stairs there. Cloaked in glamour, they went unchallenged. When the floor manager did look at them, he did so without comment. The noise increased as the workers began to engage their machines with the drive belts. Looms clacked noisily, and the throb of industry displaced all other sound.

Katriona and Tyn Lydar headed out into an external staircase boxed into a glass and iron stairwell. They went all the way up, passing by other floors also filling up with the workforce. At the top, they crossed to the other side of the building through a storage loft. There was no one about up there, only stacks of sacking and softwood crates laden with spools of thread waiting to be taken downstairs. Opposite the stairwell a raised corridor crossed over the mill's yard into the original mill. A hole had been cut into the stone to create a door for the bridge. Cold air blew down it unimpeded.

They crossed over and emerged into a dormitory full of small beds.

"This is it," said Katriona. "The Clothing and Shoddy Orphanage."

"Shh!" said Tyn Lydar. "This building is listening." Then, she added, "We must be quick. I am tiring. I cannot be away from Morthrocksey for much longer. The pain comes already."

Katriona took the boy by the hand. Although she knew it as a disguise, she was surprised the hand did not feel as it looked. "Very well. The children will be working. We shall go and see, and then we shall depart."

The dormitory had the high, sweet, stale scent of unwashed children; straw and urine. There was precious little light up there, but not so little it hid the filthy state of the bedclothes and floor. The old mill was draughty, the small windows were ill-fitting. Light shone through gaps in the wall.

They passed through the sad rows of beds, through a crooked door, and onto dusty wooden stairs that creaked under their feet. Sacks of old rags lined the stairwell walls, waiting to be plucked apart for shoddy.

On the floor below were the first of the children working at rough desks. Each child had a pile of rags by their desk which they mechanically ripped to threads, then put the threads into baskets.

Katriona's heart hurt to see cold, raw hands being worn away by a task that forgave neither age nor human flesh. The children worked in silence broken by hacking coughs. The windows were small by modern standards, leaving the middle desks in a gloom that would become near dark as the day wore out. The children wore clothes two repairs from rags. Most had no shoes, all were filthy. The air floated with fibres irritating to respiration. Hundreds of brown sacks full of more rags were piled in every available space.

None of the children spoke. The small tearing noises of cloth being ripped and ripped again overlaid the distant chuntering of machinery coming from below. The floor vibrated with the power of the machines, but the stuffy, miserable atmosphere in the room drew the energy away from even that. A boy looked up at Katriona as she passed by. His face was devoid of joy, pale, dark brown rings around each eye socket as clearly as if they had been painted on. In the eyes themselves there was none of the sparkle associated with intelligent thought, let alone the vitality of a young child. His eyes were as flat and dead as those of goat, and like a goat chewing, he did not pause at his task as she passed, but carried on mechanically plucking.

"Do not look him in the eye!" hissed the Tyn.

Arrested by the boy's dead gaze, Katriona could not stop herself, and she approached.

"You. Boy?" she said.

He blinked slowly, as if trying to recall how to speak.

"Goodman?" he said.

"How many hours do you work?"

"All day, goodman," he said in a small voice. "From dark until dark."

"Do you have schooling?"

He shook his head.

"Remove your gaze from him, before it is too late. The slipping of the glamour will startle even one so dulled in soul as this," said Tyn Lydar, tugging her away. The boy went back to his work.

"By the driven gods," Katriona murmured. "He can't be much over five years old."

"Do not do that again!" said the Tyn.

On the floor below they found similar, dozens of children carding the threads produced upstairs and picking out the resultant rovings.

The noise of the machines was very loud in there, the rasp of carding inaudible. It was an awful scene, children labouring to that all-consuming roar. Two older children stared blankly over the heads of their peers, keeping watch. The glamour put their thoughts elsewhere. Katriona and Tyn Lydar went unseen.

The ground floor was the worst of all. The ancient, water-powered machinery had been hooked up to a shaft driven by an engine outside. It was the only sign of modernity. Children darted between the dangerously exposed mechanisms. Katriona was appalled, then with a flood of guilt remembered her first visit to Mothrocksey, where children as young as these were employed to pick up swarf from the ground under the lathes. Now no child under the age of twelve would find employment in her mill. Nevertheless, her fortune was tainted by the suffering of the generations gone before.

That the children here were in far worse a state did not assuage her guilt, rather it intensified as she took in their poor condition. They were very young, and underfed, little bundles of sticks wrapped in rags, so dirty their skin was a streaky, oily grey. Unlike modern frames which could have up to fifteen hundred reels, the machines each supported only forty or so reels, and was watched over by an older child assisted by two others. Only the free labour of the children made them economical to run.

The reels rattled like bone dice in a tin cup. The drive shafts were warped and badly greased and sent out a constant whining squeal in a way that set Katriona's teeth on edge. The older children watched carefully, adjusting the machinery where necessary. The young took full reels away, brought long loops of new rovings to the frame. The smallest were employed to fix broken threads and recover mounds of fibres from under the machines while they were still running. The children's hands looked so small and delicate darting into the machines to pluck out threads and balls of greasy fluff.

"No child should have to work in these conditions," said Katriona.

"Hey! Hey you!" shouted a voice. The machines were so loud Katriona did not at first hear it. Only as a stout woman armed with a cosh and a braided whip came down the aisle in the middle of the machines did she notice. "Hey! Wait there. What are you doing in here?"

"We must go now," said Tyn Lydar.

"I've seen enough," said Katriona. She turned, and walked briskly out of the hall the way she had come, ignoring the shouts of the forewoman. The forewoman blew her whistle. Katriona and Tyn Lydar ran, their disguises flickering around them.

The forewoman hurried after them up the stairs, up to the very top where the orphans slept.

When she got there, they were gone.

EDUWIN GROSTIMAN, KARSAN Minister for Justice, looked from the thick document that he held in his hand, to the woman sat in front of him, and back again. He adjusted his glasses. He pursed his lips. He cleared his throat. He did all the things he usually did to put off petitioners to the Justice Ministry, but no matter which tic he employed, the damned woman would not stop burning a hole in his face with her eyes.

He lifted the penultimate sheet of paper, gave the last a desultorily scan. Tutting, he dropped the document onto the table and leaned forward.

"Goodlady, you cannot in all earnestness be proposing that I act upon these recommendations."

"I am in earnest, why would I waste my time—and yours of course—bringing this to you? Do you take me for an attention seeker, goodfellow?"

"No goodlady."

In a tightly cut dress of light pink pinstripes, fashionable hat and hands gloved in lace gripping a tiny clutchbag, Katriona Kressinda-Morthrocksa appeared prim and ladylike. She was so womanly, so undoubtedly female that Grostiman could not believe the steely expression on her face. He had to look at it again and again to make sure his eyes were not deceiving him. So severe, and above all determined. Uncomfortable, he looked down at the papers again.

"This is most improper," he said. "The statute you cite at the beginning here, well, it is centuries old."

"It is," she agreed.

"Then you must see that it is invalid."

"It is not," she insisted.

"There are limitations on this sort of thing," he said.

"After giving my proposal your thorough appraisal," she said pointedly, "you will have seen that the Little Agreement still has force. Or I should say, should still have force. The limitations in Karsan law on statutes are of custom, not of time. Custom has not changed."

"Customs have changed!" said Grostiman. "They have changed so much this fell by the wayside so long ago no one has even considered formally revoking it."

"So you deny that an employer has no duty of care to his employees?"

"It is arguable—"

"Have you seen the factories? The conditions?" she said forcefully.

Grostiman rocked his head from side to side and sucked air in between his teeth. "Well, well, no—"

"There we are then," said Katriona. "Sign."

"Just wait a moment please, goodlady," said the minister. He put the papers down. "This statute is not about employer and employee. It is about lord and serf. It dates from the time of King Justirion, four hundred years ago! The system of tenancy it describes is long gone." He looked at the list of values attributed to chickens, goats, dracon-cattle. "Here, the tithe value of a, of a..." he peered at the document and traced out a line with his finger, "a brace of wild dreven. They have been extinct in Karsa for three centuries. And this, the wood barter chart, log for log, by species. How many forests are there left on these isles? Payment for dwelling in kind with bushels of wheat? This is of historical interest. It has nothing to do with today's world."

"It is not the dwelling payment or the value of sticks that I refer to, but the expectations placed upon a lord for the care of his peasantry. The sentiment is still valid," she said.

He could have sworn she had not blinked once since she sat in front of him.

"But there are no peasants in Karsa any more!" he protested. "This is not applicable to the present day!"

"But there are lords. I am a goodlady, you a goodfellow. We both maintain workforces of the lower social orders." Katriona gripped the wooden handle of her bag tighter. Her lips thinned. "Look again at the definition of indentured service, and I think you will see the situation is the same, only the dressing of it has changed. You are a scion of one of Karsa's oldest houses," said Katriona. "My own nobility, although much less venerable than yours, is of equal importance. Look at page three, the copy of the original Little Agreement, look!" she said.

Grostiman flicked the papers over reluctantly. "There are legal requirements here for the care of villeinry, but come now, who even uses the word 'villein' any more? It is archaic, inapplicable!"

"Terms are unimportant. Do we not employ workers in our factories for the larger part of the year? Yes. Do we not give payment for their service in part in accommodation, foodstuffs, and clothing? Yes. Are they free to move to another master? No."

"Ah!" said Grostiman, extending his forefinger. "Well, there you are wrong. Any man might leave a contract and head to another factory whenever he so desires. I really—"

She tossed her head imperiously. "In the law, yes, in practice, no. Any person who leaves their employment is likely to be blacklisted. Can you not see? We operate a system not dissimilar to the lords of old under different names. Such a system was unjust, was it not? That was what led to the Little Agreement. Would you like to see pre-revolutionary conditions return?"

"I cannot advocate a return to such barbaric ways, no. Never."

"Was it just?" she said again.

"No," he said through closed teeth.

"So then. Our workers do not even have a codified set of protections such as those set out in the Little Agreement. Therefore, our system, supposedly born from an age of reason, is less just. We expect the same and give less in return."

"There are laws. Many laws—"

"Here and there, this and that," she said dismissively. "All routinely flouted, in my opinion because there is no overarching codification of the spirit of labour transaction. According to the old statues of indentured service, we are short-changing our workers. It cannot go on. It is, simply, immoral."

Grostiman blew out hard. He deliberately pushed away the papers.

Katriona followed them across the desk. When her regard returned to his face, she glared the harder. Grostiman felt the prickle of sweat spring upon his brow. She was uncommonly fierce.

"I realise that you have had some difficulty at your own works, owing the acts of certain agitators. Things will calm down soon, my dear goodlady, you—"

"Do not presume to 'my dear goodlady' me, goodfellow!" she said hotly. "This is not merely a question of agitation. Can you not see? The Labour Associations operate throughout our factories. What happened at the Morthrocksey Mill will happen everywhere if we do not pre-empt the workers' demands. I would say that this is not a matter of history, but one of current morality. It is true that I am motivated in part by higher concerns, however, the salient fact is that if we do not act then we shall all lose a great deal of money. Do you understand? You, you have many business concerns and investments in your own family."

"Yes, our investments are varied."

"And you are not worried about unrest in the workforce?"

"Yes. Very well, I will hear you out. What do you propose?" Grostiman laced his fingers over his round belly. He had the awkward feeling he was being talked into something that he would rather not be talked into. He resolved to stand firm.

"The old statutes allow for the formation of an inspectorate to enforce the rights of the villeinry, should they not be lived up to."

"And you want me to say that will be fine? Really?" He sat forward. "Have you taken leave of your senses, goodlady?"

"I have not, goodfellow. I want you to take a modified version of the Little Agreement before parliament. I want you to push it into law."

"I cannot authorise such a thing! At the very least, before a proposal of this magnitude could be heard, Prince Alfra would have to be consulted. Any unilateral move on your—on *my*— part would appear to be a blatant attempt to disrupt the business of my competitors. It is an abuse of power! There would be uproar!"

"In parliament. Three hundred well fed *men* may find their production costs increase," she looked at his gut. Grostiman adjusted his waistcoat self-consciously. "The alternative is tens of thousands of workers rioting on the streets. I have seen the damage that can do. Colonel Alanrys's ridiculously brutal suppression of the protests at my mill—"

"They burned down several of your buildings!" said Grostiman. "That is civil disobedience of the grossest form, not a protest!"

"So killing one hundred and twelve of my workers was the appropriate response?" she said.

"No, no, Alanrys overreacted. He has been disciplined."

"Hardly!" she snorted.

"The truth is that you only have yourself to blame, your favouring of the Tyn—"

She shut him up with an scandalised shout. "I did not 'favour' the Tyn. It was brought to my attention that they live like slaves. Shameful! Outright slavery is illegal in the Hundred—"

"For people, not Tyn."

"How are they different?" she countered. "Listen to me. Since I commenced work on the very modest modifications to their accommodation they requested, they are happier. They work harder. My human workers responded so poorly because they, too, exist in the most diabolical of circumstances, of which I was, I'm ashamed to say, wilfully ignorant," she jabbed her finger into the table. Grostiman raised his eyebrows at it. "I was so absorbed in bettering my own position, I did not see the suffering that enabled my ambition. I am a woman..."

Could have fooled me, thought Grostiman. More like a she-dracon with a threatened nest.

"... and I thought myself hard done by. I forgot that I am a goodlady, of high family, and with a great deal of money. The difficulty I have endured in determining my own course is as nothing to the daily struggle the people whom I employ must endure. Your own course is rather simpler to decide upon. Either sign the bill. Take it to parliament. Push it through—"

"Impossible," he said, throwing up his hands.

"—or I and like-minded industrialists shall lead the way in forcing change from beneath. I am not alone in being appalled. There is a stark moral choice before us. If I gather enough supporters, get them to alter our business practises, then it shall destabilise the whole structure of modern industry. And I will openly agitate for change in the factories of other businesses who do not agree. The Labour Associations are poorly funded and yet still they do good work. Imagine how much they could accomplish with real money behind them."

"You will back the Labour Associations?"

"My dear goodfellow, I shall *run* the Labour Associations."

"Now you are threatening me," Grostiman said. "That is an offence."

"A lesser one than living off the backs of less fortunate creatures. But I am not threatening you, I am threatening the established order."

"And if I don't agree? You are not a member of parliament. You cannot stand. Give it some lesser man, and it will never be heard. I hardly think your father will agree to put this forward. And for that matter, does your father know about this?" Grostiman raised an eyebrow. "How do think he would react?"

"The demonic legions of all hundred hells can blast my father's arse!" she snapped. "I am a free agent, not some dutiful, goat-eyed daughter to go sniffling after his say so. I and my father's approval parted a long time ago."

"Still, you will not get it into parliament, because I will not put this forward." He peered dismissively at the document title, "A New Little Agreement for a New Era," he read. "We might as well say we are culpable of terrible crimes, line up against the wall and shoot ourselves. No."

She smiled wickedly. "Very well. Now I am going to threaten you."

"Oh?" said Grostiman. It was his most dangerous "oh". He had an arsenal of such utterances. Better let a man hang himself running his own mouth off, he thought. An "oh" was often a sufficient noose. Not that he would employ such tactics on a goodlady, but he was so incensed he had ceased to see Katriona as a woman. Viewing her as another bullish, new money upstart made it easier to deal with her. By the gods, he would "oh" her, woman or not!

"I have been in one of your family's factories," she said. "I have seen the conditions inside. Not only do they transgress every standard of human decency, go against the spirit of the Little and Grand Agreements, they also, very provably, break today's law. I quote, and my lawyers had me learn this verbatim, 'no child under the age of six years shall be employed for more than four hours a day'. How old are the waifs in your sheds, goodfellow? Four? Five?"

"I have no idea what you are talking about."

"The Lemio Clothing and Shoddy Company factory," she said. "And the attached home for strays."

"One of many my family own. What of it? It is a small business."

"The size of the business is not at issue, only the enormity of your crimes."

"What on Earth are you talking about?"

"I see. So you would not object to an inspection by the Minister of Trade? Or a magister's sending and a broadsheet report? I can arrange all of these things." She lowered her voice. "I have been in there. The children work twelve hour days maiming themselves plucking apart better cloth than they are given to wear. Some of these children are below the age of employment. None are adequately fed or clothed. None are schooled."

"Nonsense," he said uneasily.

"So many high men are guilty of this," she continued, her eyes narrowed to a slit. "All are guilty, so none will upset the floatstone. Because of this unspoken agreement of scoundrels, all break the law freely. Well goodfellow. I am upsetting the floatstone. I will point the finger and cry havoc."

"I see," said Grostiman. "And what of your part in this little club? If we are all guilty, then so are you. Guilty by association, and very probably guilty in actuality."

"Not as guilty as some. One lesson being a woman in this day and age has taught me well, goodfellow, is to have no respect whatsoever for the unwritten conventions of men. For it is those selfsame conventions that kept me from my ambitions as keep children chained up in the dark making money for tubby parasites like you. Sign the paper, Grostiman, or I will ruin you and your entire gods' damned family. It will be incidental to my upsetting the current order, but devastating to you."

"You cannot," said Grostiman simply. "Your reputation will be destroyed. No one will deal with you. The Kressind name will be irredeemably sullied."

"Yes. I suspect it will, among people I do not care for nor respect. Whereas the poor, they shall love me."

"You will appear a weak woman, trying to expunge her guilt for a massacre that came about because of her own feminine follies. You have seen what happens when change is effected —unintended consequences of the worst sort."

"Perhaps," said Katriona. "On the other hand, convention and society have changed a great deal over the last century, goodfellow. What on the Earth or the Twin makes you think it would stop at a position to your best advantage? I am heading off a problem before it occurs, Minister. You and your ilk wander the mud blithely, ignorant of the tide. I have a boat. We can deal with this now, or you can wait for the entire city to explode. Good day."

Katriona got up. The door banged behind her. Grostiman looked at the documents again.

"Hmmm."

He picked up the bell on his desk and rang for a servant.

"Goodfellow?" his man asked.

"Send for Artibus, Dofer and Seward," he said. "That woman will be trouble."

"Yes goodfellow."

"And fetch me a decanter of red. A good one." He put his spectacles on and considered the papers more closely. "I find myself unaccountably in need of a drink."

CHAPTER TWENTY-TWO
The Unshe

NIGHT IN THE far south was a strangely luminous affair. The late spring days were long. When the sun finally departed, it dipped down behind the horizon for the briefest of rests. As it slipped to its short midnight, Heffi waited upon the summit of the island calculating the precise arc in his head. He had been a captain so long that he required a sextant only for the most precise of reckonings. As a guide to latitude, it was rough, but useful. He marvelled at the gentle declination. So far south, he had never thought to come so far south.

On the ice shelf the huts of the sea-peoples glowed enticingly with lamplight, blue through the joins in their walls, bright yellow in the ice windows. Out from the island the iron ship was lit by blazing glimmer lights and alive with an engineer's racket. Trassan had the crew working in shifts to make the alterations to the funnels, taking advantage of the calm weather and the season's light.

That far south the sky never truly darkened, the west remained tinted lemon yellow, darkening through subtle blues toward the prime meridian where the White Moon rested, nigh on a whole orb, though much faded by the promise of tomorrow. The Red Moon sped by, rosy rather than red, tracking into the east where a semblance of darkness took hold. There the sky glowed a deep purple strewn with untold stars. Heffi rested his notebook on his knee, making notes of the various constellations along with his rough reckonings as to their latitude. Longitude was harder. Only the Ishmalani had the secret of it, and they guarded it fiercely. Heffi justifiably regarded himself of something of a master of that art. To take back all this information on new stars would make him famous. It would also make him rich, given time, but he was counting on the city in the ice bringing him fortune long before then.

The lightness of the sky was redoubled by the placid surface of the ocean and the plaques of ice upon it, and so Heffi wrote without the need for other illumination. By his calculations once they passed the eighty-ninth parallel, according to the ancient science of his people, they would experience near constant daylight until past the solstice in Gannever. Heffi was content to sit and think. Occupation had forever been his personal formula for success, he was frugal with his idleness. He waited now for his meeting with the Unshe. He could do it in impatient pacing without result, instead he used the time productively. The One gave them little enough life as it was. Heffi praised Him for granting him an active mind.

Snow crunched behind him, and the breath of someone forced to climb.

Heffi shut his book gently, and tucked the pencil back into the fabric holder at the side.

"Heffi," said Trassan, stepping into view.

"Good evening, goodfellow."

Trassan sat down on a nodule of floatstone poking out of the snowcap. "Funny, surrounded by snow and freezing water. I'm almost too warm." He flipped the hood of his parka down.

"As much as I am happy to see you, Trassan, I did come up here for a bit of peace."

"And to see this Unshe of theirs?" said Trassan. "Me too. Antoninan told me that the sea peoples venerate those who are neither male nor female, and that they have great powers of foresight. I'm sorry to interrupt your dance, but I'm intrigued."

"You have not been called!"

"Have you?" said Trassan. "You did not translate what Chichiweh said."

"I will not," said Heffi, his gaze falling to the hand-written title of his book. He stroked the smooth cover. "It is forbidden."

"You are a strange breed, you Ishmalani," said Trassan. "You're a good man Heffi, I wish I could get to know you better."

"You can know me without knowing the secrets of my people. We worship the One, the Will that makes. He made this Earth, the Twin, all the stars and moons and the peoples upon them. Each sect honours him in his own way. I am bound to do so by blood and birth."

"Everyone knows that."

"And you do not need to know more in order to befriend one of us. But so many of you Ushamali feel different about it. You grow vexed at things you do not need to know, and so a distance remains. It is a pity."

Trassan shrugged. "I try not to think about it. All that matters to me is that you're a good captain, and a pleasant fellow to be with. If you're too selfish to share your religious secrets, fine! I'm rather jealous, I suppose we all are. You got to keep your god."

"This is why there is always the distance," said Heffi. "Your gods were never *real*. They were illusory, things made by men."

"I don't believe that," said Trassan. "How can men make gods?"

"Ask Eliturion, he says so often enough—they are stories told by men made flesh."

"Magic then? Which mage called them into being?"

"Magic doesn't need mages in the same way water doesn't need taps. I think he is right. There's an Ishmalani saying—fate is a story the universe tells itself."

Trassan made an interested noise and kicked at the snow.

"Have you read Eliturion's books?"

"Which one?" said Trassan. "The old windbag must have published a hundred."

Heffi smiled absently. "He has, I suppose."

"Sorry Heffi, I don't trust gods." Trassan thrust his hands between his knees. "I've met him."

"Who hasn't?" said Heffi.

"Your time is here."

Both men looked up at this third voice. There was a woman standing in front of them where no woman had been before. Nor had there been any sound of approach on the icy snow.

Trassan jumped off his perch.

"Gods!" he said.

"I thank you for it," Heffi said. He put his book away inside his parka and stood, touching his forehead with his forefinger knuckle. "This one has not been called. Shall I proceed alone?"

The woman gave Trassan a sleepy look. "If he had not been called, he would not be here. You are both to come with me."

"See?" crowed Trassan.

"This way," said the woman. She lifted a lethargic arm and pointed down the far side of the island, away from the village. "Both may come, or one, or none. The same numbers might return, no matter how many go in." She floated away in the indicated direction, leaving no mark upon the snow.

"Did you see that? I think she's a ghost!" said Trassan. "Is it safe?"

"Did you hear her message? Probably not," said Heffi. "But I am going anyway."

"I admire your demeanour, Heffi."

Heffi patted Trassan's shoulder. "I've seen too many natural and supernatural wonders in my years as a mariner to be affected by something so simple as the manifestation of a phantom," he said. "Come on if you're coming."

"You're not sore at me?"

"You heard. You were called. We don't want to lose her."

They followed the spirit down the hill.

THE GIRL WAITED for them at the foot of the island's mount where the brim of ice was narrow. She waited for them to approach and drifted along a thin path of compacted snow clinging to the rockface, dark water below.

"Keep one hand on the wall!" said Heffi. "To fall in means death in minutes."

"No fear," muttered Trassan.

Clutching at the pockmarked stone, they slowly made their way to where the ghost waited for them again. When they reached her, she pointed down a tunnel leading into the rock, and unravelled as smoke on the wind.

"Do you have a light?" asked Heffi.

Trassan pulled out a small glimmer lantern from his pocket. He worked the lever to spin the incantation wheel inside. After a few presses, light sprang up from the lens at the front. He aimed it into the hole. A rough tunnel of unfinished stone went down further than the torch's ability to penetrate.

"We better take this carefully," said Trassan. This time, he went first.

The jagged cups of broken floatstone cavities stood sharp in the light of Trassan's pocket lamp, and they had to watch their footing. The tunnel curved. Some way in, the light of the device faded, leaving them in the dark,

"This is why I dislike incantatory devices," he grumbled, shaking his lamp hard. "This tunnel is too large for the rock above the waves, it must go far beneath the surface of the sea." He felt the walls. "The rock's freezing."

"We are close. I feel a warm draught coming from below. Let's press on."

They shuffled along, feet snagging. One stumble could see them sever an artery on the razored stone, and again they held tight to the wall. Presently, the darkness lessened. Firelight shone from further in. Once it made itself known, it grew bright quickly. They stumbled, blinking, into a rough cave dominated by a blazing fire.

"By the driven gods..." said Trassan.

This was the kind of cave he had expected at the Tatama council. It reeked of sweat and cured meat. Smoke wove randomly toward gaps in the ceiling. Holes were few, and most of the smoke curled back on itself, making the air blue. Trassan blinked tears from his eyes, coughing from the fumes catching in his throat. From all over the ceiling hung severed hands on wires, brown like smoked sides of ham. Those closest to the blaze were black and shrivelled, those to the edge of the cave had fingers lengthened by stalactites of rendered fat. Stacks of bones and oceanic debris lined the chamber like a gruesome tidemark.

"Deep magic," Heffi said gravely. There was no point affecting a jaded air. Heffi, generally speaking—the non-general caveat being where money was involved—was honest and straightforward. He sensed power from the cave, and he made the sign of the One at his forehead. "We are here great one!" he called. "I can see no one," he said to Trassan.

"I do. Look!" said Trassan.

A figure skulked by the blaze.

The Unshe spoke in Heffi's private tongue. This unsettled them both.

"She has something for me," Heffi said to Trassan. "How is it you speak the language of my people?" He spoke to the Unshe in Maceriyan, his cultural disinclination to speak the secret language with a non-Ishmalan too strong to overcome.

"I speak the language of the spirit world. All tongues are snowflakes in the mouth once the master speech is learned," she said. She moved around the fire in a crabbed crouch, affording Trassan a better look. On her scalp was piled a mess of filthy dreadlocks. Over that was draped the loose skin of some kind of bird, covered in close feathers of black and white. The Unshe had painted herself to match. Her arms and face were smeared with white ash, a black bar daubed across the eyes. A second garment of hide sagged from her chest, hiding small breasts. Her arms were sparely muscled, and filthy, her hands and face were feminine, but there was a masculinity to her too, a prominent larynx in her throat, and her scent was that of unwashed man.

"I have heard of many master tongues," said Heffi. He maintained his calm, but his speech became stilted and declamatory. "Some of the less flexible members of my own kind reckon our language the master speech. Wars are made and races overthrown for the sake of truths like that."

"There are many absolute truths, Heffira-nereaz-Hellishul vovo Balisatervo Chai Tse-ban, and all are absolutely true. They intersect, they oppose. They are all lies. They are all valid."

Trassan sweated heavily. He was faint with the heat and the charnel smell of the cave. He wished to take off his parka, but he would not leave himself blind in front of the Unshe for a moment. She spoke to Heffi, but her eyes, glistening white in her filthy face, were intent on him.

"I believe in only two, the value of family, and the value of coin," said Heffi.

"What of your One?"

"If god chose to speak to us, his message would be so complex as to be incomprehensible to the listener. The One is everywhere, but he only watches. In His garden are space for all truths to take root. They flourish, but are only adornments. We are never permitted to see within His house. That is where the ultimate truth is, and we shall never know it in this life."

"You are wise, Heffira-nereaz-Hellishul vovo Balisatervo Chai Tse-ban of the Ishmalani." The Unshe tapped a finger against her nose.

"I do what I can to stay alive and earn coin. The more the better," said Heffi. "What is, is. A man who ties himself in knots about the meaning of life experiences hardly any life at all."

"Yes, yes," said the Unshe. "There is one truth from the many." She, he, it, crept around the fire toward them. Her movements were sinuous. The fire flared and glowed green. Trassan was spellbound by her staring eyes. They frightened him, but he feared what he might see in the fire more, so held her gaze.

"What of the chief?" said Heffi. "She spoke our tongue. How do you know it?"

The Unshe laughed. "Now we come to the liver of the matter. The blubber has been cut away, let others chew on that. You and I shall gorge on the richness of secrets untold."

The Unshe pulled a skin-wrapped bundle from behind her with slender hands. She unwrapped it slowly, glancing at Heffi from under the feathered skin of her cowl to gauge his reaction.

The last thong came undone, and she laid the skin flat, smoothing it out. At the centre was the head of a man.

The smell of smoked meat came off the head strongly. The skin was the non-specific yellow brown of preserved flesh, tinged black where the cold had got at it. The head could have come from a man of any one of fifty kingdoms, but the gold in its nose and ears and the lock of hair still attached to its scalp identified it as an Ishmalan.

"See, one who came here twenty winters ago. He taught Chichiweh the phrase you heard. Quell your offence, sailor. Chichiweh does not understand it, not like I."

"Who was he?" said Heffi.

"A ship of wood went far to the south. They attempted what you attempt."

"Rassanaminul Haik's final expedition?" said Heffi. "A disaster.

There was only one survivor. I knew him, he was a friend of my father's."

The Unshe shook her head knowingly. "There was not one, but several. There was dissent in their group. They abandoned three on the ice. By the time the peoples of water and ice found them, one remained. This man. You shall learn."

She took a brown stick from a hollow in the floatstone wall.

"Come, come, you must come closer." She beckoned.

Heffi and Trassan shared a glance before edging around the fire. She motioned impatiently for them to sit by her, one either side. They knelt. The shrivelled eyes of the dead Ishmalan stared blindly up at them.

The Unshe paused. "I sense the blood of Will in you, Trassan Kressind."

"My brother is a Guider, a true take from the Dead God's quarter, by which I mean he has a fair measure of mage blood. He is reckoned strong by his peers," he said. Trassan was no stranger to horror, but the head with its shrunken eyes and worm-like lips was the most profoundly disturbing thing he had ever seen. The heat of the fire beat at his back and his head like a forge hammer. His vision shifted. A drugged powerlessness descended upon him.

"And there is one who is more than that!" she rebuked. "If one in the family has the blood, all do. Remember this, and be afraid. This one will know much of you; your being casts many shadows in the realm of Will. You will not like what you hear."

Trassan turned to look at her. His head was a stone effigy grinding around on ill fashioned bearings. It was an effort to tear his gaze away from the yellow grin of the mummified sailor.

The Unshe peered right inside him. "Frightened?"

"No," he whispered his lie.

The Unshe thrust the stick into the fire. It sizzled. Oily musk smoked from it as she withdrew it from the flames. Trassan felt dizzier. She sucked in a lungful of smoke from the incense stick and breathed it into the face of the head.

"The ways of the dead are open. I open the gate." She sucked in another breath of the stinking incense and blew it onto the head. "I open the gate to the dead. Come back to the realm of being, leave behind the domain of the dead, the formless spaces." She breathed again. "Speak," she said.

The smoke gathering around the head glowed green, and coalesced itself about the shrunken features into a phantasmal image of the face that was. The fire died down.

"Speak!" commanded the Unshe.

Heffi flinched as the head's mouth opened with the click of dry bone, and a rattling moan issued from between its yellow teeth. The hands suspended over the fire jiggled, grasping at nothing.

"Heffira-nereaz-Hellishul vovo Balisatervo Chai Tse-ban!" it moaned. The eyes of smoke rolled. Behind them, dried eyelids of flesh twitched.

Heffi and Trassan stared at it in horror.

"Answer it!" hissed the Unshe. "Or it will depart!"

"I am he!" said Heffi.

"A lover of comfortable life and adventure both, to your heart's everlasting dissatisfaction," said the head. "You are known in these realms. Irony entertains the dead."

"Aye," said Heffi. "I am."

"I was Morazov-kenteaz-Varashul of the Sect of Light."

"You are not at one with His eminence?"

"I died away from land where His will holds sway. Now I am lost. Do not become as I. You seek the city of the Morfaan. The City of Ice."

"Yes," said Heffi.

"I warn you as one follower of the One to another, you must turn back. Death and worse awaits you. I have trodden the ways of the city. I know what horror lurks there."

"How can that be?" said Heffi. "My friend was father to Verenetz, the cargomaster of Haik's mission. Only he returned to the North, found aboard a ship's boat with four dead Oczerks. He told that the city was glimpsed from afar."

"The dead cannot lie," said the Unshe.

"I do not lie! Laws greater than those that bind the telling of truth between Ishamalani hold me. Do not speak of Verenetz," said Morazov. "He fled while others died. It was he that had no respect of the One's law; it was he that lied."

"Why?" said Heffi. "He was known to me, you are not."

"He was no honest man!" wailed the head. "He sought to keep the discovery for himself. Or perhaps he sought to save fools like you from what is there."

"It is our understanding that the city was unknown until Verenetz saw it, adrift and alone," said Trassan.

"Lies. You are not the first to seek it. Haik had a map, found in a wreck on the northern shores of Oczerkiya. We searched for the City of Ice, and we found it."

Heffi and Trassan looked at each other again.

"How did you come to it?"

"With difficulty. Great mountains front the water. Ice blocks the shore for a thousand leagues."

"There was no report of it during the last survey," said Trassan.

"It comes, it goes. It is there now. Mages do not see everything."

"Antoninan plans for us to head for the Sea Drays Bay," said Trassan. "Do you know it?"

"Everything can be known by the dead. The shore is inaccessible there. Ice higher than a mountain walls it from the ocean. The bay is shut."

"Tell us how you came there," said Heffi. "You will aid us."

"I came to warn, not to aid! Turn back, turn back!"

"You must be swift," said the Unshe. "It cannot lie to you. Ask and it will speak the truth."

"Do not make me! Return to the North. Do not come here again. War comes."

"War?" said Trassan. "What war?"

The face of green smoke flickered.

"Tell us of the way inside! I demand it!" shouted Heffi.

The ghost cried out. "There is a dock. Between two mountains whose peaks are close but forever apart. It cannot be seen, but it can be reached."

"What is the position?"

"Do not go!" cried the ghost. "Return home!"

"Give me the position, damn you!" roared Heffi.

The ghost spat out a stream of numbers that Trassan recognised as a designator of latitude used across Ruthnia. It spoke again, cryptic unrelated words. Heffi nodded; this was the secret longitudinal code of the Ishmalani. The measuring of longitude was a skill known only to them.

"If it cannot be seen, how do we go within?" he said.

The fire roared up behind them and died down.

"The ice will stop you! Go back!" said the ghost. "Please, no more. I beg you! You cannot go. Success beckons, but the love of gold will destroy you yet, my brother in the One!" The ghost wavered, the green light dimmed.

"What do you mean?" said Heffi. "Tell me how—"

The Unshe's hand shot out and gripped him with iron strength. "It returns to the realms of the dead. Ask no more of it, or it may drag your soul back with it."

"Be wary," said the fading face. "Go no further. The Iron Lords knock upon the door. Best never to hear the heralding. Go back to the North, to your comfortable homes. Torment will find you there. Do not die here, Heffira-nereaz-Hellishul vovo Balisatervo Chai Tse-ban or you will be marooned as I am, far from the light of the One!" It began to scream, and Trassan clapped his hands over his ears against it, but the noise passed through his hands as if they were not there. He and Heffi screamed along with it.

The scream faded. The green smoke melted away and the incense scent faded. The fire blazed high again.

Trassan took his shaking hands away from his ears. The head sat inert on its leather covering. The Unshe got to her feet and swiftly bundled it up, muttering spells against the ghost's return.

"It said it came to warn us, but you called it," said Trassan.

"Both are true. Did I not say that there are many truths?" The Unshe tied the head up with hide thongs and set it back into its alcove. "I called you here because I was meant to. I called it because it called you. All fits together, there is only one way for the world to be, and there is always a reason. Heed its warning. Go home."

"Is it right?" said Trassan.

The Unshe shrugged and sat before them, her dirty arms resting on calloused knees. "Yes. No."

Heffi narrowed his eyes. "How does he come to be here? Why is he not with the One?"

"The Southern Gods took him to be with them," said the Unshe. "All who die on the ice are theirs. Your people have no bargain with them as you do with the King of the Drowned. I could not summon him if it were not so. Those who go to your god are beyond contact."

"There are no gods," said Trassan. "They are gone."

The Unshe laughed. "Tell that to the ocean, tell that to the sky, the snow, the ice and the fire! These are the gods of the sea-peoples. I see them all around me. The great warlock drove out your gods, not ours. This is not the Hundred Kingdoms. Remember that, or the ghost's prophecy will out."

The Unshe lit a second grainy stick of incense, this one with a sweet and sticky scent. She fanned it at her guests, and Trassan fell woozy again.

"Heed the spirit! Return. Your magic is at odds with this place, it is the magic of iron, line and angle. The one who travels with you, the Red Rabbit, his presence has the spirits of the underworld in uproar. The gods of the south are angry with him, for the hurt his ancestor did to their divine cousins. Suffering awaits you."

Black spots whirled in front of Trassan's eyes. The Unshe peered at him through them.

"Go home!" She flicked him on the forehead with a dirty finger, and he passed out.

TRASSAN AWOKE ON a bed of snow harried by a freezing wind. He pushed himself up groggily, almost pitching into the black sea. He was on the narrow shelf of ice near the Unshe's cave. The night was at its darkest. Sheets of multicoloured light rippled on the horizon, reflecting green and red upon the still ocean. They crackled mightily as they danced.

"Andrade's Cloak," said Trassan.

"The spirits are angry," said Heffi, pushing himself from the wall. His tone was wry, but his face troubled. He reached a hand down and hauled Trassan to his feet.

Trassan's legs were feeble under him, and he had to steady himself against the wall. He was sure they were outside the cave entrance, but their tracks ended at his feet and there was no opening there, only a wall of weathered floatstone. He rested his hands on it wonderingly.

"I do not like this wild magic," said Trassan.

"It is not to be trusted," said Heffi, staring at the lights.

"Was I out long?" said Trassan.

"A half hour longer than I," said Heffi. "Hard to tell how long we have been here in total. The days are so long."

"Thanks for waiting."

"You are too heavy to carry, and I could not let you topple into the ocean. I am very cold."

"My apologies, and again my thanks." Trassan paused. "What should we do?"

Heffi held up his hands and shrugged.

"I wish Aarin were still with us," said Trassan. "He understands the dead."

Heffi sighed. "He is not. Even if he was and told you to go back, would you?"

Trassan shook his head. He shivered, missing the heat of the fire. "No."

"Well then," said Heffi. "Onward we go." He guided Trassan back the way they came with a hand in the small of his back. "The meeting was worrying, but propitious."

"Yes," said Trassan. "We know something that Vardeuche Persin never will. How to get into the City of Ice."

CHAPTER TWENTY-THREE
The Grand Ball

GARTEN WAS BACK in the fog. He looked out through a crack in the curtains at its blank whiteness. Only one hundred yards away from the Palace of Nations on the Place di Regime, late evening sunshine lit up the skyline of half of Perus, the rest endured an early twilight in the shadow of the Godhome. By the palace the Morfaan's mist was so thick it blotted out all detail on the massive Grand House of the Assembly. The building was identical to the palace and not far distant on the other side of the square, but its dome, the twin of the palace's and jointly the largest in the world, was an indistinct mass, and the statues lining its pediments shady silhouettes. Sun shining into the island of fog filled it with a fierce light that made the back of one's eyes throb. It was for this reason, rather than secrecy, that the curtains were drawn.

Garten let the cloth drop. "This light is awful."

Abing hoomed and hawed, rolling his glass of Girarsan whisky around in his hand. The man could not sit still. He reminded Garten of Trassan in that regard.

"It will be dark soon," said Abing. "Just count yourself lucky that the Morfaan stay here. Imagine if they were staying on the Avenue of Peace."

"I would rather not. I have had my fill of the mist." He glanced at the clock on the mantelpiece of the oversized fireplace. "How do we know Juliense will keep to his word?"

"He will," said Abing. In the ballroom downstairs, the ball's prelude played. Swelling music filtered in through the closed door.

"It will be time for the first dance soon, he cannot miss that."

"And he will not," said Abing. "I thought you calmer than this, Garten," he admonished. "Do sit down. Have a drink."

Garten left the window and dragged a chair out from the long table that took up most of the room. The room was technically Karsan territory, theirs to hold meetings in during balls such as this. Every nation had one. "Very well."

"Can I have a drink too?" said Tyn Issy.

"Yes, yes, I am sorry my dear." Abing got up, went to where Issy's box was hidden behind the glass dome of another large clock. She held out a tiny silver cup though the bars. He dripped whisky into it.

"I said I wanted a drink, not drowning," said Issy. She licked her hand noisily, like a cat.

"My apologies, goodlady," said Abing. "That's a very small cup. Now you be sure you stay quiet through all this, agreed?"

"Hmph," said Issy.

Abing poured Garten a drink and sat back down.

"Fine whiskey," said Garten.

"Yes," agreed Abing. They sipped in silence.

Someone knocked at the door. Abing nodded his head at it, indicating that Garten should open it.

Juliense was one of the most powerful men in Maceriya, some said the most powerful, and therefore among the greatest lords in all of Ruthnia, and he was on the other side of the door, coming to talk to them. For a giddy second Garten felt out of his depth. There are those moments in an official's life that prove definitive. This was one. He calmed himself, smoothed his admiralty uniform, and opened the door. The music loudened greatly. One of the Guard Comtose greeted Garten, his war panoply gleaming, a short, tasselled halberd in his right hand. Men and women in evening dress walked behind him along the balconied landing. Beyond them, chandeliers gleamed with hundreds of candles in the vast open space of the palace dome.

"Juliense, Comte of High Perus," the guard announced, and stepped smoothly back.

Juliense came in. Abing stood and offered a short bow. Garten closed the door behind him.

"I am sorry goodfellows, to keep you," said the Comte of High Perus.

"This is an important event, we understand," said Abing.

"The most important," said Juliense.

Abing handed Juliense a drink. The Maceriyan's costume was outlandish: cream satin, silver thread and mirror-bright buttons. His face was completely white, his hair hidden under a wig that must have been two feet tall. But for all his ludicrous garb, Juliense radiated a dangerous cunning. He had shrewd eyes in a hard face.

"We have minutes at most, goodfellows. So let me be plain. Karsa must back the Maceriyan candidate. I need to have your pledge in writing, this evening."

"And why should we do that, my lord?" said Abing.

"Because, your grace," said Juliense, "of the Church. You witnessed their little display at the arrival yesterday."

"You handled it artfully, if I may say," said Abing.

"Perhaps," said Juliense. "But I have angered them. Their display of ignorance might have the broadsheets hooting with laughter, but the common people rush to defend them. There will be unrest here in Perus, and in most of the other cities of the Maceriyan block. The commoners demand a share of the wealth being collected by industrialists. If it were not for them, tearing up the old order with their money and their machines, we may not be in such danger." He looked at Garten a moment. "Maybe we should follow your example, and come to an accommodation."

"Prince Alfra's father thought it pragmatic to ennoble the wealthy," said Abing. "Money has ever been the deciding factor in nobility."

"I am a pragmatic man also," said Juliense, "but our governmental systems prevent me from acting. I cannot convince the king to act as Prince Calavaion did. He is too fearful of his own position and is too timid to exercise the power he has anyway. Our House of Nobles would never countenance the acceptance of new members into the aristocracy, as yours did in Karsa. And so there is a build up of pressure, as in one of your steam engines." He looked at Garten again. "The peasants against the industrialists against the nobility. There is deadlock here. The coming of the Twin complicates matters and confounds my attempts to impose logic. Superstition is an easy outlet for the common folks' energies, and one I would ordinarily leave well alone. But now, I cannot. Zealots preach the return of the gods, and promise justice. It is nonsense. Ignorance. This is the natural order of things. Man is innately hierarchical. Were it not we as the lords, it would be some other group. But this egalitarianism it is burning through the city like a fever. Raganse is using it to hold me hostage. He will have a church candidate or civil war."

"How would our backing your favoured candidate for High Legate help?" asked Abing.

Juliense pulled a face. "Come. You know why. Raganse has fallen under Bishop Rousinteau's influence. He is stoking the fires of fear under the nobility's backsides, saying there will be riots and rebellion if a Church approved candidate is not selected as our nomination for High Legate. Naturally, such a candidate will never be elected by the remainder of the Hundred. If I have your backing, I can convince the House of Nobles that the Grand Assembly of Nations *will* elect *my* candidate as legate. If I can show you will back us, those waiting to see which way the wind is blowing will side with me. It then becomes a matter of international, not internal, politics. Your tacit approval will bring a number of the Olberlanders into line. The Queendom will likely follow your lead. And so our industrialists will trade the opportunity for change for the certainty of the continuation of Maceriyan power. I will have to parlay this into concessions, and I will be in debt to the oily hands of new money, but by doing so I can sideline Raganse, and pull the teeth of the Church. It is not a bad price."

"I still do not quite see what the advantage is for us," said Abing.

Juliense set his drink down and clasped his hands behind his back. "You have no valid candidate of your own, no Karsan has ever been High Legate. In this affair you are kingmakers, not kings."

Garten stood forward. "Then why can we not simply back another candidate from one of the other Kingdoms, one that will bring us more tangible benefits?"

Juliense smiled sourly. "Ordinarily, this would not be a valid proposition for you. It would be entirely to my benefit. But in this instance it is for the best for all of us if you side with me. If you do not aid me, there will be upheaval here in Maceriya. Already Rousinteau preaches that the other nations are jealous of our ancient empire. There are mutterings that it should be restored. And there is another thing, this woman who accompanies Rousinteau—"

"The mage?" said Garten.

Juliense appraised Garten carefully. "Yes. The mage. I have my agents chasing her, but aside from her appearances with Rousinteau they can find few traces of her. There is no mention of her in any census, no history or personal associations, and she is unknown to the Convocation of Mages. Most curiously, she bears an iron stave," said Juliense. "Which the Grand Wizard—such a ridiculous title!—of the convocation informed me by letter is an impossibility. Yet I see it with my own eyes. She is brazen now, often at the elbow of Rousinteau, whispering openly into his ear."

"An imposter," said Abing. "She wouldn't be the first to claim mageblood and have none."

"I thought so too, once. But there is something to her. She stirs up trouble wherever she goes. We have discovered that she is associated with Vardeuche Persin, which will be of personal interest to you no doubt, Goodfellow Kressind. What she is working towards troubles me, largely because I have no idea what it is. The pertinent issue for the moment is that she is a destabilising influence on an already unstable situation. I will deal with her, but first I need to prove to the people that a secular candidate is the right choice because it will preserve the power of our nation. Help me. Of the last twenty High Legates, twelve have been Maceriyan. You will lose nothing, and gain a friend."

Abing snorted. "Come now, Juliense! There has been peace in Ruthnia only for three generations. There have been five High Legates since the formation of the alliance of the Hundred Kingdoms, only two of which have been Maceriyan."

"And two of the others from Macer Lesser and Marceny." He shrugged. "Still Maceriyan, in the most important regards. You could choose to put your diplomacy behind some other nation, propel them into the Legate's house. For what? The position is ceremonial, and the heart of the continent will burn. Everyone loses. Rousinteau will use our defeat as evidence of the returning god's displeasure."

Abing scowled.

"Let me be frank, your grace," said Juliense. "There are many in the Maceriyan block who see the rise of Karsan power and your domination of the seas as an affront to our ancient sphere of influence. Khushashia dominates the east, the Mohaci snigger at us as they always have. Maceriyan pride is wounded. This business with the gods feeds off a toxic soup—change, poverty, shame, national anger, and the fear accompanying the return of the Twin. Do not make this nation lash out. We shall all suffer for it."

"What exactly is your meaning?" said Abing levelly.

"Be calm. This is not a threat. I simply have no desire to see revolution in Maceriya and the war that will inevitably follow. Peace is my only motivation. What other reason could there be? Power? Wealth? I have more of both than I can stomach. The only way I can see around this is to present a sensible candidate, and the only way to do that is make sure such a candidate will win. Any other result will be a disaster for all the Hundred. We must have this resolved, and prepare for the perigee. There is only a year before the Twin kisses the Earth. We have to stand united."

"In case the historians are correct."

"Do you doubt they are, Duke Abing?"

Abing thought a moment, flexing his left hand on the arm rest. "Very well. We can aid you, even if we decide to back another nation. We brought Countess Lucinia Mogawn here to present the findings of her scientific investigation into the Twin's approach."

"That will help," said Juliense. "But only to convince those who are already convinced. It will be small beer compared to your open pledge of support for the Maceriyan candidate."

"Who do you propose for the candidate? I think I have guessed," said Abing. He poured a generous measure of whiskey for himself. "But I want to hear you say it yourself."

"I am the only viable candidate."

"That is what I knew you would say," said Abing. "Are you sure you have enough power to satisfy you?"

"More than enough," said Juliense.

"But you're the only man for the job, is that it?"

"I find your tone disagreeable, your grace."

Outside the closing movement of the ball's theme was building to a crescendo.

"I must go. The first dance begins. You should also attend." Juliense said. "The door!" he shouted, and his guard opened it.

"Your answer, tonight," he said gravely.

Abing stood. Both he and Garten bowed.

"If I have not convinced you," said Juliense, "then we shall meet again, this time with the Morfaan. Listen to what they have to say."

"What is their position?" said Garten.

"They readily agree that Maceriya should supply the legate."

"So soon?" said Abing. "They are here barely one day."

Juliense adjusted his wig in a mirror. "Immediately. They want this done before the winter. They urge us to make preparations for next year. They talk of earthquakes and upheaval, but there is something they are not saying. In all honesty, I have the impression they are terrified by the approach of the Twin." He smiled at them. His teeth were yellow against his snow white make-up. "And that worries me more than anything else. Good evening, goodfellows."

"Your excellency," Abing and Garten said together.

The guard closed the door behind Juliense. Tyn Issy gave a dirty laugh to the sudden quiet.

"Goodlady Issy, prove your worth. Was he telling the truth?" asked Abing.

"Oh yes," said Tyn Issy sweetly. "He's shitting himself."

THE GRAND BALL was simply named, without hyperbole. There was not a greater gathering of the great and good anywhere in the Hundred. The Palace of Nations hummed to the chatter of rich men and women from all over Ruthnia, although by convention the rulers of each land were absent. Garten left Issy in their meeting room, and accompanied Abing into the throng.

The dome was the centrepiece of the palace, open for the three hundred feet from the floor to its curved ceiling, where fantastic paintings filled the spaces between massive stone ribs. A magnificent staircase of red porphyry wound around the interior to the gallery landing halfway up, where the hundred rooms of the ambassadors were situated. Either side of the dome were two enormous wings. One contained a ballroom bigger than a parade ground and as lavishly decorated as the dome. The other wing was divided into many chambers of various sizes that linked the Palace to the

Kingdom Courts, where disputes between nations and citizens from differing lands were ruled upon. From the dome wide steps led into a lobby with high glass doors, beyond which a portico opened up onto the fastidious, if monumental, precinct of the Place di Regime. Half a mile wide, the Street of Petition ran through its centre. Situated on the far side of the Place di Regime was the Grand House of the Assembly. There laws were made that affected all the kingdoms, and collective decisions of external policy, trade agreements, labour movement and suchlike. To the man on the street, the House was the source of all power in the kingdoms, but to those within the workings of the complex government of Ruthnia, all knew that the real work was done in the bars, salons, offices and the ballroom of the Palace.

Glimmerlamps and lanterns lit the place in brilliant white light; it was a palace of cut glass and crystal, ormolu and exotic woods, dragon ivory and silver. Alcoves displayed artworks of three and a half centuries of progress alongside artefacts from the various ages of antiquity.

The men split—Abing going to socialise with men of his own rank while Garten spent the evening making small talk with other secretaries and assistants to the ambassadors. He had little propensity for dancing, and left the ballroom after watching the first dance; a ridiculous affair conducted so solemnly Garten had to stifle a fit of the giggles. He went from room to room, taking care not to drink too much, to be charming, engaging yet give nothing away. He struggled to keep his mind entirely in the moment, for his thoughts kept straying to Issy in her box upstairs. She was proving her utility already, but her discovery could lead to some awkwardness.

His concerns were getting the better of him when he was tapped on the shoulder. He turned to find a woman behind him, dressed similarly to the countess in man's clothes modified to present a modicum of femininity. She was about thirty, pretty in an unobvious way. A light touch of paint accentuated her eyes, she had none of the thick white make up the Perusians favoured. Most notable was the sword at her side, a business like backsword in a plain sheath. An unfussy basket cradled the grip. A fighter's sword, not a decoration. Thick duellist's gloves were tucked neatly into the belt beside the hanger. Her hands gave away her profession. Nails bitten halfway down the nailbed, unpainted, fingers sinewy and scarred. In one she held a drink, the other she put behind her back self-consciously when she noticed him staring at her nails.

"You are Garten Kressind of Karsa?" she said.

"I am," said Garten. "Looking at that sword, I'd say you were a serious fencer. And there is one famous, serious female fencer in Perus—Kyreen Asteria. You must be her. Charmed." He performed an elaborate courtly bow.

She dipped her head. "I am she. I am offended by your description, goodfellow. The only serious female fencer in Perus? I am the best swordsman in this nation, if not the continent."

"I am sorry," said Garten. "I do you a disservice. You are correct."

She sighed, and looked around her, already bored with the conversation. "They all do me a disservice, until I slit them open. Then it's me doing the disservice," she smiled, but it was somewhat despairing. She downed her drink in one and motioned to a bewigged waiter carrying a tray of full wine flutes for another. "I heard good things about you, Garten Kressind. The money in Perus was on you to take the Karsan cup. What, six years ago? What rank did you achieve? I forget. I memorise only the names of the winners."

"Fifth was my final ranking before I withdrew from competition," he said. "I retired from competition, but have continued to fence privately. I have improved since then."

"Ah, says who?"

"Everyone I have fought, and beaten," he said. He sipped his own wine. The whiskey buzz was leaving him, and he wished to recharge it before his energy flagged, but the wine was abominably sour in the north Maceriyan way, and it curdled his stomach.

"It is hard to prove rank if you no longer compete."

"You do not compete," he said.

"Competitions are for cowards. I only fight duels; I prefer the real thing to fencing. The outcome is always much more decisive. A corpse leaves no room for interpretation as to who was the winner and who the loser. Why did you retire?"

"My father," Garten said. "He had us all learn to fence to uphold the family honour. You would approve of him, he too insists swordplay is for duelling, not for sport. I went as far as I could, and then he demanded I give up competition to concentrate on my career."

"You are a good boy then, who always does what his father says."

He shrugged off the provocation. "Fencing remains my passion. I have my own salle at home, and fight every day. It keeps me sharp, even if my sword is blunt."

"Not all of them, I hope." She looked at his own weapon. He put his hand upon the hilt.

"This one is edged," he said.

"I am glad to hear it. A man as skilled as you should carry a blade." She appraised him cynically. "A pity. You could have been somebody, and now look at you, a bureaucrat, such a waste. Well," she said with false amity. "It was nice to meet you. I like to keep an eye on men I may one day have to kill."

"I shall take that as a compliment," said Garten, and bowed.

"You should. I only fight men who I think may challenge me, otherwise what's the point? I might as well be a butcher, cutting the throats of kid goats." She smiled dangerously and offered her hand for a kiss. Garten took it and obliged. "I will see you again, I'm sure," she said, and left him alone.

"What was all that about?" Garten murmured. He followed her progress through the crowd. During the time he kept his eye on her, she spoke to no one else. He was flattered she had sought him out.

He lost her when a familiar face crossed his field of vision. He caught the briefest of glimpses, but recognition had his gaze snap back. There was no mistaking his brother.

"Guis?" he said. He pushed into the press of people. Dignitaries held low conversations, alert in case they were overheard. Goodladies affected bashfulness at the compliments of men smiling dracon's smiles. He manoeuvred around a knot of laughing bravos from Brodning. Focussed on his brother, he jostled and nudged, provoking mutters of complaint. Guis appeared and disappeared in the crowd; twice Garten lost sight of him. A wide group of tightly bunched people presented themselves, gathered around the Maceriyan god, the Infernal Duke. Much like Eliturion, he stood holding court, an attractive woman on his arm. Garten barely paid the wonder any notice, but shoved his way through the crowd impatiently just in time to see Guis exiting the building through its grand lobby. He ran down the stairs to the glass doors.

"Guis!" he shouted. "Guis wait, it's me, Garten!" But his lone voice could not compete with the orchestra in the ballroom and the combined conversations of a thousand people. He made it to the door, pushed upon the bevelled glass and ran outside. It was getting dark, and the fog had reassumed its awful pallor. He looked all around the Place, running falteringly one direction then another, then to the Street of Petitioners and the traffic there. All he saw were silhouettes in the fog.

"Guis!" he shouted. A wagon rattled past, dogs straining in their harnesses against a heavy load.

His brother was nowhere to be seen. Bemused, he went back inside. As he climbed back up the lobby stairs to the domed hall, a footman from the embassy came to him in a state of upset, he had evidently been chasing Garten.

"Goodfellow! Goodfellow! I have a message." He handed over a note. Garten snatched it, unfolded it, read it.

"What?" he said. "Now?"

"He is waiting, in Tiriton's Hall."

"Of course." Garten crumpled the note and passed it back. "Where else would the emissary of the Drowned King be?"

CHAPTER TWENTY-FOUR
The Emissary of the Drowned

A FLAMBOYANTLY ATTIRED Maceriyan footman opened the door into Tiriton's Hall, and an awful smell hit Garten hard. A stench comprised of four scents, intertwined as intimately as lovers at a revel. The strongest was of a rich, round, floral perfume of the sort that is less an adornment and more an assault on the senses, a perfume that rams itself into the nostrils without invitation and packs them full to bursting. The second scent was the attractively peaty smell of smoked meat, though the meat was not of a sort one would wish to eat. In direct competition with the savour was the stink of chemical preservatives. Finally, adding its own subtle flourish, there was the faint whiff of brine and decaying seaweed on a hot day, pleasant in some circumstances, less so in this.

The emitter sat in a chair facing a fire. Tiriton's Hall was as large and as finely decorated as all the other rooms in the palace—a riot of frescoes, statues, plaster mouldings and impractical tables groaning under the weight of vulgar bronzes. In its decorative theme of oceans, mythical and not-so-mythical creatures, the deeds of the banished sea god and his numerous daughters, it shared a commonality with the ministry of the Admiralty in Karsa, where Garten worked. The chief difference was that the Karsan ministry was tasteful, whereas it looked like a troupe of avant garde artists elated by their own self importance and hallucinogenic spirits had outfitted this room.

The emissary of the Drowned King occupied the hall, unsurprisingly, on his own. Light was restricted to a scattering of candles. The chandelier was unlit, the glimmer lamps out. The emissary stood from his chair with a creak of dried leather, and bowed stiffly. Not because of a choice of etiquette, or personal preference. His construction determined that he could bow no other way.

The emissary was a horror in a fine suit, a dried cadaver whose bones made sharp ridges under sunken, waxy skin. Black lips were frozen, drawn back over teeth made long by the withdrawal of dead gums. They were perfect teeth, bright and clean as seashells on brown sand. They attracted the attention, drawing Garten in as inexorably as a whirlpool. However horrifying the perfection of the teeth, they were better than the eyes; round, glistening balls that rolled fully exposed by shrunken eyelids, the only truly living thing about the emissary, horribly large in that dead face. The eyelids, dry as old scabs, delineated the eyes in black, accentuating their rolling moistness like macabre kohl.

"Greeting Garten Kressind," said the emissary in a weirdly human voice. He spoke warmly, but his charm was undermined by the clack of his white teeth and the rasp of his pointed, black tongue upon them. He sounded like he were a machine clacking out words, and not a thinking creature. "You must forgive my appearance. I was forced to undergo certain preservative measures to avoid decay upon arriving on land."

Garten waved away the emissary's concerns. "I had not noticed."

"Really? Many people find me somewhat disturbing. Horrifying, even."

"No, not at all," said Garten. An attempt not to breathe through his mouth for politeness's sake had him nearly gag.

The emissary laughed. He held up a handkerchief to his mouth when he did in a bizarre display of good manners. "Yes you do. Why do you think I sit in here alone? I am invited to every ball and dance, every banquet. I cannot dance, I do not eat. My attendance provokes revulsion, but I come anyway. There are always matters of state to attend to, and these gatherings are where so much of import is discussed. I am always afforded my own room," he said. He held up his arms and his leathery hide squeaked. "A good choice, is it not? For the same reasons I do not show myself openly, I will not ask you to shake hands with me. I will stress that this is not a display of ill feeling on my part, nor a calculated show of enmity. I refrain from physical contact in deference to the sensibilities of others."

"You are very kind, goodfellow."

"Naturally. Undeath does not have to kill manners."

The emissary did, however, approach him. He walked very slowly, and with difficulty. Never had Garten seen so arid a being, but his fashionable shoes left moist prints on the tiled floor. The quadruple scents of smoke, perfume, formaldehyde and the ocean swelled in time with the music playing in the ballroom, making Garten faint. He heard the pounding of the waves under the music. He placed his hand upon a table to steady himself.

"What can I do for you, goodfellow?" Garten asked.

"Goodfellow? I suppose I am now. But who knows what I once was. Sailor? Merchant? A lowly gleaner, caught unawares in the tide? A criminal even, left pegged out to drown? I am who I am. Who I was when I was alive is unimportant. In truth, I remember little. When a spirit goes from one form to another, it leaves behind its former being. The drowned forget everything. Whoever I was, I am not he, and he would be horrified by me. I am what I am, as we all are." He put his handkerchief to his nose again, perhaps in admission of his own stench. "It is strange to be here, on the dry land. I often ponder that it must have been natural to me once. Now it is the most alien of habitats. It was unpleasant to be made fit for this role, and I can no longer go back. I am, if you will, a fish out of water." The tight black lips creaked into an awful smile. "Alas, although I myself bear you no ill will, I have been tasked with delivering sorry news, and I have been ordered that it must be delivered to you, no other."

"Very well," said Garten.

"A little under three months ago, your brother's ship, the *Prince Alfra*, crossed the domain of the Drowned, to whit, the Drowning Sea, wherein is located the court of my lord. I will cut to the chase and say Trassan Kressind did this without the proper authorisation. My master is greatly displeased."

"Trassan was in possession of the correct papers."

"He had papers. He presented them. They were correctly composed, but they are not to the spirit of our treaty. No ships to pass the Drowned Sea, or to venture further than two hundred sea miles south of the Isle of Skelpy without permission of the Drowned King."

"We are within our rights to issue Licenses Undefined to whomever requires them, so long as there is a need. Exploration is a valid reason."

"Your ship engaged in battle with my lord and our border guard."

"I am shocked. But the *Prince Alfra* is not a warship."

"Nor is it a solely an exploration vessel," said the emissary. "I read the broadsheets, goodfellow. I pass on the news to my lord under the sea. The target of this ship and that of the Maceriyan Vardeuche Persin is an intact Morfaan city. This is a matter of industrialists' rivalry, not a scientific expedition."

"And Persin?"

"He did have the correct papers, in accordance with our treaty with the Kingdom of Maceriya."

"How?" said Garten. "If one expedition is to be allowed, why not another?"

"I cannot discuss the details of agreements struck with another sovereign nation, you understand."

"Yes, yes. What occurred? Was anyone hurt?"

"A great many of my master's subjects were hurt," said the emissary, "but I assume you express concern for the welfare of your brother?"

"Brothers. There were two of them aboard."

"Ah, yes, the Guider," said the emissary. His bog brown face lacking the flexibility necessary for the majority of facial expressions, he conveyed his sympathy by gesture. The way he tilted his head then suggested a sardonic streak to his character. "Now he did have proper permissions, by merit of the standing agreement between his order and my master for access to the Final Isle. An agreement also violated by his guiding of one hundred and twelve servants of my master into the realms of the dead. The agreement between the Sunken Kingdom and the kingdoms of the land is and has always been that the drowned belong to the Drowned King. Is that not so?"

"Well, yes, but—"

"Then you will be forced to admit, Garten Kressind, that your brothers have committed an act of aggression. Be thankful my master has not yet decided upon a course of action. Sanctions will be forthcoming. Our agreement with the Guiders is also under review, though we are willing to write off Aarin Kressind's transgression as a rogue act."

"These are strong accusations. I cannot imagine my brothers acting without provocation."

"The drowned were the ones provoked, goodfellow," said the emissary.

"Why not tell this directly to the duke. You and he are of the same rank. He would hear you. He has been expecting a summons to audience."

"Yes, that. Among others, the licence had your signature upon it. As secretary to the Duke Abing, Lord of the Karsan Admiralty, we naturally suppose it was you who pushed through your brother's Licence Undefined. We hold you personally responsible. The greed of your people has become insatiable, and nowhere is that clearer than in the actions of your family. You epitomise the overreaching arrogance of the Karsans." An apologetic cough rattled in his throat. "The king's words, not mine. With this act of nepotism you push us too hard. I apologise but my master wishes that you tell the Duke Abing of what I must import as a punishment to you. He bears grudges strongly. You are fortunate that his fury stops at that."

Garten took in a deep breath, the stench of the emissary nearly choked him, and he spluttered his words out. "Hang on a moment! I warned my brother time and again against crossing the Drowning Sea, but he would not have it. I told him of the risks, I informed him of the agreement."

"Then we concur."

"We do not concur, goodfellow," said Garten. "His documentation was legally proper and signed by the highest authorities in the land. I did not push it through. My signature is upon the paper as issuer of the licence, nothing else. If there was a clash, then it would have been for good reason. I refuse to believe your accusations."

The emissary shrugged, a horribly slow and noisy movement. "And we do not believe you. I do not believe you, to be frank. The treaty was flouted and we were attacked. I am sorry to inform you that should your brothers set sail on any sea again, they will face the wrathful retaliation of the drowned. Wherever they go, we shall find them. Furthermore, if there is another incident of this severity again, it will lead to the rescinding of the treaty and, I fear, war between the isles and the drowned. Karsa suffered hundreds years of reaving at the hands of unghosted sea dead, until the signature of the treaty with your people. Two centuries of peace, goodfellow, and you want to throw it away for the chance to burgle the houses of the Morfaan. Such lack of foresight, the squandering of one true advantage for the slim chance of another. You let the wrong anguillon slip the hook. None of us wish to find ourselves in a situation where the drowned are once again permitted to walk upon the land.

"Pass on this news to your duke, Goodfellow Kressind. Pray do it sensibly. Although my master would welcome a war to replenish his army with the bodies of your sailors, I have no wish to see innocent men die." The emissary looked down at his body, his neck creaked and popped. "I do not recall any other existence, but I know what I am. I would not wish this unlife upon the blackest of souls. Now I have delivered my message. I have other appointments to keep, and would like to look at the fire a little longer before I must speak again. There is nothing like it under the sea."

Garten clicked his heels and bowed. He left, tense with an anger he could not display. Out in the hall of the dome the ball was becoming livelier. Under the influence of sour Maceriyan wine, goodfellows and goodladies alike became as raucous as decorum allowed. Garten decided to join them. Today was a day that demanded a drink, followed by several more. Damn his stomach.

CHAPTER TWENTY-FIVE

A Second Important Meeting

PERUS AND ITS many shadows had always held a terror for Guis, and so he had avoided it. When a man is running from the darkness, the worst place to be is where the sun shines rarely.

None of that mattered any more. The Darkling rode the flesh of Guis Kressind and the man was locked away.

The creature strode quickly, relishing the pumping of Guis's blood, the play of muscles under Guis's skin, the thrumming of its stolen heart and whoosh and roar of breath in its lungs. Carnality delighted it. After several months in the stolen body, it had come to see itself as Guis. The corporeal form of Guis Kressind belonged wholly to the Darkling. The library of the man's memories, hopes, dreams and fears were its to peruse at will. Guis's fears especially made it laugh, for it was the dreaded culmination of them. The more the Darkling steeped itself in Guis's life, rolling in the filth of his mind like a dog in the spoor of its prey, it identified with him. Guis Kressind was the name it was forced to present to the unsuspecting mortals it encountered, and so Guis Kressind was the name it had come to associate with itself. This too was a thrilling novelty. The Darkling had never had a name before.

As far as the Darkling was concerned, Guis was he and he was Guis. It was Guis that crossed the road. Guis who dodged a thundering carriage, Guis who winked at a beautiful girl walking the pavement, making her hurry by. He liked the look of unease on their faces. The pretty ones were the most reactive. They were the ones who had weathered the leers of others most often. He enjoyed the paradox some presented, dressed up to be attractive, outraged when their efforts attracted the attention of those they would rather avoid, angry when no one noticed them. The mortal world was steeped in such small hypocrisies.

Guis was someone anyone would avoid. The Darkling's possession disturbed the flesh. Guis's skin had become pallid and greasy, his eyes sunken in brown rings, his frame gaunt, though the Darkling often gorged itself for the pleasure of eating. Often it forgot to wash. The Darkling had little idea to begin with that mortals needed to toilet. Its skills were not perfect yet, and Guis smelled because of it. His clothes were in disarray and hair lank.

Nevertheless it was Guis, Guis Kressind, not the Darkling, not the nameless creature of the Dark Lady, not the servant of misrule, but a man who went to the door of the house of the Infernal Duke. So what if a new and abominable soul steered the body? Guis was what it called itself.

Guis let himself in. A potent combination of his innate magical ability and the Darkling's uncanny arts brushed aside the duke's defences. There was no one home. A residue of magic sparkled in his nostrils; the trails of unthings whispered into being to cook and clean. The duke had become parochial, employing parlour tricks to do his housework for him. The psychic geography of the house slipped through his mind as cool pebbles slip through fingers; the shape, texture and colour of each impression telling a different story to one skilled enough to read them. There was a stain of dismay on the weave of the house, of shame, of ecstasy, and the sickly taste of unreturned love. Faded thoughts and feelings, bleached away by the wash of time. A fresher tint, less nuanced but taking on complexity, overprinted all the rest. He shut his eyes and licked his lips. "Madelyne," he said, tasting the name on the fabric of the world.

She was not present. There was no living thing within. No insect or vermin or life of any sort made its home in the duke's abode. The duke's insubstantial staff would never have to dust away a cobweb or chase away a lizard from the pantry. His presence alone kept small things away. It was a dead house, partly divorced from the world, though anchored to its soil.

"Like the duke," giggled Guis. "Lost at sea." He whistled a tuneless song as he wandered down the hall, drawn directly to the tower of the north wing. As he passed under the bedrooms of the girls the duke had entertained, he touched upon their pleasures and their pains, old and worn emotions. A spike of fear tented reality's weave as he passed under Madelyne's room, but that too was quickly gone as he sauntered by. Muskier sensations, less human more animal, tickled at him as he entered the tower. During the day the interior was bright, tall windows up the stairwell on three sides bringing an abundance of light at odds with the animus loci of the tower. It was a nocturnal building, slothful in the day. He trailed his hand along the door of the ground floor room where Madelyne had languished that first night and several since, and dozens of other women on hundreds of nights before her. Sorrow, excitement, embarrassment, uncertainty, terror, arousal and a dozen other emotional notes tinkled in Guis's mind. He drew in a delighted breath, flexed his hand as he drew it back and looked further. He sensed more satisfying fare above. He mounted the stairs. The first floor echoed with raw sensation lost in the confusing territory between agony, shame and ecstasy. The room on the floor after was massy with magic and throbbed with the most extreme of emotions. Few of the duke's consorts had been admitted through that door. Not all of them had come out.

"Tut tut tut," breathed Guis, resting his face on the door and drinking in past pains and pleasures. "You have been busy."

Upon the third floor Guis passed the duke's personal bedroom. He could not resist peeking inside—the other rooms might be the more theatrical, but this was the duke's personal space and so he cracked the door and peeked. More insight could be gained from what he felt there than any number of sensual torture chambers. He found it disappointingly prosaic. A large bed built for the duke's size occupied the centre of the room. A chamber pot the size of a small cauldron poked out from beneath. The covers were askew, the nightstand heaped with books.

Guis sniffed and licked at the air using senses possessed by no man, solely for his own entertainment. Sniggering at the duke's pretensions to mortality, Guis pushed the door quietly closed. What he required was at the top of the tower.

The tower rose over the roofs of the other buildings on the Place Macer. The stair ended on a landing that allowed one to stand right by the last window, and Guis spent a long time gazing at the city. He picked out the twin domes of the Grand House of Assembly and the Palace of Assembly on the Hill of Roses, the vulgar mausoleum of Res Iapetus crowning the Ardsmont. The plunging cleft of the Foirree and the steel bridges over it. The city disappeared in places, sucked down into its deep cavernas. Away on the tallest hill was the Pantheon Maximale. The pinnacle of the cupola on its dome resting, by chance arrangement of perspective, exactly on the rim of the Godhome.

The thing in Guis remembered Perus from the old times, and it found the changes not to its liking. The stone and the sky had become stained brown with industry. The Godhome's shadow put half the city in the dark, and the streets there twinkled with glimmerlight even though the sun was high. "For freedom Res Iapetus did this," said Guis. "From the city of the morning to the city of shadow. Well done, humanity." Guis's parasite was a wicked being through and through, but its evil was of a particular kind. To see Perus so abused sorrowed him.

Guis left the view. He paused a moment before the double doors of the final room. Flexing his fingers, Guis undid the magic around the place piece by piece and opened the door without discovery. Inside he discovered a temple to the lost gods.

Eleven thrones were arrayed around the circumference of a room rounded and outfitted to resemble the Yotan in miniature. A clear glass dome capped it, through which the pointed attic of the tower's conical roof was visible. Ten of the thrones were occupied by man-sized statues of the gods. The eleventh, carved from dark stone and decorated with vile scenes worthy of the original was empty. This was throne of the Dark Lady—Guis's and the duke's mistress.

Insolently, the Darkling settled Guis Kressind into the empty throne, and waited.

Several hours passed before Guis heard the Infernal Duke climbing the stairs. The footsteps slowed as the duke approached the door— Guis had left it deliberately ajar. He imagined what was going through the duke's mind. Had his sole servant, Markos, finally betrayed him?

Was it his latest plaything going where she shouldn't? Guis stifled a laugh at the thoughts racing round the duke's cavernous mind.

The door opened silently. The duke's massive shoulders and horns were silhouetted in the aperture.

"Hello, your grace," said Guis.

"Who are you? What are you doing in here? How did you come in?" said the duke in a low and dangerous voice. He bullied his way through the door, as if it must be shoved aside to admit him. Guis saw his anger rise as red wings from his shoulders, threatening as a snake's spreading hood.

"Don't you recognise me, your grace? Your senses have dulled." Guis sniffed. "But this world is not what it was. It has taken on the appurtenances of solidity so much that little difference remains between the World of Will and the World of Form."

"It is in the nature of extremes to equalise, entropy is inherent to life," said the duke. He stepped nearer. "It is you," he said. He drew back. "How do you come here?"

"How else? Your magic is strong, I could not breach it. Fortunately for me, the door was open," lied Guis. "I would be more careful of your choice of companion in future, duke. Or else cease allowing your harlots access to your secret chambers by way of testing them. Either way, your precious human failed. They do not listen, and will betray you in the end."

The look of fury that crossed the duke's face gratified the Darkling greatly.

"Get out of here, thing," he said.

"Thing no longer. I have a name," Guis said proudly. "A name to go with my form."

"You were never of a degree to have true form," said the duke.

"Not true. We all were, once. You will be surprised what we have learnt on the other side of death's gates."

"Once was a long time ago," said the duke. "What do you call yourself?"

"My name is Guis Kressind."

"I see," said the duke. "Guis. Get out of the mistress's throne. You commit blasphemy."

Guis lifted his arms and looked at the chair he sat in. "How can I commit blasphemy? There are no gods in this world. And there has been no news of the Dark Lady since our expulsion."

"How have you come back? No riddles. I have no patience." The duke was agitated at this news, and Guis found that hilarious.

He smirked as he replied. "The Gates of the World are leaking. The wards the Morfaan put in place to close the ways are dying. The World of Will gives up its last claims to the name. Its essence becomes equal parts form and will. The creatures that infest this world draw too much on the spirit of the Earth, forcing it from potential to actual. Therefore there is insufficient magic in the aether left to hold the gates closed. Their opening will not occur for some years, but a way can be forced for the first time in eight millennia. I was able to come through by manipulating this creature." He gestured at his body. "He has some power of his own. It worked against him. Rather ironic."

The duke blew out a breath and shook his horns, looking for all the world like a dracon-bull twitching flies from its muzzle. "If this is true, the gates will collapse moments after they are opened. You will not return, and I will be left here alone forever," said the duke.

"You know, I never understood how it is that you escaped. Old Eliturion, we all know why he remained. There are the handful of other, lesser things that clung on when Res Iapetus lost his stomach for the hunt. But you? You were here in the city when the expulsion began. I never had you for a traitor, or thought you might come to an accommodation with the mortals for your own gain. You were a loyal servant of our Dark Lady. Why are you here, while I and every other servant of the gods faces dissolution in the wastes of the formless?"

"I do not know," said the Infernal Duke. He lowered his head.

Guis's stolen face lit up impishly. He wagged a finger. "Ah-ah, I think you do, your grace. I think you really do."

"I do not," the duke said fiercely. "I was in the city, visiting with the matriarch of the Dark Temple."

"Visiting? You have become coy," Guis raised an eyebrow.

"We had our duties," said the duke. "I was in her bed when I saw the Godhome slide out of the sky and come to rest with its rim upon the hills of the Royal Park. In clarity I felt the removal of our fellows from this world. I left, and waited upon the Avenue of Triumphs for Iapetus to visit my own extinction on me. I had no chance of defeating him, but I wished to make account of myself. I was ready to fight him. He never came. Instead I witnessed him depart the Godhome to begin his purge of the lesser Y Dvar."

"You should not use that name," tutted Guis.

"And why not? What are we but slaves to mankind's fancy if we forget what we really are? Gods! We fool ourselves."

"Fools or not, we are something different now." Guis sat back in the throne. "The gates will not collapse, not for a while. There is enough Will left in those that remain. Enough to allow the gods to return."

"And if we might reestablish ourselves here, will not the Draathis attempt a resolution of their war? The World of Form comes closest next year. The last two occasions have seen them visit ruination on the Earth."

"They mass," said Guis. "Another shadow slipped into their world before my arrival here: a spy is in the world. The Draathis have anticipated this weakening. They will be able to use the gates, and will fall on this world with their full number. Not invasion, but migration. They see this world as their birthright."

"The people here are not ready for it," said the duke. "The Morfaan barely exiled them, their last incursion was a lesser thing. Both attacks destroyed civilisations."

Guis grinned. "I know, marvellous isn't it? There is a small place where the actual Guis Kressind clings on, buried deep in the extensive architecture of the human brain, an oubliette of the subconscious. He knows what I know, and grows frantic, howling and crying for release. The Draathis's hatred of the Morfaan and all their beasts is unbounded. They will exterminate and take their place as overlords of the worlds of Form and Will both. Mankind's tenure here is over."

"We should warn them. We will die without them," said the duke.

Guis pulled a disgusted face. "You have grown weak. Where is the cruel lord of hell I once knew? What is this that you do here, spanking girls? Ritualised cruelty you are desperate for them to enjoy? In ages gone you would have ravished them then torn them apart to feast upon their flesh before their dying eyes."

"I am not who I was. That was not what I wished to be."

"We are none of us how we wish to be. We are what we were made to be. Once the vermin are removed, we shall be free of the forms they pushed onto us. Do you not see, these people that you wish to defend are the ones who have made you? Hate them. Then you might return to purity of Will, and we may restore the creation gifted us. The Draathis will not stand before us."

The duke shook his head. "There is no return. We are tainted, changed as the twin worlds are changed. Form and Will cannot remain strangers forever, what has been altered cannot be put back. We are, as you say, what we are."

"Well then. You will not help them. That is the will of Omnus."

"And the Y Dvar of the other paths. What of them?"

Guis laughed. "Now to speak of slavery, look to them! Slaves of man and slaves to themselves. They will perish at the hands of their children. We are the ones who preserve the legacy of the creator. Within us alone remains the seed of his intent. Humanity should never have been brought here. They are weeds in a garden. Let the Draathis reap them. Once the Draathis are done, we shall expunge their taint. Then we might do away with the sorry developments of these last aeons, and set things aright."

"Why should others suffer," said the duke, "when it is the Y Dvar who are to blame for squandering the creator's gift?"

"You and I are no longer Y Dvar. That name means nothing." He leaned forward. "You and I are the servants of the gods of this world. War is coming, and our masters are returned for vengeance. You should remember whose side you are on."

Guis slipped out of the throne. "Well, it was so lovely to catch up with you. The last two hundred years have just flown by." He rubbed his hands together. "I must admit, I can see why you enjoy living here down among them. I intend to go out now and enjoy the flesh of this being a little more, before it and all like it are rendered into dust. I'll show myself out."

CHAPTER TWENTY-SIX

Lavinia

"U<small>P UP UP</small>! Get up you lazy little bastards! Come on! Work's waiting. Get up, get up get up!"

Desperately, Lavinia clung to the last shreds of her dreams, but they split and fled, skittish as ghosts, from the angry voice of the overseer. "Come on little Mohaci girl, get up!" Her bed shook as it was kicked. The woman was not cruel, but she was often tired, and short of time, and that made her angry and quick with her whip. Lavinia caressed the letter from Tuvacs she kept under her pillow. The paper had become smooth as velvet she had stroked it so many times. She could still make out the words, but they became fainter, and she tried to stop touching it, but there, in the dark, chilly dormitory of the Lemio Clothing and Shoddy Factory, it was a reminder that there was someone out there that loved her.

She grimaced as she put out her legs from under the thin blanket. Cold. That was how every day started, with the cold, and that was how it ended. She slept in her clothes at night, and it was still not enough. Her garments had become so ragged and dirty from constant wear she should have been ashamed of them, but the cold drove all that away. Shame had come to seem such a trifle in the face of the chill of the isles. She was never warm in Karsa. When the sun rarely shone it soothed the skin, but it did not dry the damp from her bones. Winter at home might have been hard, but summer was glorious, hot and dry with long days that lasted the night through. In Karsa City it rained. When it wasn't raining the sky was often dim with thick brown fog that burned her throat and made her eyes water. When the fog had gone they had all cheered. None of them got to enjoy the few days of sunlight that came afterwards.

She hated Karsa City. Sometimes she thought she hated Tuvacs for leaving her there. That frightened her. If she hated her brother, she had nothing left in all the world.

The children were subdued. They did not chatter or laugh. Overseer Agna did not take kindly to unnecessary noise. What sound there was had a smooth feeling to it, like she was underwater all the time. Noise did not stick in her ears. More and more she had to ask that people repeat themselves, although she dared not ask Agna because she would think her stupid. Frequently she misheard, and she thought Lavinia was stupid anyway. Lavinia's ears hurt whenever she went into the lower workshop, and because she was good at loading the rovings into the machines she was in there often. The pain afterwards lasted all night.

"Didn't you hear me, lazy little Mohaci? Get up!"

"Sorry goodwife Agna. I will be quicker," said Lavinia. She ducked her head respectfully, made herself small, doing nothing to set off the woman's temper.

"Hmm," she tapped her whip on her leg. "See to it you are. Time is money, and it costs keep you urchins fed."

A half-tun of freezing water was set out for the children to wash in. Many of them splashed on the least amount, but Lavinia took her time to wash herself properly. She only wished she could clean her clothes too. She had two dresses which she wore, one on top of the other, and only one pair of wool leggings. It was all too small for her. This last year she had grown a few inches, and her skirts were rising past her knees. When the director brought the orphanage's benefactors around there he lamented the lack of funds to buy better clothes. Promises were often given by the horrified goodfellows and their ladies. If the money arrived, the children gained nothing from it.

Two trestles were set out at the end of the room by the older children, well on their way to becoming as mean and empty as Agna. Others put wooden trays mounded with stale black bread on the board, and small, greasy bowls.

Someone tapped her shoulder; Marta, a girl not much older than Lavinia. Eleven or twelve perhaps.

"It's sunny!" said Marta.

"Sorry?" said Lavinia.

"Sunny!" said the other girl. Lavinia followed her pointing finger through the open doorway, to where the sun shone through the dirty glass of the bridge.

"Quiet back there!" shouted Agna.

Lavinia wanted to leave the line and stand in the light, let it warm her. But she dared not. She tried to stop her teeth from chattering. Boys behind the table slopped weak milk soup into the bowls. The food was unappetising, but the children ate it ravenously anyway. They slurped and gulped, gobbling their gruel down, watching each other shiftily in case someone attempted to take their ration. Sharp elbows jutted as they hunched over the soup, ribs showing in skinny chests. They would not eat again until nightfall.

They were taken downstairs to the picking floor. The children lined up for roll call in sorry lines, not one of them speaking. Agna read out the names of them all, despondent voices answered. After calling the name, Agna assigned the children a task.

"Gerrion," Agna said.

"Here."

"Picking floor," Agna said.

"Marta."

"Here."

"Carding floor," Agna said.

Lavinia hoped that she would not be sent down into the spinning room again. She closed her eyes and clenched her fists, trying to will the world to be the way she wanted it, like a mage. The stories Tuvacs and Tuparrillio had told them back in Mohacs had been magical, simple, populated by men and women who could change the world if they did not like it. Stories made sense of her life, and imbued their dreary existence as gleaners with wonder and hope. She was reluctant to remember the stories now. If being a gleaner had seemed hard, this was far worse. The stories reminded her of better times, and they lied. The truth was much harder than the stories promised. Often she wondered if this awful life was worth her journey to Karsa. The long trek across Ruthnia, the waiting in Macer Lesser for a train to smuggle themselves aboard, living in filth. People came from all over Ruthnia to the isles, drawn in by the new industries' rapacious appetite for labour. Her brother had seen a possibility of work, of safety from the criminals running the gleaning gangs in Mohacs-Gravo's filthy canyons. Like the stories, he had promised so much. Now she was alone, cold and hungry.

"Lavinia! Lavinia!" shouted Agna. Her voice sounded far away. Lavinia opened her eyes in time to see Agna draw back her hand and strike her across the cheek. A hot iron flavour filled her mouth.

"Are you here girl? Stop your daydreaming, there is work to be done!"

Lavinia swallowed a mouthful of blood. It made her feel sick. "Here goodwife."

"Speak up quicker next time! Time costs!" She picked up her clipboard from where it hung off her belt on a string, and ticked her name. "Spinning room," she said.

"Yes goodwife," said Lavinia miserably. She probed the front of her mouth with her tongue. Her teeth had bitten into the inside of her lip.

Goodwife Agna finished her reading of names and assigning of jobs. Lavinia struggled to hear her murmuring.

"To your work, all of you! You have to work harder, do you understand me?" Many of the children were immigrants to Karsa, and did not speak the language well. Goodwife Agna spoke to them all as if they were mentally deficient, loudly and slowly, aiding their understanding with the whip. "You are not productive enough. You cost Goodfellow Mroten Grostiman money. Work harder, or you will be on the street."

"Yes Goodwife Agna," the children chorused. The same threat, every day. Maybe it was true, maybe they would go onto the street. Lavinia was numb to it. Some of the children stayed on the picking floor, dragging rags out of the sacks by their benches before wearily taking their seats. The rest filed out in two silent, single lines. One line peeled off at the next floor, into the carding room. The final flight of stairs beckoned Lavinia. The treads rumbled under her feet as the machines started up, welcoming her in. She felt as if she were descending into the first of the hundred hells.

The noise of one machine alone was bearable. The rattle of bobbins on their spindles and the click-clack of the guiding arms was almost soothing, but dozens of them together became a torture. The rattling settled into the bones, engulfing the pounding of her heart. The trembling floor set up a pain in her joints, like a dozen tiny hammers chipped away at the knuckles. Below notice at first, but with persistence insufferable. When she left the room at night and the drive shafts span down, she could still hear the bobbins rattling, still feel the thrum of the machines in the soles of her feet and her legs.

Lavinia attended one of the spinners. An older boy named Karll watched the arms that stretched the rovings out and twisted them into thread, winding them finally onto the infernal bobbins. Lavinia's job was to watch the rovings as they unwound from broad spools. If they were not turned properly in the spooling room, they snagged. If they had not been picked from the card and rolled correctly, they broke. The rovings unwound, their thick twists shifting back and forth across their spools like long anguillons dancing in the water. They passed through pegged teeth on the weaving frame, and there they might also snag, or snag then break. Being made from unpicked cloth, the rovings were of poorer quality than fresh fibres, and snagging and breaking were common happenstances. If anything went wrong, then Lavinia must work quickly to set it right, or risk a beating come the evening. They were rarely hit during working hours, because it slowed production. The lashes the children were to receive at close of day were chalked up on a large board at the front of the room so that they might better anticipate them. Goodwife Anga stood close by the board, watching for infractions. They all dreaded the production of the chalk.

Lavinia watched the rovings unwind, sway sway sway sway. She jumped as a hand clasped her shoulder. Karll was saying something into her ear. She shook her head.

"Pettria is late with the spools!" he shouted as loudly as he could. He pointed to the rovings. The spools were almost empty. Pettria was supposed to deliver fresh from the spooling room every half hour for Lavinia to replace the empties, but she had not. "Go see where she is! I can watch both ends for three minutes. Go on!"

She nodded. First she must get permission from Goodwife Anga. She had to shout to make herself heard. Anga produced her chalk, and Lavinia's stomach flipped. The mark scratched down next to Pettria's name, and Anga waved her out.

The storeroom was off the second workshop on the ground floor. The spinning machines were old, water-powered devices adapted for steam. The roving twisters in the second workshop were ancient. A rope lift brought sacks of twisted roving down, children dragged them over to wood and iron spooling devices, operated by hand wheel. Fibres of cloth sparkled in the rays of light slanting in through a pair of dirty windows.

"Where's Pettria?" she asked. One of the others mimicked her voice. She never mastered languages as quickly as her brother, and spoke with an accent. She ignored the insult

"Through there," said Garristion, who was something of a leader among the children. He pointed off to the storeroom.

The storeroom was mercifully quiet after the noise of the weaving room. Spools were threaded onto poles slanting up from the walls. Pettria's hand truck was in the middle of the aisle between the two rows.

"Pettria? Pettria, where are you?" There was no reply. Thin passages lined with roving spools opened up off either side. "Pettria!" she said, becoming angry. "We're about to fall behind. Angry Anga is out to whip you. Pettria!" She became frightened, worried that she too would be beaten. She went to the end of the store, looking down every gap between the spool racks, but she could not see the other girl. "Pettria!"

She turned back, exasperated, to come face to face with Pettria's dirty face under her dirty hat. Older than her by four years, she was much taller, with a ropey strength in her arms.

"Shh!" she said. She clamped one hand over Lavinia's mouth and the other behind her head and pushed her between two racks. Lavinia flailed at Pettria, knocking the rovings swaying, but Pettria impelled her backwards, half lifting her from the ground, slamming her into the wall and winding her.

"Shh!" she said. "I've been watching you, Mohaci maid. You're beginning to flower, take on the pretty. Might find you a good man to take you away from all this. Be a shame if someone ruined that lovely face." There was a gap in Pettria's upper jaw lined with decaying teeth. Pettria's hands smelled bad, and her breath was feculent. "About time someone taught you the facts of life. I'm bigger than you. You give me what I want, or I will take it off you."

Lavinia shrieked into the dirty hand as Pettria pushed her head into the wall, pinning her.

"Shh, shh! There's another way. Another. Shhh! Don't say I ain't your friend. Listen! You give me half your ration in the morning, and I'll keep off you, even keep the others away. Especially the boys. They'll be a problem for one like you soon enough. Pretty's a curse in a place like this. I can protect you. That a deal?"

Lavinia shook her head emphatically.

"Bad choice, Mohaci maid. I'm going to hurt you." Pettria pinned Lavinia's head against the wall. She drew out a dagger made of glass cracked out of a window, the handle wrapped with stolen cloth, and held it up by Lavinia's face.

Tuparrillio had always warned her to be careful, back in Mohacs-Gravo. He had warned them all, but especially the girls.

"Or you could just give me your bread. Your choice."

Tuparrillio had done more than warn her. Her guardian had been a soldier, once, and he had shared his skills.

Lavinia bit hard into the edge of Pettria's palm, digging down until she tasted blood. Pettria screamed shrilly, tugging at her hand to get it from her teeth. Lavinia would not let go until Pettria banged her head hard on the stone. Lavinia saw stars, but her jaw slackened only a little. Pettria yanked her hand out, ripping the wound.

"You little bitch!" Pettra said, aiming the dagger at Lavinia's face. Lavinia ducked it, and Pettria's dagger shattered on the wall. Bending low, she raked at Pettria's face, scratching a furrow in her cheek, then barged the bigger girl with her shoulder. She was heavier than she, so she struggled her hand up to Pettria's face, clawed at her face to find her eye, and pressed hard with her thumb.

Pettria went down shrieking. Head spinning, Lavinia stepped over her and ran for the door. Garristion looked at her wide-eyed as she sprinted from the storeroom.

Karll gave her a questioning look as she returned to the weaving machine. Lavinia's look killed his curiosity dead. She shook her head and held up a finger to her lips, nodding meaningfully at Goodwife Anga. The rovings were nearly done. It the spools weren't swapped, there would be trouble for her regardless of what had happened. She waited for them to run out. Karll stopped the machine, and she set to unloading the empties in a daze, hoping that the spools would magically appear and save her.

She unhooked the last. Someone handed her a full replacement. She looked up. Pettria stood there with her cart, bruised and bloody, her weeping right eye covered over with a rag. Lavinia got the machine reloaded, Karll started it up again, and Pettria pushed her cart on.

Goodwife Anga chalked up three more marks next to Pettria's name.

So it went, day after day. Spring wore on. Lavinia's heart should have been gladdened by the return of the sun, of the warmth—such as it was in Karsa. Spring meant the lines between Karsa and the far east should be open. Spring should have brought her news from Tuvacs. Spring brought only despair. She grew skinnier as her insufficiently nourished body continued its struggle to turn her from girl to adult. She felt herself begin to fade as if she were passing from life into non-existence, so that it would be as if she had never been.

And then, one day, it stopped.

She was working the weaving machine, watching the hypnotic uncurling of the rovings sway and sway, when sudden light intruded into the dark world of the orphans. The large double doors at the far end of the weaving shed opened. A group of men came in. Several wore the tall hats and coats of the constabulary. One of them held up a sheet of paper before him. Other men and women, not police, came with blankets and kind words. One of the constables went to the master lever at the edge of the room and disengaged the gears of the drive shaft. The machines slowed, and stuttered to a stop.

"What are you doing? Explain yourselves!" said Goodwife Anga.

Another man that Lavinia had seen two or three times came forward. He was stooped, and had a hunted look about him. He wrung his hands over and over. "Shhh, Anga, shhh. There's nothing we can do."

The man with the paper walked down the aisle. "By the order of the Ministry of Justice, on behalf of Prince Alfra, lord regent of the Isles of Karsa, all production is to cease at the Lemio Clothing and Shoddy Factory immediately!"

"Why? What is happening? This is a charitable institution."

"This factory is closed upon charges of child exploitation and defiance of labour ordinance number eight hundred and four, signed in the year of 452 by the assembled prime ministers of the three houses."

"Goodman Grostiman," said Anga to the hunched man, "your cousin at the ministry, what..."

Grostiman silenced her with a look. "He signed the order himself. I've carts outside waiting. Get rid of them."

The constable watched the children being rounded up.

"You are to be taken from here," said one of the people. "Freedom awaits you."

"Why are you doing this?" said Anga. "Do you know how much it costs to keep these wretches? We are performing a public service!"

"I do not know," said the constable, rolling up his writ. "And I do not care. I put the law into action, I do not write it." He thrust a piece of paper at her. She looked at it questioningly.

"A warrant. You are not to leave the city. Prepare yourself, you will probably be arrested. Good day, goodwife."

"How can I be tried for past actions under a new law?" Agna demanded, but the constable ignored her.

Lavinia followed the others tentatively. The weak spring sunshine felt deliciously warm and unbearably bright. Kind men and women shepherded the children towards waiting carts. They were helped up and packed in tight, wrapped in new blankets. Someone gave her an apple. She looked at it stupidly. The colour was ridiculously red after the grey of the mill. Then the drays heaved, the cart pulled out. It was all over so quickly.

By the time the millgate was behind her, she realised she had left Tuvacs' letter behind. The apple rolled from her hand, and she burst into tears.

CHAPTER TWENTY-SEVEN
The Room of Hands

A HUGE HAND wrenched Madelyne out of bed, hauling her up by her hair.

Terror chased sleep from her.

"Your grace, what is happening? I—"

"Silence!" roared the Infernal Duke. "I will have my due for your lodgings."

He had changed, his eyes blazed coal red. His clothes were gone, his vaguely human form shed with it. He walked upon a goat's legs, his skin was deep red, and shimmered with heat. The fingers of his single hand circled her waist easily, and burned her. He shoved out of a door too small to encompass his divine bulk and stormed along the corridor. Fires burned in the carpet where his feet touched. He trailed his free hand along the wall, causing paintings, hangings and doors to burst in flame.

"Faithless creatures, all of you!" he growled. "I gave you the freedom of my house, and would have granted you that of my heart. Now I must punish you. Where you would have experienced pain to shrive your soul and bring you closer to the divine, now you will have it only to suffer."

"I have done nothing wrong!" screamed Madelyne. She swung from his wrist, arms burning with the effort of keeping the weight from the roots of her hair. Her eyes streamed from the smoke of the burning mansion. "Please, your grace!"

Somehow he could walk down the corridor, though he had grown far too large for it to accommodate his body. The mismatch between his dimensions and that of his home caused Madelyne's head to spin. Through the door and up the stairs he bounded, lighting the way with his fires of wrath. Beyond the walls the city went about its business ignorant of what went on within the duke's mansion. Hearing the sound of a carriage thundering by outside heightened Madelyne's terror, for it rooted her experience in the real world, as unreal as it seemed.

"No one can hear you. No one will come. You shall suffer for your impertinence."

"What have I done?"

"You are human. You are a woman," he said. "That is enough."

He kicked in the door to the second room upon the first floor. Like the Room of Dawning in shape, size and decoration, there were within no normal article of furniture, but a collection of devices from a torturer's lair. With his free hand he smashed a heavy wooden chair to flaming pieces and flung her to the floor. The door slammed behind them, untouched. Fire sprang up in the fireplace, roaring high with unbearable heat. The fire dogs glowed cherry red. Madelyne tried to rise, but the duke kicked her sprawling. Pinning her in place with a sharp hoof, he unlooped a chain from a hook in the wall, and lowered something from the ceiling. He reached down and lifted Madelyne by the head, swinging her into a collection of iron objects hanging from chains. She beat at his arms in panic, sure he meant to kill her, but he stunned her with a slap and tore her clothes off. They ignited and fell to ashes, leaving her naked in his iron grasp. He was as hard as stone, immovable as a tower.

"I have done all you said!" she screamed. "I have done nothing wrong!"

"You are a liar. Your motives are impure! You are as treacherous and evil as all your breed."

Heavy manacles snapped about her ankles and wrists, a belt about her waist. He swung a loop of metal up between her legs. She shrieked at this. He snapped it closed to the belt, locking all the restraints in place with heavy, oily padlocks, then locked her head upright with a heavy metal collar that engulfed her neck from collarbone to jaw. Now she was trapped, he unhooked the chains and hauled on them with one hand, lifting her up until she was level with his flaming eyes. Iron on her crotch, wrists and ankles bit into her uncomfortably.

"This is what you expected from me, and so this is what you shall receive," he said. The friezes around the tops of the walls writhed, the plaster figures trapped inside tormenting and assaulting one another. He took something from a wooden mannequin's head, some kind of mask, close fitting and made of pale leather. As he held it up, she screamed. In his hand was the skin of a woman, peeled from her flesh.

"Does this fit your prejudice? Is this what you know of me?" he said.

Madelyne's horror mounted as the features on the mask moved, the mouth gaping in a silent scream. The duke slipped the hood over her head, yanking the lace ties tight and tying them off. It blinked for her, its lips squirmed over her own, disgustingly intimate. He was aroused by all this and she shrieked again. If he meant to take her, she would die. She tugged futilely at her chains.

He walked around her.

"I admit I enjoy this," he said. "But it is my preference to explore these sensations with a willing partner. You could have trodden worlds of exquisite pleasure, but now you shall have only pain."

There was a rack of whips in full sight of her. With great deliberation, he selected one and walked around to her exposed back. She struggled, unable to move, dreading what was to come.

"Twelve lashes you will receive," he said. He swished the whip three times, each pass made her flinch, so that even when he struck her, it came as a surprise. "That was a taste. Let the twelve begin. Six for your humanity. Six for your womanhood."

Hot pain flared across her buttocks.

"I did nothing, please your grace!" she shouted.

"One," he said. "Two." Again he hit her, and she cried out. The second stripe overlay the first, then the third came, and the fourth, striking out a burning cross hatch on her buttocks and back. Her skin split, and blood ran down her back.

"Please!" she wailed, and began to cry.

"I do not care for your tears."

The mask's mouth closed over hers. The eyes shut, sealing themselves completely, and the leather constricted, clinging to her head so that it seemed to become one with her own skin, her face eyeless and voiceless. She threshed madly, the blows from the lash lessened in importance, for now she feared she would suffocate, but the nose of the flayed woman opened, and she drew in a panicked breath.

"Nine," said the duke. "Ten." With each hit, he put more of his strength into it. Her head buzzed with the pain, the constriction of her face was suffocating. "Eleven." He paused, swishing his whip one more time without impact, causing her to flinch. He laughed.

"Twelve," he said, and laid the whip across her shoulders so hard it wrapped around her chest and cut into the underside of her breast.

"Tonight you will be judged," he said. "I shall leave you with my many hands. If you live when I return, then I am in error, and I shall be sorry. But I am rarely wrong, Madelyne, so I shall bid you farewell now." He paused. "It is a shame, you were promising. I was growing fond of you."

He left her hanging, the choking mask wrapped around her face. She passed in and out of consciousness, before being woken by sibilant voices on the edge of hearing. They spoke to her, but she could not understand what they said. The words were elusive, and if she caught one, it seemed to change into an unfamiliar tongue that she could not understand.

The fire roared behind her. Sweat stung her cuts. Her back throbbed pain so intense it ceased to hurt and instead became stimulating, as if her senses had been so overloaded with hurt that her body registered only the sensation and not its quality. The iron strap bit into her inner thighs. Her hands went numb from lack of blood flow, and she tried to shift her weight to ease the load on them in turn, but succeeded only in provoking a storm of protest from her limbs. As the pain of her cuts subsided, that in her arms and thighs gew, pushing through the floor of her consciousness as a seed grows upwards, until it flowered with agony that dominated her thoughts.

She sobbed. Her tears had nowhere to go, trapped between the dead woman's skin and her own. The whispers grew louder. Something brushed past her. Madelyne jerked in shock, setting the chains rattling. The touch was cool, almost unpleasantly cold. An attempt to speak came out as a panicked, muffled nothing—her jaw was clamped shut by the mask.

"Is she a good choice?" hissed one voice.

"Let us see," said another.

"Death if she is not," said a third.

"Ecstasy if she is," said a fourth.

She felt cool hands all over her, and other things, ropey limbs and pulsing organs that caressed and prodded her. She struggled against them.

"Shhhh," they said. The invasion of her mind she anticipated did not come, or if performed was so subtle as to be unnoticeable.

"We see good things"

"She is untrustworthy," said another.

"Our lord is upset. He sees amiss. His anger is not the whore's fault."

"Taste her soul."

"I have. She does not lie," said the third. "She has done nothing wrong, not yet."

"Not about this. There are other lies inside her."

"Master says is she a good choice. This other lie he did not ask of. If he knows, if he doesn't, if he cares, is not our business!"

The others laughed chillingly.

"She has not seen inside his temple, it has not been profaned by mortal presence."

"She has obeyed his rules."

"Will she fulfil him?"

"Possibly."

"Ecstasy then," said the first voice.

The hands all pressed into her at once, and became insistent. Where they touched, the pain ceased to be painful, but became an unbearable pleasure. Alarmed, disgusted, she moaned in spite of herself. They lifted her, taking her weight. The chains clinked. The strap across her sex fell away. Strange limbs stroked and moved within her, opening her body with multi-jointed fingers. She gasped, deep in her throat, until that was invaded also, appalled at the warmth spreading up through the base of her stomach. The mask writhed with a delight of its own. Madelyne wanted to scream, to throw them off and flee, but she was held fast by the fetters and the hands of the duke's servants; her body was melting into a cocktail of extreme sensation, and her mind blurred into nothingness.

Again and again, they brought her to climax, more times than she could have thought possible. In the end a species of numb ecstasy overcame her, and she fell into the embrace of the hands listlessly, without demure.

When they had done, they took her down, unclipping the manacles and bearing her across the room so that she felt as if she floated. Only a little awareness was left to her. She had no idea that such a state could be induced through physical contact. She was glad that it was over.

The mask remained on. A collar was placed around her throat, a chain attached to it and she was laid upon the floor. A fur was draped over her, its soft hairs a hundred thousand petty blisses on her wounds.

Madelyne fell into a sleep the like of which she had never known.

When she woke the next morning, the mask had come off. She picked it up fearfully, sick at what she might see. No maiden's face or human skin greeted her, but a simple hood of kid leather, laced up the back, with open holes for eyes, mouth and nostrils. She felt a strange disorientation, before realising she had been moved into the Room of Dawning. As usual, Markos came in with clothes and unchained her. He tended to her whip cuts. They stung as he rubbed a salve into them, awakening her sex against her will, and she shifted uncomfortably, confused at this new reaction to pain. Markos kept his eyes from her nakedness as he worked, and left without a word, leaving the door unlocked.

Madelyne sat there in a pool of fur, sunlight warming her listless body. She felt exhausted, exhilarated, ashamed, violated.

She had never felt such an intensity of physical excitation. The duke had not lied to her, she had done nothing wrong and so she was spared. The punishment was nothing compared to the reward. She had lived her entire life to rules less severe than that.

There were plaster faces in the frieze among the roses today, innocuous and still. They smiled smugly down on her.

She shivered. What in all the hells was happening to her?

CHAPTER TWENTY-EIGHT
Ilona Discovered

A SHIP AT night is a kingdom of small sounds. Iron creaked and pinged with differences in temperature. Men's laughter from the common room swelled as the door was opened, cut off again when it clanged shut. The engines, powered down but never deactivated, sent their sighs out through the ribs of the double hull. A hammer banged three times, then stopped. A moment of silence in which Ilona imagined the wielder critically examining his work. Three more bangs came, then three more.

Ilona crept along the main corridor. Doors opened on each side. She hurried past a cabin door as it cracked open. Inside someone snored. She glanced in. Four bunks, two empty. An Ishmalan sprawled on the top of the occupied pair. Another settled himself back into a lower bunk to read by glimmerlight. He glanced up at Ilona's shadow dancing silently past. She ducked into an alcove holding firefighting equipment and held her breath. The man came to the door, looked down the corridor, shook his head and went back in. Her heart pounded. Quickly, she ran down toward the galley. She had removed her shoes to move quietly, and her feet were cold on the iron of the decks. How she had come to loathe the smell of iron, like the smell of cold blood. Her hair and hands were dirty with grease and black oxides. She supposed she must look a fright, and smell twice as bad. She had little energy to care about something so superficial as her appearance; she was hungry. She had to eat.

She gained the door of the galley without being seen only to find it tightly shut. A press of her ear against the door revealed little. Noises were conveyed from all over the ship by the metal. She hesitated over the lever that kept the door shut. Her thoughts returned to the large stocks of food in the holds, but she had no way to get into the barrels and crates there without betraying her presence. No one would notice a little pilfering from the galley. There was no choice.

The lever slid back and up easily, the motion sliding two horizontal bars out of their slots. A pull brought the door out smoothly, rubber seal smacking like lips. She stepped over the high lintel and into the galley.

She shivered at the sudden warmth, unbearably hot after the unheated aft hold. The galley was close to the engine room. A bank of pipes delivered heat to the room's ovens. Three long steel tables bolted to the floor took up most of the space. Pots and pans occupied racks, their handles hung on tall hooks, bellies held against the wall by tight netting. Two huge ranges filled one wall. A pair of doors to the left of Ilona, toward the stern, opened into a dry store and a cold room. She was in little mood for dry rice. She hankered for meat, for cheese, for something substantial. Tyn Rulsy seemed to think she should subsist entirely upon soup.

After so brief a moment of warmth, it made her miserable to step into the cold room. Trassan had adapted some other man's invention to refrigerate his stores. Rows of pipes covered in frost filled the ceiling. A liquid growling came from the walls. The air was sharp, the floor cold. She hopped from foot to foot to stop her toes burning.

A wide smile bloomed on her face. A barrel of salt meat was open in the room. A wheel of cheese sat on a table by it, its wax peeled invitingly back and a large slice removed, revealing creamy flesh within. A knife had even been provided for her!

She moaned with relief and fell upon the food, plunging her hand into the brine of the barrel and pulled out a large piece of meat. She bit into it and spat. The meat was wet cured, not cooked. Never mind, the cheese remained.

It had been her plan to steal food and make a swift getaway. All thoughts of retreat fled as she cut into the cheese. She nibbled a piece, then another, then cut a large wedge and stuffed it into her mouth. Her careful cuts became an undisciplined sawing and she gobbled it down in ragged slabs.

Whistling came from behind. The door opened. Ilona looked up, eyes wide with fear, her mouth crammed with cheese. A cook's boy stared at her as if he'd found a cockatrice in his lunchbox.

"Who the hells are you?" he managed.

Both their eyes strayed to the knife in her hand.

"I don't want no trouble!" he said, as panicked as her.

Ilona leapt and barged past him. She collided with a net of pans and sent them clattering. She recovered before the cook's boy mastered his surprise, was out the door and sprinting down the ship's corridor.

The boy emerged.

"Stop! Stop!" shouted the boy. "Stowaway! Stowaway! Stop!"

Doors opened. An Ishmalan put out his head only to draw it back in shock as a wild, filthy woman hurtled toward him, a knife in one hand and a large piece of cheese in the other. Others spilled out into the gangway. Many shouts joined the boys. A bell rang furiously.

She skidded around the corner that would take her into the stairwell. A blond man with a drooping moustache stepped into her path. He wore the light leather armour and uniform of a Karsan marine. As a girl she had constructed daydreams around such men, now he was a great danger to her. She sprang forward in a desperate knife thrust. The marine stepped out of the way of the blow with a surprised look on his face, and she slammed into the stairwell wall. He caught her knife hand with both of his, one on the wrist, the other wrapping round her fingers. He bent her hand back toward the top of her forearm, her fingers opened without her volition, and the knife dropped. With her wrist locked, he pushed up and back, upsetting her balance, and tipping her into his arms.

"Release me!" she screamed, kicking at her captor with her legs. He grappled with her. He was so much stronger, and forced his arm down onto her thighs.

"Get off!"

"Calm down!" he said. "I'm just trying to hold you still!"

Her captor relaxed his grip. She took the opportunity to tear a hand free and elbow him hard in the mouth. His teeth bit into her skin, hurting them both.

"Lost fucking gods, ow!" he yelled. He spat blood. She ducked out of his arms, but he grabbed her and pulled her back. There was no escape anyway. Below, above and back into the gangway there were men. They were variously frowning, laughing, goggling disbelief, nudging each other suggestively.

The man grabbed both her arms hard. "I'm not going to hurt you! What the hells do you take me for, woman?" He was offended, and pulled her roughly toward him. "I want you to stop kicking me! Hey, hey! Stop. You are going to hurt yourself, girlie."

"Never address me in that way again."

"Oh oh, now you play the goodlady. Driven gods!" He spotted a Maritime Regiment uniform in the crowd. "Forfeth, get me some bindings, she punches like a docker."

The gaggle of men laughed and whooped. Their smell was harsh in her nostrils.

"You best come with me," he said into her ear. His moustache tickled her and she cringed from it. "I'm an honourable man. Not all of them are."

"Take me to Trassan!" she said.

"Oh I will alright," said the man.

"I am his cousin!" she shouted.

The man's grip relaxed. "Ilona?"

"You know me?"

"I know your cousin Guis very well. We have met before, a long time ago." He looked her up and down. "You've grown."

She bared her teeth at him. "I'll tear your throat out if you lay a finger on me!"

"Hey there! I meant nothing by it. I am Bannord. Harimus Bannord Thriven of Donnelsey."

Ilona's face creased. "Harimus?"

"You can see why I go by Bannord."

Forfeth pushed his way through the men, a rope in his hand. "Here you are lieutenant."

"That won't be necessary," said Bannord. "Alright you men! Fun's over, back to your business."

The crowd dispersed slowly. Bannord shook his head at a couple of ill-favoured Ishmalani. They touched their top knots and went away.

"I remember you," she said. "You used to pull my hair."

Bannord manoeuvred her towards the stairs. "Did I? Sounds like the kind of thing I'd do. Sorry. You just bust my lip, so now we are even. Come on." He motioned for his man to open the door. Cold air blasted in.

"I can't go outside!" she said.

He looked at her feet. "For the love... Don't you have any shoes?"

SPREAD OVER THE table of the stateroom was a large map of the lower kingdoms, the Suveren sea, the Sorkosan peninsula and the Sotherwinter beyond its curling southernmost tip. A brass model of the *Prince Alfra* marked their current position, far from any land. Most of the features past Karsa's Final Isle had been recently pencilled in.

Trassan leaned on the table with both elbows, fingers tracing over a heavily annotated blueprint. Five others listened as he described the recent modifications.

"I've run heating pipes out of the ship, up the exterior of the funnel, and about the whistle. The heat will prevent the ice forming around the release pipes. I have endeavoured to take from the centre of the ship, away from the parts of the ship we use the most, but it will be colder."

Drentz the boatswain tapped the plans. "Without the heating pipes," he said. "it will be unbearable in the forward quarters."

"Unfortunate," said Heffi. "But they will just have to deal with it. Without heating, the release pipes will ice up and then we're going nowhere."

"The modifications are finished?" asked Antoninan.

"Yes, goodfellow," said Tyn Gelven, the head of the expedition's small band of Tyn. "They are completed. My iron whisperers are satisfied that the alterations are sound. We may depart when we wish."

"Tomorrow," said Trassan. "It must be tomorrow. We have wasted enough time here."

"That is good," said Antoninan. "We are outstaying our welcome. It has been made known to me that the Tatama are uneasy about Vols' presence here for so long."

The mage blinked uncomfortably.

"I do not know what to say," he said.

"Your ancestor's fault, not yours," said Trassan. "But the gods here are angry with you."

"Bannord would say you are a liability," said Volozeranetz.

Trassan made a noise in his throat. "Bannord isn't here. Antoninan, let them know we're going at first light. Now, as to where. After our conference with their magician, we were given some valuable insight. Heffi."

Trassan rolled up the blueprint and Heffi came forward. He ran his finger along the coastline of the continent of the Sotherwinter. Large parts of it were blank. Other sections were dotted, the high and low watermarks both covered in question marks. Where it was solid, someone had scrawled 'Ice or land?' next to the coast.

"Here," he said. "There is an entrance to the interior."

"How did you come by this knowledge?" asked Antoninan. "No one has stepped upon the continent and returned."

"Their Unshe is a breed of Guider. Through her, we learned that that is not the case," said Heffi. "Rassanaminul Haik's expedition made it to through the ice. They have been to the city."

Consternation and surprise murmured round the room.

"The stories of Verenetz?" asked Volozeranetz.

"Fabricated, in part. For what reason was not revealed to us," said Heffi.

"Servants of the One do not lie!" said Drentz.

"This information comes from a servant of the One," said Heffi. "They cannot both be correct."

"You deal in necromancy, against the teachings of the One," said Tolpoleznaen.

"Well, as I understand it," ventured Vols, "your religion does not expressly forbid the—"

Tolpoleznaen glared at him. Ardovani rested a hand on his shoulder. Vols shut his mouth.

"Listen to me, Tol. This way is the only way. Our planned route," Heffi's fingers moved along the paper to another isolated section of solid black coast, "takes us two hundred miles overland. This way is much shorter."

"Aye, a short route to death!" said Tolpoleznaen.

"This is madness," said Antoninan. "Your steersman has it right. The Sea Drays Bay is the only reliable landing point. We should head there as planned."

"But the survey, goodfellow!" said Heffi in exasperation.

"We will not know for sure until we sail there to see for ourselves. The ice may have shifted," said Antoninan.

"Goodmen, please!" said Trassan, sensing a full-blown argument. "It is not unusual to be informed by the spirits. As expedition leader I—"

The door swung open. Bannord came in.

"What happened to your face?" asked Trassan.

"This did," said Bannord. He beckoned and Forfeth pulled Ilona into the room.

"Ilona?" Trassan pushed round the crowded table to her, and took her gently by the shoulders.

Her face went from abashed to outraged in a second. "Don't you Ilona me!" she shouted, and kneed Trassan very hard in the balls.

Trassan collapsed with a pained sigh.

"For the driven gods' sake, goodlady!" exclaimed Bannord. "I thought you were calm!"

"You bastard! You complete bastard!" Ilona screamed at Trassan. "We had an agreement! You were going to take me with you! You left me behind with my crazy witch mother! She was going to marry me off! Marry me off! You gods damned selfish wanker!" She kicked him in the ribs. Trassan moaned.

"Hey, hey," said Bannord softly. He pulled her away from her cousin. Ilona's face wavered and she cried, more from fury than from sorrow.

"I've been locked in the hold for two months! Do you know what that was like?"

"To survive so long without detection is impressive," said Heffi. He touched his forehead. "The One watches over you." The other Ishmalani mirrored his gesture.

Trassan's hand slapped on the table. He heaved himself to his feet with a groan. "Stop smirking Bannord, this is a small disagreement between me and my dear—"

Ilona went for him again. Bannord yanked her back in the nick of time. Trassan flinched as her foot grazed the hand protecting his face.

"Please stop doing that," he said.

"I told you I'd kick you in the balls. And I have!"

"Indeed you have," said Heffi. "Well then. It seems we have a new crewmember. Tell me, do you have any skills you might offer our venture?"

Ilona frowned. "Skills? I—"

"Every man, and woman now I suppose, must pull their weight aboard a ship," said Heffi. "And I, as captain, must assign you a job. What can you do goodlady, other than booting your cousin very hard in his privates?" Heffi's men laughed.

"Do you see, Ilona?" said Trassan, riding the waves of pain throbbing out from his testicles. He felt sick. "I couldn't bring you with me."

"What? Because my entire life no one has thought to teach me anything but needlepoint and dressmaking? Because I'm a girl?"

"No, dear cousin. I—"

"Well I'm here now. You have a sailmaker, don't you?" said Ilona to Heffi. "He sews."

"It is not the kind of sewing you are accustomed to." Heffi said, uncomfortable that his attempt to patronise Ilona into submission was backfiring.

"Then teach me!" she rounded on Trassan again. "I will not be a burden. And you will regret doublecrossing me."

"It was for your own good!" protested Trassan.

"I shall decide what is for my own good and what is not!" she shouted.

"Where do we put her?" said Bannord.

"See, women on board ship are nothing but trouble. Now you need your own cabin," said Trassan.

"I have managed perfectly well in a freezing hold with a wooden pallet for a bed."

"You can always go back," said Trassan.

"I will move one of my people from the common room. We can make space for her there, and I will watch over her," said Tyn Gelven.

"Sleep with the Tyn?" said Ilona.

"Do you have a better idea?" said Trassan. "It is a good job you were uncovered when you were. A few hundred miles further south and you would have frozen to death."

Tyn Gelven gazed at her with large brown eyes. Ilona mastered her distaste. "Thank you goodtyn."

"Is the correct response!" said Heffi cheerfully. "Let's find the poor girl some clothes."

"We've spare parkas and cold weather gear in the stores," said Drentz. "I'll send for something."

"That settles that then," said Trassan. "Bannord, get her out of here. We've business to attend to, and it can't wait."

A knock sounded on the door jamb.

"For the love of all the driven gods, what is it now?" demanded Trassan.

Issiretz, the lookout, put his head into the room. "Forgive me goodfellow captain. There are lights on the horizon. Ship's lights. We're being followed."

"Persin," said Trassan.

THE SHORT NIGHT was nearly done. The moons were gone and the Twin was lowering itself below the eastern horizon. The sky behind its black bulk glowed with the promise of the sun. Drentz took Ilona away to kit her out for the cold, coaxing her to follow with promises of a warm bath. Trassan and Heffi trained their telescopes to the dark blue northern sky. Lights twinkled where sea met sky.

Trassan snapped his eyeglass shut. "Persin. It must be. We're being followed."

Heffi kept his trained on the horizon. "I count three, maybe four ships."

"His ships are faster than I feared," said Trassan. He cursed and performed a quick calculation. At the top of the wheelhouse they were fifty feet above the water. The maths was simple. Persin was only six miles away. "We're leaving. Now."

Heffi nodded. "All crew, prepare for immediate departure!"

The order emanated out from Heffi, through the first mariner, the second, the third, out to the heads of the teams under their command, then into the teams themselves. The ship erupted with action. "Antoninan, get a message to the Sorskians, thanking them for their hospitality."

Possessed by the urgency of the moment, for once Antoninan had little to say and hurried off to see it done.

"Bannord," said Trassan. "I am entrusting you with Ilona's safety."

"I have enough to handle without being your cousin's babysitter," said Bannord. "If Persin's got three ships, how many men will he have? I'm going to have my hands full keeping the marines sharp enough to take on twice their number. I don't need the distraction."

"I don't give a damn!" said Trassan, rounding on the bigger man. "I am the one paying you. Keep her safe!"

"If you insist." Bannord adjusted his sword belt.

Trassan calmed. "Persin will not attack us. He will seek to overtake us, to reach the city first. If we get there before him, then perhaps we need to worry about fighting. He and I can come to some arrangement."

"Fair enough."

"I do not think she needs much care," said Trassan. "She's assaulted both of us in one night. Perhaps you best capitalise on that." He squinted at the lights. They were drawing closer. Persin might have relied on floatstone for his ships, but he was getting more speed from them than most others could. "Teach her to fight."

"Are you serious?" said Bannord.

"If I get you to teach her some of the more masculine arts, perhaps it will blunt her fury at me," he said. "The women in my family! None of them seem content with their lot. She reads too many books."

"There is your sister, yes. Another frightening woman."

"To be frank, I blame Katriona for encouraging Ilona."

"Do you think Katriona helped her aboard?"

"I doubt it. She would think Ilona's actions the height of idiocy, she would prefer Ilona go to school and become a yellow band thinker. That's not Ilona's style. She'd rather go to war. But it'll be Katriona's example that has inspired my little cousin to take this course. Gods' shit! And I thought she was not present at the departure because she was angry with me."

"She is angry with you," pointed out Bannord. "So you want me to put a sword in the hand of a hot-tempered girl in order to wriggle your way back into her good graces? She kicked you in the balls not ten minutes ago. Had she a sword she'd likely have cut them off."

Trassan lowered his voice. The dark shapes of the crew went to and fro on the deck below, preparing the ship for departure. Steam wisped from the funnels, growing thicker by the second. Without the new glimmer engines, they would never build steam in time to evade Persin.

"She is the only human woman on a ship of two hundred men," he said. "There's more at stake here than me ingratiating myself."

Trassan glanced at the blue-tinged steam. The ship's main lights were out, but if Persin had not seen the *Prince Alfra* before, the flag of vapour lightening the night overhead would tell him exactly where it was.

"We need to get far ahead of him, or he'll follow our steam all the way to the Morfaan docks. I'm going below," he said, and left Bannord alone to watch Persin's expedition drawing closer.

"Marines!" Bannord shouted down to a pair of his men on the main deck. "Send out the order, to defensive positions." He raised his telescope to his eye. Persin's expedition focused into three individual vessels. "Just in case," he said to himself.

CHAPTER TWENTY-NINE

Further into the Sotherwinter

WITH PERSIN HARD on their tail, the *Prince Alfra* maintained full speed. Lookouts posted up the mast and at the prow kept watch for icebergs. Trassan confidently asserted that they were the only things that posed any danger to his ship, but Heffi was taking no chances, instructing his men to watch out for ice dragons and leviathans. Midsummer approached. The sun lingered long in the sky. During the brief nights they kept nervous eyes astern, searching for the smoke plumes and lights of Persin's expedition. They saw no sign of their rivals, and when Trassan was sure they had outpaced Persin, he ordered the ship's powerful glimmer lamps activated so that they might press on through the brief night. The weather grew colder. Ice thickened on the ship's structure.

Bannord was good to his word, and instructed Ilona on the use of the boarding cutlass. Seeing his charge take such delight in his lessons, Bannord grew enthused, and only partly because Ilona was such a very pretty girl. He taught her the rudiments of small sword fencing, sabre fighting, and shooting. She was a quick learner, and he found her sharp tongue entertaining. When the weather closed in, forcing them off the deck, he had part of the hold where Ilona had been hiding cleared so that they might fence there. The aft became something of a gathering place, where men off duty came to practise their swordsmanship and bet on the outcome of bouts. Despite the Ishmalani's reputation for pacifism and their holy book's ban on warfare, many of them were adept knife fighters, and from them Ilona received further instruction. Ardovani and Vols Iapetus attended often, Vols showing a wholly unexpected appreciation of fencing. His excitement at the more technical matches helped endear him to the crew.

All the while the engines of the *Prince Alfra* throbbed, steam turbines turning screw and wheel. For three weeks the ship headed south, entering waters few vessels had plied, and fewer had returned from. The sea became gelid and sluggish, covered from horizon to horizon in jostling plates of thin ice that the *Prince Alfra* smashed its way through. Icebergs became more common, and soon thicker patches of pack ice were forcing short detours that made Trassan swear and Heffi roll his eyes.

One rare fine day Bannord and Ilona fenced on deck. The skies were clear and a strong sunlight blazed from ice so dazzling white it appeared like no earthly substance. In the sun they were hot, though the day was frigid, and to spar they had removed their parkas, exercising in their felt undershirts. Ilona fought with a short broad sword, better balanced than the cutlasses the marines favoured, and a thin stiletto. They were real weapons, though the edges were protected by leather sparring covers. Bannord fought with but a smallsword, his arm out behind him for balance. Tyn Rulsy warmed her back on the warm middle funnel, eating dried fruit while she watched. She wore a cut down parka that made her look like a child from behind, unnerving when she turned her wizened Tyn face upon whoever challenged her.

"Adjust your stance a little," Bannord said as Ilona circled him. "Keep up your offhand. You want to be able to threaten with it one instant, make your opponent forget it the next. When he does, that's the time you can bury the knife up to the hilt in his ribs."

"Or her ribs," said Ilona.

Bannord smiled at her. "Sure."

"Perhaps when I get home, I will open a fencing school for women. There must be more like Kyreen Asteria in the world."

"I hear she's more man than woman," said Bannord.

"She is more than a man, I think," said Ilona. "Would you teach in my school when you leave the army?"

"As tempting as it is to face the sharp blades of women rather than their tongues, you must keep my name out of your plans, if you would goodlady," said Bannord. "My poor old man's heart is weak."

She let out a sharp laugh and leapt at him. Bannord parried her sword and the knife that followed. "Steady!" he said as the knife passed near his ribs. "Under the rebating cover that thing's properly sharp."

"Fight better then!" she taunted.

A cry went up from the lookout's nest. "Land ho!" Other voices passed the shout back along the ship. The whistles wailed triumphantly.

Bannord dropped his guard and craned his neck to see forward. Ilona swiped at him again. He sidestepped. Over balanced by her blow, Ilona fell over.

"Are we there already?" said Ilona as Bannord pulled her back to her feet.

"Let's go and see," Bannord said. They put their parkas back on, and went to the front of the ship, Rulsy trailing after them.

To the south the frequent teeth of icebergs merged into a white band that stretched out of sight. Black mountains crouched over the ice like a battleline sheltering behind shields.

Bannord cupped his hand around his mouth. "How far?" he called to the lookout.

"Twenty miles or more," came the lookout's reply, sharp as glass on the cold air.

Whistles blew and sailors ran about. The ship drew to a halt and Trassan, Heffi and Antoninan came out onto the wheelhouse balcony and began talking animatedly. Bannord and Ilona watched them until they went back inside. With a rush of steam, the ship's port wheel chopped into the water. Once more it began to move, turning so that it was parallel with the shoreline.

"Well then," said Bannord to Ilona, who was looking at the distant ice.

"Well what?" she said.

He slapped her backside with his blade.

"Ow!" she shouted.

"How dare you handle the goodlady so!" said Rulsy.

"I didn't slap your arse, Tyn," said Bannord. "If you want to stop me doing that, Ilona, you better get back to your lesson. Come on."

"Do we have to?" she said. "My arms ache."

"I've got nothing better to do, and neither do you. If you were in a battle, you might have to fight all day. Trust me, then your arms would hurt properly, and if they did you would be dead. As women are weaker than men, strength and stamina are areas of your training we have to work especially hard on. I need to muscle you up, my girl."

"I'm no one's girl," she said darkly. "Who'd let me fight in battle anyway?"

"Apart from the Pristians—who insist women are superior to men—the Fethrians who have no sex, and the Amaranth who make no distinction, there's the Sorskians, Ferroki, Marovese, Suverese and the rest of the southern kingdoms. So, nobody at all," he said. "But then, nobody at all let you on this ship or invited you on this expedition, and here you are, so I'd say there was a good chance of it wherever you are. Come on girl. Guard up!"

"And I thought you were against all this," said Ilona, readying her weapons.

"I am," said Bannord. "Giving women weapons is madness. Why do you think I don't live in any of those places?"

The hull of the iron ship squealed through broken pack ice. Trassan stood atop the wheel house, his eyeglass fixed to a mount on the railing he had cobbled together. Summer had done for the ice what no human agency could, shattering it to pieces. Long leads of bright blue water snaked their way between icebergs. On these, Trassan and his crew kept a nervous watch. They glided by on their way to the shore, glowering at the intruder to their domain, threatening to huddle in to one another and crush the ship between them.

Tolpoleznaen was a deft steersman and steered the ship past with inches to spare. That he could gauge the depth of water over the berg's hidden lower portions seemed miraculous to Trassan, but the ship never once touched them. An occasional piece of the ice pack stubbornly barred the *Prince Alfra*'s way. In those instances, Trassan shouted warnings down the speaking tube into the wheelhouse, but the ship passed through without incident, the ice shattering before the ship's strengthened bow.

Heffi came up the stair onto the wheelhouse roof. Cheeks ruddy with the cold gave him the appearance of some minor, jolly god of good fortune.

"The ship is performing well," said Heffi.

"And we've no icing on the whistle bells or inside the funnels," said Trassan.

Heffi made an equanimous gesture. Parts of the ship were almost unbearably cold now the heat had been rerouted. He was not going to bring that up again. "I was referring to our ice-parting capabilities."

"The *Alfra* has not been tested properly yet," said Trassan darkly. "These fragments are no more than four feet thick. By my reckoning the ice is five times thicker in winter and some thicker portions might survive as late as Gannever. I am unhappy with the build up around the paddlewheels and prow. That could slow us significantly. We are lucky that Persin's boats are even less well suited to this kind of sailing."

They drove on past another huge iceberg. In its bright shadow the temperature dropped. Heffi shivered. "There are more of these large bergs."

Trassan pointed ahead. "And more ahead. If they close in too far we will have to go around. How far is it to this double mountain?"

They looked over towards the shoreline, indivisible from the ice. The mountains were taller than they had appeared, blasted free of snow by wind coming from inland that carried long sheets of white from their summits in falling plumes. A gap in the mountains marked the bay they had originally intended to land at, but against the whole coastline the frozen sea was rucked up into jagged embankments.

"According to the last survey," said Trassan, "this wall of ice was not present."

"It is tidal, I'd guess," said Heffi. "Stacked by successive Great Tides."

Brown ravines gashed the wall. Huge overhangs hung on the point of collapse. There was no clear road through.

"Climbing that would be impossible," said Trassan.

"We should go no further toward land," said Heffi, "but sail back out to clearer water, and come inshore when closer. Sailing through this will impede us at best, risk the ship at worst."

"Antoninan wants to head for the shore," said Trassan.

"For what?" said Heffi. "To prove to Antoninan that his preferred landing site at Sea Drays Bay is inaccessible?"

"Life would be easier if he accepted my judgment without making all this fuss," said Trassan.

"This ice might have blocked the harbour the spirit told us of as well," said Heffi. "What then?"

"We shall deal with that when it comes to it," said Trassan.

"There might not be a way," said Heffi. "We should discuss the eventuality."

Trassan frowned. "There is always a way, Heffi. Always."

IN THE END, after much argument with Antoninan, Heffi and Trassan had their way. The *Prince Alfra* ran alongside the thickening maze of icebergs clustered about the Sotherwinter continent, and stuck to clearer water. The banging of ice from the hull became a constant. The men chipped at ice coating the ship, the ice in the ocean chipped back. Icebergs growled warnings at them. Eerie noises whooped and rumbled over the sea. Every night loud booms carried from afar would wake half the crew in fear that they had struck an obstacle.

Midsummer approached. Some vagary of the current during Gannever's White Moon tide cleared berg and pack ice away from the shore and allowed them closer to land for a while. The mountains intimidated them, their blue tongues drooping insolently from hanging valleys. Still the shore was hidden by ramparts of ice, and soon enough wide skirts of pack ice spread out again upon the ocean surface, this unbroken, and the *Prince Alfra* was forced further away. This was finally enough to satisfy Antoninan, and they sailed onward for the docks the spirit told them of without further debate.

When the double mountain they sought came into view they seemed small and unimpressive. Heffi checked and double checked their position again, finally declaring them to be the correct peaks, made tiny by distance.

Once more, the prow of the ship was set towards the Sotherwinter continent.

CHAPTER THIRTY
A Secret Deeply Buried

UPON THE FINAL Isle Aarin did not dream. Oblivion awaited him when he slept, and he rose every morning unrefreshed. He came to dread retiring to the damp cell he and Pasquanty shared upon the ground floor of the monastery. Without windows or fireplace, the walls were constantly damp, the lines between the stones picked out by spongy mosses that glowed eerily when the candle was out. At the highest tides the waves boomed against the foot of the mount, not far from the walls. Being awake in the cell was oppressive, sleeping worse. To rest there was to sink beneath the dark waves.

"Is this how the drowned feel?" Pasquanty said every few days. The deacon became pale, his eyes bloodshot and red rimmed, crusted with an unhealthy scurf. Aarin was irritable.

They spent their days pacing the chilly cloisters, or atop the windy tower. Twice Aarin attempted to climb the knoll of the island, twice he was driven back by freezing, horizontal rain. Despite the season, the sun paid only fleeting visits to the Final Isle. From the summit of the tower blue fringed the horizon, but never made it to the island. It wore a shroud of clouds as if in protracted mourning, and the temperature never rose beyond the norms of early spring, although they were approaching the beginning of summer. Aarin could not imagine being warm again. At the times his patience was thinnest, he would go to the prior's steward's office and ask to know when the prior would see them.

The steward never looked up from his piles of ledgers. He did not stop writing. He was not bound by the monks' oaths of silence, but would always say just one word, and would not be drawn to speak again. "Soon," was all he would say.

So it went on for weeks. Even at the times they were permitted to speak the monks of the island had little to say to Pasquanty and Aarin or each other. The Guiders ate with the monks in their refectory—it was a small mercy that the food, culled from the sea, was hearty, if repetitive. Only at mealtimes did the monks pull down their black hoods to reveal faces trapped in black wrappings. Their necks and heads were hidden, the black bandages covering even their foreheads. The severity of the monks' dress robbed them of individuality, making all save the most extreme of their features unmemorable. After weeks on the island, Aarin only recognised a handful of their faces and had come to identify them by their gait, habits and size—the limping monk, the fat monk, the hurried monk, the slow monk, and so forth. He rarely matched a face to these characteristics.

Following mealtimes the priests of the island withdrew to the north wing of the building, where they remained until well into the short night. Candles shone in the barred windows. A persistent tapping of chisels could sometimes be heard. Aarin knew nothing else of their work, and for most of the day he and Pasquanty were left alone. Boredom set in, loneliness followed close on its heels. Sleep was always elusive, and unpleasant.

Their routine appeared the beginning of a dull eternity, until one night a loud knocking upon the door dragged Aarin back from his nightly struggle against the dark.

Pasquanty rasped a flint and iron together, setting alight a wad of fire cotton and lifting it to their candles. Made of sea dragon tallow, they gave off a fishy odour that permeated every room of the monastery.

The banging continued at the same rhythm.

"Who is it?" mumbled Aarin. He swung his legs out of the bed, clenching his jaw as bare feet hit the freezing floor.

"I will see, master," said Pasquanty. He left his bed, candle shielded by his hand. "Who is there?" he said, not a little tremulously.

"I have come from Prior Seutreneause," said an emotionless voice. "He will see you now." The knocking stopped. There was no lock upon the door, but the monk did not attempt to enter. "Bring your dead charge."

The news banished Aarin's tiredness. "Quickly Pasquanty!" he said, clambering from his bed. "We must be quick! Finally, we are to have answers!"

Pasquanty helped Aarin dress as fast as he could. For his meeting with the Prior, Aarin put on his Guider's robes, not the demi-habit the monks had given him. Aarin drank a glass of water, dashed more on his face and yanked wide the door. There was no one there.

"By the dead!" said Aarin. "He's gone. Quick! We must not miss our chance. Get Mother Moude, get the box!"

Pasquanty thrust the candle at Aarin, and dragged Mother Moude's heavy, iron-bound chest out of the corner of their room.

Aarin fairly ran through the dark monastery, Pasquanty lagged behind with the chest.

Not knowing where to go, Aarin headed to the doorway to the north wing of the monastery. Always locked before, he found it hanging wide. He hesitated, started forward, then turned back. "Pasquanty! Get a move on!"

"Coming master!" called the deacon. Pasquanty caught up, straining at the effort. Aarin looked through the door. Candlelight shone from around the corner. He blew his own tallow out and set it down in on a shelf.

"Let me take a handle."

Pasquanty set the box down. The two of them lifted it again.

"Thank you Guider Aarin," said Pasquanty.

"I do not think we need to hurry," Aarin said. He moved forward, Pasquanty shuffling awkwardly on the other end of the chest. The door opened onto a small vestibule. A second door was situated in the wall at right angles to the first, also open. From beyond came the yellow glow of candles and the sound of pens on paper. The tap of chisels on stone rang at the edge of hearing.

About half the monastery's complement sat in rows at high, angled desks, writing on sheets of vellum. The pages were richly decorated, the characters they wrote in the centre of each too small to be made out without a lens. Aarin looked about questioningly, but the monks ignored the two Guiders.

"Where is the prior's office?" he asked eventually.

A single monk turned to regard them, his face floating like a ghost in the centre of his hood. The monk raised a finger and pointed to a door, almost invisible in an unlit corner of the hall. Aarin and Pasquanty hurried to it.

The door was of a single panel of closely fitted planks, deeply carved with an image of the Dead God gazing balefully from his cross. There was a huge lock, but its deadbolt was withdrawn from the iron staple in the frame, and the door pushed open at the slightest touch.

A stairwell descended into the earth. A strong draft slightly warmer than the air in the monks' hall blew from below. The sound of tapping grew louder.

"Come on," said Aarin.

"Yes Guider," said Pasquanty in a small voice.

The stair spiralled down around a central pillar carved from the living stone of the island. The steps were slippery, the light from the infrequent candles inadequate.

"What is that tapping?" panted Pasquanty. The steepness of the steps forced him to bend uncomfortably over, his hands almost between his knees. The weight of Mother Moude's box pulled on Pasquanty's shoulders, the forward edge of it dug into Aarin's arms.

"Chisels," said Aarin.

The stair emerged through an archway that looked like it had been built for a larger staircase. Rich carvings of the Dead God in his many guises wound their way up freestanding pillars to an arch that joined with the stone of the island's roots. The Guiders passed under into a vault, very long, carved directly from the stone and lit by smokeless firebowls whose light was directed onto the walls and curved ceiling by polished bronze reflectors. This illumination was so strong it was easy to see that the stone was covered in tiny script. A scaffolding bridged the vault two thirds of the way down. Two open-sided towers with many floors allowed access to the walls. A long walkway joining them gave access to the ceiling. Men worked all over the scaffolding, chiselling at the walls or lying on their backs, carving the script into the ceiling above them. From the far end, where the vault receded into darkness, the draft came, stronger now and carrying a hint of decay.

To their right was a solitary door set into an arch as richly decorated as the entrance to the vault.

"This way, Pasquanty," Aarin said. The crossed a floor buffed to a high shine. A few feet away from the wall the script became legible. It was proved to be name after name, letters as big as a child's fingernail crammed close together in lines equally miserly spaced. A lozenge between each name divided them, otherwise they were so tightly written the names would have run into one another. Without this, Aarin doubted he would have recognised them so quickly for what they were. The majority were Karsan.

"What is this?" said Pasquanty.

"A list of the dead, I would guess," said Aarin. He bade Pasquanty set the chest down. He ran his hand over the letters.

A cough brought his attention to the door. It had opened without his noticing, and a monk stood there. He wore white, his hood was down and his head was unwrapped. Unlike every other inhabitant of the isle, he had a warm expression. "This way, Guider Aarin," he said. "Leave your charge, we shall collect her upon our return."

They followed the monk into a hallway lined with statues. A sole, sweet-scented candle burned between the feet of each. "The former priors of the Final Isle," the monk explained. Aarin counted thirty. Empty plinths continued where the statues stopped, awaiting future occupants.

"This must be an ancient place," said Pasquanty.

"It is," said Aarin. "These statues represent hundreds of years of leadership going back beyond the formation of The Hundred, to the time of King Brannon."

"They do," said the monk. "There have been members of our order here since before the Isles were settled."

"Are we under the sea? This vault and hall extend past the limits of the isle's mound."

"You have your father's capacity for practical observation," said the monk approvingly. "But you are not under the ocean. You are beyond it."

The monk had said more words during this short conversation than all the others had throughout their stay on the isle. Questions jockeyed with one another in Aarin's mind, tripping over each other in the race to get to his tongue and snarling it in the process. He stuttered, began asking one thing then switched to another. "Beyond? Metaphysically?"

"We are the wardens of death," said the monk serenely.

"How, do you have mages? Why is this not more widely known within the order?" he asked. Pasquanty huddled close to his back. For once, Aarin did no rebuke him for his timidity.

"In good time. You have been judged worthy, Guider Aarin Kressind. All will be revealed to you shortly."

"The names on the wall, what does they mean?"

They came to a door covered in bronze, graven with dozens of representations of the Dead God, all with the same dolorous face.

"All will be revealed in good time," said the monk. He opened the door. "Enter. The prior will see you now."

The prior's office was well appointed, surprising Aarin after the austerity of the rest of the monastery. Thick carpet muffled their footsteps. Books lined the walls. A large fireplace made the room the warmest he had yet encountered on the isle. A nest of sofas circled the fire. At the far end was a large desk, the four legs carved with the Dead God, his staring, miserable face prominent. Behind the desk sat the prior. He had a sheaf of papers arrayed before him, but his pen was in its pot, and he watched them over laced fingers.

"Prior Seutreneause!" said Aarin. He strode down the length of the office, leaving the timorous Pasquanty behind.

"Guider Aarin," said Seutreneause. He opened one long hand and gestured to a chair set facing his desk. "Sit."

Aarin went to the chair and sat. After so long in the cold of the monastery he felt ridiculously hot, although the room could not have been any more than comfortably heated. His impatience chafed at him. "Prior—"

The prior held up a finger for silence.

"You too, deacon. Come sit before me. This concerns you also." Seutreneause was of Macer Lesser, and spoke Maceriyan in the idiosyncratic manner of that land.

Pasquanty came forward, his nervous eyes darting around the study, his larynx bobbing in his throat.

The prior considered them. "Guider Triesko recommended you to us, Guider Aarin."

"He told me to come here," said Aarin, doing his best to rein in his impatience. "To bring Mother Moude with me."

"Do you know why?"

"I went to him for help. The dead I guide have become erratic. Fewer ghostings are required, but those spirits that need help do not go easily. I wished to know if this were normal. My attempts to speak with other notable Guiders came to nothing. My readings in the libraries of our order brought me no answers. To be frank, I did not wish to trouble Triesko with this knowledge, and waited until I had exhausted other lines of inquiry before approaching him."

"I see. Why?" asked the prior.

"He was good to me when I was his deacon."

"That is not all."

"I was concerned he would report me for my use of Mother Moude," admitted Aarin. "She was put into my keeping, I assume to keep her from less trustworthy hands. But I used her. I was the one who was not to be trusted."

"You were supposed to use her," said the prior.

"So Guider Triesko told me," said Aarin irritably. "I am sorry prior, we have waited here for a very long time. Triesko told me nothing, other than to imply that I did right in doing wrong. Why was I sent here? Why have we been kept waiting?"

The prior reached out to rest his hand on a large paperweight. Preserved inside the glass was the skeleton of an anguillon elver, no bigger than a finger. "You are aware of the dwindling of the Dead God's quarter?"

Aarin shrugged. "What of it? The number of fourth sons sent into our service grows less every year, so I have been told by the Master of Inductions. These are irreligious times. Once we were priests, but they are not popular. There is no god to minister for. Only the necessity of our calling stopped our order collapsing as the churches of the other gods did after the Driving. I am not surprised fewer are attracted to the role. It is a lonely vocation, funding is not what it was and we are not as respected. The world has changed."

"The quantity of the quarter is less than it was, but so is the quality," said the prior. "Traditionally, the fourth sons of mage-tainted families have always had the gift of communion with the dead, whether the talent for magic showed itself in their generation or not. Once, the third brothers of the greatest mages were powerful wielders of magic in their own right. Now there are few mages, and few fourth sons with the Guider's gift."

"The magisterial colleges attract them," said Aarin. "It is a matter of custom, surely?"

The prior shook his head. "Not only custom. The mage taint weakens, many families have lost their touch altogether, and those who are gifted are rarely capable of becoming true mages. Res Iapetus was the greatest of his kind, but also one of the last."

Pasquanty interrupted. "Is it some punishment of the gods for their banishment?"

Aarin frowned at him.

The prior gave a reptilian smile. "The gods are not in any position to punish anyone. I shall be frank with you both. The very nature of magic is altering, fundamentally. That is why the dead fade away or do not go easily. Those souls that are strong-willed enough to manifest will not be commanded, because we do not have the strength to command them. Those souls that do not manifest after death cannot gather the power to make themselves appear. The fences of the dead become higher, their realm is withdrawing from ours. Look into the realm of death, and you will see no way through. The gates of death are closing."

"How do you expect me to believe that magic is leaving the Earth?" said Aarin. "The streets are full of machines powered by metaphysical engines."

"But what he says is true," said Pasquanty.

"Be quiet!" snapped Aarin.

"If you expected answers from me, you will be disappointed. I have performed my own investigations," said the prior. "All we of the inner chamber have. We are not alone in noticing this dwindling. Alas the magisters that speak up on the matter are silenced by the vested interests of their own colleges; the Lord Magisters would cast the triumph of the magisterial way of magic as proof of its superiority rather than it being a consequence of magic's weakening efficacy. Others are too removed from the art to see anything amiss. Their devices work. The magisters ply their trade. The bereaved take the lack of ghosts as a sign of a peaceful departure. The world continues to turn."

"Triesko did tell me one thing," said Aarin. "He hinted to me that there were more than two gods still abroad in the world."

Seutreneause shook his head in disappointment. "He was premature in telling you this, but what harm is there in it now?"

"The god of death?" guessed Aarin. Seutreneause gave the slightest nod. "He was not driven out by Iapetus?" said Aarin.

"He lives here, in this world between worlds, under the Final Isle."

"Then, if the god of the dead is still among his servants, why do you not speak with him?"

"We have tried. We have failed."

"Then why have I been sent here?"

"Can you not see?" said Seutreneause. "Through your mother your family carries the mage taint. Your talent as a Guider is unsurpassed in the current generation. You were sent here to speak with Tallimastus. You were sent here not to receive answers, but to provide them." The prior picked up a small silver bell and rang it.

"I'm sorry?" said Aarin.

"Come," the prior said. "There is no time like the present. With a little luck, soon all our questions will be answered."

Not knowing what else to do, Aarin allowed Seutreneause to lead them out of his chambers and into the vault. Three monks waited there, two already carrying Mother Moude's chest. The group walked toward the dark end of the hall, under the scaffolding. The scent of decay intensified there. The workers tapping mechanically away were not men, but animates, dead whose ghosts had been trapped within their corpses. All of them wore the black habits of the monks.

"This work was done in ancient times," said Seutreneause. "The names are the names of all the dead of Karsa, each carved with precisely four hundred and forty four strikes of the chisel."

"It is a form of binding?" said Aarin.

Seutreneause nodded. "You are very astute. With so many ghosts failing to manifest for their departure we cannot be sure of their fate. Old doctrine tells us they make their own way to the other side. But there are so few now, there are among us those who fear they dissipate, and find no rest."

"That's... terrible!" said Pasquanty.

"And must remain secret," said Seutreneause with a stern look. "The nature of the afterlife has always been shrouded to all but the most powerful mages and Guiders, and accounts of journeys there are garbled. Some suggest it to be a terrible place, but it is a place. Imagine then if the populace suspected there was nothing after death. Soldiers would refuse to fight. No man would take any risk. Others might throw off the shackles of civilised society in their despair, and let run their animal urges in a riot of indulgence. These things cannot become common knowledge."

"I swear, prior, I shall never speak of it!" said Pasquanty in terror.

"You are preserving their souls," said Aarin.

"By binding them in a small way to the mortal realm, we might give them time to persist, until the crisis is passed and the gates of the dead open again."

Aarin looked up at the dead men working the walls.

"And you keep your own safe in their shells."

"We have done so for one hundred and fifty years."

"It has been going on that long?" said Aarin, shocked.

"Longer, since the time of the Driving," said the prior. "You are far from the first to notice. Since Res Iapetus's time, over four million men and women of Karsa have passed on. The population increases, our work becomes a heavier burden."

"Why only Karsa?" said Aarin. "You are of Macer Lesser. What of your own people?"

"We cannot save them all," said the prior. "This place was founded by a Karsan, it is funded by the Ministry of Death."

"They know?" said Aarin.

"Naturally," said the prior. "You are percipient to have noticed what few have, but I did say you were not the first."

"Who built this place?" asked Aarin.

"Ah, here we are," said the prior, evading his question. They reached the far end of the vault, well out of the light illuminating the scaffolds. A yett was set into the wall. The prior took out a key of bone on a bright red cord. It squeaked loudly in the lock. His hand came away red with flakes of rust.

"Down we go," said the prior.

Aarin paused upon the threshold. The air was noisome.

"Do you wish to find the answers you sought, or are you going to abandon your quest at this late hour?" asked the prior.

Aarin looked behind him. The monks crowded he and Pasquanty, blocking the way back. Pasquanty pleaded with his eyes that they leave. Aarin shook his head slightly, and looked back into the pit.

"Lead on," said Aarin.

The prior went first, taking one of many lanterns hanging from greened bronze hooks and striking it alight with a flint and steel wrapped in oil cloth on a shelf beneath. Aarin bade Pasquanty do the same, so the deacon took up a second lantern. He himself kept his hands free. The lead of the three monks took a lantern to light the way for those carrying Mother Moude. Together they went down a short tunnel cut into the stone of a place far from the world.

The tunnel opened out in the face of a cliff comprised of white rock columns shot through with gleaming veins of glimmer. The far side—if there were one—was invisible. Stairs unguarded by rail or line cut down across the rock formations at a steep angle. Either the work was poor, or the rock was rotten, for the steps were uneven. Each was a crumbling invitation to trip, while overhead the upper part of the sheared columns were poised like pistons ready to thump down. They kept to the wall. Aarin put out his hand. The rock was chill and slick as butcher's fat and his fingers came away greasy.

"Careful here," said the prior unnecessarily. Pasquanty whimpered.

The stairway angled downward in a straight line, taking them far out from where the island would have stopped. The stone was like nothing Aarin had seen on the surface. He could not believe the sea to be above them. The prior had not lied, the caverns were buried in no earthly soil. The void ate up the sounds of their descent, the clink of chains on Mother Moude's chest, their breath, the slap and gritty slide of sandals on the steps. Though the rock was running with moisture, there was no drip of water, nor any sound of wind from the unvarying, foul-smelling drafts blowing upwards. The presence of the monks was an imposition on the void's unnatural stillness. A building sense of anger emanated from the dark.

The stairs eventually ended, as all things must. A broad platform of pitted paving slabs held up by iron girders jutted into the void from a small room scraped back into the cliff. The stairs stopped a little way beyond, odd marks still in the stone, as if whoever had made the stairway had intended to go further, but had turned back.

Three slender piers of stone extended further into the dark from the platform's edge. Rusted iron rings were sunk into the very ends. To these, the prior pointed.

"Set Mother Moude on the central pier. Deacon, you must go to the left, Guider, to the right."

"No. This is not right. We will go back," said Aarin, wary of the prior's intentions.

"Oh thank you!" whispered Pasquanty.

"You must," said the prior.

Aarin backed away. A dagger tip in the small of his back halted him. A gentle prod informed him of its deadly sharpness, the point pushed through his clothes and pricked at his skin. Pasquanty looked on, the little lantern bathing his aghast face in yellow light. He looked so like a character from a badly acted melodrama, Aarin would have laughed in other circumstances. The two men carrying Mother Moude had their free hands inside their habits, ready to draw their own daggers. Had Pasquanty been a different man, Aarin supposed, he might have smashed one in the face with his lantern, while he could step round quickly and disarm his captor, and so might they have effected escape. While Aarin considered his course of action, Pasquanty froze. If Aarin acted alone, he would die.

"To the piers, please," said the prior. "If you do as we ask, you will survive this, Aarin. Triesko had every faith in you."

"I trusted him," said Aarin, rocked by betrayal.

"You were right to. He did not send you here to die. You are our hope, Aarin, not a sacrificial lamb. Now give us the keys to Mother Moude's chest."

Aarin took out the necklace from his robes and held them up. The monks set Mother Moude down. One came forward and yanked the chain from his neck.

Another prod in the back inched Aarin forward. Pasquanty was shepherded onto the leftmost pier by nothing sharper than a hard look. He trembled so much he was in danger of falling, his eyes closed against the endless drop. Aarin stared ahead, and took his place calmly. The pair of monks stayed behind them on the platform, daggers drawn.

The last of the prior's servants placed Mother Moude's chest onto the middle pier and shoved it out. The rasp of metal and wood on stone broke the silence, and the sense of intrusion grew heavier. The monk balanced the chest carefully, unlocked it, and opened it wide, exposing Mother Moude's bones and her chain inside. He looked to the prior, who nodded to him. The monk opened his robe and unhooked a heavy steel hatchet from a belt inside.

Pasquanty looked at Aarin helplessly.

"Call her forth," said the prior. "The Dead God requires a sacrifice. You shall not pass without one. A dead soul for the Dead God."

Aarin looked at the sorry collection of brown bones. He had always meant to find a way to free Mother Moude. Her enslavement was unjust, punishment meted out in a less enlightened age. He had always held back for fear of what havoc she might cause. He wished he had been braver.

"Do it!" said the prior. "If you do not, you are of no use to us and you must perish for what you know."

"Please Guider," whimpered Pasquanty. As much as the deacon irritated him, in that moment Aarin felt sorry for not being kinder to him too.

"Mother Moude," he said quietly.

She did not stir.

"Louder!" hissed the prior.

"Mother Moude!" Aarin shouted.

At the second call the witch's ghost shot out of the chest. She wore her youthful form, naked and voluptuous. The hook on the end of the chain pierced ethereal flesh that bled smoking blood. Before she reached its fullest extent, the monk swung his bronze hatchet, smashing the chain, and Mother Moudee soared high. She shrieked in joy, looping around and around, the chain snapping after her like the tail of a kite.

"Free! Free!" she shouted. "I am free!" She came to a halt a short way out from the stone piers. "No chains, Guider Aarin? No chains?" She stared down at him triumphantly.

"I set you free, as you have asked me to do so many times," he said quietly.

"And you will regret it. Do you think I shall go gratefully to the far lands? Do you think I shall grovellingly accept your mercy and lift the veil, ducking under and away with nary a whimper? You are wrong, wrong! You shall face my anger!" she shouted. "Four hundred years have I languished in that box, imprisoned, used, my life and afterlife taken from me. Such torment will I visit on you, the last of my captors! I will haunt you to the end of your days. All you love shall perish by my hand!"

"I am sorry," said Aarin. Tears welled from his good eye and ran down his cheek.

"Oh Tallimastus!" intoned the prior. "Accept this gift of the dead. Open the way for the living!"

The wind from below blew stronger. Mother Moude dropped a foot. Alarmed, she looked about her. "What is this place?"

"I am sorry," said Aarin again.

A groan resounded from the void. A voice moaned upon the wind. "The first lock is open."

Aarin had seen terror on the face of the dead before. It was his duty to ease it, to help them from this world to the next. The Guiders of his day might hide the holiness of their calling and name it a moral duty, but it was and always would be a sacred one. There was nothing he could do for Moude. She reached out her arms.

"Please!" she said. "Please!"

With a piercing scream, she was yanked away from sight. A phosphor trail danced in the black and was swept away. The wind blasted strongly, rocking Aarin back on his heels.

"Now the second gate," said the prior.

The monk guarding Pasquanty's pier strode up behind him and cut his throat with a swift, clean movement. Pasquanty's hands shot up to his neck, arterial spray jetting between his clutching fingers.

"Pasquanty!" shouted Aarin.

Aarin's cry was cut short. A noose of red rope was placed around his neck and drawn tight. He grabbed at it but it would not shift. He turned around. A monk held grimly onto the knot. He reached for the monk holding the noose, grappling with his arms, but the man had been chosen for his strength and reach and would not release the rope.

As Aarin choked, Pasquanty gurgled horribly, eyes wide with fear. He reached out for Aarin with one hand, blood bubbling between the fingers of the other. The monk who cut him put his foot on Pasquanty's backside and shoved him off into the dark.

"Oh Tallimastus!" shouted the prior. "Accept this gift of the living, open the way for the dead!"

The wind roared again, reeking of corpse gas. The other two monks joined their comrade and took up the end of the rope around Aarin's neck.

"The second lock is open. The gate is wide. You may pass," said the voice.

"To meet with the god of death, one must die," said the prior. "You have one unliving eye," the prior said to Aarin. "Look through that, and come back to us."

They pushed him from the edge then. Feared that his neck would snap he grabbed for the rope above the slipknot, but they kept the rope short. He fell only a foot, banging his shins on the stone. He lifted his legs, his feet scrabbled at the pier but were kicked away, and they lowered him down until all he could see was the abyss stretching infinitely down. His muscles burned with the effort of holding the rope slack. Tears blurred the sight of his good eye.

For five minutes he hung on to the rope, keeping his own weight from his neck. He tried to cry out, to beg to be lifted back, but all that emerged was a strangled gasp. His feet kicked. He found no purchase.

"Hurry him along!" commanded the prior.

"Yes master."

Something hard and cold whipped into Aarin's fingers, and he could not hold on any more. The rope jerked him, the knot slid tight, crushing his throat closed and shutting his veins. Black spots whirled, his vision flickered, and Aarin was gone from the lands of the living.

CHAPTER THIRTY-ONE
The Dead God

AARIN FELL AWAY from himself and into the void and the wind. Above him his body kicked on its line of red rope. The immensity of the wall overcame the small scene, until it was lost in an unending gloom, and it seemed to lose all relevance to him.

Aarin had glimpsed the lands of the dead. Some of what he had seen had unsettled him, some cheered him, the disparity between the two extremes had hardened his resolve to perform his duties better. He would leave no soul to wander lonely, or be sucked up into the dark vortices that troubled the marches of the world between the realms of death and life. It pained his heart to know he had failed two such souls in a matter of minutes.

This was not the realm of death. The forbidding immensity of the void became claustrophobic from his current point of view. A definite idea of centre was inherent to it, even if the edges appeared infinitely far away. He rushed on, reaching untold velocities, until he flew at the same speed as the wind, and a false calm descended. A thread, red as the rope that strangled him, unspooled from his heart, linking his spirit to his corporeal form. As long as that held, he might return whence he came.

Time became erratic. An eternity beckoned, bottled by the dark. There was none of the rushing light and sound he had seen as he guided other souls onto the next phase of their existence. He skated along the curves of time's cage, neither truly living nor truly dead.

A light winked brightly ahead, and receded to a point bright as any star. Perspective shifted, the light exerted an attractive force upon him. He accelerated. The light burst, becoming a confusing display of dazzling, interlocking circles.

Light died. Motion ceased. He had arrived.

Aarin stood upon a smooth plain of silver, whose rounded horizons suggested a globe. Upon the plain was a throne. Upon the throne was a mighty figure divided medially in two. One half of the figure was as familiar to him as his own face; a long head, a dark beard, blind eye, a supply muscled body pierced at wrists and ankle by nail marks. Tallimastus, god of death and creation, glared the doleful glare Aarin had seen upon a thousand representations.

At the midline of his body, the smooth bronze skin gave way to desiccated corpse flesh, sunken onto angular bones. The face that side was a death's head, shrouded in shrunken skin, the eye hollow and clotted with dark matter. The crucifixion wounds were hard black slits, little different to the god's eye on that side.

"So another comes into my prison," said the god. The living side of Tallimastus's body remained motionless as every statue Aarin had ever seen of him. It was the dead half which spoke, words hissing through locked teeth. "Welcome, Guider Kressind."

A dusty cough served it as a laugh.

Aarin fell to his knees, and pressed his head against the silver. "I come to beg your indulgence," he said.

"As they all have come," rumbled the god. Ennui strangled his words of life. "Speak."

Remembering the prior's command, Aarin looked up with his good eye shut, and squinted through his bad. He expected to see nothing, he had been blind in his left eye since he was six years old, but through it he saw clearly. Through his dead eye the stylised representation of Tallimastus's right half and cadaverous left were replaced by a careworn man, still titanic, but human somehow. His face was lined with worry, both eyes milk white, his beard long and full. A red line across his forehead marked the crown stolen from him by his son. In all regards, size excepted, he appeared as a deposed monarch, a blind king in exile. The wounds in his limbs wept slow blood.

Around him were crowded a depleted court. Mother Moude was

at his right hand, Pasquanty, his face full of accusation, at the left. Behind were nine others Aarin did not know. Three of them were Guiders like himself.

Tallimastus turned in his throne. "You see them?"

"Yes, my lord," he said.

"Then you are mighty in your art. The others did not." He pointed out the Guiders. "They gained the knowledge they came for, then they remained, as shall you. Amuse me before your vitality flees and you become a dumb ghost. Ask your questions, the answers will do you no good. There is no escape from this place."

With difficulty Aarin kept his good eye closed. He had not attempted to do so since he was a child, when he spent hours every night hating his brother and willing his sight to return, and he found the action hard. The muscles twitched with unaccustomed effort.

"How did you come to be here?" Aarin asked.

"This place?" Tallimastus lifted his eyes into the endless dark. "Res Iapetus. Next."

"He banished you to the realm beyond. I have seen through the veils and into the lands of the dead which border those others. This is not that place."

"Well done," said Tallimastus. His manner changed, becoming more conversational, less imperious. "I tried to stop him, you know. Even though he gave my bastard, usurping son the punishment he deserved, I couldn't let him get away with destroying the Ruthnian gods. I thought to best him, and take my place again as king. Did you know that?"

"No, my lord," admitted Aarin. "The accounts of what happened in the Godhome are incomplete."

"And all derive from what that arrogant dog Res Iapetus had to say, I assume."

"Yes, my lord," said Aarin.

"I'll tell you how I came here. I am the god of death and creation. I was made to be by you imaginative little people. I had a purpose foisted upon me. When Res Iapetus drove out the others, he cast out my living aspect. But my deathly aspect could not be and never was contained in the Godhome. After the expulsion, he hunted this diminished part of my soul tirelessly through realms mortal and ethereal. There were several times when I lost him, but he was tenacious, I'll give him that. Clever as well, he had this place all set up, ready to accept my essence, all built with knowledge scavenged from the Morfaan. He caught me, and here I have been ever since, for two hundred, long, lonely, tedious years."

"Why not banish you entirely?"

"I am the god of death. I am an absolute. The others were more abstract, their stories fanciful. I am in my way more real than the lot of them put together, that is why, when the myths grew around us, they made me their king, to begin with. All things must die, and every creature fears it. I'm sure new versions of my children coalesce somewhere now, around luckless cores. They will not be the same. But death is and will be forever. Had he not imprisoned me, I would have leapt into being again after a few years and gone after him. Not just as death, but reborn as the vengeful Tallimastus entire! I'd have pulled his guts out of his anus. Slowly. By trapping me, I cannot reform. I cannot be replaced because I am still here. It was, I grudgingly admit, rather clever of him."

"The legends say you were mad. You are not."

"What is madness but a differing point of view? I was mad because the stories called for me to be mad. I am somewhat isolated here. I am freer than I was. The turning of men's minds have less effect on me than they did. I no longer have to conform, though I can never be as I once was. That is the worst part of this punishment, to be sane again after so long, without being permitted to be myself." He laughed bitterly. "I am sure you did not come to ask me about my woes. What is it that has you betray your deacon and condemn this abused woman to share my boredom?"

Aarin guiltily avoided Pasquanty's dead eyes. He had not known for certain what would happen, but Pasquanty's death had seemed likely to him as soon as the door in the vault had opened. He could not pretend otherwise. "I could not turn back."

"Apparently not. Your time runs out. If you wish to know, you better ask."

"The guiding of the dead has changed."

"Oh, that," said Tallimastus. "I was hoping for a new conversation. Is that the only thing you people are interested in?"

"Those ghosts that are reluctant are harder to banish," Aarin persisted, "but there are fewer ghosts to guide overall. Mages dwindle, the Dead God's quarter produces fewer true Guiders. What is happening?"

"Magic," said the ex-king. "The answer lies with magic. You must know that. You are of the true quarter. The mage taint is strong in you. You live in an era of new machines, all of them fuelled by the glimmer, which draws upon the magic of the world."

Tallimastus was displeased at Aarin's bafflement.

"Magic is force, surely as the gravity that drags at your feet or the magnetism that swings the compass. But it is unique in its inconstancy, it is a product of the spirit. Where it is found in one place, it may not be in another. It waxes and wanes to its own rhythm. You, your people, have disrupted that rhythm with your cleverness." He gave Aarin a slow, insincere clap. "Your machine age begins here, as it has in myriad other times and places. The time of gods is done. Bravo."

"Explain more," said Aarin.

Tallimastus sighed. "Magic is finite. You are using it up for your own selfish ends. To reach the realm of the dead requires magic. To manifest a soul as a ghost requires magic. If there is less magic, both are harder."

"But the reluctant souls—"

"The selfish and desperate gather to themselves that which others might use. These ghosts will be more powerful, for a time, then they shall also fade."

"What happens to the dead?" asked Aarin. "Oblivion?"

The Dead God shrugged. "I do not know. What are gods before people worship them into being? Where will I go when people cease to believe in me? There are many answers that are by their nature unknowable. I try not to let it upset me, or then I really would go mad."

"It is not the approach of the Twin?"

The Dead God tilted his head back and thumped at the arms of his throne. "No, there's a whole other problem for you there!" He looked wolfishly at Aarin. "We can discuss that together, although you won't be doing much talking. The dead are poor conversationalists. Time's up. Your thread is fraying. Let me cut it for you."

Tallimastus pushed himself out of his throne. Aarin looked at the cord tying him to his mortal body. It had faded to the faintest red. He stooped and grabbed at it in panic. A gentle tug told him it was still there, but not for long. The cord was became more insubstantial as he gripped it.

"Res Iapetus put me in here. All for the love of his dead wife." Tallimastus's voice became deep and awful. He grew until he was eight times the height of a man. Aarin's good eye snapped open, and he saw the god in his divided form again. The corpse half shambled forward, dragging the unmoving living side along with it clumsily, reminding Aarin horrifically of his father. Aarin yanked at the cord he was holding. It burned in his hand.

The Dead God lunged for him, swinging the stiff living side of itself about like a door.

"You are very gifted!" the god said. "But you'll not escape. Go on, my companions. Welcome your brother to his new home!"

The ghosts in attendance swarmed forward at the god's command, darting into Aarin's face and about his legs. The older were vacuous, dim eyed, nothing but hunger. Pasquanty jabbered at him in silent accusation. Moude wept. Aarin batted at them, his hands chilling as they passed through their insubstantial bodies. His limbs were turning green as the ghosts', losing their definition. He gave the vanishing cord one last final tug.

The cord tugged back.

Aarin was yanked back, slipping through the fingers of the Dead God, toward the world of the living.

"You'll not escape! You can't!" shrieked the Dead God. He grew larger, matching the speed of Aarin's ascent.

"Do not pursue me! I will return!" Aarin promised. "Perhaps you can be released."

"You won't! It doesn't matter. Even Res Iapetus could not win against me. I had the last laugh at his jest! I had my own trap for him, as he had his trap for me. He languishes in it even now!"

The filthy wind sprang up, roaring in Aarin's ears.

"Res Iapetus lives?" shouted Aarin.

"Not quite," laughed the god, his voice tinged with the insanity he was famed for.

"Then where is Res Iapetus?" shouted Aarin.

The Dead God loomed over him, growing ever bigger, until his feet were barely accommodated by the silver orb. When he spoke, his voice filled every corner of the infinite void.

"Res Iapetus is the Drowned King."

The Dead God opened his mouth to swallow Aarin, but the Guider was torn away, his cord sending shooting pains into his chest as it heaved him away. He sped from the roaring god, until he and his prison orb were a star again, then nothing.

The pain in his chest became a pain in his neck.

"Get him up! Get him up, gently!" said the prior excitedly.

Aarin's eyes opened. He was choking, suspended over the bottomless void.

Rope dug into his neck as he was pulled upward. Hands grasped him under each armpit, and hauled him back onto the platform at the base of the stairs. Someone loosened the rope and tugged it free from his neck. Aarin took in a fiery, whooping breath, and rolled, coughing and retching, onto his side. The prior leant over him, face alight with excitement.

"You have returned! What did you see, what did he say?"

Aarin tried to talk. His windpipe was a bruised tube a straw's breadth down the centre of a trunk of pain.

"Water, get him water!"

A canteen was put to his lips. Aarin spluttered as cold water gathered in his mouth. He could swallow only a few drops, the rest spilled down his front.

"You knew." He spoke in a barely audible, reedy croak.

"What?"

"There are no modern devices here, no machines, not even paper. There is nothing of the new world in this monastery. You know why the dead do not go easily. Res Iapetus made this place. It is his legacy that funds it."

"So he told you, good. That proves you saw him," said the prior. "What else did he say? What can be done to arrest the unravelling of the veil?"

"I did not ask. I had little time. He ranted. He wanted to keep me."

"You saw the others."

A nod set an invisible knife sawing at Aarin's neck.

"What else did you learn?"

"Nothing. I learned nothing."

Seutreneause tensed with fury. "You lie. You passed into his gaol and you spoke with him." He signalled to his monks. "You will tell us of all that transpired. We have plenty of time."

Aarin pressed at the floor with his hand. New pain shot up his arm. Three of his fingers were broken.

"You would not go," said Setreuneause. "If you wish your other fingers to remain unbroken, then next time you will let yourself be strangled. Take him away!"

The monks hustled him out of the cave, up steps that were longer on the going up than the coming down. In the vault he saw a new animate, fresher than the rest, dressed in clean robes.

Pasquanty's ruined neck smiled the smile his slack face no longer could. The unliving deacon watched with dull eyes as his former master was dragged past.

Two of the monks took him to a monk's cell. There was no lock on the door, and two beds set out inside. On one was laid a new habit of black.

"The sea is as effective a barrier as any to escape," said one of the monks. "The master says you can work with us and remain occupied, or languish between visits to the Dead God in discomfort and boredom. The choice is yours. I do not care."

"We are all Guiders. We only wish for the dead to rest easy," said the second other more gently. A flicker of guilt crossed his face.

Aarin feigned hesitation, then gave a tiny nod of acknowledgment.

"Good," said the gruffer monk. "Our goodbrother physic will be here to see to your hurts in a while. Do not leave, or we will put you in a place less to your liking." They shut the door behind them, leaving Aarin alone.

The habit waited for him on the bed. He would put on their garments. He would labour alongside them. When they were complacent, he would escape, and take the Dead God's warning to the world. He would do these things, and more, for he was not only a Guider.

He was a Kressind.

CHAPTER THIRTY-TWO

Braving the Ice

THE *PRINCE ALFRA* hooted loudly, and with a churning of wheels the ship rode up on the pack ice, forcing it down and apart with doomy crackings that resonated throughout the ship's hull. Funnels huffed glittering steam as the ship drove on forward. The ice screamed. Dry snow blew sideways in a strong breeze to sting exposed flesh. Men with long poles were stationed by each wheel housing and at the prow. Trassan dashed to and fro between them.

"Get that piece there! Keep it out of the wheel!" he yelled.

Three men jammed their poles into a roughly hexagonal piece of ice, pushing the side closest to the wheel down and forcing the opposite side free of the water.

"Shove it away! It'll go into the paddle!" he yelled. He grabbed a pole from the hands of one man, and shouldered him aside. "Heave!" he yelled. "Heave!"

The ice slid heavily sideways, threatening to drag the sailors over. The paddlewheel bit the water, stirring it to foam, crunching smaller pieces of ice to fragments with shocking noise.

Trassan thrust the pole back into the man's hands. "Keep the ice away!" he barked.

He marched back across the deck. Bannord approached him, a slighter figure in tow. Only when he was close did he recognise his cousin, bundled up against the weather.

"Bannord!"

"You sent for me?" said Bannord.

"Get your men to the poles. There's not enough out here."

"I will leave five of them on watch." Whiteness surrounded them, the peaks of icebergs emerging without warning from the snowstorm. "For ice as much as anything."

Trassan muttered something in the manner of angry, impatient men.

"What might I do?" said Ilona.

"Do?" said Trassan. "You have done quite enough."

"I am trying to make amends, cousin," she said, wary of his mood. "What else should I do? It was you who reneged on our arrangement, and I who, as a result, spent weeks in a freezing hold."

"Why is she trailing about after you like a puppy?" he said to Bannord.

"Because you asked me to look after her, and because she's learning. She's much better company than you."

"Don't go easy on her. Give her something to do, Bannord." Trassan caught sight of something that displeased him and jogged off to the prow, shouting at a sailor as he went.

"You can stand watch. Over there." Bannord pointed to a section of gunwale forward of the starboard paddlewheel. "With Darrasind."

"What do I do?" she said.

"Stand. Watch," said Bannord. "Specifically for fucking enormous pieces of ice that might hit the ship and sink it. Fairly simple."

"Alright," she said.

"Now," said Bannord.

ILONA KNEW ALL the marines, but none particularly well. She had exchanged few words with Darrasind. He was a quiet man in his late twenties who said little and avoided her eyes, so when he greeted her cheerily she was instantly put on her guard.

"Good morning, goodlady, and what a fine morning it is too!" he said. He had his blanket-muffled ironlock cradled in the crook of his arm, his other hand he waved in greeting. Fatter snowflakes were coming down, catching on his lashes, beard and brows. His normally quiet eyes danced with mischief, his cheeks were redder with something other than the cold.

"I have been told to join you on watch, marine Darrasind," she said, affecting a hauteur to cover her wariness.

"Then watch together we shall!" he said with an extravagant bow. He stood too close. It was very cold, and all on deck wore their full winter gear. Darrasind seemed innocuous. With his proportions distorted by his bulky parka and mittens he looked like a child's soft toy, but the look in his eyes made her nervous. "I will look that way, and you shall look that way." His pointing finger made an angle in his mitten. "That way we can cover twice as much, and move half as less. I mean, half as little." He struggled in a deep breath, half-swallowing it. "You know what I mean."

"Have you been drinking?"

"Only a nip, now and then, to keep this thrice-damned cold at bay!" he said. "Do you want some?" he added slyly. He reached inside the neck flap of his parka and pulled out a bottle. "The lieutenant need never know. Finest Girarsan whisky. Bloody awful country, full of swamps and poets. But they make a fine firewater. Fedrion gave it me," he added in an exaggerated whisper.

"No thank you," said Ilona. "And you better have no more either."

"Suit yourself, Goodlady," he said. He took a provocative swallow

"Goodmaid," she said automatically.

"Not married eh?" he said. There was a pause. "Think a man like me might have a chance with a girl like you?"

"Never," she said. "Watch."

A part of her demanded that she leave immediately, but the greater succumbed to pride. If she left this one relatively simply but important task, the crew would never take her seriously and all Trassan's dire pronouncements about her being a disruptive influence would be proved true. Furthermore, Darrasind was drunk, but ordinarily inoffensive. She feared to leave him at his post and she was reluctant to report him.

Instead she tried to blot the man's presence with the business of watching for peril in the driving snow. To a degree it worked. One part of her face was exposed to the breeze and became so cold shooting pains fizzed across her cheek. The snow deadened even the dreadful cracking of the ice and groaning songs of the bergs. The shouts of other men became indistinct, their bodies camouflaged with dappled grey and white and blurred about the edges. The hard lines of the ship receded. Calls she could not make out the words of went up from time to time. The ship slowed, the huffing breath of its engines lessened. When the whistles sounded, they came from far away. She was alone, isolated in a soft-edged white circle no more than four yards across.

The problem arose when Darrasind noticed it too.

A cold hand pulling back her parka hood took Ilona by surprise.

"Darrasind!" she yelled, rounding on him. She tugged her hood back up.

Darrasind's mitten flopped back against his arm. He had removed the under glove also. His exposed fingers were red as raw steak mince in the freezing air.

"You're so pretty," he said. "Might I have a kiss? Just a kiss, that's all." He smiled almost sweetly. "It's been such a long time. Since I kissed anyone, I mean. I don't mean nothing by it. Just a kiss."

"Get away from me!" she shouted. In her panic, all her training with Bannord went from her mind and she shoved ineffectually at Darrasind. His smile turned maudlin.

"No need for that, sweetheart," he said. "Only a kiss, please. I'm sick of the sight and smell of men. I want to smell a woman."

He lunged awkwardly for her, dropping his rifle in the process. He stumbled and slid a few feet from her and recovered with a dopy laugh.

"Making it hard, eh?"

She stepped aside, tried to clear her mind and get herself under control. Her training. She brought Bannord's lessons to mind. When he came at her again she was ready to fight. He received a punch to the kidney that staggered him.

"Why'd you do that?" he said, genuinely hurt.

Too late Ilona caught sight of a tall pinnacle of ice come sailing from the snow behind Darrasind's head.

"Darrasind!" she screamed. "Behind you!"

He didn't turn around. "Yeah, I've heard that one before. Letting me down easy. Go on, just one kiss, then I'll leave you be, I promise."

He leaned in. Ilona hooked a leg around his ankle and pushed hard, sending him back into the snow heavy tarpaulin covering the ship's boat.

"Ice!" she screamed. "Ice to starboard!"

Her cry was taken up. The ship's whistles cried alarm. Thick clouds of steam pumped from the funnels as more water was introduced to the reaction chambers of the boilers. The port wheel slowed and spun backwards, the starboard turned forward, and the port side increased speed, swinging the ship's prow to port so quickly Ilona staggered.

The iceberg glided past. Ilona breathed a premature sigh of relief. A roaring grind shrieked out as the ship met the ice. The poles of five of the men snapped against the pack ice they were punting at as it was suddenly crimped by the pressure of the iceberg and the ship. A sixth pole was caught between wheel and floe, lofting its wielder screaming over the gunwales into the water.

The ship juddered as the iceberg ground along the outside of the wheel housing, ripping free half the panels covering the paddlewheel. A final judder threw a second man from the rails and into the freezing ocean.

Darrasind picked himself up. "Now you've done it! All I wanted is a kiss. Now we've hit a berg. That's on you, goodmaid."

Ilona stared at him disbelievingly. The whole ship was in uproar. Men crowded the starboard railing, pointing and shouting. Ropes sailed over the side, only to be drawn in wet with burning cold water. Out they went again, and then again. One dragged taut, and the Ishmalani and marines heaved at it, drawing a sopping, half-dead man up over the side. The rescued sailor was swiftly wrapped in the dry coats of his comrades and bundled inside.

The other rope flicked out again, and again. Each time it came back without a passenger.

The men fell silent.

Bannord dashed around the machinery at the midline of the boat. "What the hells happened here?" he demanded. "You were supposed to be on watch!"

Darrasind stood to attention. "She distracted me, sir. I did my best to resist but," he shrugged. "She—"

Bannord grabbed Darrasind by the parka and propelled him backwards into the ship's lifeboat. "You're lying. I'm going to flog you, Darrasind. Ilona!" he said over his shoulder. "What happened?"

Ilona's eyes flicked between Darrasind's face and Bannord's furious countenance. "I... Do not flog him, I beg you. It is my fault."

"Your fault how? Did you come on to him?"

Ilona's face set, she had a choice to save Darrasind, or to tell the truth. "Never. He demanded that I kiss him."

"Sir, I—"

Cold fury froze Bannord's gaze. "You what, trooper?" He sniffed around Darrasind's face. "Is that whisky I smell on you?" He slammed Darrasind against the boat. Darrasind didn't know where to look. He flushed bright red with shame. "You stupid little prick. Look what you've done!" Bannord threw the smaller man to the deck. Darrasind put out his ungloved hand to arrest his fall. The bare skin stuck to the metal, tearing free as he rolled. He yelped, and cradled his bleeding palm.

"I only asked for a kiss, it's all, I swear. I would never harm a woman that way."

"Shut your fucking mouth and give me your gun, now!"

Darrasind's ironlock was three feet from his uninjured hand. For a second Ilona thought he meant to go for the weapon and discharge at his superior, but Darrasind did not have it in him. His injured hand pressed against his chest, he retrieved his gun and handed it to the lieutenant.

"Get inside," said Bannord. "Get your hand seen to by the physic then get to quarters. If I see you outside the barracks, I'll shoot you myself. Do I make myself clear?"

"Yes sir."

"Go. Now!"

Darrasind headed off, pushing through the crowd gathering around the scene of the altercation. Trassan took her elbow to drag her to one side.

"Do you see why I did not bring you, why I could not?" he hissed.

"Trassan, I was entirely innocent. Had it not been for him, I would have seen the iceberg in better time."

"If you had not been aboard, Darrasind would not have been distracted!" growled Trassan. "Can't you see what your presence here means among these men? You've thrown the fowl in with the dracons, and you, dear cousin, are the damned fowl in this case!"

He looked around at the men. Several still stood by the rail, searching for the lost sailor. A few of them stole looks toward Ilona. Most were curious, more than a few openly hostile.

"Leave it!" shouted Drentz, "he's dead, he'll not last more than two minutes in this cold. He's with the One now."

One of the men wept at the news. Others shouted at this ruling.

"He's dead!" bellowed Drentz. "Back to work!"

"Damn it! What is the damage!" shouted Trassan. His engineers and Ishamalani looked over the side of the ship. "How is the wheel?" he said. He turned on Ilona in his anger. "You're in serious trouble, cousin. Already I have my marine officer playing chaperone."

"It is not necessary."

"Apparently it is."

Tolpoleznaen appeared at the wheelhouse railing. "News from the engine room, we're clear. No leaks. The wheel turns true."

"The outer panels have been ripped off, but the wheel's turning as it should, goodfellow," confirmed a man at the rail.

Trassan took in the crowded sea, the bergs lurking in the snowstorm. Invisible in the storm, the cleft mountain was nevertheless tantalisingly close.

"This is never going to work. Tol! Tell Heffi to reverse course, we'll be smashed to pieces if we go on."

"Then what?" called back the first mate. "We're nearly there!"

Trassan worried at his lower lip. "I've another idea. I'll be in in a minute. And fetch me Vols! It's time he earned his keep. You, get yourself back to your cabin."

"Why should I?" said Ilona.

"Really, Ilona?" he squeezed her arm tightly. "You're a giant temptation to everything with two legs and a cock on this boat. You are to stay in your quarters from now on."

"I refuse."

"You will not."

"Don't order me."

"I'll order whoever I want," he snapped. "Go on, get below. Or must I assign more men to protect you?"

"This situation would not have come about if women were accorded a more equal role and you had a few more aboard."

"From where I'm standing, more women means more trouble," said Trassan.

"Tell that to your sister," said Ilona right into his face, "without whose ironworks this vessel would not have been possible." She yanked her arm free of his grip and walked away shaken.

"A man has died, Ilona!" he called at her back.

His words hit home hard, but Ilona stood tall. If she did not, Trassan would have won.

CHAPTER THIRTY-THREE
The Room of Time

MADELYNE'S NEXT WEEKS only served to confuse her further. The day after the night in the room with the hands and the mask, the duke came to her contritely while she walked the grounds, the first time he had ever joined her outside. He fell in beside her. They walked side by side for a few moments. Though she was frightened she did not show it, and when she neither spurned him nor fled from him he bowed his head as he spoke.

"I was enraged," he said. "I apologise. It goes against the spirit of our agreement. You have done nothing wrong. I had no right to punish you like that. You passed the test. In my anger I was sure you would fail. I thought you had opened the door to my fane and let him in. I... Something is happening, something..." He stopped on the path, fists clenched. Madelyne slowed and regarded him. "I am sorry," he concluded abruptly and departed, and she did not see him again for some time.

For the rest of that day she wandered around the house, debating whether she should leave now before it was too late. The duke's residence showed no sign of the previous night's occurrences. No scorches marred the walls or carpets. Nothing was out of place, everything was like it had been before the night of the hands. Only the bruises on her back and deep lassitude told the truth of what had occurred. She expected every twinge from the bruises to be reminder of her ravishment, but they were worse, for instead she remembered the pleasure of the hands, and it awoke in her a hunger for more. She grew fretful when the duke did not reappear. She disturbed herself by wishing to see him. The feeling only grew, and her thoughts strayed often to the ecstasies she had experienced. The duke was not the first male to abuse her, but he was certainly the first to apologise afterward, and none had lifted her to such peaks of sensuality. The more she thought on it, the more she became troubled. She should hate the duke, but she did not. Quite the contrary.

She decided to go the next morning, packing her things in preparation. But when the morning came, she went for breakfast, and then the library, sure she would depart. It was evening by the time she admitted to herself that she was staying another night. The next day, the same thing happened, and the next, and the next. When a week went by, she conceded she was staying, and abandoned the pretence.

One afternoon she sat in a window seat, staring out over the rose garden where Gaffne worked, through the fence to the Place. Madelyne was a woman who understood her mind. Her self realisation had kept her well, sane and alive. She unpacked it to examine the contents. Her life she portioned up into tiny crates full of memories, that when stacked in the warehouse of her mind made her who she was. That was how she envisaged it. She went within this construct, to try to understand.

There was her time as a child in the poorhouse orphanage with Harafan, where authority was to be feared, and the time after, when no authority had led to disaster on more than one occasion. After she had grown too old for the orphanage she had felt lost without the harsh rules that set the tempo of her early life. In the first part, there was no love save that of her Harafan, the little boy who had become dearer to her than a brother. In the second she had a surfeit of affection, not understanding until later so much of it was the false love bestowed by selfish men on pretty girls. In that time she had done so much she wished she had not. With the duke, she had a good measure of both affection and boundaries, for he was affectionate to her, she could not deny that.

All her life she had run from rules—she had been a gambler, a thief, a fighter, and more than once a whore. Had she been mistaken, and fled from the thing she craved the most? Here she knew what she was to do, and would be punished if she did not. The duke's punishments were trying, but so were those in the poorhouse. Here there was no arbitrariness, no going back on promises. His desires were odd but by no means unique. He was kind to her when she pleased him, and above all he was honest.

She sighed, looking down at the needlework in her hand, the rich dress. This wasn't her. She hadn't thought it was, at any rate. Was this who she was? Needlepoint? Mooning over a man who wanted to spank her bottom like some dirty old man paying a coin per slap? She put it aside. Best go read instead, she thought. These questions were not the right questions. She should be trying to figure out how to extract the information she needed from him. Her mind was dulling from lack of use.

But though she waited outside at noon every day for a half hour, when Harafan finally sent her a message she pretended she had not received it, and buried herself in the library.

On the fourth day the duke returned. For a week, they spent most of every day together, talking about this and that. The duke had researched her background thoroughly, and with a few well timed questions he had her opening her heart to him. She surprised herself by discussing her life in a way she had with no one else, not even Harafan. He was sympathetic and helpful, offering his advice and wisdom.

One night he told her, "It is time," and he took her back to the second room. He restrained her again, and whipped her, but gently, enough to bring the blood to the skin and excite the flesh. Then he pleasured her until she thought she could take no more. In between surges of physical ecstasy, she anticipated him going further with trepidation. But he made no move to undress, and demanded no pleasure for himself. For four nights he did this, until every movement during the day brought tiny bursts of pleasure and she began to long for the night.

On the fifth night, he took her to the third room. He did not tell her where they were going, but the way he behaved forewarned her that they might ascend to the next floor, and when he led her with great ceremony past the door of the second room up the flight of stairs, she knew she had been right.

"This is the third room, the Room of Time," said the duke. He took an iron key from his belt, and inserted it into the lock with a tiny click. "I open it to you now." He turned the key and pushed open the door. "Take off your shoes, and step inside."

"Yes your, grace," she said. He smiled indulgently at her.

The room beyond was bare of all adornment, no windows it had or other exits. The floor, walls and ceiling were covered in firmly padded satin. Madelyne's feet pressed into it pleasingly when she stepped inside.

"I will not ask you what you think. I do not wish to draw you into a trap." The duke went to a ring handle set flush into the wall, opening up an inbuilt cupboard. Inside were a collection of his favoured implements, some for pain, other for pleasure, he ran a finger along them idly, sending them swinging on their hooks. "In this room, I might control the flow of time. If I punished you in here, every pain would last an eternity. Or I could make it fly, so that all strokes blurred into one sharp moment, and slow it again that you might enjoy the after-effects of excitation without the initial discomfort. The moment of physical ecstasy can be prolonged to last almost as long as time itself. Here, in this room, you will learn to open your soul to the immensity of creation through carnality, for only from the body can true appreciation of the spirit come. Should you succeed, then you will join me by my side, forever."

"How?"

"It will take time," he said earnestly. "Years, maybe. Entering here is but the first step. But it is the first step of the final stage. Well done, Madelyne. Very few women have been permitted in here." He paused bashfully. "And none so quickly."

He went behind her, and unlocked the cracked leather collar she had worn since she had come into the house. From his pocket, he took a fantastic collar of bright metal links, studded about with blood red rubies. He set it about her neck and spoke to her tenderly.

"I have given only six of these to my consorts. Each has been unique. All are made of the Morfaan steel. It is impossible for your people to cut or work. But I can." He closed it. The links fit her neck perfectly. She felt a tiny key slide into the link at the back of her neck.

"But," she said, touching it gently. "This is priceless. I could buy a duchy in the Olberlands with this!"

He laughed richly and turned her around. "I would hope my duchy will suffice, and that has bounds far wider than any upon this Earth." He looked into her eyes, proud and loving. "This is a mark of my commitment to you, not simply a sign of my ownership. You gave yourself to me freely. Freely in return I give you this, and with it my pledge. While you wear the collar, you are under my protection. No harm can come to you."

"None?"

"Nothing," he said. "Not the gods themselves or Res Iapetus or the black gulfs of eternity and the things that swim there could touch you."

He embraced her; she went into his arms willingly, breathing deeply of his hot scent. A intense sensation ran through her, then departed, a slow wash of contentment built in her chest and flowed out into her body, slow and sweet.

"I have slowed the clocks of creation," he said. He spoke unnaturally slowly. Light took on a queer quality. When she moved, she felt her muscles uncurl and tense, fibre by fibre. The duke's words hit her one at a time, like warm rain, every syllable a pleasure. "Tonight I shall make love to you for the first time. Tonight, you will experience something only a handful of mortal women have enjoyed."

He commanded her to undress. She did so gladly. It took forever, the threads of cloth bumping delightfully over her skin one by one as her clothes fell their long way to the floor. When she was finished, he followed suit.

They stood disrobed before one another. He was magnificent to look at, and she was unafraid.

An infinitely slow step brought him to her, and he took her into his arms again. The unnatural heat of his hands bloomed on her skin.

With her collar on, she did not feel naked.

AFTER THAT, THEY made love often. He had no cause to punish her again, but sometimes he restrained her, for the look of it he said, and sometimes he whipped her or did other things that, in her previous life, would have sent her flying out the door, but which she came to desire. With expert application of pleasure and pain, he rose her up to heights undreamed of, and in the nights they spent in the Room of Time, she scaled peaks of sensation as high as the stars.

Midsummer approached. The month of Gannever opened hot and glorious. Harafan sent messages to her constantly, but she ignored him. She came to share the duke's bed, at first occasionally, then nightly. Her aim at being in the mansion retreated from the forefront of her mind, niggling only when another message from Harafan arrived, all of which she dithered over before discarding. When the time came to gain the knowledge she needed, it was unexpected, almost done as an afterthought.

Madelyne nuzzled into the duke. Such a powerful presence beside her. Perversely, she felt safe with him despite what he sometimes did to her. After the incident with the mask and the hands, she had seen his face when he struck her and saw only concentration, the desire to awaken all her senses, perhaps anxiety that he went too far, maybe a little hope that she would be the one. There was no trace of the brute lasciviousness she had seen that one and only time.

"What is it like, being a god?"

The duke pulled her closer, and she snuggled into his enormous arm. The curves of its muscles fit into her back perfectly, big enough to be a bed for her all by itself.

"That is a peculiar question," he said.

"You cannot say you have never been asked before."

"Yes! Yes, I have." He laughed drowsily. "But it is still peculiar."

"Yes?"

"Do I ask you how it is to be a woman? It is impossible to answer."

"No," said Madelyne. "But you are a god, unique. I am one of millions of women."

"You are still unique," he said. "All things are."

"Maybe, but I am not so special as you."

"You are to me."

"Did you answer these other girls when they asked?" she said, a touch jealously.

"Yes. And I will tell you. I told you that I would hold nothing from you."

"So tell then!" She gave him a playful slap.

"Truthfully, I cannot answer well. How do I explain what I am and how I feel in terms you would understand? Another person cannot really do this truthfully to a second, so how can I? I have been many things, but I have never been mortal and the state remains a mystery to me."

"So you pursue romance with women without knowing their minds?"

"Oh, I know their minds, and their hearts, and their bodies." He ran a pointed nail down her back, drawing quivers of pleasure from her muscles. "But I cannot claim to be human. Being a god is lonely. I am alone. Hence all this."

"There is Eliturion."

"Eliturion is a sot who thinks himself a poet, and they are the worst kinds of sot of all. He was above me in the pantheon—I am a lesser god at best, not worthy to be worshipped. I was the servant of the Dark Lady, not a deity in my own right. Being a god then was..." He searched for the words. "Playing a role. A repetitive, dull charade."

"Eliturion says stories made you."

"He does. He tells everyone who will buy him a drink that. It is not true."

Madelyne propped herself up on her elbow. "How so?"

"You cannot make something from nothing. Every time something is created, something else must be taken away. To make fire, wood must burn. To sate hunger, food is consumed. To water a factory, a river must be drunk dry."

"But, but it's magic. Magic makes something from nothing."

The Infernal Duke shook his head. His horns caught on the fabric of his pillows. "It does not. As your magisters and engineers are discovering, magic can be harnessed through the medium of glimmer. Once that is used up, then what is left? Sand."

"What was used up to make you?"

"Something that is long dead," he said sadly. "I was not always this way. None of the gods were. Once we were free; we coursed the atmosphere without form, beings of Will. You know the balance of Form and Will?"

"No," she said.

The duke shifted, bringing his arm up around Madelyne so that he could gesture with both his hands. "All things are made of two components. Will, that is the ineffable," he said, lifting his right hand, "and Form, which is the solid." He repeated the gesture with his left, bringing his fingertips together to make a cage. "Both are real, both are actual, but one is perceptible, the other is not. All thinking beings comprise a deal of Will; it coalesces into something approaching substance to give us our souls. Whereas Form is the crude matter of the universe. You men and women who call this Earth your own, you approach a balance between the two, and that makes you dangerous, for you can call upon the strengths of both. We gods are—*were*—mostly Will; the Morfaan somewhere between us and you. All things were created to rest somewhere on this scale of spirit to matter. A rock has more Form than a bird, a fish more Will. There was a beauty to it, but its pattern, whatever it was intended to be, is disrupted. We are not made of stories, Madelyne. We gods were imprisoned by stories. Stories wove cages round our spirits, divorcing us from our purer state. It is partly our own fault, but I did not ask to be this way. I am not comfortable with what I have become—the Infernal Duke! Lord of the Fifteenth Hell!" he declaimed ironically. "My essence, such of it that remains, fights against this imposition but every year, as the stories become legends and the legends feed history, and the stories are repeated again and again, I become less and less what I was, and more as people expect me to be. Res Iapetus saw the gods as tyrants, but he did not comprehend our nature. We are slaves, doomed to preset paths of myth and the retelling of myth in ever less subtle variation, until you are done and we are used up. So you see, I thank Res Iapetus, in a certain way, for he freed me a little from the trap."

She gave him a questioning look.

"I am no longer venerated," he said simply.

"But who created all this," she said, "if you are not gods?"

"The Ishmalani believe in the One, the creator, the spirit of the world. They are also incorrect."

Madelyne, sensing her opportunity, pursued her questioning. A fresh thrill excited her mind. Now was the time to uncover what she had suffered for. But she had to force herself to ask. It was not so important any more. "To me, you are a god, and to everyone else..."

"Every human else. Try asking a Tyn sometime what they think of me."

"Every human else," she agreed. "You are powerful, magical, dangerous. If our stories really did trap you, they also made you strong."

"Agreed," he said. "Though we were not feeble beings before."

"So how did Res Iapetus drive you away?"

"Do you know why he did what he did?"

"Something to do with his wife, they say."

"That is true. She died in childbirth. Her ghost was collected from her deathbed, as the legends say should happen and so therefore did, by Alcmeny, goddess of love and perfection. It was her custom to take the ghosts of women who had died so into her service. They became handmaids to her, while their children's unformed spirits became flowers in her garden."

"That's... that's sort of awful."

"Not according to your ancestors. They thought it a great honour. By the time of Res Iapetus, two hundred years ago, the intellectual revolution that led to this modern age was well under way. Men began to question what came before life. They started to look beyond the veil of death to what might be next. Ghosts rose, where did they go? They did not find out, no one ever will, but the first Rationalists formed an inkling—half right I have to say—that the ghosts who went on continued on, and that corporeal life might come again to them. Freedom was the watchword of this new mode of thought. The fate of those half-formed souls transformed into flowers, and the weeping mothers set to wash Alcmeny's feet for eternity with their tears ceased to seem like such an honour, and to none more than Res Iapetus. He petitioned Omnus, the lord of the gods and the master of us all, to release his wife and child so that they might pass into the next world, and be free to continue through the cycles of existence. Omnus refused. Iapetus threatened him. Omnus appeared then in person, and destroyed Res's fastness in a battle that lasted a day. In response Res retreated, disappearing from our knowledge for several years. The gods thought him done, but he returned more powerful than any mage before him, breached the Godhome and banished the gods."

"As simple as that?"

"As simple as that. I still do not know how he became so powerful. It was unprecedented, though he had help gaining entry to the Godhome. We will not see his like again in this age. Do they not teach you this?"

"I didn't get much schooling in the poorhouse."

The duke shifted. She ducked his narrowing gaze.

"You do not appear uneducated. You reinvented yourself well. It is one of the reasons you intrigue me." He settled deeper into the cushions and gave a loud yawn.

"Iapetus was a long time ago," Madelyne prompted.

"Two centuries is an eye blink to me," he said sleepily.

"To you. To us poor mortals it might never have happened."

"It happened!" The duke's laugh rumbled in his chest, and Madelyne's whole body trembled with its vibration. "Mortality need not be your fate, Madelyne, if you continue to please me, then twenty decades will come to seem like nothing."

"Yes, your grace." She became quiet. The duke said no more. His chest began the steady, slow rise and fall of a sleeper. She almost left it there, content with this thing she had found but had not sought. But the talk of the poorhouse reminded her of Harafan, and guilt drove her on.

"Your grace?"

"Mmm?" the duke said. He sighed with pleasure as Madelyne nestled further into his side.

"How did Iapetus get in, to the Godhome. Who helped him?"

"Eliturion," the duke said, falling asleep. "Eliturion struck a deal with Iapetus. I don't know why. He betrayed us. All of us..." he said, drifting away again.

"Your grace? How?"

The duke whispered. "All of us had a key, a phrase that brought us into the Godhome."

She knew this, but acted surprised. "What was his phrase?" she asked in a playful way, though her heart was in her throat.

"Hmmm?" he came awake a little. She stilled, scared she had

asked him too much. There was no going back. She smiled at him, he smiled back, his eyes hooded. They slid shut again.

"What was Eliturion's phrase?" she whispered. "Go on, tell me," she made her voice teasing, though she felt no playfulness. "I shall tell no one. I promise."

"Hnh," said the duke. "You'll never believe it." His smile permeated his voice, making it warm and soothing as heated mead. The Infernal Duke's words were thick. Madelyne had to lean close to hear. And then he told her, a short poem, each word spaced by deep breaths.

"Is, is that it?" she said.

"Indeed. My reaction precisely. Stupid, isn't it?" said the duke.

Madelyne let him drift away to whatever dreams gods have. She repeated the phrase again and again to herself in order not to forget. Her pulse thrummed in her chest. This was what she needed. She could leave. But she found herself conflicted at the prospect. She was content, happy even, in the arms of the duke. He encircled her, larger than the world. To be in his power had stopped being terrifying. He had become comforting, a shield against all the hardship she had been forced to endure in her miserable life. She could stay here forever, she knew.

Then there was Harafan, the only person who had ever cared for her, waiting for her to get in touch.

Waiting for her to betray the duke.

CHAPTER THIRTY-FOUR
Threading the Needle

"THAT IS AN insane idea," said Captain Heffi. He sat back in his chair in the stateroom with his hands crossed over his belly. The other expedition leaders kept their lips buttoned, waiting to see where this would go.

"No more insane than getting torn to pieces trying to go through," said Trassan.

"Yes, but *under the ice*? Are you serious? Really Trassan, I understand your eagerness to get to the shore, but this is too extreme. What if the ice falls in on us?"

"It won't," said Trassan.

"How do we know the ice does not go all the way to the seabed? Or that the entrance to the docks isn't frozen solid? If that happens, we will be stranded."

"We'll have time to get out well before the tide comes back in."

"Another objection," said Heffi. "The tide may go out too far for us to come close to the dock. What then?"

"I don't believe the Morfaan were such shoddy engineers. But again, we will have plenty of time to get out. If the worst comes to the worst, Goodmage Iapetus here can clear the ice from over our heads."

Heffi looked at Vols doubtfully. He did not look at all well—grey skinned and drawn.

"Come on!" said Trassan, slapping the table. "We all know he can do that."

"Yes, but so much of it—"

"I can do it," said Vols. "It is simple."

"I have full faith that he can," said Ardovani.

"Tell them what you have seen, Vols," said Trassan.

"Goodfellow Trassan had me perform a sending," said the mage. "You must forgive my appearance, but projection of the soul is among the most draining of all acts a mage might perform."

"You were successful then?" said Heffi. "I do not mean to be rude, goodmage, but you have had precious little success in reaching Karsa."

"I was successful this time." He cleared his throat and relaxed into his chair. His eyes became unfocused, looking through the walls of the ship, his voice dreamy. "The ice sits on the water. It is thick, much thicker than the pack ice—that is the correct term?" he looked dazedly to Antoninan for confirmation.

"It is."

"Wrinkled and stacked. It whispered its creation to me, for a man unbound from his flesh is open to all the voices of the world. *Many tides pushed me*, it said, *many tides made me climb*."

"I admit, I'm impressed," said Bannord. "Did you think to ask it if it would hold?"

"I did," said Vols proudly. "'What happens to you when the tide goes out?' I asked it. *I become the sky*, it said. *I become the sky*. I passed through the ice and into the sea, and gratefully, for the ice is so cold it affects the soul, hard as iron and more unforgiving."

"Tell them what you saw under the ice," said Trassan.

"Thick pillars of ice. Platforms of ice, tunnels and caves of ice."

"Do you see?" said Heffi. "A labyrinth to catch and kill us."

"But there is a way through," said Vols. "Several. On the far side of the ice is a large cave. The docks are there."

"Tell us what the docks are like," said Bannord.

"They are shielded from my vision by ancient wards. But I did leave the place, and soared high. I saw the city from above." His eyes shone. "A city made all of ice."

"We stick to our original plan, and go overland," said Antoninan.

"There is no way. This is the way," said the mage. He blinked, coming out of his half-trance.

"Well," said Heffi. "Well, well, well."

Trassan looked around the faces of the men in the room. It was so full they obscured the light of the lamps on the wall, making the room a dim cave. "I am not going to force this course of action on the expedition," said Trassan. "It is risky, so I have called all of you here—the leaders, foremen and knowledgeable goodmen—to put the plan to a vote. I repeat that is shall be a risk. But I believe a greater risk would be to wait, or to turn back, or to seek another route through to the city. If we cannot get through, we shall turn back. Tolpoleznaen, can you take the ship through?"

"Mage," said the helmsman, "can you provide me a map of the way through?"

"I can try," said Vols. "I am no skilled draughtsman, but I should be able to give—"

"With a map, I can do it," said the Ishamalani. "To refuse would be an affront to the One. The One put this challenge before me. I will prove myself equal to his task."

"It cannot be seen, but it can be reached," said Trassan. "This is what Heffi and I learned from the shaman of the sea people. So, we have a choice. We turn back now, or we try the passage under the ice. The next close approach of the Twin is in two nights time, and comes with the White Moon. There will be a Middle Great Tide. Then we shall attempt the crossing under the ice." He shrugged. "Or not. It is not a choice I will make alone. I have no right to. But if you decide against, then all we have worked for will be in vain and we shall return home poorer than when we left. Who is in favour? Give me a show of hands."

Heffi's chief officers, Tolpoleznaen, Volozeranetz, Drentz, and Suqab all raised their hands, some more quickly than the rest. Bannord put his hand up right away, as did Antoninan. Ullfider the antiquarian's hand shot up, for he was most keen to get his hands on the Morfaan's secrets. Kororsind the alchemist hesitated for a good second. Tyn Gelven shook his head. "We should go back," he said. "We are being told something. We should listen." The cook, Henneman, looked bewildered to have been invited to the vote. He shook his head, staring at his hands which remained curled upright in his lap. His Tyn counterpart, Charvolay, put her hand up slowly, glancing at the others as if asking permission. The physic Mauden simply said, "No." Trassan's engineering chiefs, Goodman Ollens and his assistants, agreed unanimously. Trassan smiled with satisfaction and raised his own hand.

"Well Heffi?" asked Trassan.

Heffi grumbled and stuck his own hand up too.

"To the hells with it," he said. "I could do with a fright to put me off my food a while, I'm getting fat."

THE SNOWSTORMS SPUTTERED out. Two days of preparation went by in a frantic blur. Gelven had his iron whisperers interrogate the ship until they were ill with the touch of it. Ardovani slept little, spending his time renewing the protective wards carved into the ship's decks. "All this iron makes protective ritual hard," he would tell anyone that would listen. "But a little is better than nothing." Antoninan began preparing the expedition's equipment to go ashore. Vols spent his time meditating, clearing his mind of the certainties of reality in case he should need to change it, given confidence by the recent ease with which magic came to him, which he confided only to Ardovani. Much of the crew busied themselves hacking the ice from the ship, working with such energy that it was soon clear from prow to stern. Trassan paced impatiently, shouting when asked a question, taking over tasks in irritation when he deemed them performed imperfectly. The rest of the time he had his glass to his eye, scanning from east to west and back again in search of his rival, but Persin remained elusive.

On the day of the attempt, the Twin rose in the early hours of the morning, its wan orb growing perceptibly in the predawn sky as it sped toward the world. The White Moon rose afterwards, moving up obliquely across the Twin's glowering face, until it looked like the second world would swallow it whole. Under the influence of both bodies, the tide went up and up, turning the ocean before the wall into a treacherous mess of frozen reefs and whirlpools sharp with fangs. Teeth of ice flashed white in the short night as slabs of frozen water were heaped in layers atop the barrier. The mountains shook and cascades of broken glacier fell from the continent, though they felt no tremors upon the ship. This was the Great Tide.

For a several hours the ship held its position as close to the ice as was safe. After a day, the Twin swung around the planet on its steep course and travelled away from their segment of the sky, to bring its army of water to other shores.

A convulsion on the surface announced the tide's retreat. A wave as smooth as one cast into a ribbon bellied out from the land, raising the ship several feet upon its glassy surface.

The tide went out.

The ocean tilted as a mountain of water was hauled backward behind the Twin; a monstrous conquering god dragging the seas off in chains.

The *Prince Alfra*'s wheels churned at the water at full power; still it was dragged backwards from the wrinkled wall of ice blocking the way to the continent. The pack ice lifted up when the tide went out, colliding with a noise like metal snapping. Sheets large as counties slid backwards, sucked out into the wider sea. The wave steepened. "Full power," said Trassan into the engine room speaking tube. "Immerse all glimmer cores." He looked at Heffi. The Ishamalani watched the dials on his desk climb toward the red segments of the their circles.

"All reverse," he said. The orders bell clanged tunelessly.

"All reverse," repeated Heffi's aide.

The ship whined with the increase in power. The pounding of the engines, often unnoticeable in the wheelhouse, became an insistent throb. Towers of white steam rolled high from the ship.

The *Prince Alfra* clung to its gradient as the ocean fell past the regular level of the ice and uncovered the underside.

Tolpoleznaen worked the wheel, face forward, sparing only the smallest glance for the dials at his own station. His hand twitched back and forth up the wheel, the other adjusting the rotational speed of the wheels, dextrously jinking the ship to avoid broad white ice plaques that defied logic and floated up the wave past them, hauled back after the Twin. Every one Trassan thought would hit; every one Tolpoleznaen deftly avoided.

The angle of the ship's pitch decreased. The mountainous wave of the tide rolled away across the ocean, foreshortening the horizon.

A new world was revealed to the crew of the *Prince Alfra*. The wall had become an overhang. Beneath were the blue dark depths of a world under the ice.

"Take us in," said Trassan impatiently. He looked out of the wheelhouse's rear windows, not trusting the tide not to come rushing back unexpectedly.

"Trassan," said Heffi. He nodded at the engine room speaking tubes. Trassan shook off his misgivings and bent to it.

"Retract glimmer core one. Power down, three quarters," he ordered.

"Aye aye, goodfellow," came Ollens's reedy reply from the engine room.

The bergs and ice had been scattered all across the ocean, the pack ice in particular fragmented, and the way was clear. But new perils presented themselves. The Great Tide had piled broken laminates of ice along the wall's rim. Some of this would stick, Trassan surmised, becoming part of the barrier. A lot slipped off in sudden, thunderous avalanches that rose high spouts of water and punched foaming circles into the sea. Their wash rocked the ship. Trassan watched the looming wall anxiously.

"Take us in, twenty degrees starboard," said Heffi. Tolpoleznaen's eyes had narrowed. The helmsman was deep in his art. He responded wordlessly, shifting the wheel a touch and sending the ship forward. Out on the balcony, Vols and Ardovani stood waiting. Against such a sudden, elemental force as the ice falls, Trassan doubted their magic would do much good, but their presence reassured him.

"Full ahead, Heffi, get us out of reach of these falls," said Trassan.

"Half ahead," said Heffi quietly. "Let's do this softly. Noise brings down avalanches. Let us play our role, goodfellow, you do yours."

Trassan's jaw worked. He gave a tight nod. Heffi was right, but Trassan disliked having no control.

The ship moved toward the gaping cave under the ice. Everyone fell silent. The chopping of the wheels and the rumbling of the engines seemed dangerously loud. All eyes went to the shelf of ice high above. Water cascaded from it, running from hidden reservoirs within breached by the upheaval of the tide. Trassan was not the only man to wince when a man-tall icicle fell like a spear and exploded on the deck with a bang.

A curtain of shade cut the sea in two. On one side, the water was deep blue, on the other a mysterious green. The *Prince Alfra* passed through it, its paint going from dazzling to dim. For a second it was a ship made of two halves captured in different times—one asail on sunny seas, the other voyaging deep in the night. Then they were past, and into the cavernous underworld. Cold groped for them. Trassan shivered with the abrupt change in the temperature.

The *Prince Alfra* sailed into an alien world.

"I have seen many strange things in my years on the ocean, but this... I do not have the words," said Heffi. Everyone looked up, mouths and eyes wide like children at a carnival. The ice had indeed become the sky. Only Tolpoleznaen stared dead ahead, lost to the rigours of his task.

A roof of ice as high and artful as any basilica to the gods arched over the *Prince Alfra*, carved into whorls and smooth sculpture by the actions of the ocean. Faults threading the ice were lit up by sun, turning the ice-sky into an abstract mosaic of blues and blacks divided by a tracery of eye-aching white. Pillars of the finest blue, the legacy of earlier tides, held up the mass above. They grew more numerous as they headed within, cutting the space into a labyrinth of curving walls and soaring, convoluted spaces that groaned and creaked frightfully.

"Tolpoleznaen, we are in your hands. Steady as she goes. No undue noise. No whistles!" ordered Heffi.

Immediate danger past, Vols and Ardovani came back into the wheelhouse, breath steaming in the doorway as extravagantly as the ship's exhaust swirled upwards to embrace the blue. The *Prince Alfra* brought clouds to this aqueous sky for the first time.

"It is beautiful," said Vols. "More so in the realm of Form than it was in the Will."

"Is it stable?" asked Trassan.

"I think so," said Vols. "Well, let me qualify—I sense no desire on the environment's part to fall on us."

A tocking like that of a monstrous clock knocked overhead.

"Then I hope we all get what we want," said Heffi uneasily.

The ice spoke. Great tickings and sighs, squeaks like greatly amplified string instruments, and stranger, howling noises boomed through the caverns as the ice settled. The rumble and splash of distant collapses thoomed through the passageways, amplified to a terrifyingly immediate volume. Heffi followed the breath of the *Prince Alfra* up to the cavern's high ceiling.

"There's not enough heat in it to melt the ice. We won't destabilise it," said Trassan, with a confidence he had to manufacture.

The great, shimmering beauty of the under ice awed them all, striking them dumb. Frequently they would pass a feature that drew comment, causing them to forget the peril they were in. Mighty arches of ice, tunnels rippled like the skin of the desert, walls that glittered with rainbows of refracted sunlight, shallow water of dazzling blue, deep black holes under the water, and once a perfect circle in the roof that gave out to the true sky, shining with such ferocious intensity that the men shielded their gaze.

Wonder could not put the pressing, gargantuan weight of the ice from their notice completely. The feeling that it could, at any time, collapse and destroy them induced a queasy fear that demanded attention, and the more attention it got the greater it became. Trassan was glad then for the steely determination in Tolpoleznaen's bearing. Every glorious sight was nothing; he cared for nothing but the correct passage, the quickest path. His eyes flicked down to examine the compass pedestal to the left of the wheel and Vols' rough map, pinned to the station in front of him by a magnet. They were all he had to guide him through the maze, but he behaved as if the route were familiar to him as the ride up the locks of the Slot.

They entered into a tunnel that bored deep into the ice. The glorious blue faded from cerulean, to azure, to the colour of twilight sky, and thence to that of night. Trassan ordered the prow and wheelhouse glimmer lamps activated by Ardovani. The magister went out, and brought the lamps' magic to life, and white beams stabbed out from the ship.

"Careful, Tol," said Trassan nervously, "the walls are getting narrow."

"Do not tell me my business, Ushamali," said Tolpoleznaen. It was his only utterance during the passage under the ice.

At his gentle command, the ship twitched port, then starboard. The quiet rasp of contact was increased by nerves and the tunnel's acoustic properties to the proportions of disaster.

"Watch out!" gasped Trassan.

Tolpoleznaen ignored him, and spun the wheel. The ship shuddered, a terrific squealing vibrated down its length as metal pressed into ice as hard as stone.

"Give me more power," said Tolpoleznaen.

"Full ahead," said Heffi.

"Are you sure?" said Trassan.

"Leave us to our business!" said Heffi. "Full ahead!"

The ship huffed and shuddered. White clouds of steam, the sparks of dying glimmer in them clearly visible in the dark, filled the tunnel. The squeal returned, and became a groan, though of metal stressed by ice or vice versa it was impossible to tell. The middle mast scratched against the ceiling, rigging twanging like the strings of a guitar.

Suddenly, the *Prince Alfra* lurched forward. The steam whirled upward, and they were out of the tunnel in a cave of stupendous size.

"I see rock!" called the lookout. "Land ho!"

The ice there was so thick there was little light. Above, untold millions of tons of water made solid rucked up into a hollow mountain range, and they were far beneath it.

"This is it," said Vols breathily. "This is the place by the cleft mountain."

Trassan hurried out. He grabbed the handles of the wheelhouse searchlight from Ardovani and panned it around. The dim black line at the far side of the cave became clearly defined, a band of rock between water and ice. The water there was mirror still, until the *Prince Alfra* approached, sending wavelets to caress the granite.

"Take us to one hundred yards out!" said Trassan back into the wheelhouse.

"Which way?" said Heffi. Tolpoleznaen still wore his mask of fierce concentration.

"Vols?" asked Heffi.

"To the left. That way," pointed the mage. "That was where my vision was blocked."

"Tolpoleznaen, hard a port," said Heffi.

"Aye aye, captain."

The wheels span counter to one another, turning the ship on

the spot. Their slapping of the water echoed around the cave like applause.

Trassan played the light along the walls, looking for a hint as to the entry to the Morfaan docks. He saw nothing, and began to doubt the truth of the ghost's account. How could they build a dock here? He expected something like the Slot, but saw no locks or passage.

For long seconds Trassan felt the touch of failure, then they rounded a promontory and his heart leapt.

Before them were the docks of the Morfaan.

Two giant heads rose from the sea, mouths wide, the lower jaws under water so they peered out from the sea like swimmers. Between them a square canal had been carved into the rock, shearing through the mountain's roots and up all the way to the sky. The faces were confrontational, a warning against entry.

Trassan knocked on the window and pointed forward. Heffi nodded, saying something inaudible to Trassan outside. The ringing of the order bell penetrated the glass. The ship turned, the chuff of the engines and wheels chopping water dominating the cavern.

Cautiously the ship nosed its way toward the canyon.

The passage was lined with glass-like material. "It is like the pass at the Glass Fort," commented Ardovani. "Have you ever been?"

"No," said Trassan.

"I did the once, quite remarkable, but I believe this trumps it. I have my own theories as to how the Morfaan made their building glass. Perhaps we will discover the truth of it here?"

The heads loomed bigger. A trick of perspective had made them seem smaller than they actually were, and they grew to a staggering size as they approached. The ship lined itself up with the canyon. Black water stirred inside, wavelets white with crescents of light. The top of the slot was four hundred feet above. A crust of snow had formed over it, for the most part it glowed blue, too thick to permit the sun, but it was holed in many places, and from there shafts of light streamed down, reflected off the walls, then shattered on the water.

The *Prince Alfra* moved ahead.

Lights flared in the eyes of the statues. A moment later, Vols stepped out from the wheelhouse and joined Trassan and Ardovani.

"What is happening?" said Trassan. "Are we in danger?"

"I do not know, goodfellow," said Vols. "But it would be better if you returned inside. The iron will provide a modicum of protection against magic."

Reluctantly, Trassan agreed. The three of them went back inside. Fuggy air embraced them tightly. Condensation streaked the windows.

"Any ideas yet, goodmage?" said Heffi.

"None, I'm afraid," he said. "I sense no building of power that might directly harm us, but... *Gnk.*" Vols went rigid. He blinked rapidly. "I... I... oh dear."

Anger slammed into the navigation watch, staggering them all. Between the stone heads a living face materialised. Spun from golden light alive with glimmer spark, huge and wrathful in countenance. A cacophony of a hundred languages poured from its lips. Vols became pale, several of the men gripped at their ears and shouted. Nothing could be heard but a crowd of dead voices. Until, one by one, they fell silent, leaving a single, strong voice they could all understand.

"Go back, go back!" it intoned in Karsarin, although the lips of the head spoke another tongue, and moved out of time with the words. "This place is forbidden. Return whence you came, or suffer the wrath of the masters. Go back, go back."

Trassan gritted his teeth. "Keep going Heffi!"

The ship approached the head. Through the translucent planes of its alien face, they saw the canyon walls, and the canyon slot. They were coming alive with shooting sparks of glimmer blue energy that shot along the walls, changing directions at hard right angles.

"Go back!"

A second flood of anger assailed them, filling their minds with images of terrible fates. Trassan saw Kressind Manse ablaze, his siblings dead, the world in smoke and fire and his dreams smashed before him. The vision imposed itself upon his sight, but through it he saw the wheelhouse, each man troubled by private hells. All except Tolpoleznaen. He stared forward, jaw clenched so hard the veins on his forehead stood proud. "The One guides me. I rise to the challenge of the One. I will not fail the One," he was saying, lips moving over grinding teeth, his face turning purple with the effort.

"Go back, go back, or all you cherish shall be laid waste."

The ship passed into the face. The visions brought pain. Trassan doubled over, the world was a shadowplay behind the fires consuming his family. Dimly, he perceived one of the Ishamalani grab at Tolpoleznaen's arm, wild-eyed and brandishing a knife. The helmsman pulled out a small ironlock squeezer pistol from their sash and shot him dead without looking aside from their course.

"The One the One the One," he said, with fanatical determination.

"Go back!" it roared.

The visions ceased. Trassan blinked afterimages away. Vols Iapetus stood on the balcony forward of the wheelhouse, raised hands shining within a nimbus of light that reached out and touched the Morfaan image. The face wavered, its voice cracked and fell silent. Glimmerlight raced madly around inside, and the face faded, and disappeared with a flash. The ship passed through the space it had occupied.

Trassan got to his feet. Others stood shakily. The corpse of the Ishamalani sailor lay on the floor, his blood collecting in the corner of the wheelhouse.

"The One, the One, the One," chanted Tolpoleznaen under his breath. The lights in the glass walls went out in threes and fours until they were gone.

Trassan looked at Heffi. The captain raised his eyebrows.

Outside, Vols leaned on the railing, breathing hard. Ardovani went to his aid.

The snowy crust blocking the canyon top parted into white drapings, revealing a river of sky. A bright line marked the canyon's end, the restricted view giving little clue to their final destination.

The *Prince Alfra* steamed on, wheels and screw turning, the crew silent, many tearful, others sunk into a despondency that was slow to lift. Soon they approached the exit to the canyon. Beyond it Trassan saw four tiers of what could only be docks, stepped into the side of a giant bowl so that, similarly to the docks in Karsa, they might be used at various heights of the tide, only the Morfaan docks were made of unmarked black glass, free of rubbish or debris, pristine even after so many thousand years.

With a triumphant wailing of its whistles, the ship left the canyon.

The dock pool opened out a mile wide. To one side a stream of water flowed upwards through a channel alive with glimmer light. Tolpoleznaen headed for it, the iron ship shattering the thin covering of ice as it sailed forward.

After a brief consultation with Heffi, they decided to chance the unusual lock, and the ship sailed to the foot of the water. The prow nosed onto the flow, there was a lurch forward, a grumble of settling steel, and they were sailing uphill. A look of purest pleasure spread across Trassan's face.

"A road of water, without locks. It is a fully functioning Morfaan device. It is unlike anything I have ever seen before. It is beautiful!"

"It is, goodfellow," said Ardovani. "It is."

Frozen canals led off at the four level of the docks, running around the back of the quays so that at various tides they could be accessed from both front and back. Leading off the canals open rectangles marked berths for vessels. Trassan imagined finding an example of a Morfaan craft left behind, waiting for a new master. He saw himself returning not in a ship of iron, but in one wrought of the Morfaan's imperishable metal. To his disappointment all the berths were empty, their waters frozen white.

They reached the last level of the docks. At the top a second round pool opened out, square docks extending radially from it, each of these bigger than the ones below and closed off by a lockgate.

The city of ice was before them, half a mile back from the dockside.

Giant pentagonal beams canted at uniform angles formed an immense latticework. One, single edifice, no individual buildings, but a palace at the base of the world to dwarf that of the richest emperor. Diamond white, this was not the building glass or metal the Morfaan were known for, but ice, clear as water. Murmurs went around the crew, then shouts, then cheers. The entire complement came out on deck to look in awe upon their destination. Men slapped each other on the back. Trassan caught sight of his cousin hugging Bannord.

"We've made it," said Trassan. "We've actually arrived."

"Does it live up to your expectations?" asked Heffi.

"I cannot describe how I feel," said Trassan. "Put us in."

"Tolpoleznaen, make for that berth there. Slowly. A shame the gate is shut. We will have to tie up alongside."

But as they approached, there was a cracking of ice, and the door slid down to allow them access. The *Prince Alfra*'s prow broke the ice on the surface of the dock, sailing in as if it were returning home. Heffi had the whistles sounded one last time, then gave the order to stop. The *Prince Alfra*'s wheels stilled. The engines quietened. The steam rising from its funnels reduced to a trickle.

Tolpoleznaen blinked, looked about in confusion, down at the dead man covered in a blanket by the wall, and slumped against the wheel. Heffi grasped his shoulder gently.

Trassan took in the vista of the city again, and his eyes were drawn to another berth occupied by a wild shape of spun ice. At first he took it for a natural formation, but within was a shadow. Trassan squinted at it, until the riddle unlocked and spars, masts, and hull leapt at him from a confusion of icicles. He took out his glass, ran it over the shape, then snapped it shut.

"We're not first to come here," Trassan said. The cheers died down. Heffi came to his side. Everyone looked to where he was pointing. "In that ice, there is a ship."

CHAPTER THIRTY-FIVE

An Adventurer's Fate

TRASSAN, FLANKED BY Bannord and three of his marines, approached the entombed ship. Vengrise, one of Ullfider's two assistants, came with them. As did Ilona. Trassan fumed about her inclusion, but Bannord had argued her case.

"She'll probably be safer with us than at the ship," he had said.

Looking at the second ship in its casing of ice, Trassan doubted that, but Bannord was insistent. He had even given the girl a gun. Trassan walked to the ship, shoulders tense with wrath. He blamed himself. His idea to have Bannord teach her had backfired. He had hoped she would find the repetitious nature of swordplay drill tiresome compared to the fantasy of her novels. The opposite seemed to be the case. Trassan felt a fool. The satisfaction in being able to say "I told you so" to a close relation is rarely matched and he would not get to say it.

She is happy, he reasoned, and being useful. The crew like her. Stop being such a selfish, curmudgeonly arse. If Katriona heard me say half of what I am thinking, she would stab me to death with sharp words. It'd take a while, but she's persistent.

Ilona might die, he argued back against himself. She will die. What will I do then?

Presentiment of death filled his heart with ice and boots with lead. She was there, there was nothing he could do about that. She was armed and more or less capable. Not the ideal situation, but there was no way she would let him lock her in her cabin until he had delivered her safely home.

Maybe if I knock her out...?

He dismissed the idea. A curse of silence on Kressind women, he thought. I have friends with sisters and cousins who actually know their place.

The day was overcast but sharp, with a clarity that made a lie of perspective and carried sound for miles. Every shout made Trassan wince as if it would bring an army down on their heads. Around the *Prince Alfra*'s dock there was a lot of noise. The steam crane peeped and huffed. Men called out directions to one another as they lowered pallets of supplies onto the quayside. Antoninan's dogs barked excitedly where he exercised them away from the ship, kicking up clouds of snow as they chased each other. Amid all the bustle of unloading, there was laughter and loud conversation. All of them—man, Tyn and dog—were giddy with being ashore again, but away from the *Prince Alfra*, with the silent City of Ice looming over them watchfully, Trassan was nervous, and wished they would all be quiet.

The snow was dry, and the flawless surfaces of the Morfaan offered little purchase for drifts. At the dock the dark gloss of building glass shone through the snow where the wind had cleared it away. It was very cold, but still, dry and crisp. The party barely felt the low temperatures.

The crunch of their boots on snow stopped. The silence redoubled.

The ship was locked solidly into its berth. Ice encased it completely to the depth of several feet, so that the actual shape of the vessel was elusive to the eye. Strip the ice away, and it was much smaller than the *Prince Alfra*, half the size abeam, a little over half as long. Much lower to the waterline, and with an insignificant displacement by comparison.

"Most interesting," said Vengrise.

"What is?" said Bannord. Trassan could tell he felt the same way about the city. He had his gun ready to fire, and looked often towards the dark cave of the entrance.

"The ice, goodfellow, do you see? It is sideways. Have you ever seen icicles like that? They are horizontal."

"It is quite obvious when one looks at it in that way," said Trassan.

"Hmm," said Bannord. He picked up his pace so that he walked ahead of the others, examining the vessel. "Definitely Ocerzerkiyan. No one south of the High Spine makes ships of wood like this, and I should know, I've boarded enough of them. This is a small one, not a ship of war. Fast though."

Trassan braved the intense cold radiating from the ship to squint into the ice. A thirty degree tilt to port obscured a view of anything but the hull, but he made out a gunwale topped by a balustrade with finely carved spindles. A line must be rigging, and a round shape a barrel. There were all manner of objects in there, but all were off the deck, frozen mid-explosion.

"Trassan! Come and look at this!" Ilona called from the prow.

"Stay together!" muttered Trassan to himself. He took up a lumbering jog to reach her side. Seeing her like that, with the ominous columns of the city dome behind her, rekindled his fears for her safety.

"You shouldn't wander away like that. What if there are beasts here, or..." he trailed away.

"Or what?" said Ilona. "There's nothing here. It's deserted."

"I'll feel happier accepting that when I know what happened to this ship," said Trassan.

"There's a piece of the puzzle right in front of you, cousin," she said. Being under Bannord's tutelage had done her good. Some of the light had come back into her eyes, and though she attempted to repress her spirits round Trassan in case she provoked him, she was finding it harder not to talk back; the part of Trassan not fretting about the safety of his expedition was relieved, and decided the sword swinging from a hangar at her left suited her. He imposed a scowl on himself to scare off his positive feelings.

Ilona looked away from him to avoid giving away her amusement—Trassan always wore his feelings on his face. She pointed up at the prow. The wood had only a thin sheath of ice, the bowsprit erupting through it to stand proud, though on the lee side the prow had its odd jacket of horizontal icicles like the rest.

"Yes?" he said. "A ship's name."

"You said you had read Rassananimul Haik," said Ilona. "We talked about it at my house. When we made our deal, remember?" she said, unnecessarily smugly as far as he was concerned.

"I have, but not in Oczerk. Who speaks Oczerk?"

"Well cousin, I do. As a matter of fact. What?" She pouted at the look Trassan gave her. "There isn't much for we goodmaids to do, you know. I had tuition. That is Oczerk. It says—*Hakkainma Kre*, or *The Shining Dawn*," she said excitedly.

"She's right," said Bannord. "I read the letters, I speak about fifty lines worth of Oczerkiyan, mostly variations on 'Surrender or die', but I can make out a name. I know this one."

"This is the last ship of Haik himself," she said.

Bannord shifted his gun. "Didn't he vanish, what, forty years ago?"

"Twenty-seven," said Ilona.

"Then how did he end up here?"

"His book, which I have read in the Maceriyan translation," said Trassan pointedly, "was an account of his expedition to the polar south three decades back."

"Yes, I read it too. I think we all did," said Bannord.

"Well," said Trassan loudly. "He departed again three years later with much winking and implication to his countrymen about a great mystery he had discovered—he was such a braggart he could never keep a secret. And he never returned. One man survived, the Ishmalani cargomaster Verenetz. He always maintained the expedition never made landfall, although he spoke of a marvellous city he saw made of ice. The shaman of the Tatama Awa-Ata had... a different account."

"Hers might be the truer account," said Bannord. "Verenetz said they saw the city from the ocean. You cannot see the city from the sea."

"Verenetz was never really believed," said Trassan. "Until Vand uncovered the Morfaan map at the Three Sisters. Vand had the money and the influence to get a sending performed. Nine attempts it took, and a fortune in silver, but he was successful and I was commissioned to build the *Prince Alfra*."

"So Verenetz was lying then, only not in the way everyone thought."

"He wasn't telling the whole truth," said Trassan. "That's for sure."

"Then what happened to Haik?" said Ilona. "Do you think he might be in there, entombed in the ice?"

"Let's take a look around the far side. Slowly, and carefully." Trassan lifted his arm and waved back at the lookout's post on the *Prince Alfra* to indicate they were going out of sight. The flicker of a red flag responded. "Come on."

He led the way around the prow. Ice reared over the ship in a wave studded with a thousand spikes. Thick cylindrical sections of icicle lay broken all over the dockside under a scrim of snow. Debris and objects cluttered the interior with dark shapes. The listing of the boat brought the gunwale right down to water level, and made a ramp of the deck. Snow blanketed much of the ice on that side, but in the few clear spots many more objects were visible trapped in the ice.

"Hang on," said Bannord. He held up his hand and pointed to something sticking out of the ice by the aft mast. "Drannan, Forfeth. Check that out will you."

"Is that a corpse?"

"I reckon so. The crew has to be somewhere, don't they? Kolskwin, keep watch here will you?"

"Sir."

Forfeth looked back. "It's a body sir."

"There we are," said Bannord. He shouldered his gun and he, Ilona and Trassan, went to look.

A man's upper torso, shoulders and head protruded from the ice, one arm was frozen in the mass, the other was held across the remains of his face to shield it. His flesh and skin had shrunk, freeze dried, and become hard as cured leather. This, more than his resting place's frigidity, kept him in the position of his death. His clothes were faded by harsh polar sunlight and tattered by winter storms, but below the level of the ice, man and clothing were eerily intact. Bannord leaned closer and lifted up a long braid, checking the beads at the end.

"Ocerzerkiyan alright, one of their warrior-sailors, a bit like our marines, but not proper soldiers. They usually run." He looked closer. "There's at least one more in there."

"There are more up there sir, look," said Drannan.

Trassan looked to where he pointed. Bannord scrambled up the ice, it was so ridged with icicles that he climbed it easily enough. He moved over the tilted deck, brushing snow away, ordered Drannan to help him, and together they cleared a wide section of snow.

Ice tinkled down the slope to the dock. Ilona covered her mouth and stepped back.

Within the ice were dozens of bodies, all frozen during the act of falling. Weapons flew from still hands, never to land. Fingers shielded faces, some had turned and run. All had been hit by a tremendous force and then captured by it, imprisoned for three changeless decades.

"Now this, I do not like," said Bannord.

"Nor me," said Trassan. "Any idea what might have happened to them?"

"If you're asking if I know, then I don't. If you're asking for a guess, well," Bannord looked at the city, "I do not think this place is as deserted as it looks."

A DAY LATER Ilona paced the deck along the railing of the ship. Snug in her arctic gear, her exposed face was thrillingly cold. The long day was coming to an end, its last light dying in the sheets of ice hanging from the *Prince Alfra* in glorious display. Two weeks from midsummer, a single brief hour of night awaited. On the ice were numerous tents established by the expedition in anticipation of housing finds from the city, glimmer lamps on hooked poles marked out paths through the camp and its perimeter. Just beyond the lights, the great sleds of the drays were set up ready for morning. The dogs lounged on the snow, grateful to be out of the hold, restrained by pegged leashes that could not possibly hold them, Ilona thought. The ropes were an odd formality, it seemed to her, a mark of the agreement between master and hound, not intended nor suited for genuine restraint.

The mood of all was up, and that had taken genuine restraint on the parts of Trassan, Antoninan and Captain Heffi to defer the first foray into the city. After their inspection of Haik's vessel they had drawn into council, from which she was excluded, and had been there for hours. For now the rest of the crew celebrated, the ship alive like at no other time on the ocean. Ilona found the stillness of the land unsettling. The ground seemed to swell and rock in a way that made her feel sick. It was a trick of the mind after so long at sea, the Ishmalani said, but in a place like that it was difficult to put aside thoughts of bewitchment.

A door in the superstructure opened. Bannord came out, and made straight for the ladder hanging off the side of the ship, unaware of her watching him. He had his men out to patrol around the ship, a hundred yards between them, always in sight of each other. He visited them all one after another, his gun over one arm. The snow was bluing in the light, making of him an unreal shape starkly highlighted in orange by the sunset, like a puppet in a theatre. Such a strange man, very masculine in that aggravating manner so many of them had, dismissive toward her weaknesses—as he saw them— patronising, but at the same he had encouraged her. At first, when he began to teach her the sword, she had thought he was holding back. He assured her when she asked that he had not, and as far as she could tell he had applied himself to her education diligently. And then he'd make some awful, crude joke, or slap her behind or call her weak or do something else that made her blood boil.

She coloured at the length of time she watched him for and became cross at herself for mooning at him like a girl just into her womanhood, and pointedly looked away, back to the ship. The deck was quiet but for a couple of sailors covering over the forward steam crane with a tarpaulin. Comforting yellow light spilled from the windows of the wheelhouse and the doors when they opened and closed. There was hint of festivity to everything, as if they had reached the Yule Feast of First Iapetan half a year early. The weather was fit for it, though that date was far away. Midsummer Night was so much closer. With the cold and the snow it did not feel like it. Winter here must be a terrible thing indeed, she thought.

She continued on her thoughtful stroll and came across Magister Ardovani at the stern of the ship. His strange rifle was propped up against the rails and he was engaged with setting up a long astronomer's glass upon a tripod. The brass of the tubes was already spidered with frost that grew with each breath that caressed it.

"Good evening, Goodlady Kressinda-Hamafara," said Ardovani. He spared her a brief, genuine smile, and a polite bow, then carried on setting up his equipment. Ilona thought him good company, kind and enthusiastic in all he did, unstinting of his praise of the merits of others. He was handsome in that Cullosantan way, small but well proportioned, with long, agile fingers, and finely groomed. He had kept his beard short despite the cold. His warm, caramel skin looked so out of place in the frigid wastes. She looked into his eyes and saw dusty roads and dark green cypress neat as topiary rather than reflected snow.

"Are you not celebrating?" she asked.

"I will, but I wish to perform some observations of Andrade's Cloak from an unmoving platform," said the magister. "The aurora has not been documented from so close to the pole and never here in the land of the midnight day. If I learn nothing from it, well then, I have the privilege of looking on its beauty."

His eyes lingered a little too long on her face. Ilona looked in the direction the telescope was pointing. "I find it eerie, goodmagister."

"All the finest things in life are frightening," said Ardovani. "A little. 'Love without fear is not love.' That is what we say in Cullosanti. It goes for all things."

"Being a magister especially, I should imagine."

"Indubitably," he said, sighting down his telescope. He adjusted the spread of the tripod's legs, pushed wooden pins into holes to hold them in place, and stood back. "That should do it," he said, and gave his full attention to Ilona. "Now I only have to wait."

"I suppose that is the default position for a magister, courting danger."

He laughed. "A romantic view."

"Tell me, what is the difference between a magister and a mage? I always thought them to be much the same. But I see that you and Goodmage Iapetus are different."

"Well, perhaps you were poorly informed."

She bridled only a little. Ilona had been patronised by many men during her young life and was therefore particularly sensitive to being talked down to, but she took no offence from Ardovani. His laugh was so bright and joyous and he seemed to take delight in their conversation. "On the contrary, Goodmagister Ardovani. I believe myself well informed. I read widely. I thought the difference exaggerated by the parties involved to accentuate their superiority over one another."

"There is a large amount of bad blood between the two branches of our calling, more's the pity," he agreed.

"So then it is as commonly held, that you are some sort of magical engineer, and Goodmage Vols is, for want of a better word, a wizard."

"Never call him that!" said Ardovani. "He won't thank you."

"Tell me the difference then, or I shall be forced to call you both wizards."

He flashed her a white smile and leaned back on the rail. "Neither of us are. There is but one wizard, and he is jealous of his title. I will describe the difference for you. It is true that many of we magisters specialise in the utilisation of magic in engineering. But then so do many without the mage taint. Your cousin, he is a sort of magical engineer, but he does not carry the blood himself, although I understand others in your family do. We magisters and mages are both true mageborn. Magic is all an act of will, you see. Broadly speaking, the difference between a mage and a magister is in the way that we use our gift that makes us either one or the other. Magisters employ rituals of proven efficacy, procedures if you prefer, in order to create a certain effect. These are generally lesser than the great magics you read about in the histories, but the use of prescribed formulae bestows greater ease and reliability on the practise of magic. The fabric of the world becomes used to these changes, enacted as they are by many minds, and the more a formula is used, the easier it becomes. This is why in stories and the like, witches and other users of magic employ fetishes or familiars; it is a focus, you see, and mages too make use of such techniques. It is true that now many of my brethren specialise in engineering, but it is possible to be a purely immaterial magister, whose works are not so very different to those of a mage—on the surface. But whereas we magisters rely on rational experimentation to create a given effect of incremental power, a mage attempts to alter reality by force of will alone. We all influence the world, collectively, through our thoughts and our dreams. We are all mages to some degree."

"Then is what the mages do lesser? Is that why there are so few of them?"

"On the contrary. What a mage does is by appearance much cruder, but far more effective, and far harder. Not only must he convince himself that the world should be a certain way, but through the medium of his power alone he must also convince the world that it is in error. The world is alive, unresponsive, unconscious, but it has a spirit. The Ishamalani worship it, and its creator."

"Yet you must also use this spirit."

"We do. And our road is easier, if less dramatic. Magecraft has become harder as the population grows. Other people make a mage's work difficult. In populous areas they must assert their own version of the truth over that held by the many members of the human race; not only convince the spirit of the world that he is right, that the world is wrong, but also that the unthinking opinions of the many other people around him are also incorrect. It is why, I imagine, Goodmage Vols and the other mages dwell so distantly from concentrations of the population. In truth, their gifts are greater than that of the magisters, or the Dead God's quarter, or any of the others who are blessed with the knack of magic. Among my school, there are a goodly number who might once have been apprenticed to mages, but not all magisters have the requisite ability to be so, and fewer still the correct set of mind. The gift of a mage is mighty, but to wield it they must either be insane enough to believe the world is different to how they perceive it, or supremely confident that they can change it to match their own caprice. Preferably both."

"Vols is neither, is he?" said Ilona. "The others, they say things about him."

"Bannord?"

"I'm afraid he's not very flattering."

Ardovani placed a hand on Ilona's shoulder and guided her to the starboard side of the ship's stern. He searched for something a moment, then pointed. "Do you see that?"

A column of whirling snow travelled along the ground, looping out from the ship and back again.

"That," said Ardovani, "is Vols Iapetus. He has transmuted himself into a living embodiment of this place and roams freely through it.

Have you not seen? His powers have grown away from the swarming Isles. Imagine his burden. His ancestor was the greatest mage of all time, the Goddriver himself. No matter his ability, Vols would find it impossible to live up to that. People look to the past, and they look to him, and they compare, judging him harshly for who he is not. They do not favour him for who he is. They have no confidence in his power, and sadly nor does Vols. Do not underestimate him, Ilona. His gift might be erratic, but it is my opinion that Vols Iapetus is the most dangerous man in Ruthnia. Should he find his confidence he will be the finest mage of this century."

A crackling popped in the heavens. Green waves of light uncurled across the horizon like dancers coming on to a stage.

"Andrade's Cloak!" Ardovani exclaimed. "Glorious, and visible before full dark." He hurried to uncap his telescope. "Come now. Why don't you help me with this? You can aid me making the notations. You know mathematics?"

"Yes," said Ilona. "I was taught many useful skills I was never intended to actually use."

"You can use them now. Bannord has been teaching you the arts of combat, I am sure there are things that you might learn from me— the movement of the stars, the patterns of the Earth, the sympathies between magic and matter. There is the mage taint in your family. Perhaps helping me might awaken yours, if it is present?"

"I will help, but please do not tease me, goodmagister."

"I never tease on important matters," said Ardovani gravely. "I would be glad of the company."

CHAPTER THIRTY-SIX

A Shock in Perus

Ambassadress Chiwil of Pris faced Lucinia Veritus of Mogawn over afternoon tea in the Karsan Ambassador's Room in the Palace of Nations. Between them were coffee, heavy with perfumed flavourings, lemon biscuits, and a world of entirely different expectations.

Chiwil's coyness at speaking her mind was annoying Lucinia, so she spoke it for her.

"You are going to offer me a place in your Queendom," she said.

The ambassadress showed a brief half-smile. She was like no woman Lucinia had ever seen before. In skin tone and size there was nothing remarkable about her, she was short and somewhat stocky, her hair long on the scalp and left side of the head, shaved down to a half inch around the back and right side. Her exposed ear was studded with five earrings of rank. She wore britches and stockings and a close fitting jacket. This style of men's clothing had spread from Maceriya over the last forty years, but the ambassadress's were not men's clothes cut to fit the female form, nor were they feminised according to the mores of the western kingdoms, but something else that presented a look familiar and yet utterly different.

And that, thought the countess, was the Queendom through and through. Alien underneath.

The ambassadress moved with the easy confidence of someone born to power. Lucinia had seen it often in men, never in women. She had known women who fought their way to influence or found themselves imbued with power by a quirk of fate, but they exercised it guilefully, or with overstated force—a failing she knew well for it was her own—or they were crushed. Ignored, married off, driven mad. Chiwil's acceptance of her privilege as a right was something new.

A pair of male servants stood guard. Fine specimens, well-muscled, tightly clothed, kohl-eyed, and silent. Lucinia tried not to gawk at them. It was rare to see a male of Pris outside of the country. The ambassadress paid them no more attention than if they had been extraneous dining chairs.

"Why else would I be here?" said the ambassadress. Pristians only ever had the one name. She knew little more of them than that. Her knowledge of Pristian customs was limited to the lurid rumours told on the streets of every city outside its borders. "You are the foremost mind in the field of astronomy alive today in all of the Hundred. We will gladly offer you whatever funds you deem necessary to relocate, and the post of Mistress Celeste at the university of Prishna."

"Heavenly Mistress?" said the countess with an arched eyebrow.

A stone possessed more humour than Chiwil's face. "Tradition is fundamental to our national identity. Our ways can appear quaint to outsiders. It is a teaching position. Prishna is—"

"The foremost institution for geographical, astronomical, and philosophical instruction in your country. I know, it is well known. I have read papers from there."

"By whom?"

"Shelfosh. Marchina. Someone else, I think. I do not recall."

"You do not sound as if you were impressed."

"Forgive me, but my own researches have far overtaken anything I have read from anywhere."

Chiwil sniffed the coffee, wrinkled her nose and clapped her hands. One of the males came forward dutifully. "Take away this decadent Maceriyan swill. Fetch us wheaten ale. Chilled, I cannot stand it warm."

"Goodmistress," said the man.

Chiwil watched his buttocks moving in his tight trousers as he left. "Such a pretty thing, don't you think?"

"Delightful," said the countess. Though she enjoyed the man's backside, for once in her life she was taken aback at another woman's behaviour. There was nothing light or charming about Chiwil's comment. Lucinia decided there and then that Chiwil was a brute. "I prefer my men with a little more spirit."

"We have spirited men. We would be grateful for someone to occupy them," said Chiwil.

Ah, though Lucinia, *was that a joke?* She drank her coffee. She found it palatable.

"If you were to accept the role, you could have your pick," Chiwil went on. "You would be of high status, higher than countess in Karsa. We treat our educators very well. Any man could be yours. If it would sway you, we can outfit you with a stable of fine consorts, all you would have to do is say."

"I hear your men cannot refuse a woman's advances."

"That is the natural order," said Chiwil. "Women bring life, therefore we are the arbiters of how it should be lived. Alas, we are the only nation to live as nature intended."

"That seems poor sport to me," said Lucinia archly.

"I see," said the ambassadress. "If that is not attractive, perhaps you might find yourself a lifemate? A woman like you would be much pursued. There are many women who find your life story thrilling, why—"

"You may find it hard to believe," interrupted Lucinia, "if you believe only half of what is said about me, but I am not interested in bedding women."

"I understand same-sex coupling is frowned upon in Karsa," said Chiwil sympathetically.

Lucinia laughed. "And if you'd heard even a little of me, you will know I don't give a dracon's shit for convention."

"You cannot dismiss the option until you have tried," said Chiwil. "You could find yourself a partner. You would make an excellent mother. Any donor would be proud to father your children."

"What kind of empiricist would I be if I had not tried the love of women?" said the countess. "Of course I have tried! It was pleasant, but failed to set my heart racing. I like men, ambassadress, and I like them to be free to think. I like men whom I can pursue, and who might refuse me. It makes bedding them all the sweeter when they do not. If you are here to lure me to your kingdom with the promise of domesticated males and limitless tribadism then you should try harder."

Chiwil frowned. "You would not say that you pursue these men who might rebuff you only to prove to yourself that you are not unattractive? You do not invite them in to your bedchambers so that one of them might, just might stay? You do not shock public opinion in order to test the boundaries of your acceptance?"

Chiwil's assessment of Lucinia's drives was uncomfortably accurate. "You are better informed than I supposed," said Lucinia icily. The servant returned, and handed Chiwil a fine glass tankard of cloudy beer. He bowed and offered one to Lucinia. She accepted. She had never tried wheaten beer before.

"We lag behind in the celestial sciences, but we are quite adept at psychology," said Chiwil.

"Evidently," said the countess. "Your beer is also good, better than your sense of tact."

"You are not known for tact either," said Chiwil. "We have limited time, we are not here expressly for this one purpose, and so these side issues, however important, must be dealt with expeditiously. There is no reason to dodge the tide, we must plunge in. Were you to come to Pris, all these things that humiliate you in your own land would cease to be important. You would be free, and feted. In Pris the true order of the race is maintained. Women are mothers, they are moulders, we are leaders. Come and see how life should be."

"And you'd like the chance to turn me to your side of the bed, is that it?"

The ambassadress puckered her lips disapprovingly. "You are as obsessed with sexual matters as you are talented. The offer is genuine."

The countess drained her beer. "Well thank you, Medame ambassadress, but it is not for me. As for the difficulties you are so sure I experience, if you are such a magister of other people's minds, how can you be sure I do not define myself in opposition to them? I would be quite adrift if everyone were kind."

Lucinia and the ambassadress stood. "It had crossed my mind, countess. My report on you was thorough."

Chiwil put her palms flat on her hips and made a strange little bow.

"The offer has been made, it will remain open."

"I have said no."

"It remains open," repeated the ambassadress. She extended her hand. Lucinia took it. The ambassadress shook in a male Maceriyan style, fingers gripping fingers.

"Good fortune with your lecture, goodlady. You will need it, most of these men would rather pull a dracon's tail than take sound advice from a woman."

"Now that's what makes it fun." Lucinia curtseyed ironically, clicking her heels like a man.

She exited the Palace and headed across the Place di Regime toward the Grand House of the Assembly, annoyed by Chiwil, but intrigued with her offer. Maybe it was time to move on from Mogawn. She treated the place like a refuge, darting out to shake her backside at the world, then running home to hide. For all the resistance she had encountered, her trip round the Hundred earlier in the year had suggested the possibility of change. If not Pris, why not somewhere else? Perhaps the more relaxed northern kingdoms and their pleasant climates. Why not Perus, even?

Perus agreed with her. People bowed to her and looked at her curiously more often than they wrinkled their faces in scorn. She was spared insult here and had been mildly surprised at the enthusiastic reception she had received from certain ladies, and surprised at the fad for clothes aping her own. She had no illusions. Fashions in Perus sprang from one ridiculous extreme to the next; he who was lauded one year could easily find themselves prosecuted in the courts the next for licentiousness.

"Fickle, flighty, foolish," she said to herself. Amazing that these people had once run half the world. The comment was not fair; the men and women on the square moved with a purpose only exhibited by those with weighty matters to attend to, though they were all dressed like clowns.

She reached the Grand House. Being an exact likeness of the Palace, it gave the unnerving impression of arriving at the place one had set out from. Was that a mathematical possibility? she wondered. Then she groaned inwardly as she spotted that damned fool of an ambassador, Mandofar, hurrying down the stairs toward her at the head of a phalanx of footmen. "Goodlady, where have you been?"

"At the Palace, declining an offer I had to refuse," she said. "What are you fussing about? I am on time. They are not due to hear me for another hour."

"You were supposed to be in the Grand House twenty minutes ago! There are matters that need discussing. Your dress, your—"

"What is wrong with my suit?" she said.

"It is, well... it is unfeminine," he said. "We need to present you in a certain—"

"Damn your balls man!" she said loudly. "This is a fine suit. I'll wear what I bloody well please, now go away. I need to shit before I talk."

"Goodlady..." Mandofar's whole face bulged comically at her vulgarity.

"Do you not understand 'go away'?" said Lucinia. "My, you are as stupid as Abing says. How about this?" she placed a finger in the middle of his chest. "Fuck. Off. Ambassador. Now. Is that clear enough?"

Mandofar blanched. "I... I... I have—"

"Never been so insulted? You obviously don't get out enough. I will be waiting in the antechamber to the speaker's stage after I am done with my toilet. Get one of your flunkies to bring me my pipe and get a quart of wine set out for me. Believe it or not, I'm actually rather nervous."

THE COUNTESS CHECKED her glass slides again and again while she waited, putting them back into and taking them out of their leather-clad box several times. She smoked her way through a half pouch of tobacco without noticing. The wine she put aside when she became lightheaded. The antechamber was a bar, really. A man sat behind a counter with racks of bottles. The seating was arranged around four small tables. Besides her and the server, the room was empty. A couple of pompous looking Maceriyan civil servants passed through, all made up like their lords but wearing sober black clothes. One nodded at her, another ignored her. That was the sum of activity.

She smoked, she drank and she waited. The man on before her went over by five minutes that seemed to last an age. This was not like her, she reflected ruefully. She had taken her presentation to the Royal Institute far more lightly. She came to the conclusion that she was nervous not because this was important, but because she was beginning to be accepted. Failure had never worried her before because she was outside the normal run of things. To fail on the terms of others was no failure at all. But here she was now, about to present to the assembled representatives of all the kingdoms, in a country whose people mimicked her dress, only months after a good reception from her own—exclusively male—peers. She was no longer an outsider, and failure's risks had become very real indeed.

A muffled round of applause, quiet at the clapping of birds' wings, shook her from her thoughts. She doused her pipe, and took one last sip of wine. Presently, a door opened and a young Karsan man came out. He smiled at her. Ordinarily she would have behaved saucily with him, but she was not feeling herself.

"Countess, if you would come with me, they are ready for you. I am Jonn Moten, I will show you to the podium and I will change your slides for you while you speak."

"Thank you," she said. She followed him through the door from the antechamber into a corridor. Affecting a carefree air, though her head was light with nervousness, she said, "Have you done this before?" and examined her words as she spoke them. Strike up a rapport, make friends, make them like you, be one of them. At that moment she hated herself for her artifice.

"Oh yes," he said. "Never to so full a house, but it is among my duties to assist the Karsan representative, the ambassador usually, when they speak to the house."

"You are not nervous, Goodman Moten?"

"No, goodlady. There is nothing to what I do. You have the difficult role. But do not be concerned, I hear your talk is favourably anticipated. We are here."

The corridor terminated in a tastefully decorated room. Double doors opened into the hall of the Assembly, a set opposite led back into the hive of offices and meeting rooms of the Grand House's southern wing. Two sofas and a pot plant marked a feeble attempt to bring domesticity to the room. The sofas looked like they had never been used. This was not a place to loiter, but a transitional space between nerves and terror.

"Are you ready, goodlady?"

"As I'll ever be."

"Then we shall begin."

Moten took the box of slides gently from her and opened the doors. A flight of dark wooden stairs led up to a podium. Moten went first. As she reached the top a stave was banged upon the floor and a loud voice announced her.

"Lucinia Vertisa, the Countess of Mogawn speaks on behalf of the Three Houses of Karsa and Prince Alfra, sovereign lord of the isles."

She emerged blinking into bright limelights. An octagonal space was walled in with a panelled rail, a lectern at the front. Moten showed her to the front. A magic lantern with a glimmer lamp inside was set on a table at the back, the thick lens of its eye dazzling. Morten left her and busied himself with this as she set out her papers. Did it matter that she had not told him they were numbered? She supposed not, he looked like he knew what he was doing. She would find out soon enough.

Polite applause greeted her. She squinted past the lights. She wished she had spent more time on her appearance. She felt vulnerable and too hot. The representatives were arrayed below the pregnant swelling of the Grand House's dome in three tiers of wooden galleries. There were only one hundred representatives, but there were many others in the hall—the ambassadors, assistants, servants, advisers, specialists of countless disciplines and the one hundred men and women of the Assembly Guard. The Karsan embassy was seated in the Petitioner's Quadrant below the podium, sharing space with the delegations from three other nations whose people were addressing the assembly that afternoon. She caught sight of Garten coming in late, the Tyn's box in one hand. Abing tutted at him as he sat down at the far end from his fellows.

Above the Petitioner's Quadrant was a small balcony housing the Morfaans' thrones—they were there watching, almost enshrined their box was so heavily decorated—and next to that a much larger, if less grand, box for the Maceriyan government. In the Maceriyan box there were ten thrones, the highest and most ornate was always empty, reserved for their powerless king. Convention, and the execution of three of his predecessors in coups, discouraged him from attending. Three thrones for the comtes of Perus, five for the ducal lords of the country's fivings, and the tenth for the primate of the Church, left vacant since before the union of the Hundred, when Res Iapetus had sent his holy lords packing from the Earth. She gave all her attention to that single chair. It was to stand against the terrors of religions, feckless gods and associated superstitions that she had agreed to appear. When she spoke, she addressed these idiocies of the past and not the dignitaries of the present.

"Goodfellows and goodladies of the Hundred Realms of Ruthnia," she began. The lectern glowed with magister's marks, and her voice was amplified tenfold. Her nerves jumped—she literally felt a tingling in her arms and legs—and serenity descended on her. On the lectern were her notes, her life's work condensed into simple language. Why should she feel nervous? She was the mistress of her art. Her confidence was a shell over her insecurities, but it was thick and strong. She felt it forming around her, and her voice rose in power.

"I am here today to present to you the findings I have made through my extensive study of the Twin, also known as the Dark World, and in the most ancient of texts as the World of Form. As you are all aware, next year, 461 of the new calendar, on 32nd Takcrop, the Twin will make its closest pass to the Earth for four thousand years. This perigee has heralded great upheavals in the world in the past. The legends surrounding its approach fascinated me as a girl." Did she imagine the sniggers there? She shut them out. "As an empiricist, I will prove to you today, that the approach of the Twin must be prepared for. But that talk of it heralding the return of the gods—as rumour upon the streets of this very city suggest—is a nonsense. The danger, however, is very real," she paused. "We may be living in the last days of the present age."

Raganse, Comte of Outer Perus, made a loud noise of disapproval and noisily left, as did a few other representatives.

A murmur rippled through the crowd. Conversations started up that did not die away, and so she raised her voice to be heard over them. "I believe, through observations of the Twin's movements, and more importantly the tides, we might mathematically prove the existence of a strong, attractive force as fundamental to the workings of the universe as magnetism or magic. If we look to my first slide..."

Morten placed the slide in smoothly. It was the correct glass, the right way up and the right way around. Good boy.

"... we can see here the orbits of the Twin and the two moons. They are—"

There was light, bright and painful. She felt weightless, as if flying. She wondered a moment if she had dreamed all this, and she was being awakened unexpectedly. The confusion persisted for less than a second.

She slammed down. Something weighty landed on her outflung arm, pinning it in place. Ringing in her ears subdued all other sound, there was grit in her eyes. She tried to rise but could not for the weight. She shakily turned her head and saw her arm swallowed to the armpit by a splintered section of bench. A sensation of wetness spread across her leg, and she looked down her torn clothes to see a wound in her thigh spilling blood into the rubble.

Fire leapt up from the wreckage where she had been standing, and leaned hungrily toward her.

CHAPTER THIRTY-SEVEN
Over the Wall

VARDEUCHE PERSIN STALKED through the boiler room of his flagship, the *Marie Sother*. Stalls full of coal ran down one side, dark iron furnaces down the other, their doors open upon their fiery hearts. Sweating godlings threw hundredweights of fuel into roaring fires by the sack full. The temperature on deck was well below freezing, but down there it was hotter than the hundredth hell. The comparison was obvious, but apt. The Torosans were black from head to foot, demonic in the orange light of the furnaces. A leaking joint hissed superheated steam, the room reeked of hot metal, the bitterness of coal and sweat.

"Stoke them higher!" he ordered the foreman. He was a short, wiry fellow from the Three Lands on the Ellosantin sea, his home a world away from the freezing mountains of Toros. But he was dirty as his workers, the whites of his eyes startling in the black of his face. It made him a silhouette; hard to see he was a real man and not some dark thing crawled out of the pits of the afterlife.

"Mesire, if we do so then we will risk rupturing the pipes. We already have a leak."

"As the one who designed and built this ship, I think I am in a better position than you to judge its tolerances. More coal!"

"Yes Mesire Persin," said the foreman.

Persin finished his inspection and headed up. The *Marie Sother* was one of three ships, all carved from single pieces of floatstone. Floatstone was a far superior material than wood to make a ship with. It was rigid, light, and practically unsinkable. A king's fortune paid for each, and now he risked losing his prize to a man equipped with a vessel made from iron. Persin ground his teeth. He hated Arkadian Vand, and therefore he hated his protégé Trassan Kressind. The prospect of ceding the city in the ice to a young whelp with an unproven ship design made him rage, and his temper had become foul.

The decks grew colder the further away from the fires of the boiler room he went. Coal was cheaper than glimmer, and to his thinking more reliable, but despite his best efforts he had not managed to get a hold of Trassan's designs for the *Prince Alfra*'s engines, and his estimation of their capabilities was woefully conservative. The iron ship had set out after his own expedition, but had soon passed them by. Only once had he caught sight of the rival vessel. For an elated moment, Persin thought he was beginning to gain on the *Prince Alfra*, but it had drawn away, and within two days its steam plumes had disappeared beyond the horizon.

He went up the tower at the centre of the boat, informed the captain that he was to order the other ships to full speed, then stomped off into his cabin, hoping to rest alone.

It was not to be. Adamanka Shrane sat cross-legged on a rug in the middle of the room, her staff across her knees and her eyes closed. A stove kept his quarters warm, so he shucked off his furs. He poured himself a drink. Windows around three sides of it allowed good views of the sea, the *Marie Sother*'s deck, and the expedition's other two ships, the *Shadow of Perus* and *Maceriya's Glory*. All three of them were smooth skinned, unlike ordinary floatstone boats. He had the cavities on the outside filled in with a durable plaster of his own creation. Their drag reduced by this simple measure, at first the ships had sailed swiftly through the oceans, but then the ice had begun to embrace them, clogged rigging made them top heavy, and the stone's inherent roughness encouraged formation of ice on the hull. They had become sluggish in the water. Mountains of ice sailed by them. Sheets of ice clogged the water, and a wall of ice blocked access to the continental interior. Seeing the black rock of the mountains poking over the rumpled pack ice sent him mad with frustration. There was nowhere to land.

Vardeuche Persin loathed ice.

He sat down, and put up his feet. "Shrane!" he said. "Shrane!"

She let out a noise of irritation. "I am engaged in a seeing. Can you not see I am busy? This is a delicate act and I cannot be interrupted."

"You are talking to me now. Tell me what you have seen."

"I have found the iron ship. They have made landfall upon the Sotherwinter continent."

"Where?" said Persin, torn between exploding with annoyance and eagerness. The others had got there before him, but he had more men, and now they had shown him the way. "We shall follow them, and take what is rightfully ours."

"We cannot. They pass under the great wall of ice that blocks access to the coast, and up into a port of the Morfaan."

"Then let us do the same!"

Shrane sighed and opened her animal eyes. "We cannot. By the time we reach the port, the tides will not be right for another thirty days. To pass that way, we must wait until after the next Great Tide."

"I will not let a lackey of Vand take my prize!" snarled Persin. He downed his wine. "There must be another way." He looked at Shrane. "Is there?"

She smiled slyly. "There is."

"THAT'S IT?" SAID Persin. He slammed his telescope closed against the palm of his gloved hand. "That is impossible."

Four miles away, through a shifting morass of deadly icebergs, was a dip in the wall. Persin could make out a way from the shore up over the mountains fronting the ocean, he could not conceive of a way to get to it. The ice on the water was jammed in close, groaning and shrieking as it ground against itself. "We cannot get there! We will be trapped, and carried off in the current. With pressure that immense, I cannot safely conclude that the ship will not be crushed like an eggshell."

"All will be well," said Shrane. She wore only the thinnest coat out on deck, no hat, no gloves, for an inner heat radiated from her. Wherever she went, ice glistened with water. "You have completed the transfer?"

"All material for the expedition has been moved to the *Marie Sother*. The men we require are aboard. The other ships will head for the docks you described. But whether we go in one ship or three, we will not make our way through that ice."

"We are not going through it," she said.

She planted her staff on the top of the tower, spread her feet, closed her eyes, and began to mutter.

"What by the drunken god are you doing?" he asked.

"My magic saw us through the realm of the Drowned King without detection, it will see us through this realm of ice. Silence."

"How will mist and obfuscation help us against that?" grumbled Persin.

"My magic is not so limited," Shrane said. She began to chant, low, breathy, on the inhalation and exhalation. Persin watched her dubiously. Shrane's magic was powerful, but he had had dealings with mages and magisters both. And at some point their claims always exceeded their abilities.

A green spark cracked from the iron of Shrane's staff, scorching the low wall around the tower's top. It was the first of many, gathering dancing threads of power that played loudly around her hands, mouth, eyes and the tip of her staff. Clouds raced across the sky, drawn towards the *Marie Sother*. They boiled over the mast. The ship groaned, and tilted to one side. Persin searched for a wave, but saw none. He took in an apprehensive breath.

"Stand ready!" he shouted down to the deck, three storeys beneath him.

She smiled as she chanted. A curse on all users of magic, he thought. They never could tell a man what they intended. They were hooked on theatricality, every last one of them had a puerile need to amaze. He looked down again, hoping to whatever god still gave a shit about the world that his men wouldn't panic.

Thunder rumbled from the *Marie Sother*'s private storm. Lightning of the same green hue as the sparks around Shrane's staff threaded through the billows and curves of the cloud.

The ship tipped forward, then back. The men waiting on deck made unhappy noises. Water ran noisily off the sides as the *Marie Sother* lifted upwards out of the sea and flew slowy forward. Persin was afflicted with a sudden attack of nausea at the sight of *Maceriya's Glory* and the *Shadow of Perus* shrinking behind them. The dogs in the hold bayed madly. Shrane's jaw clenched. The ship leaned forward, and Persin got the distinct impression that Shrane was like a potboy running to catch up with a collapsing stack of dishes, trying to outrun those toppling forward before they could fall. The ship accelerated, until it hurtled forward at a great rate. Jagged icebergs whipped past, the mountains became large and clear. The space behind the dip in the ice covered in scree, close enough that he could see the individual rocks making it up. Then they were passing low over the ice wall, which gnashed and clattered beneath the keel. Rising up, they passed its upmost reaches, and approached the bare stone of the mountain.

Never had landfall been a more appropriate phrase. With sickening speed, the ship contacted black rock, shattering its prow into powder. Rigging snapped and fell, prompting alarmed yells from the crew. The stern of the boat lowered, then dropped and banged twice onto the ground, leaving the *Marie Sother* at a steep angle. With a terrific grinding it slipped backwards. Persin ran to the back of the tower, hitting the railing there with winding force. The sea was three hundred feet below them. The scree slope steepened, leading directly into the sharp landward edge of the ice wall. The ship bounced toward it, the floatstone crunching on the harder granite as it skidded uncontrollably backward.

"Shrane! Stop us! You'll kill us all!" he shouted.

The boat turned on its keel, tipping sideways. Men's screams ceased awfully as they fell out and were smeared to paste under the sliding hull. Supplies and sleds, so carefully stowed for the landing, broke their ropes and fell overboard; crates smashed, scattering their contents down the slope. The scree banked up under them. Persin hoped it might reach a sufficient mass to stop them, but a small avalanche rushed out from under the rupturing keel.

"Shrane!" he shouted.

Lightning arced around Shrane's staff. She still had her eyes closed, muttering her strange words to herself. The ice wall came closer. The snow of it was dusted brown, the crevasses were deep and a stunning blue. Persin watched them rush at him, arrested by the colours, sure this was his final sight.

The boat lurched, and slowed. Shrane held up her staff, and turned it slowly. As if hand and the ship were the same, the *Marie Sother* followed, righting itself to the scree. The ride became smoother, the horrible crunching of broken floatstone lessened.

Almost delicately, the ship came to a stop in the angle between ice and scree at the foot of the slope. Boulders rattled down into the hull, bouncing in decreasing numbers until finally, they stopped.

A slew of debris described their path, the rocks marked with the chalky white of pulverised floatstone and the red of obliterated men. The deck was in disarray. There would be more casualties there.

Shrane stopped chanting, and sagged into her staff. Persin grabbed her.

"You have wrecked my ship."

"We are upon the Sotherwinter continent, where few men have ever trod," she said wearily. "The prize is yours for the taking, and you have two other vessels to bear you home. No venture can be completed without a little sacrifice. Now leave me be. You have witnessed a great work of magic, and I must rest."

She moved slowly toward the tower stairs. Persin moved to follow her, but she stopped him with a dangerous stare.

He went to the rail, and began shouting orders down to his men to prepare for disembarkation.

CHAPTER THIRTY-EIGHT
Aftermath

GARTEN PUSHED A broken body from his chest. Shouting and alarms rang under the dome of the Hall of Assembly. Soldiers ran pointlessly from place to place, yelling, weapons out. Garten was drenched in blood, already drying sticky on his face. With trembling hands he probed his body, relieved to find no shock-numbed wounds. So far as he could tell he was, miraculously, unharmed.

He wished he could say the same for Lucinia. The speaker's podium was a mess of twisted iron and blazing wood. Tongues of orange flame twisted where she had been standing.

"Fire, fire, fire!" someone called, far above. A bell rang, then another. The soldiers ran, some fled. Those with a presence of mind hurried to the epicentre of the explosion, the end of the Petitioners' Quadrant. Garten's seat had been upended by the blast, and he struggled to locate his original position. When he did, his stomach flipped. There had been four other embassies in the quadrant along with Karsa's: Macer Lesser, Mudai, Rodriana, and Tellivar. Members of the smaller groups were scattered willy-nilly, strewn like corpses in a melodrama. Two men sat blinking, holding their bloodied faces in their hands, another clawed at the splintered remnants of his left leg, screaming without taking a breath. The rest of them lay still. They might have been alive or they might not, but it was the Karsans who had been closest to the blast, and they were all certainly dead. Scraps of them adhered to the walls. The ivory shrapnel of teeth studded wood. Garten picked his way through scattered limbs and shredded finery, searching for Abing. He stood on something soft, lifted his foot to see a hand adorned with Mandofar's ring of office. He was staring at it, unable to move, when a groan spurred him back into action. He followed the pained sounds, overturning an upset bench to find Duke Abing.

"Damn it Kressind!" he said. His thunderous voice had faded to a pained whisper. "Damn it all!" His hands were bright red, his sleeves soaked in blood. A length of bent iron protruded from his gut. Blood flowed around it, so slowly it looked almost decorative; a lazy, pulsing fountain in a summer courtyard, not a sign of harm.

"The Morfaan! Get them out of here. I don't trust any of this lot. Not one!"

Garten looked up for the first time. The force of the blast had directed itself upward, reducing the Maceriyan box to a bottomless square. Planks of wood and bodyparts dangled from it. The Morfaan balcony had fared better, and both the emissaries lived. The male looked to be having a seizure or a fit of panic; the woman's face was a picture of outrage.

Living soldiers reached the Maceriyan balcony—all those guarding it had been flung outward, colourful and dead as a scattered bunch of cut flowers.

"The Comtes are dead!" one was shouting.

"Secure the house. Get that fire out. Send for the physics."

"At last one of those bloody idiots is showing some wit," said Abing. He grunted in pain. "I'm going, for the love of all the Earth, I'm going! Gods damn it, not like this!" he said. He gritted his teeth, his lips parted to show teeth stained crimson. "Get to the Morfaan Kressind, get to them and get them out of here before someone else finishes the job."

Garten nodded and backed away. "Whatever you say, your grace."

"Bloody lucky you were late, or you'd be dead too. There's just you now. They got the bloody lot of us! Hold the fort until help arrives from home, and don't do anything bloody stupid."

"Yes your grace," said Garten. He hurried away, past his seat. On his way out he turned his ankle. He felt it go and flicked his foot out before he could put his weight down and twist it, kicking aside a small, brass bound box in the process. "Issy!" he said, and plucked up her case. "Issy, Tyn Issy, are you hurt?" he opened the door. Issy stared back at him, her hair rumpled but otherwise unhurt.

"Take more than that to kill a Tyn of my degree. I am tougher than lesser beings."

"I'll take that as a no then."

"Wait! I slipped and tumbled though. I think I broke a nail," she said peevishly. "After all I did. My art saved you."

"You?"

"How else do you think you still live, by which I mean not dead? Foolish man. Ungrateful. And you forgot me."

"I did not," he lied.

"You did."

"I'll give you flowers when this is done," he said. "Thank you."

Garten stumbled over the bomb's wreck. A spine glinted whitely from the red ruin of the floor. There was an inch of blood in the bottom of the Petitioner's Quadrant. He never knew so much fluid was contained within the human form.

He exited the box. Away from the blast the effects were superficial, debris tossed from the explosion, not structural damage. He had enough of his family's affinity for engineering to see that. He took the stairs up to the balcony at a run. There should have been two soldiers guarding the Morfaan box, but they had fled or gone to the carnage in the Maceriyan balcony. A scabbarded sabre lay discarded on the floor. Not his favoured weapon, but Garten retrieved it before pushing through the curtain unmolested.

The curtain was a divide between two degrees of order. On the side of the corridor, there was no sign of anything amiss. On the other, devastation. The ornamentation of the box had been blasted into a thin spread of plaster glittering with scraps of gold leaf. Splintered wood poked dangerously from broken beams and panelling.

The male Morfaan was cringing into the female, weeping like a child, her clothes bunched in his fists and pressed into his face. Garten stepped back. The woman heard him and whirled round, provoking a fresh round of wailing from the male. There were representatives still in the building, and some had stopped to point from the galleries above, astounded by this performance from the erstwhile masters of the Earth.

"You must come with me, now," said Garten. He held out his hand, ridiculously feeling that he had intruded upon a private moment.

The female—Josan—looked imperiously at the scabbarded blade. He held it in the same hand as Tyn Issy's box, leaving one free.

"You come here armed. You may wish us harm, we are safer here," said Josan.

"I think not," said Garten. "I cannot say that the bomb was intended for you, but it is likely."

The male began to titter. "Bomb, bomb, bomb."

"Yes," said Garten, "an explosive device, most likely a mixture of glimmer and iron, it—"

"We know what a bomb is," said Josan.

"So clever you have become," said the male wiping tears from his face with the back of his hand. "We are very proud of our protégés." He turned his face to look at Garten. His eyes were rimmed red with weeping, and although they were inhuman, there was no mistaking the madness in them.

"My lord, are you hurt?" Garten asked.

"My brother is shocked," said Josan defensively. "That is all."

"Please," Garten said, "come with me. I will take you wherever you wish. I am Garten Kressind, the sole survivor of the Karsan embassy. My lord's dying wish was that I see you safe."

The woman's odd nose flexed. She looked up to the faces peering over the balcony at her and her simpering brother.

"To our rooms in the palace," she said. "That is far enough away from here, and guarded by more than men."

By now the outflow of people had become an influx. Soldiers, physics, Guiders and the curious came into the dome from every entrance. Soon those soldiers who had come to help were occupied with holding back the crowds and keeping order.

"This is a mess. Which way do we go?" he said to Josan.

"I will show you, Garten of Karsa."

She parted the curtain, and moved out of the remains of the box with difficulty, for her brother still clutched at her skirts. A long hall led back from the Hall of the Assembly. Toward their end, staircases swept up from it to the circles and boxes of the representatives. Josan moved very quickly, half-dragging her brother. Josanad had stopped weeping, and peeped at everything with fearful eyes. Encumbered, the Morfaan moved faster than a human could walk and Garten jogged to keep up. Men rushed past them in both directions, bearing the wounded, shouting. The assembly was an ant's nest disturbed.

"How did you come away unscathed?" she asked Garten.

"I have a friend."

Josan eyed Issy's box. "You have an Y Dvar guardian? Those of the half-will?" She slowed, putting space between herself and Garten.

"A lesser Tyn," he said. "She is under many geas, do not fear."

"One should always fear the Y Dvar," she said.

They went down a fan-shaped stair that opened into a lobby area, and headed for the doors. Josan slowed, yanking her brother back.

Outside, the sun was shining. She approached the edge of a rhombus of sunlight on the carpet and looked fearfully skyward.

"The mist! It is gone!" she said.

Josanad blinked myopically. "Gone, how?" he straightened, changing completely. A different man emerged from the cowering thing of a few moments ago.

"The mage," said Josan. "The one at the rock. The lackey of this ridiculous church."

"Shrane," said Garten.

"You know her?"

"She has been causing trouble. Have you not been told?"

"We have been told very little," said Josan.

There was shouting outside.

"What's this?" said Garten. He drew his sabre. "Get back."

A line of men were advancing up the steps, armed with a motley collection of weapons. A soldier moved to confront them. One of the men raised an ironlock pistol and shot him down.

"Get away from the doors!" said Garten.

A bullet shattered the glass.

"Sister!" said Josanad. For a second, Garten feared the return of the frightened boy, but the Morfaan shook off his cloak and drew matching swords of strange design from his belt. To Garten's surprise, a second, smaller pair of arms emerged from slits in his tunic, and plucked daggers from crossed baldricks.

"We will fight together, goodfellow," said Josanad.

There was no time to think on this change in the Morfaan. Their attackers opened fire, destroying the glass of the doors, forcing the Morfaan and Garten round the corner into cover. The men ran in, expecting their quarry to have fled, but Garten and Josanad were waiting.

"Karsa!" Garten shouted. Josanad added a cry in a high, piping language, and they ran into the knot of assailants. Garten despatched two before he had finished his charge, opening one's face as he fumbled his gun up. The second made a pathetic attack with his sword that Garten evaded easily, skewering him through his throat.

Josanad moved with amazing speed, swords blurring, hacking down men as he span. Garten would never advocate turning one's back on the enemy as the Morfaan did, but Josanad came through it unscathed. In seconds, he had incapacitated or killed five men. The three left threw down their weapons and fled.

Soldiers thundered into the lobby, and trained their guns on Garten.

"Lower your weapons!" demanded Josanad, stepping between the guards and Garten. "This one fights for me!"

An officer ran down the stairs. His jacket was soaked all down one side in blood.

"My lords Morfaan! I was told you departed by the south exit."

"And I by the north," said another, coming to join them.

"Distractions. There are agitators in this building." said Garten. He hunted about the wounded, and grabbed a man clutching a deep gash in his arm. "You!"

The man spat at him. Still energised from the fight, Garten hauled him up and pressed his fingers into the man's wound, making him scream.

"Tell me why the Morfaan were attacked," demanded Garten.

"Gladly!" said the man. "I have nothing to hide. The gods! They insulted the gods! The Assembly, the Morfaan." He snarled. "You will all die for it."

Garten shoved him back. Disgusted with himself, his rage abruptly left him, leaving him feeling ill.

"Round these bastards up," said the officer. "Get them to the physics, those that look like they'll live, then deliver them to the

Fortress," he said. Soldiers pushed past Garten. Two lived. He pitied them for their fate. "Get the Morfaan back to their apartments via the south wing tunnel. Keep them out of the sun. Triple the guard. Men of good standing only, no foreigners."

"This is a matter for all the kingdoms," said Garten.

"It will be my head if they die, not yours," said the officer. "Only those men I know personally will watch over them."

Josan looked helplessly over her shoulder at Garten as they were hustled away. Everywhere there was shouting and bells. More and more soldiers were coming into the building, flooding past him like the tide past a rock.

Now the excitement of combat was leaving him, a weight of dread drew Garten's gaze to the dead on the floor. Their wounds were bright scarlet ways into the meat. Their most intimate parts were unknown even to themselves, revealed for all the world to see. It was abhorrent, this lack of dignity, worse than death in its way.

These bodies were opened by his blade. He screwed his eyes shut against the sight, but the images remained. He had trained with the sword all his life, but he had never yet killed a man. Not until now.

Garten's sword clattered from his hand.

CHAPTER THIRTY-NINE

The City of Ice

THE SOLSTICE WAS a week away. The nights were a bare purple bruise on the western horizon before they drained away. The effect on the men of so much light was simultaneously energising and enervating. They had little desire for rest, and the few hours of sleep they took were fitful. When awake and engaged at their tasks they went at them with a feverish intensity, but when not gainfully employed many of them fell into a nervous, twitchy daze. Between them Bannord, Trassan, Heffi and Antoninan kept the crew hard at it, preparing the camp and sleds to bring back whatever wonders were within the city, and surveying the outer bounds of the dome. Ullfider and his assistants chipped away at Haik's icy tomb. The city waited, but Trassan did not give the order to investigate. Fights broke out, especially between members of the more radically opposed Ishmalani sects. Other men became maudlin.

Bannord grew concerned at the wait, and sought out Trassan. The aft hold had been emptied of the larger items of equipment. Although the walls were still lined with shelves of supplies not needed on the ice, there was sufficient space for a modest workshop.

Trassan spent most of his time there when not dealing with the day-to-day running of the expedition. Sure enough, Bannord found Trassan with his sleeves rolled up, tinkering on a device Bannord didn't recognise.

"We," said Bannord, "are going to have a problem if we don't get in there soon."

Trassan sighed and leaned on his workbench. "I agree, lieutenant, but what's to be done? The Ishmalani have to observe their rituals, and we have to set up camp. I've learned enough from the writings of Haik about the importance of a proper base in the Sotherwinter."

"The weather's fine," said Bannord. "The city is five hundred yards from this perfectly adequate dock. We've enough supplies to last us months. We're not camping on shifting pack ice."

"Are you challenging my judgement?"

"Hells yes I am. What are we doing sitting out here?"

Trassan wiped his hands on a rag. "Bannord, to be frank with you, I've not idea why Guis recommended you over Captain Qurion—"

"I do," said Bannord.

"Don't interrupt, please," said Trassan wearily. "I do respect what you have to say, Bannord, but there have been only a handful of successful recorded voyages across the Drowning Sea to the Sotherwinter. Others have tried, and the King of the Drowned has pulled them under or the weather has made them founder. Haik is the only man to have crossed the Sotherwinter Sea twice, and his second attempt doesn't seem to have gone so well. I may look like I'm dawdling, believe me, I want to get into that city so much it's making my teeth hurt." He hung the rag on a hook on the table and rolled his sleeves down carefully. "I am an impulsive man. You know my brother, it runs in the family. I've learnt the hard way to know when it pays to be careful. Another few days is not going to hurt."

"I disagree."

"And I am expedition leader."

Bannord made a conciliatory noise and crossed his arms. "Look, I'm not suggesting that we go in half-cocked. Fuck that. But we need to do *something*, get the more belligerent and active men out and doing work with a bit of balls to it. I say, let's scout the city."

"I've had scouts go in a way."

"Only the entrance cavern. Let's go inside in force," said Bannord. "Something bad happened to our Ocerzerkiyan friends over there in the other dock. I'd rather find out what it is before we go in with a train load of civilians."

"Whereas I'd rather you didn't go in there mob-handed and destroy a lot of valuable material you don't understand," said

Trassan. "Haik's ship is being examined. I don't want to go before we've learnt all we can from it."

"Really? As Ullfider tells it, there is nothing of interest aboard, and if there is it's all frozen solid. The scouts sent into the city entrance report nothing. Empty rooms swathed in ice. Notice a pattern here?"

"They've barely penetrated the city. There could be anything in there."

Bannord pointed a finger at Trassan. "We agree on something. Yes, anything. Some anythings carry swords. If there is a presence in the city, I would rather face it now, and not give it time to prepare. That kind of mistake gets men killed, and if you lose the marines, we're all dead."

"That sounds like a threat."

Bannord let out a groan of frustration. "I'm not talking about abandoning you! You're as stubborn as Guis. What do I have to do to get you Kressinds to have a conversation without wilfully misunderstanding me? Listen, Trassan. I get the impression you don't like me much."

Trassan stuck out his lip and shrugged, not a denial.

"But I do know what I am doing. As a marine, I'm often harnessed to duties that involve civilians. It's unavoidable. I've been guarding merchantmen most of my life, or acting as some ambassador's guard more times than I can remember. And I'm telling you, my men are getting fractious, and the others are too. We have been cooling our heels here for a week without so much as a poke into the city. We're going to run out of time."

"We are doing good science on the ice. Persin cannot get under the ice wall for another four weeks. We'll be away before he gets here, and if we're not, we'll be ready for him."

"Assuming he comes this way."

"There isn't another way," said Trassan.

"How do we know? I am trying to help you, goodfellow. Anyone would think you don't want to go in after all that effort. The crew are whispering that you've lost your nerve."

"It's not nerve."

"Perfection, then. Remember the bloody whistle? Perfection is dangerous in a place like this."

"Preparation," countered Trassan. "Dangerous not to have that."

"When are we going in? Let me get together a scouting party in force, and we can at least range ahead a way."

Trassan picked up a screwdriver by the tip and knocked the wooden handle thoughtfully against the top of his bench. "Alright. We'll do it. But I want one of the alchemists and Ullfider along. Ardovani and Iapetus too."

"Fine," said Bannord. "Ardovani has proven himself in a fight, Iapetus seems to be getting his head out of his arse now we're here. Both of them will be useful if the Morfaan have left any nasty tricks. How many of my men should I detail to remain here?"

"Half. Ten," said Trassan.

"I've got sixteen left. Dellion is sick."

"Eight then."

"Very well," said Bannord. "The morning?"

Trassan nodded and went back to the parts of his machine.

"Well, I'll go make the arrangements then." Bannord folded his arms and looked around the hold. "You stay down here doing... whatever it is you are doing. Do not trouble yourself."

"Bloody arse," said Trassan as Bannord left, just loud enough for him to hear. Bannord flicked the Dark Lady's horns at him by way of response, and so parity was restored.

ILONA FIDGETED IN her uniform. The arctic gear they wore made them sweat, and wool was rough against her skin.

Bannord adjusted her baldrick over her parka, checked the hang of her sword. "Stop wriggling, trooper," he said.

"It's itchy."

"Goat's wool is good enough for the heroes of Karsa," he said. He whispered close into her ear. "Get some silk lining put in, or wear a shirt beneath, otherwise it'll drive you crazy."

"What is Trassan going to say?"

"You're forgetting something," said Bannord.

"Sir," said Ilona.

Bannord grinned. "Trassan is going to say precisely... nothing. He cannot say anything. You are a stowaway, you need to work. I've found it for you. Those are the laws governing Karsan shipping. You are now a member of *Prince Alfra*'s Maritime Regiment."

"He'll go mad."

"He can go fuck himself," said Bannord. "The man's so driven he pushes on into danger one moment, becomes a dithering prick the next."

"He is my cousin."

Bannord raised his eyebrows and tilted his head.

"Sir," said Ilona.

"Let me handle him. Darrasind!"

Darrasind jogged up from the unit of marines standing ranked upon the ice and came to attention between Ilona and Bannord.

"Sir," said Darrasind, purposefully keeping his eyes front, and Ilona out of his field of vision.

"Darrasind here is going to show you how we do things in the Maritime Regiment. Isn't that right Darrasind? You're going to make up for your embarrassing behaviour."

"Sir, yes sir!" shouted the trooper, flushing bright crimson. His comrades sniggered.

Bannord smiled. "It's his way of an apology," he said in a loud stage whisper so that both Darrasind and Ilona could hear him. "Isn't that right, Darrasind?"

"Sir, yes sir!" said Darrasind.

"Have you something to say to the goodlady... I mean, Trooper Kressinda-Hamafara?"

"I am sorry. Really sorry." His face turned even deeper red. "I don't know what go into me. I mean, you are so pretty and all and—"

"I'd say it was about half a quart of good whisky got into you, wouldn't you, Darrasind? Darrasind here is off the booze until I say otherwise. Anyone catches him on it, it's thirty lashes for him."

"Sir!" he said. "Thank you sir!"

"You have any trouble, you tell me," said Bannord.

"I will. Sir," added Ilona hurriedly.

Bannord's face softened. Ilona liked this Bannord, even if his behaviour made his other side all the more infuriating by contrast. "Ilona, Trooper Kressinda-Hamafara. This is the last time I'm going to show you any personal favour. After this, you're one of the men.

You do what I say, and you do it quickly. Do you understand?"

"Yes, sir!" said Ilona, standing to attention.

Bannord pulled a face at her posture. "We'll work on that," he said. "You two run along now."

Darrasind held out his hand to indicate that Ilona should go first. "I really am completely sorry," Bannord heard Darrasind saying as he led Ilona to the unit of marines. "Truly."

Trassan was deep in discussion with Antoninan, the latter holding a freshly drawn map in his hand. The Maceriyan explorer had taken his dogs two days to the east, then to the west, while the ship's crew had prepared. There were, Bannord had been told, no traces of the Morfaan in either direction, nothing but trackless snow and black rock. There was only the city.

Trassan handed Antoninan the map back as they approached.

"Are you ready?" he asked Bannord.

"I've picked my men."

Trassan looked past Bannord to where the marines were dividing themselves and collecting equipment for the expedition. Mild interest became a frown.

"What's my cousin doing there? You haven't told her to come have you?"

Bannord could not stop his smirk. "I ordered her to come, actually."

"Ordered?" Trassan's face fell. "You have not recruited her!"

"I have. She needed to pay her way, now she is."

"You can't do that!"

"I did."

"But there are no women in the Karsan army!"

"There are now," said Bannord. "I'm the ranking officer here. Military affairs are my purview."

"You arrogant bastard!" said Trassan. "I don't believe this!"

"There is precedent," said Bannord. "Women have served in the Karsan army in the past..."

"Only in times of dire emergency!"

"... and regularly do so in the armies of some of the other kingdoms."

"What?" said Trassan. "I'll report you. I'll have your commission stripped if you don't stop with this nonsense this instant!"

"Too late now, she's signed the paperwork."

"This is ridiculous."

"Do you really think I care?" said Bannord. "I've won half a dozen medals, Trassan. My father is poor, but he is still in the House. I'll be reprimanded, but so what? And if Ilona proves herself, then they will be too embarrassed to say anything whatsoever. Taking her out of the army will draw censure from the Queendom. Seeing as they're our number one ally in central Ruthnia at the moment, my superiors will be keen to avoid that."

"Only if they find out about it."

"What makes you think they won't?" said Bannord. "Ask your brother Garten, his department oversees the Maritime Regiment. I am sure he will agree with me."

"You said she was a liability. You didn't want to train her."

"As with all men with a good education and the wit to use it, I reserve the right to change my mind." said Bannord. "She has spirit."

"You're doing this just to spite me." Trassan jabbed an accusing finger at Bannord. "Ilona!" he called. "Ilona!"

"She has her orders, she won't come."

"Get her over here then!" said Trassan.

Bannord nodded. "Trooper Kressinda-Hamafara!" he barked, but he kept his smile and his gaze glued to her cousin as she jogged up. If Trassan was appalled by her carrying a rifle before, to see the blue and black uniform visible at her throat under her parka made him livid.

"Ilona, you don't have to do this."

"Trassan, you moron," she said. Bannord laughed. "I want to do it. Please let me be useful."

"What if you get hurt? What if you are killed?"

"There's a chance of that anyway. The weather. Persin. The Drowned King. Whatever is in there. Anything could kill me. I understand that. I could have stayed at home and died of boredom instead. I would rather die as a useful member of the crew with a weapon in my hand than as a stowaway screaming and needing protecting at every turn. It is my choice, Trassan. You are so thick-headed sometimes. You know why I came on this voyage."

"Yes, well. I did go through that with you. I am going to be married, Ilona. There's nothing between us, not any more."

She punched him hard in the arm. "By Omnus's hairy balls! Gods! Listen to you! Did you not hear anything I said to you at my parents'? I came here because I wanted to make my own choices, not because I'm some lovesick girl!"

"Ah," said Trassan, embarrassed.

"You told Bannord to teach me."

"I only meant for you to be able to defend yourself, not go on the offence!"

"Fine. Too late. I'm a soldier now. Live with it, or don't. It doesn't make any difference to me. Can I go, sir?" asked Ilona of Bannord. "The civilian leader of our expedition is getting on my nerves."

"As you were, marine," said Bannord.

Ilona executed a clumsy salute and walked off.

"By the bloody gods," said Trassan. He dragged his mitten down his face. "Her mother would kill me if she were here. Then eat me."

"I am not doing this to annoy you, despite what you might think," said Bannord. "She is better employed, I think, than left idle. Real mischief would come of that."

"You may be right," said Trassan. "Very well. If anything happens to her, it is your responsibility."

"As her commanding officer, that goes without saying."

"Right," said Trassan. He watched his cousin swapping jokes with her new comrades. They appeared to have welcomed her into their ranks. "Whatever. Be ready in fifteen minutes," he said, and went back to talk some more with Antoninan.

"Now that went better than I expected," said Bannord to himself.

CHAPTER FORTY
An Honourable Man's Burden

SHORTLY AFTER THE explosion in the Hall of the Assembly, Duke Abing died. He did not go quietly. When he could not control the agony, he screamed his frustration at the world, and when he could he spent hours whispering frantic advice to Garten. A day after the explosion, he spoke his final words.

"I am not bloody ready!"

As he was in life, so he was in death. He produced a wild and powerful ghost that took two Guiders to send on, taxing them to the point of exhaustion. When they finally had him pointed the right way, Abing shot away from this existence to the next still mouthing advice to his successor.

Garten's world was pitched into chaos. He found himself the acting ambassador, representative and special envoy to the Assembly of Nations all at once. Mandofar's secretary, under secretary and Karsan liaison with the Three Comtes had perished in the explosion, leaving Garten with staff of the most junior sort. Luckily, all were capable; they would not have found employ in the diplomatic service had they not been. The pressures of foreign affairs, even more than the army, tended to weed out incompetent sinecurists and leave only the talented behind. One international incident was usually sufficient to ensure the expulsion of inadequate staff. They left with their lives, though not their reputations.

Garten threw down the sheaf of paper he was reading onto Mandofar's desk. The deceased ambassador's office was his base of operations, a fine room, though nowhere near as grand as his offices in Karsa City.

Mandofar's position was the kind he had aspired to all his working life. But it was not his, he had not earned it fairly, and the stamp of the other man was on every object. He sat at Mandofar's desk, looked at Mandofar's pictures while he drank Mandofar's liquor from Mandofar's glasses.

"Damn room smells of Mandofar," he said.

"Temper temper, Garten dear," said Issy. Her larger case had been set up on a side table. She sat inside, taking alternate bites from a cake and the scrunched up technical specifications for a new kind of steam hoe.

"I do not know where to start!" he said. "In two days the new ambassador will be here and the whole things is a gods' damned mess!" He rubbed his hands over his face.

"You are tired."

"I've not slept for a week."

"Not technically true," she said.

"Alright!" he snapped. "Two hours snatched here or there don't constitute a good night's rest!"

"Do not shout at me. Sleeping is a weakness. I do not need to sleep. It is not my fault you are weak."

"Tyn sleep," said Garten. "You sleep."

"You think I sleep. But what am I really doing?" Her pretty lady's face leered at him. He could easily imagine her peering at him from the bole of hollow tree when she did that, before ripping his throat out.

"Do you have to pull that expression?"

"You object to my face now?"

"No, no. I am sorry." He ruffled his own hair. "I could do with some exercise. It would be good to hold a sword in my hand." As soon as he said it he realised he didn't mean it. The dead faces of the men he'd killed haunted him yet.

"Be careful of your desires, you do not know where they will lead you," said Issy, and took another huge bite of paper, crumpling it into her mouth bit by bit until her cheeks bulged.

There was a knock at the door.

"Come in!" barked Garten.

Jonn Moten poked his head around the door apologetically. Garten's mood softened. Moten had been very useful to him these last days, despite his injuries. The left side of his face was mottled by scabs. Moten hadn't mentioned it himself, but he had been four hours in the hospital having all the debris dug from his flesh, and had had to go to a healing magister to ward off infection.

"The Countess Lucinia Mogawn is here to see you."

Garten nodded and opened his gritty eyes wide so as to appear more awake. "Send her in, thank you Goodman Moten."

Moten bobbed his head and opened the door. Lucinia Veritus of Mogawn limped in, leaning on a stick she gripped so hard her knuckles were white.

Garten hurried up and pulled aside a chair for her and held her arm while she awkwardly got into it. She settled into it gratefully, shoving her splinted leg out in front of her.

"Drink?" said Garten.

"I look like I need one, don't I?" she said. The shiny scars of minor burns mottled her face. "I'm a blasted mess." She smiled at her own joke. "Do not worry overly much, Garten, luck was with me. The break is simple, has been set well and seen to by a magister so will heal soon. The burns will also fade, although I am hoping for a discrete scar. It would only enhance my reputation."

"I am so sorry that this happened to you."

"I flatter myself that they were after me," she said. "No one has ever attempted to assassinate me before. I consider it a badge of honour."

"Maybe," said Garten.

"If it were not for Moten..." she tailed off. The countess had been trapped. Moten had dragged her out before the fire could kill her. "I will have that drink, I think."

"Good idea." He went to a drinks cabinet. "Mandofar has a fine selection here. Any preference?"

"Something strong, not too sweet," she said. Garten selected a decanter and poured them both large measures.

"Thank you," said the countess.

"You are leaving today?"

"Yes. I would stay—"

"You must return," interrupted Garten. "I insist. If you are a target then you are not safe here."

"I do not care, goodfellow," she said. "If you need me to remain, I am willing, if not entirely able for the moment." She tapped the splints on her leg with her cane.

"You will go home."

"Well, one does live in the most inaccessible fortress in all the Isles. I will be safe there if nowhere else. I have disseminated printed copies of my speech. It will lack the power of a spoken presentation, but needs must." She raised her glass. "To you," she said, and drank half of it in one swallow. "How are you faring? I imagine this is the kind of office you had in mind for yourself, even if I doubt you intended to gain it so precipitately."

"I am not the holder of this office. I am to be relieved in two days."

"Quick, by bureaucracy's standards."

"Indeed. I am not comfortable here. There is a scent a man leaves behind him, on the role and on the room. Were this to be mine I'd rip it all out and have new brought in. The smell of that man is insinuating, just like he was. It cloys the back of my throat."

"The only throats he is irritating now are those of the worms," said the countess.

"If only it were not so. I could do with his knowledge. I am certain Raganse was behind the bomb. He's condemned the militant side of the church while pulling the bishop closer in. The chances of a moderate being chosen now for the Maceriyan candidate for High Legate are practically nil. The sons of Juliense and Arvons are in their minority; Arvons' is barely one. Until they are of age, Raganse is de facto ruler of Maceriya."

"The last thing Ruthnia needs now is to lose focus," said Lucinia. "We must be ready for the coming of the Twin next year, not banging tambourines to welcome the gods back."

"That is the least of it, countess," said Garten. "There will be dissension in the hundred. Deadlock. I cannot see this devolving into armed conflict, it is unthinkable."

"Perhaps because it is unthinkable, you should consider it," she said. "The threat of war is greater now than it has been for decades."

Garten was glum at the thought. "You are becoming involved in all this, I thought you said the end was nigh, all that."

"I have lived my life in opposition to the prevailing wind, my dear Garten. Just because I believe Ruthnia to be doomed, does not mean I will not go down without a fight." The countess finished her drink. "I must be away. My train leaves soon, I move slowly and you are busy." Garten moved to take her glass, then she offered her arm and Garten helped her up. She leaned in and kissed his cheeks gently.

"Be careful, Garten. You may have guessed that your brother behaved poorly toward me, but you are a good man. I wish you well."

Moten returned to help her out. There was a wheeled chair just outside. Garten caught a glimpse of it as the door swung shut, he guessed he was not supposed to. The countess was proud. He was sorry to see her go.

Garten sank into endless reports gathered by agents of the Karsan intelligence ministry working in the city. Every one seemed to concern the Church and its growing appeal, each report was worse than the last. Gloom enveloped the room and he absentmindedly hunted about for candles, still reading. Another knock at the door shook him from his concentration.

"What is it?" he shouted. He looked outside. It had become foggy.

"Begging your pardon, goodfellow," said Moten. "It's the Morfaan, Lady Josan she—"

Josan pushed past into the room, her odd way of moving and long skirts making her appear to glide. A wide hood concealed her face, but she pulled this back. Underneath she was heavily made up.

"Leave us," she said to Moten.

"Yes my lady Morfaan," he said, closing the door behind him.

The papers drooped in Garten's hand. "Lady Josan."

"You will listen. I have need of you," she said. From her such an imperious statement was a simple fact, something a forester might say to a tree before felling it.

"Yes?"

"You helped us after the explosion." Her speech was stilted, delivered oddly, without the usual array of human ticks. The less extreme facial expressions of the Morfaan were inscrutable to him, when he registered them at all.

"I have enquired about you. You are a good swordsman. I require someone whom I can trust, and who knows how to handle a blade."

"A blade?" said Garten.

"Yes," she said, wrinkling her face at him like she had not realised he could speak. "A blade. Tomorrow, at dawn in the Meadow where we arrived. My brother has been asked to duel."

"A duel? Who wants to fight the Morfaan?"

"I have said this. It has occurred before."

"Not for three hundred years," said Garten.

"Nevertheless, there is precedent."

"Please, Lady Morfaan. This is a trick, so soon after the bomb, the attempt on your life—"

"Was it an attempt on my life? Is that so? Do you have proof?"

"No, I surmise."

"Leave supposition to minds greater than yours," she said. "We were masters of this Earth for aeons. There is no threat. A matter of pride and honour, foolish, but sincere. If we decline, our position weakens. We will appear frightened, and a Morfaan fears nothing. I have been told that since Josanad's last victory, your rules of fighting have changed. I understand that currently it is legally required to have a companion present at a duel."

"A second," said Garten.

"Yes. A second to fight in his stead if he be wounded. Do not be afraid. Josanad has never been beaten, by man nor Morfaan nor any other being. You will not have to fight. But you are necessary."

"Might I ask who his opponent is?"

"The woman, Kyreen Asteria. She is arrogant. You will have the privilege of seeing her die."

"Lady Josan, Kyreen Asteria is the finest duellist in the world. She has never been beaten. And your brother, if you will forgive, if he suffers from one of his—"

"There is nothing wrong with my brother!" she said. She reared back, like a snake about to strike. "You presume too much."

"I... I apologise," said Garten.

Her anger passed. Her neutral expression returned.

Garten sat down heavily.

"You wish me to act as second?"

"Yes," she said. "You have demonstrated your loyalty. You are skilled with a sword. I trust you. You accept?"

"As an honourable man, I must," said Garten. "I cannot decline."

"Very good," she said. "I shall see you tomorrow." And then she left.

"I told you to be careful what you wished for," said Issy.

Garten held his hands up. They were shaking.

CHAPTER FORTY-ONE
The Ice Warriors

THE EXPEDITION STRUCK out into the City of Ice. They took all three sleds, and all the dogs, the members of the party riding sat on either side, feet on the runners. Three marines accompanied each sled, four on the rearmost if Bannord were reckoned among their number. Trassan went out on the front sled with Antoninan and Ullfider. The mage and the magister rode the second with the alchemist's apprentice, a lad named Marlion, and Antoninan's groom.

The head groom's son drove the dogs of the last sled. He had no reins as a driver would on a dray wagon, but shouted directions to the dogs. They responded flawlessly. A couple of Heffi's burliest Ishamalani sailors rounded out the party. The sledges were made of heavy wood that seemed too large for the dogs to pull, but they managed both vehicle and cargo at a brisk trot. Valatrice called out to them from time to time, barking and yipping orders, occasionally resorting to human language when describing an easy route or warning of potential dangers.

Snow hissed under the runners. The dogs panted. Small noises in a wilderness of white silence that filled the world side to side. And ahead, the rainbow glitter of the City of Ice's prismatic cover curved over to hide the sky.

The city seemed more of an artificial cavern than a city built by men. The interior was a broad space half a mile wide lit by bright light and broken rainbows scattered on snow. The dogs' panting became louder as they pushed into the city's silence. Four hundred yards in, a wall blocked off the interior. The cavern was a vast porch to a giant's building. A gateway opened in the frozen wall. This was of more familiar Morfaan style than the crystalline lattice of the city's high roof, but still of ice. The gates were open, massive slabs incised with Morfaan characters.

A long road opened. Buildings sheltered under the artificial sky. The scouts had come into this, the city proper, but had stayed near the entrance. Now the plan was to head as far as the road permitted, then work their way back toward the ship to create the map of the city needed for later, systematic exploration.

The buildings were like no human construction, but fluted, strange undulating things that resembled the stems of unfamiliar plants. They crossed over one another and interlocked, with increasing density toward the all-encompassing roof, so that they resembled the interior of a sponge or coral. Toward the road the spurs split, pushing out into air on their own like the twigs of a tree. Some were very long, proceeding for a hundred yards or more without visible support. Bannord had listened to the reports of the scouts, but this was the first time he had ventured through the gates, and none had gone further than this. He grudgingly admitted to himself that Trassan had it right, waiting until they were properly prepared. The place was a labyrinth, and all of it, without exception, seemed to be made of frozen water. There was no trace of metal or building glass, nor of the finely wrought stone the Morfaan utilised elsewhere. Apertures that might have been windows and doors pierced the building limbs, but they were set at strange heights that would make them useless as such. A few opened at street level, permitting a view through into the dark spaces of the buildings' interiors. The expedition were silent. The alien buildings had a certain beauty, but their unfamiliar nature disturbed them. The ever-present sensation of being watched had faded from the docks, but it returned stronger now they were inside.

The city went back, further than the extent of the exterior, which Antoninan had circumnavigated, suggested. Trassan called a halt to consult his maps and perform calculations. Bannord took his men off the sledges, sending them in twos to investigate the interiors of the mysterious buildings. They came back baffled, reporting empty halls and rooms and staircases that went nowhere. All of them experienced a suffocating silence, and the sense of watchful eyes grew oppressive.

The party refreshed themselves, and passed on, leaving the piss of the dogs bright yellow on the snowy roadway.

Eventually the furthest wall appeared, the roof lowering itself and bowing to meet the floor. The ceiling lost its regular sweep, taking on undulations to match the buildings below. The woven nature of the dome's construction smoothed. Where it touched the ground it was as solid as a castle wall, and there another gate awaited them.

The sleds pulled up. The party got down, staked the dogs in place, and went to investigate.

Two interlocking teardrop gates made up a circular whole. A smaller circle in the centre bore a device that resembled a flame. Three small indentations were set beneath it. The joins where the gates met each other and the walls were solid, and it appeared to have simply been carved from the ice of the wall.

"This has no counterpart on the far side," said Antoninan. "It is a sham, decoration."

"It is not. We've already come a mile further than the outer dimensions should allow," said Trassan. "This is Morfaan magic. Perhaps those holes are for keys."

"We have no key," said Antoninan, "and the buildings are empty. I say it is a carving."

"We have a Vols," said Trassan. "Goodmage, your services, if you please."

The mage approached the gates without comment. He placed his hands on them, and withdrew them almost instantly in surprise.

"Magic?" said Antoninan.

"Assuredly," said Vols. "It is ice, but it is warm. You are correct, goodfellow, this area we are in is not attuned to the normal state of being. The world here has been, er, well... Been extended somehow."

"The Morfaan come from beyond," said Ardovani excitedly. "To Perus, from out of nowhere! In the fullness of their power, they could walk between worlds. Could this be one of their gates? Who knows where it might lead?"

"Those are legends," said Bannord.

"Legends are history in fancy clothes, so we say in Correados," said

Ardovani. "The facts of the Morfaans' abilities are well-established in the older chronicles."

"Open it," ordered Trassan.

"Very well," said Vols. He closed his eyes and put his hands back onto the door. The area around the gates thickened with magic.

"Stand ready," said Bannord. Ten ironlocks pointed at the gate. A shimmer sprang up from the top of the gateway, sudden as a spring bursting from rain-sodden ground. Light poured down the join in the gates, reached the floor, then shot upwards around the gateway. The impressions of cracks became cracks. With a moan, the gates parted, rolling off into sockets in the wall. A warm wind blew outwards, perfumed with a scent none of them had experienced before.

"Smells like flowers!" said Fedrion in wonder.

"Smells like trouble," said Redan.

The tunnel it revealed also appeared to be of ice, but of a different kind to that making up the rest of the city. This was partly clear, with large, leaf-like structures trapped inside in multiple layers, making it translucent. The tunnel appeared like a hollow cylinder rather than a tube bored through a solid mass. At the far end, light shone, bright as sunlight.

"Could you have missed an exit?" Trassan asked Antoninan.

"No," he said. "I did not."

"That light is not daylight," said Ardovani. "It is the wrong colour." He fished about in his pack, drew out a wooden box and took a complicated eyepiece from inside, comprised of several lenses mounted in series. He put it to his face, clicking different coloured lenses in and out of place. "Not daylight," he said eventually.

"We go in." Trassan looked back at the silent buildings. "And I was beginning to worry there was nothing here."

"Aretimus, Drannan, you up front. Kressinda, Darrasind, guard the rear."

"Yes sir," the troopers responded. Aretimus and Drannan advanced cautiously, guns ready. Their hammers clicked as they cocked them.

As soon as they stepped over the threshold a voice boomed out.

"Stop!"

The face of the Morfaan from the dock gates blurred into existence, filling the wide tunnel top to bottom, more solid than before.

"This city is the domain of the Morfaan on Earth. You were warned to depart."

"Wait!" shouted Trassan. "Listen to me! We come as seekers of knowledge."

If the head could understand, it showed no indication.

"You shall all perish," it said, and faded away.

"Shit me," said Drannan. He looked back to his lieutenant. "What do we do no—"

He fell dead, a spear of smoking white ice through his neck. Aretimus discharged his gun with a yell and leapt back from the tunnel entrance.

From the corridor walls, things climbed, uncurling themselves from the shapes in the ice like children creeping out from piles of leaves in games of autumn hide and seek. They were made entirely of ice, with smoothly sculpted features approximate to men but vastly bigger, all of them taller than nine feet. They carried bows of ice with strings of crackling energy, and spears with barbed points. Their bodies steamed, hot like the gates, and where they walked snow melted.

"Everyone away from the gates!" screamed Bannord. "Marines, fire to cover our retreat!"

They fell back from the tunnel, running for the doors of the deserted city, Bannord's men firing into the mass of ice warriors filling its length as they retreated. Forfeth and Timmion covered their comrades, blazing blue bullets smacking into the chest of an advancing warrior. The ice warrior's chest cracked, and steam whistled, but it did not stop until two more ironlocks spoke. The ice construct shook with releasing pressure as it turned to find its assailants, detonating with a rush of heat that showered the area with scalding water and pointed fragments of steaming ice.

The ice warriors let out a strange, whispering cry, and charged.

"Run!" shouted Bannord.

The piteous yelp of an injured dray squealed out behind him, and he turned to see a dog thrashing in its death throes, a trio of arrows melting into its fur. From the buildings behind more of the ice warriors emerged, unpeeling themselves from the walls. They were flat when they came free, seeming only to pop into rounded being as they walked. Steaming water pattered into the snow from the buildings as they passed, and the air around them danced with heat. Ilona and Darrasind opened fire from a building, but did not slow them.

"The dogs, save the dogs!" shouted Antoninan. He ran for the sled with the dead dray. The dogs were tense, about to flee. He drew his knife as he ran, and fell on the dog, slashing its traces through.

The boy groom yanked out his the dogs' pickets and shouted for his team to flee. Arrows whined weirdly at him, piercing him through many times. His commands cut off. He blinked, blood poured from his mouth and he drew in a retching gasp that could not fill his punctured lungs. The sled jerked forward and he fell backwards, dead before his head touched the snow. His father yelled, sprinting for him. Men looked to the creatures coming at them from both sides. The dogs of the other two teams barked and whined, yanking fruitlessly at their tethers, biting each other in fear.

"Hold the line!" shouted Bannord. "Keep your nerve!"

The party disintegrated into disorder. They scattered, dodging between ice warriors advancing from behind.

"Get into the cover!" shouted Bannord, hurling himself into the doorway sheltering Darrasind and Ilona. The alchemist's boy was there with them, looking out. Further back, where the room it abruptly stopped, two Ishamalani sailors crouched.

"Get the fuck down!" bellowed Bannord at the alchemist's boy. He grabbed him by the parka hood and yanked him back. Half a second later, a spear of ice roared into the outside wall and exploded with a gush of escaping steam.

"Gods fucking fuck it!" Bannord shouted. He leaned round the door jamb and fired his ironlock. He hit an ice creature square in the head. It strode on two steps, but its head wobbled and shattered. It toppled forward, boiling water spilling from its core.

"Reload this!" said Bannord. He plucked a bag of shot from round his neck and shoved it at Ilona along with the rifle.

Ice creatures chased down fleeing men, spearing them as boys spear frogs. The sled with the dead groom's blood on it bounced past, dogs yelping in panic. Antoninan's head groom grappled with his own drays, trying to stop them from fleeing while still attached to the sled. He cut them loose one by one, and they ran off, skidding in their panic. Those still in traces tossed leapt and tugged, snarling and snapping. For all the man's experience, there was only so much he could do to control a four hundred pound dog, and he was flung to one side as one slammed into him. The remaining dogs tried to run, yanking each other in opposite directions before their leader got them going, but they charged right at three of the ice creatures, and were speared to their deaths in a flurry of sickening blows. The third team were calmer, held in check by Valatrice's presence as Antoninan hurried from dog to dog cutting their harnesses while Valatrice gnawed at the leather of his own.

"One, two, three, four," counted Bannord. His eyes darted about, each glance revealing a new horror. In the doorway opposite, Kolskwin shattered the arm of a creature trying to gain entrance to his building only to fall back screaming as boiling water jetted into his eyes. A bullet shot from the room, punched right through the construct, but it was not hindered. The water froze over the hole in its back and in its stump, and it continued methodically jabbing with its spear. "Eighteen," finished Bannord. "I count eighteen."

"Seventeen," said Ardovani. He crouched behind Bannord, and took aim with his strange gun, shooting out a roaring beam of yellow energy. An ice construct vanished in a pillar of steam.

"Can I have one of those?" said Bannord.

"Alas, it is a prototype, and cost a great deal of silver," said Ardovani. "I did offer the plans to the Karsan army, but it was outside their budget."

"Fuck that, I'll pay for one myself," said Bannord.

"Twenty thousand for the raw materials only," said Ardovani apologetically. "Then there are the preparations that must be applied, alchemist's fees, and my time." He snapped off another shot, the crystals fitted to the length of the odd barrels glaring with searing light.

"Maybe not then," said Bannord. "I need to get my men in order. Cover me."

The situation was deteriorating rapidly. The party was divided, beset at every place, the remaining marines ineffectually scattered among them. He held out his hand. "My ironlock, trooper."

"Sir," said Ilona, and shoved it into his hand.

"I'm going to help the others," he said quickly. "Get ready for my orders."

Bannord kept his head down, and dived out from behind the doorway. His men were scattered about. *That*, he thought ruefully, *is the bloody problem with ambushes.* Arrows of steaming ice sped at him, narrowly missing his head. Another beam of magical power blasted so close it singed his hair as he ran for the monster that had blinded Kolskwin. The one-armed creature exploded, and Bannord threw himself forward, skidding on the slick surface of the floor into the room. There were four of his marines inside, and three others—Ullfider the antiquarian and two sailors. One marine lay on the floor, the spear that had killed him melting quickly. His ironlock was clutched across his chest defensively, mangled into scrap. Kolskwin writhed in agony at the back with handfuls of snow clamped to his face. Only Timmion and Fedrion remained unhurt.

"Lieutenant!" Fedrion said. "What are we going to do?" He was close to losing his courage, his face whiter than the snow.

Bannord belted him around the head. "Get your pissing act together. We're going to have to fight our way out, or we're all going to die."

Fedrion rubbed his ear. "Yes sir, sorry sir."

"We're split, we need to get together, drive them back with a fusillade, alright? They're not proof against our weapons. We can stop them, if we concentrate our fire."

"Yes sir!" they said in unison.

"Any of you others armed?" said Bannord. The Ishmalani patted their knives, no good. But the antiquarian took out a long, finely made ironlock revolver.

"This do?" he said.

"More or less," said Bannord. "One of you Ishamalani take Kolskwin's gun. The other take my revolver."

They looked at each other.

"It is forbidden," one said. "We are not permitted firearms, by the laws of the One, and the laws of Ruthnia."

"Fine. Die then."

That put their religious bans into perspective. One of them

snatched up the rifle and joined the others. Bannord held out his pistol to the other. He hesitantly took it.

"That's better. Listen. We'll all open fire. The others should get the idea, I hope. Keep them off Ardovani; he's got the best weapon. It will not take them long to figure that out. We ready?"

They nodded.

"Right then, that fucker there," he said, pointing to a construct with a crest of upright icicles for hair, "bring him down."

The five of them trained their guns on the construct bearing down on Ardovani's position. The magister was occupied with another, and ignorant of its approach. He fired his gun, his energy beam cutting a leg from under a warrior, sending it crashing to the ground.

Ilona and Darrasind fired from behind Ardovani at the monster Bannord had picked out, but it did not slow. The creature raised its hand. From its palm issued a gout of steam that solidified into a mass of spiked ice, partly blocking the door around Ardovani. The magister scrambled backwards. Bannord now understood what had happened to Haik's vessel.

"On my mark, aim, fire!" Bannord shouted.

Five ironlock guns spoke, shooting out bullets of glimmer. The barrels were rifled, a recent innovation, but the bullets remained large in order to generate a sufficient charge from the iron pin of the hammer penetrating their silver skin. They smashed into the back of the construct en masse, breaking it to pieces. A sheet of hot water poured from inside, a mighty blast of steam roaring from the back and turning to white clouds of ice on the cold air. The construct fell to its knees, and toppled sideways, dead.

"Reload!" Bannord shouted. Timmion had his bullet slotted in through the breach quickly, then helped the Ishamalan do the same. Bannord made himself two promises. Firstly, he would petition the admiralty to arm the Maritime Regiment with self-loading carbines like the sauraliers carried. Secondly, he would save enough to get Ardovani to make him one of those devices. If he had to steal the money, he would.

The men sounded off their readiness.

"Aim!" Bannord shouted. "Fire!"

Another round of bullets cracked out, demolishing a construct attacking Trassan's position. When it fell, the engineer had his men rush out and reinforce Ardovani. An ice warrior soared overhead, spinning helplessly into a high wall where it exploded, quickly followed by another. Vols' work.

Things were turning their way. Bannord counted only seven of the constructs. "Come on," he said, and exited the building.

He stepped out, right into the path of a ice warrior. It raised its spear. Bannord fumbled his gun, his shot going wide. He backed away, drawing his sword, but then Valatrice was there. Howling chillingly, he and one of his pack mates leapt at the warrior, knocking it from its feet and sending it crashing into the wall. Its shoulder burst. It attempted to get up unsuccessfully, collapsing back into the wall, feet peddling uselessly at the floor. The rest of Bannord's small unit came out of the building, backed off to a safe distance and filled the construct full of bullets. The warrior collapsed into its own steaming heart. Its magic disrupted, it melted away to nothing.

Bullets sped in from every direction at one of the last creatures, breaking it open so that it exploded outwards with immense force.

"Where shall I put these?" called Vols. Bannord found him, a hundred yards away. He held his hands over his head. Three of the constructs floated helplessly over the street, unable to move.

Bannord grinned triumphantly but it died quickly. There were bodies everywhere of men and dogs. Antoninan's draymaster wept over the body of his son. Red flowers bloomed on beds of white snow.

"Good job Bannord," said Trassan.

"Not good enough," said Bannord. "That cost us dearly."

"Sir!" Timmion spoke. "We're three marines dead. Five others. Antoninan's lost half his dogs, and Kolskwin..." he swallowed. "Kolskwin's blind sir. Cooked his eyes in his head."

Kolskwin's screams attested to the pain of that.

Bannord spat into the ice. "Have him remain here. All civilians too. I want you all in a building. Darrasind, Aretimus. You stay on guard. Timmion, get Ranost and help round up the dogs."

"Sir."

"I assume we are going further?" Bannord asked Trassan.

"You assume right," said Trassan shakily.

They returned to the corridor, ready for attack, but nothing more came against them—Trassan, Vols, Ardovani, Bannord, and Ullfider, who refused to be left behind. Antoninan would not speak with them, but went about furiously seeing to his animals, thereafter setting off in pursuit of the fleeing sledge. His ire increased when Valatrice declined to be harnessed again or to help, but insisted on going with the party down the tunnel.

"This wonder I have fought for," he said in his perfect speech. "My packmates will return. In the meantime, I will see beyond the tunnel for myself."

The corridor's walls moved with the play of light. No cavities remained to show where the ice creatures had come from and the constructs themselves had melted completely away.

The tunnel was not long, and soon they found themselves in a vast, spherical room at the centre of which was a platform of Morfaan steel mounting a freestanding, circular portal also of Morfaan steel, though otherwise very much like the gate of ice they had come through.

Dozens of doors led off the room. A gallery ran round halfway up the wall, more leading off that. Ullfider hurried to these while the others approached the gate.

"It is a gate," said Ardovani. "Can you sense the magic?"

Trassan could. He could smell it. It numbed his teeth and made his spit taste of metal.

Vols approached. He put his hand against it and nodded. "It is a gate. This whole place bends the laws of time and space, making accommodation for the city and this room. But beyond this door, beyond this door..." He looked up at it. "Here lies another world," he said wonderingly. He pressed his face against it and shut his eyes. "I can see it. A world of ash and fire, dark."

At that moment Ullfider came out excitedly from one of the rooms, hobbling as fast as his aged legs would allow. "Goodfellow Kressind!" He swallowed hard, he was so excited he could barely speak. "This room, it is crammed floor to ceiling with intact Morfaan devices."

The spell of the gate was broken. Trassan rushed past the antiquarian into the room he had come out of.

Inside were hexagonal alcoves, like the cells in a hive. Sheets of thin foil covered them over. Ullfider had ripped a number open recklessly. Inside each cell was a pristine artefact. Trassan pulled out a musical instrument, then some kind of weapon, and other devices of featureless steel that hummed and clicked when touched. Ullfider followed Trassan back into the room, practically dancing with excitement. Trassan turned round and round giddily. There were dozens of the cells.

"The other rooms?"

Ullfider's grin nearly split his face.

In the next were vehicles parked in rows, sophisticated versions of the charabancs colonising the streets of the Hundred. In another, flat discs were stacked in neat rows. In another, endless shelves of trays containing Morfaan silver, the enigmatic beads discovered at every ancient site the creatures had inhabited. Trembling, Trassan ran down the length of the racks. Hundreds of trays, thousands of beads. But they were not what he was looking for. At the far end, in a cell of its own, was a small device the size of a travelling bag. It consisted of a flat deck to the front inset with a solitary hole big enough to accommodate the tip of a finger. From the rear rose a pair of elegant metal horns, seamlessly integrated with the deck, between which spread an interlocking web of metal strands of varying thickness. He picked it up, hardly believing his luck. It let out a musical chime when touched. A film of light formed in the space between the wires. Tonal sounds sang from it.

Hesitantly, Trassan reached for the nearest tray of silver. It pulled out smoothly, resting on invisible runners of force. At random, he selected a bead.

Bannord burst through the door, lively and bright eyed.

"Trassan!" shouted Bannord, his and Trassan's animosity forgotten. "This place is full of material. Every room, both levels are stuffed from floor to ceiling. This place must be some kind of store, and it is pristine."

Trassan withdrew his hand from the tray and pocketed the bead.

"Strip it," said Trassan. "Strip it all. I want it all in the ship, in the hold, by this time tomorrow. Someone get Antoninan to calm down, we're going to need his dogs."

"I shall speak with him," rumbled Valatrice. "He will not go against me."

"What's that?" asked Bannord, nodding at the device as Trassan left the bead chamber.

"I don't know," said Trassan with a forced smile. He opened his satchel and placed it inside. "Who knows what half these artefacts do? Quickly now everyone, get this back to the ship! If we must leave, then we shall carry away the treasures of the ancient world!"

"It must be catalogued, sketched in situ before we move it. We shall miss the subtler story if we ransack the building!" said Ullfider in anguish.

"Very well," said Trassan. "Begin your sketches. We'll make notations of where everything came from, and box it up by room. Don't worry Ullifder, I won't let us miss unlocking the power of the Morfaan because I dislike bookkeeping."

Ullfider was mollified. "I shall send to the ship for assistance."

"We'll be sending for a lot more than that," said Trassan. Excited shouts came from every room, dispelling the expedition's fear.

"Vols! What of the gate? Can you open it?" he asked, imagination already buzzing at what else may be on the far side.

Vols stepped back from the portal, shaking his hands out with a worrisome expression. "I suggest we do not, and that we hurry in clearing the chambers," he said slowly. "There is something on the other side of this door, it has noticed us, and it desires greatly to come through."

CHAPTER FORTY-TWO
The Duel

THERE WERE FAR too many people in the Meadow to fit around the duelling ground. Few would see the fight, but that didn't seem to worry them. For the population of Perus the duel was an opportunity for an impromptu holiday.

The mist had returned, clinging to the edges of the duelling ground. Past its dank confines a late spring day warmed Perus, and the sun turned the mist a flat, headachey gold. Outside the clearing the usual raucousness that accompanies large gatherings had set to, inside it hush prevailed. The barkers and salesfolk were kept away from the lords and ladies of Perus. Only the wealthy were permitted in, although the trees about were full of less wealthy spectators. It was all so genteel, like a stilted garden party or a revel at a modest wedding. Bizarre to think, Garten thought, that someone might very soon be dead in the centre of it.

Around the ground men and women of high station talked quietly about swordplay and strategy and duels they had witnessed to impress their companions. All of it was a sham, the opinions of armchair-warriors. There were one or two Garten saw that might have conceivably fought, but these days real duels were rare. It had become the norm for people like Asteria to fight other professionals. Matters of honour were saved for the courts and settled with money. As Garten's father Gelbion had once dryly remarked, it was less messy that way.

Packed clay covered with graded sand made the finest bouting circle Garten had ever seen. He stared at it dumbly, suffering from a lingering sense of unreality. Images of the carnage at the Palace superimposed themselves on the scene. His sword dragged at his hip. It had gone from an extension of his arm to an alien limb, keen to force him to its deadly purpose. He needed time to acclimatise himself to his new status of killer, yet here he was, about to fight again, seconding for a creature out of myth. The affair was absurd.

On the far side of the circle Josanad stripped down to his shirt and went through a series of complicated stretches, his subsidiary arms hidden away. The president of the match and his assistants conferred on the paved area to one side of the circle. A pallid, worried looking physic waited in a chair under a parasol, even though there was no sun. A Guider in full regalia waited solemnly a few feet further on. Near him was a young man with a sword, surrounded by women that he was too nervous to flirt with. Asteria chose her seconds on the basis of who pleased her most in the bedchamber, it was rumoured. By the look of the boy Garten could believe it. He was no swordsman. Youthful arrogance was melting under the heat of the moment, exposing inadequate ability. The boy caught his eye and nodded at him. Garten returned the gesture then looked elsewhere.

A ripple of polite applause went up from the crowd. Kyreen Asteria had entered the ground from the pavilion. As more people caught sight of her they added their voices to the crowd's greeting, until all were shouting and cheering as loudly as decorum allowed. The applause spread out from the clearing, travelling hand-to-hand into the greater crowds, until all those out of sight on the Meadow had joined in.

Asteria strutted with supreme confidence. Her sheathed sword was unhooked from her belt and held before her so that the crowd could see it. The weapon was a backsword, shorter than a rapier but longer than Garten's own favoured smallsword. Unlike his weapon, hers had an edge, being sharpened for half the length of the blade either side of the point. Primarily a thrusting weapon, it could be used for cutting also, and demanded a hybrid technique. Asteria was beyond such things as technique and school. She had a style all her own.

Josan came after Asteria from a second door in the pavilion and approached the ground. People made way for her and bowed but did not dare address her. She exchanged a few words with her brother, then joined Garten at his side of the circle.

"Your people have changed a great deal since our last visit," said Josan.

"Some say it is a sign of our growing sophistication," said Garten.

"Some say the same in my land also. They see it as a sign of hope," she said. "I am not convinced."

"There are more of you than two?" asked Garten.

"Why would there not be?" she said. She was tense, affecting calm as the worthies around the field affected knowledge. He glanced over at Josanad, seeking some clue to weakness there. The craven, child-like being he had seen in the Grand Hall of the Assembly had not given another showing, but Garten was wary of its reappearance. He had once relished the idea of fighting Kyreen Asteria. Confronted with the possibility, he was well aware she would kill him. This was a match best kept to daydreaming. He hoped Josanad could keep his head.

"When acting your dreams, reality has a rude way of spoiling a man's life, in this case terminally," said Issy smugly through her viewing slit. The case rested along with Garten's fighting gloves on a table provided for his use. Wine, food and tobacco were laid out for him, none of which he had touched.

"Are you reading my mind?" he asked.

"Might be," she said.

"Do not trust it," Josan said. "The Y Dvar are older even than we. They are rotten in their hearts."

Issy blew a raspberry at the Morfaan.

"Be quiet, Issy, you'll be noticed," said Garten.

Asteria took off her jacket. Buttons and sparkling crystal charms dangled from its seams, and her hat was similarly lurid. The fabric of the shirt and britches she wore underneath matched that of her outerwear, but they were practically cut and free of ostentatious decoration. A flunky appeared and took her coat, a fat goodlady snatched her hat from the arc of its flight when Asteria tossed it aside and held it up triumphantly, displaying it to envious friends.

Asteria lifted up her arms and paraded around the circle, waving her hands upward to encourage the crowd to louder cheering.

"She is confident," said Josan. "She will die. No human has ever beaten a Morfaan blade to blade."

Garten hesitated, unsure if he should speak his mind.

"My lady Morfaan, forgive me," he said. "I do not think your brother should have accepted this combat."

"Why? He is unbeaten."

"I saw him in the Grand House of the Assembly. He was different. Is he ill?"

Josan's alien features displayed an unreadable emotion. "He was not himself. A passing moment. The shock of the bomb. Our senses are more refined than yours."

Garten dared to push further. "You were unaffected."

"Our women are stronger than our men," she said. "Enough questions. Wait here until you are needed, in silence." She distanced herself from him.

"Uppity," said Issy quietly. "Never change, the Morfaan."

"How much do you know about them?" said Garten.

"Lots," said Issy. "But I am sure you can guess what I will say next."

"You can't say because of—"

"Geas."

Asteria finished her lap, hooked her sword back to her belt and strode to the centre of the circle. "Greetings citizens of Perus!" she cried. "I have come today for the fight of our lives! More my life than yours," she said to appreciative laughter. She shone with the attention, her smile bright as the White Moon. "You will not witness a contest like this again. No human has fought the Lord Josanad for three hundred years. To see me fight, you are blessed. I am the finest swordswoman of the age!"

The crowd clapped and cheered, "Hear hear!"

"But to see a Morfaan fight, well. Well! You shall pass the story of this match down to your great-grandchildren's children. Such finesse the Morfaan have, such fine movement, such speed!" A grave expression replaced her smile. "I am going to have my work cut out for me. Lord Morfaan Josanad has agreed to fight me not for grudge, not for vengeance or hate, but for spectacle, and such spectacle I have waited all my years to experience. Never have I experienced such honour. Goodfellows, goodladies and goodfolk of Perus, as challenger I welcome Lord Morfaan Josanad to the Meadow duelling ring!"

The crowd burst into wild clapping and shouting. Their blood was up. All eyes were on the challenger and the Morfaan. Garten stood there waiting like the seventh dray in a team of six. Josanad entered the circle. Asteria had the grace of a dancer, but the Morfaan's poise was beyond human. The crowd fell silent. Asteria drew her sword and saluted him.

Josanad drew his paired, triangular swords but did not salute. He glared about the crowd with naked disgust. Josan flinched.

"I come to this world that my people once claimed as their own. I am insulted as an affront to the gods," he said. "I am attacked with explosives, and now I am called to a duel by this woman. She says it is a matter of honour for her. Would she die by my hand for the sake of death's thrill? Dead is dead, goodlady. Whether cheered by the crowd or in the corner of a field far from home. Why do you put me to this distasteful task?"

"You have killed already this week," Asteria said. Her amicability cracked, but it was cool calmness that showed beneath. "What does it matter?"

"I kill those that would kill me. This is a pointless game," he said.

"Then why play it?" she said.

"I cannot refuse, pointless or not. When you die, it will be your own choice."

Asteria laughed. "Lord Morfaan, your argument is flawed. I do not intend to die today."

"Then you will be disappointed." When Josanad saluted her at last, bowing his head and crossing his swords in front of himself, he remained disdainful. She saluted again, and the president came to the side of the circle to begin his recitation of the conventions of the match.

"And now, is your brother himself?" asked Garten. Josan ignored him.

It was obvious that Josanad and Asteria intended to fight to the death, but the president stated it baldly. His four assistants spaced themselves around the circle, to prevent the duellist quitting the field and to judge hits on points should the duel be resolved inconclusively, chiefly if one of the participants sued for mercy, or was too wounded to continue fairly or, as commonly occurred, both struck simultaneously and died together. The latter was the fault of poor fencers, and Garten did not expect that outcome.

The president concluded the regulations and raised his arms out to his sides, a handkerchief held in each hand between forefinger and thumb.

"Stand ready!" said the president. "Take your guard!" Asteria and Josanad adopted fighting stances, she a variation of the Tellivarian school's opening posture, he a contorted position a human could not accomplish, one blade held low, the other high. Hush fell. Out on the main Meadow a gentle hubbub persisted. A man called out the sale of pastries and a string band played. It was so quiet on the duelling ground that the stirring of young leaves in the breeze sounded loudly.

"Begin!" called the president. He dropped his handkerchiefs, and withdrew.

"How exciting," said Issy. It was impossible to tell if she meant it or not. People glanced over, looking for the voice.

"Shhh!" said Garten.

Duels always began the same way whatever the level of the combatants' skill. They circled each other. Weak fencers sought to delay the inevitable, or to set up a bluff, or to display strength they lacked. The strong read their opponent. The result was the same, a measured pacing around the edge of the sand, feet spread and crossing nimbly, legs bent to provide thrust, swords points held firmly at the opponent or held deceptively off target. Garten had seen this preamble to blade contact go on for ten minutes. Frequently, that was all there was to the bout, circling, an attack followed by a flurry of parries and ripostes, ending without warning with one man lying dead or wounded.

That was not going to happen today. Asteria surprised no one by making the first move. She was an aggressive fighter, often employing a headlong rush to force a reaction so that she might gauge the defence of her opponent.

Asteria's speed took the Morfaan by surprise. She arrowed across the circle, blade out at full stretch in a dazzling fleche. Josanad's weapons blurred in a cage of steel around his head and torso. At the last moment, Asteria dropped her point, going for the Morfaan's left leg. He moved it just slightly so that the point hissed past his knee, stepping around and back to face Asteria's new position. She recovered nimbly, whipping her sword upward, seeking the Morfaan's groin. He parried with one sword, and extended the other in an attack of his own. She turned the movement of her blade as she pivoted back into a guard and stopped dead, hand pronated, sword curling round into an unusual interpretation of the first position, point down. Josanad responded, his twin blades slicing across each other. Asteria kept her guard in the first, parrying the swords with delicate sideways sweeps, his weapons clicking quietly on hers as they were deflected for all the fury in the blows. Asteria twisted her hand so the palm was uppermost, sending her sword darting out at full stretch in the fourth position at such speed it was hard to see the move.

Josan hissed. Maybe Asteria was good enough to beat a Morfaan. Josanad attempted to break the weapon with a crosswise sweep from both swords. Sparks fountained from the metal. Asteria's blade held and she disengaged. She made two more attempts to pierce his guard, he defended the first, counterattacked into the second by swerving his body around the sword. He was preternaturally quick, swaying in a fashion that put Garten in mind of a serpent. Snakes came often to mind when he was with the Morfaan. Asteria could not match his reflexes, but she was wise to the ways of the sword. Her arm and weapon moved as if inseparable, moving in to tangle Josanad's upper blade, prising, and sliding down along its short length at his exposed shoulder. Josanad's other sword batted it away, and he riposted with an arcing slash at Asteria's belly that would have gutted a lesser warrior. The crowd gasped as Asteria stepped back, evading the blow at the last minute. At the fringes men muttered as they hastily relaid their bets. But if the crowd didn't notice, Garten did—Josanad's riposte was clumsy. Asteria saw that too, and she smiled.

They parted further, and circled again. This time Josanad attacked, weapons blurring, Asteria could not afford to take the full brunt of their hits against her more delicate weapon, and the way she twisted it just so or moved the forte of the blade a fraction to deflect the attacks made Garten envious of her ability. Josanad's weapons were heavy, unbalanced looking things. By all rights he should have lacked finesse, but he wielded them dazzlingly, and Garten could only wonder how fast the Morfaan would be with a lighter sword.

The end came so quickly that Garten struggled to phrase the movements. Asteria panted and dropped her shoulder, a feint of body not of blade. Josanad took the bait, one sword smashing her weapon aside, the other sweeping for her arm. She turned only a little, allowing the edge of his leading weapon to open her shirtsleeve and scratch the skin beneath. They were close, almost body to body, a difficult position to land a hit, but Asteria held her right arm back, twisted awkwardly and high. Josanad's lesser arms sprang out from their hiding place beneath his shirt, surprising the crowd more than Asteria. Josanad plunged the daggers held in his smaller hands at the woman, but Asteria was already moving away. Still with her sword angled downwards, she twisted and thrust, removing herself from the reach of Josanad's blades and taking him through the shoulder. Six inches of needle sharp steel poked out of his back, dripping a pale blood. She withdrew sharply and leapt away.

Composure dropped from the Morfaan like a mask. Josanad snarled. Josan cried out an anguished warning, but he did not heed it. Enraged by the hit, he went into a whirling attack with all four weapons. Asteria waited until the last second, then drove forward, evading his blades by twisting and coming in from the side, piercing him neatly through his heart. He swung drunkenly three times, she moving side to side to dodge. Swords fell from limp fingers and he looked down at them stupidly. His eyes clicked closed, then open, and he collapsed. Asteria pulled out her sword as he fell to the ground. Josanad curled up on himself, shuddered, and lay still. Alien blood tinted the scuffed sand pink.

A terrible cry went up from the crowd. The true significance of the afternoon's entertainment became apparent. Josanad, lord of the Morfaan, had been slain by mortal hand against all expectation. Horror filled the duelling ground, quick and cold as a flood of water. Asteria's face blazed with triumph, oblivious to the mood of the audience.

Josan screeched. She ran to her brother, her poise lost, head bobbing like that of a charging battlemount.

"I declare the winner Kyreen Asteria, by dint of death of her opponent, Lord Morfaan Josanad!" proclaimed the president. Muted cheers greeted the announcement, quickly silenced.

"No!" shouted Josan through the shock of the crowd. "No! It is not over! The second will continue the bout!" She glared with ferocious yellow eyes at Garten.

"Do you consent?" asked the president.

"Yes, fifth best in Karsa, and possibly a little better than that. Do you consent?" crowed Asteria. She wiped watery blood from her blade with a cloth and tossed it into the crowd. Noble onlookers abandoned their manners to scrap over it.

Garten was surrounded by a sea of expectant faces already judging him for cowardice. To face Kyreen Asteria one-to-one was tantamount to suicide. Luck might see him through, but he doubted there was that much luck in all the world.

His honour, or his life.

"Do not engage her!" hissed Issy. "Do not fight!"

Garten drew his sword. "If I die..."

"When you die," corrected Issy.

"If I die, get yourself sent to Katriona, my sister. You'll get on with her, you are very alike."

He saluted the Tyn, and was gratified to see genuine sorrow on her face behind the slit.

"You are an idiot," she shouted. "I will tell all your brothers! I will! I swear."

"It will be old news," he said.

The president nodded at him. Garten saluted. Asteria grinned at him, flushed with exertion and victory. She saluted him back.

"A smallsword?" she mocked. "A weapon for jabbing at urchins and pickpockets." She tilted her backsword. "I prefer this."

"I like the speed. We all must make do with the preferences we were given when we are made."

"Never take what you are given, but take what you want. The only other way is unsatisfactory, and in this arena will lead to death." Asteria pointed her blade at Josanad. "Speed served him poorly. You will see that too, when you are transfixed by my sword."

"Doubtless," said Garten. Desperately he tried to ignite the flames of aggression. To go into a bout with anything less than a certainty in one's own ability was to ensure defeat, and here that meant death. He looked at Asteria, gloating still, and he knew he could not beat her.

"Stand ready!" shouted the president, retrieving his handkerchiefs. "To your guard!" Garten adopted his favoured stance, basic fencing posture, hips sideways, shoulders turned forward, sword out and up to attack and defend according to circumstance. Basic, but effective.

"Begin!" the president cried.

Garten advanced quickly. He told himself he wished to surprise Asteria, and to take advantage of her winding. Truthfully he wished to get this over and done with as quickly as he could. He had already given up, and Asteria saw it.

Josan crouched by her brother, a knot of people around them. The Guider hovered nervously over her, unwilling to brave Josan's wrath and unsure of how to guide the ghost of a Morfaan. Josan sent the crowd back with a glare, sheltered her brother's body with her own, and began whispering into his ear. The atmosphere thickened. Garten's ears popped as he attacked.

He would not give up. He would not die quietly. He would give Asteria something to remember him by.

Never had his sword moved so quickly. Asteria's eyebrows rose. Her expression changed from mockery to appreciation. "You have a swift attack, very good. Now let us see you recover from its failure." She parried it easily, bringing her own sword in to the left of his. Garten caught the disengagement and attack to his upper chest just before it came too close to stop, parrying it and attacking in his turn. She parried, feinted, remised. He ignored the first, and caught the second, rasping his sword up her blade in a return thrust to her arm. She dipped her forearm out of the way, stepped aside, causing him to stumble with the impetus of his own attack.

"Maybe fifth best is not that good after all," she said, and went at him. He regained his feet in the nick of time. A broad, upward swing of his sword sent her blade sailing out of the way. He moved to punch with his off hand. She ducked out of the way and stabbed hard toward his kidney. He parried close in, too close to effectively riposte, and they parted. They circled again.

"Not bad at all," she said. "When you die, you can tell your relatives in the realms beyond that you were killed by the best swordswoman in all Ruthnia. It might salve your pride."

He was expecting the attack after the jibe, but little prepared him for the speed and power of it. Her sword hissed at his face. He dropped low and lunged off his front foot, sending himself shooting past her. He recovered well, turning as he went, his sword snaking back into guard.

It clinked against hers, now pressed firmly against his throat.

"Do you call for mercy?" intoned the president. The crowd fell silent.

"Is it offered?"

"I'll let you go if you beg," said Asteria. "Life is far too dull for mercy. I prefer a little humiliation to spice it. If I don't get the kill, I need something to remember."

"Charming."

"Charm? I had no time for finishing school. I was too busy learning how to slaughter fools like you. So, what's it to be, fifth best in Karsa?" she said. The razor tip of her sword broke his skin painlessly. A droplet of blood trickled down his throat. "I give you the fool's choice—life, or honour?"

"I will not beg."

"I thought not. If you were clever, you would never have taken me on. Do you know why I win?" she said.

"Practise?"

"A glib man so close to death, though I suppose you can take comfort your ghost will certainly find its way," she said, twitching her chin at the Guider. "I win, Garten Kressind, because I like to kill."

He saw he muscles tense, her eyes dilate, saw the intent to end him swell like an ugly canker throughout her being.

He refused to close his eyes. Reality took on an intensity that was overwhelming. He heard, smelled and saw with such clarity he became painfully aware of how precious life was, and how he had squandered it.

"Brother! Brother!" Josan wailed.

The crowd drew a collective breath. The pressure of magic

squeezed at Garten. Issy shouted. Josan gave out a chilling wail. Space convulsed, and the crowd was gone.

Garten fell sideways into a dark place, bounced off a rough, wet, wall. His sword jarred from his hand with a clatter. Unceremoniously, he fell down, and landed on his backside in an inch of water.

He stood, trembling. It was too dark to see. He had no idea where he was.

Garten was lost in the black.

CHAPTER FORTY-THREE
A Plan in Action

ON THE OTHER side of the park from the duelling ground, Madelyne waited for Harafan. The precinct was far from the safety of the Meadow and other heavily frequented places. The stone bench she sat on was choked with ivy that ran up the trees and halfway across what was once a path, though she could tell only by the ornamental edging pieces of fired clay poking up through the leaf litter. Where the path was not hidden by ivy it was covered with nettles and other noxious weeds. Black-skinned trees leaned over it, their limbs contorted into ugly poses. She had the fancy they were dancers immolated mid-step, leaving twisted, charcoaled corpses behind. That image was too much, and she turned away from them, and stared at the small, clear space in front of the bench. The Royal Park covered hundreds of acres, but large swathes of it were abandoned. So much of it had been swallowed up by trees, weeds and rumour so long ago it had the feeling of a place deliberately designed to depict the mercilessness of time. Such a thing was possible. Perus had more than its share of eccentric noblemen with the means to make such a monument. But the truth was that since the driving of the gods, the Royal Park had become dangerous.

The area reeked. There was supposedly a lake nearby. She did not know of any person who had actually seen it, but the weedy, noisome scent of stagnant water was everywhere. Things rustled in the undergrowth. She saw rats and other vermin, but heard no songbirds nor saw any dracon-birds flitting through the branches.

Visited only by the foolhardy or the reckless, the 5th Precinct of the Park was among the most desolate, shunned by all that was good and clean, too close to the point where the Godhome touched the Earth to be safe. The great tilted plate of it rose over her like a hand poised to swat a fly. She had never been this close. Very few people dared.

A loud crackling had her jumping from the bench. The duke's latest marks brushed tantalisingly against her clothes. She wore nothing but the finest garments now, the worst of them so much closer woven and luxurious than the best dress she had ever worn, but even their whispering touch on the welts on her legs troubled her with intermingled pain and arousal.

Harafan forced his way through the stand of black trees, waving his hands at a cloud of gnats.

"Gods! What a fucking miserable place!" he said. He unshouldered a large pack and dropped it on the ground. He smelled of mouldering wood and long dead leaves.

"You chose it," she replied.

He pawed a gnat from his tongue distastefully and licked at his clothes to remove the taste, slowing as he took notice of Madelyne's outfit.

"Wow, Madelyne. You look very fine. Those are beautiful clothes. You could pass as a goodlady, really. And your face!" He looked closely at her. "There's something different about you. What have you been up to?"

She stepped away from him. Again her clothes brushed her. She was acutely aware of every movement on her skin, cognisant of her body's basest desires in a way she never thought to be. Need stirred in her. She turned away so Harafan could not see her flush.

"Are you alright?" he asked, becoming concerned.

She did not reply. How could he understand half of what she had undergone? Away from the duke she feared he had enchanted her, when she was near him she could think only of his touch.

"Fine then," he said to her silence. "I take it if we are here, you have what we need. That is all that matters." He looked up at the Godhome's underside, leaden in the gloom. Either side of it the skies were lemon yellow with high evening, but just there, so deep into the dominion of its shadow, the sun could never shine.

"Yes," she said, more coldly than she intended.

"Look," he said. "I know you have been through a lot, but it will all be worth it. We go in, we take what we want, and we leave rich. No problem. Seriously Mads, have you been alright? I've sent you five messages in the last month. I'd heard nothing until you got in touch last week."

"I haven't been able to reply. Come on. We should get going. If you only believe half of the stories, then it is dangerous to be here after evening."

"Are you hiding something from me?" he asked. "Are you sure everything is alright? Mads, come on. How long have we been together?"

"Sixteen years," she said. "Since we were eight."

"Haven't we always looked out for each other? Haven't we always been friends? Have you been holding out on me?"

She nodded, bit her lip. A deep sense of shame had her hide her face. "He told me three weeks ago."

"You've known for three weeks? Why didn't you say anything?" he said, hurt now mingling with his concern. "Were you going to go in yourself? Like that, on your own? After all we've suffered?" He threw up his hands. How much he was like a little child in that moment. Madelyne hated him, wanted to be away from his petulance and hopeless dreaming. She struggled with her reaction. Harafan had been her friend for always. There only ever had been him.

"It's complicated," she said finally. "I would never cheat you, Harafan. You're the only family I have."

"Don't tell me you're actually falling for the demoniacal bastard! That'd be hilarious," he said.

"Screw you," she said. "You can't tease me about this. You don't know. You can't... I..."

"Shhh! Alright, alright!" he said. He came to her and took her upper arms in a soft embrace. He was being kind. He was always kind to her. He could not know that his hands pressed against skin made tender in her nights with the duke. "I'm here. We're here. When this is done, you can get out, find yourself a good man, and I can find myself twenty bad women!" He tried out a smile on her. She blinked back uncalled tears and nodded.

"Now, what is it?" he said eagerly. "I'm dying to know. Is there a staff or a key, or a crystal? Remember when we robbed that magister's house, and his key was a clockwork dracon-bird carrying a strawberry? What terrible taste."

He laughed, she joined in, more subdued than he.

"It's words, Harafan."

"Words?"

She nodded. "Just words."

"Fine. Whatever. They were gods. I suppose it could be a puff of air. Do you know them?"

"Memorised. I can say them right."

"Huh," said Harafan.

Madelyne became caught up in the moment, and started to speak like she once had when they had an important job, quick and excited. "The drunken god betrayed the rest of them, can you believe it? He gave Res Iapetus the words to get in. Why would he do such a thing? He's been living in a box ever since. I wonder if it was worth it?"

"Sometimes," said Harafan, "we're our own worst enemies." He shivered, and looked up at the looming Godhome. "We better not say the mage's name again around here. Call me superstitious, but I don't think the Godhome likes it." He examined her dress, almost lasciviously, and Harafan never looked at her that way. "That is pretty. Can you run in it?"

"I can run in anything," she said.

"That's my girl." He went to his pack, and took out three folded bags, a leather satchel, and a small knapsack. He put the satchel on, and replaced the pack on his back, then unfolded the knapsack, adjusted the straps and handed it to Madelyne. "You carry the sacks in there. I've got some stuff to get ready. If what that woman Shrane told me is right, we're going to have to be very careful, and make sure we do this right."

They fought their way through last year's brambles, light turning green in the shadow of the Godhome. They snagged at Madelyne's coat, but it was so finely made it never tore. Harafan was less fortunate, his trousers were shredded. Both of them were harried by squadrons of gnats as they pushed on up the path. Trees leaned into the way, clawing at them with sharp twigs. Water dripped from everything, soaking them both. To begin with, the path was well defined, if overgrown, but it narrowed between its broken edging, until that too vanished in the middle of a stand of stooped, gnarly trees little taller than two men stood one on the other's shoulders.

Without the Godhome to guide them, they would quickly have become lost; as it was, they were headed toward the one place in all the city everyone avoided.

"We've got to get nearer," said Harafan. The Godhome was very close, a metal wall that shut out the world. To their left miniature hills creased the land, covered in thickets of the black trees and impenetrable wild roses. They climbed the first, coming down the other side to another overgrown path, the only evidence of which were paving stones pushed through the turf by roots, and a gate in a fence of iron rails rusted reed thin. Wild roses and blackberry tumbled through between them. On the other side was a cemetery. Tomb roofs of rain-whitened lead poked over the undergrowth.

"What a sight," said Harafan. "I've heard about this place. It was the burial ground of the old Maceriyans during the era of Resplendency," he said. "Imagine what treasure you could pull of out the ground here with a shovel and a lick of courage."

Madelyne took his hand and turned him to face her. "Do you think you are the first to have that idea? You said we had to be careful." Madelyne pointed.

Only feet away from the gate was a skeleton imprisoned by brambles. The remains of its clothes were in tatters and the bones yellow from exposure. Ivy wound its way around the ribs, and out through the jaw and eye sockets. Harafan wrestled his way past the gate and went to investigate. A bag, rotted mostly through, was beside the dead man, tools still inside. An iron chisel stained the leaves with bright orange rust. The tomb was unharmed. No one had taken the lead from the roof. The door seal was whole.

"Alright, alright," said Harafan. "I guess the stories are true then." After a moment's rearrangement he put his pack and satchel on the ground, and took out a belt upon which were two fat bags tied with string. He set these above his hips, before resetting the rest of his baggage on his shoulders. "The minute you see anything strange, let me know," he said.

"What is in the bags?" she asked.

"Iron filings, laced with a tiniest amount of dust from the Black Sands. When I start scattering it about, don't tread on it. I've heard glimmer and iron is not volatile at this ratio, but let's not take any chances. It's to keep the Tyn at bay."

"When did you start learning magic?"

"I haven't. I had a pay a magister a pretty amount of coin to get that secret. Apparently, it's the only way to get close to them without them tearing you apart."

"What did you tell him?"

"Nothing, don't worry. I said I was writing a book on Lesser Tyn. He thought I was mad. He was happy enough to take my money though."

They pushed on. The skeleton was not the first body they saw in the cemetery. Others lurked in secret places, as if engaged in a macabre version of hide and seek. Some were fresher than others, having scraps of flesh adhering to their bones under clothes that had yet to perish. There was no sign of the living.

Madelyne and Harafan fell into step with the tombs marching over the small hills, following paths dense with thorny plants into dwarf valleys that must once have been serene, but now were the epitome of desolation. The tombs became grander and more elaborate as they went deeper, many sporting elaborate ghost catchers or enchanted warning horns should a revenant find its way back from the lands of the dead.

"They say this place was used right from Morfaan days until the God-Driving. Thousands of years of the dead, all here, packed into the ground." Harafan meant to scare her.

"Don't," she said. He took that as success, but she wasn't scared. He was ignorant of the things she had recently experienced.

"There are catacombs beneath. I heard that if you go far enough into them, you come to the place where the Morfaan placed their dead before the Old Maceriyans and that there are wondrous things there, buried with them. But though lots of people have gone in, nobody has ever come back."

"Then how do you know what's in there?" she asked.

He grinned. "Good point. That's the problem with all rumoured treasures, isn't it?"

They climbed a final hill taller than the rest. Upon its summit was a church to the gods, modest in size but lavishly decorated. The roof had tumbled in, taking out the nave as it fell. Shards of dusty, coloured glass lay like jewels all around the end. From windows down each side the stern faces of Omnus, Alcmeny and the rest still looked out.

From the top of the hill, they saw the full extent of the cemetery. Back the way they had come they made out the lighter green of healthy woods and meads where the Royal Park was still worthy of the name. Where the shadow of the Godhome never lifted only weeds and sickly trees grew. They were close to the source of the shadow. On the hill opposite rested the rim of the Godhome itself. The top portion resembled a city, but that side presenting itself to the ground was a wide, convex circle of flawless Morfaan steel. Dark reflections played over its surface. The Godhome must have weighed millions of tons, but its edge rested as lightly on the ground as a cloud. It had ploughed up a low bank when it had fallen, furzed over with low brush now, and the tombs there had been smashed into squares of white stone scattered like teeth by a hammer blow. The damage it had done to the earth was otherwise minimal. Nevertheless, seeing it like that, teetering on the edge of oblivion, both of them understood like never before the danger the Godhome presented to the city should it ever fall. Most of it was situated over the park, but not all, and the impact alone would shiver buildings down to their foundations miles away.

"Right then," said Harafan lightly. "Let's get this over with. A couple of hours of terror, then we'll be rich forever. A fair trade, in my opinion."

Throughout the earlier part of the journey, they had talked, Harafan keeping up his usual endless patter. Madelyne's less than favourable reaction to his first few questions about the duke had him avoid the subject, and he commented instead upon the desolate sights of the cemetery. Caution took his voice as they descended into the shallow bottom of the last valley. They threaded their way between its glorious tombs silently. Wicked vegetation pulled at everything, as set on engulfing them as it was on smothering the grave markers, and it took a long time to make the final approach. They hit the base of the last hill late. The Godhome hinged over their heads, now the totality of the sky. They became colder more than the deepening shadow could account for. Thick undergrowth barred their progress, and they were further delayed seeking out a way. Scratched, sweaty and fearful, the stumbled upon a flight of shallow steps between the tombs that had remained almost clear, and they scrambled up this, tugging their feet through the grasping weeds.

Hard, semi-musical clacking accompanied every footstep, for there were bones everywhere, the remains of hundreds of people interlocking with one another to make a rough pavement under the brush. Madelyne watched her step but paid the bones no more attention than that for a long while, until she chanced to look down. The uneven texture of a long leg bone had her reach for it. It was coarse under her fingers. She brought it up to her eyes, and saw the saw-toothed marks of little teeth in the surface.

A rapid rustling in the bushes behind filled her with dread.

"Harafan!" she said in a high whisper. "Harafan!"

He stopped a dozen steps ahead. "What?"

"Movement."

She caught sight of something speeding through the brambles that made her palms sweat. Someone spoke off to the left. The voice put her in mind of the duke's invisible servants, a whisper, just audible, but of a type that insinuated itself poisonously into the psyche. Another movement rushed through the bracken. Something tittered behind a tomb.

"Harafan!" she said.

"Don't stop," he replied without looking back. She reached him as he withdrew fistfuls of powder from the bags on the belt. He held his hands away from his body a little, and let the filings trickle free.

"Follow me, stay between the lines of iron. Don't stand on them if you can avoid it."

She saw things in the bushes, heard a tittering and saw the flash of wild yellow eyes not far from her legs. Startled, she moved closer to Harafan. They continued together at a quickened pace. The Godhome filled the world with steel. It looked near, but judging its distance was hard because of its enormousness and they closed on it far too slowly.

A high trumpet sounded, and the undergrowth erupted with movement. Things burst from the brambles on wings. Tiny Tyn rode out onto the stairs mounted on the back of rats and small dracon-birds. Larger, impish creatures emerged from behind the tombs, looking lecherously at Madelyne. The cemetery was all a twitter with their speech. Wild Tyn of every conceivable shape and kind gathered around them. Some clutched spears no mightier than pens, others drew tiny swords hammered from discarded nails. Their clothes and gear were the cast-offs of mankind, shreds of cloth stitched into parti-coloured trousers, gloves repurposed as little suits, the thumbs cut off. There were Tyn no bigger than insects riding moths, others the size of human infants, several with flat faces like bats, one had three heads on the necks of serpents. They had feather, furs, scales and rocky skin. There was one that looked like a tiny, jewelled dragon. Some appeared human, but with the reverse jointed legs of fowl. Some glowed, some were shadows, some vanished and rematerialised elsewhere. Wide mouthed, thin mouthed, toothy and toothless. Some with a dozen eyes, several with none. They were glum, elated, suspicious, mocking, surrounded by an overpowering smell of leaf mould and magic.

"Stay close!" hissed Harafan. He cast a handful of sand behind him. A knot of lesser Tyn drew back with small cries of alarm. On both sides, the Tyn pressed in, whispering threats in a dozen tongues. But they stopped short, curls of dissipating magic boiling off an invisible barrier over Harafan's mix of iron and glimmer rich sand when they came close.

"We're going to have to run!" said Madelyne. The black sand dribbled from Harafan's hands too fast, she had to quash the urge to scream at him to close his fists tighter. "How much do you have?"

He thrust into his pouches and drew out more. "Not enough," he said. "Are you ready?"

Madelyne nodded.

"If we don't make it, we can say we tried. On three, two, one!"

They broke into a mad sprint, fear propelling them up the hill toward the Godhome. The Tyn let out a wicked war cry, and surged after. Tyn riding birds, beetles moths and broken butterflies swooped upon Madelyne, tugging her hair free from its dressing.

Those mounted on flightless beasts galloped alongside their prey, ululating and brandishing their tiny weapons.

Harafan thrust his hands into his pouches and threw out a sifting of sand. Where it touched upon Tyn skin they howled and fell back, smoke pouring from their bodies.

They approached the Godhome. The ground became difficult. There were mounds of bones all around it, tangled with the black bushes and the stone of toppled tombs. The bank the fall had thrust up broke the ground for twenty yards before the steel wall of the Godhome's underside. Harafan stumbled, punching the ground painfully to arrest his fall rather than spill the precious sand.

The Godhome's wall was ten yards away, eight. It let off a strange vibration that shook the roots of Madelyne's teeth. She and Harafan practically ran into it. When she touched it, the metal was freezing cold. When she breathed on it, her breath spidered into short-lived frost.

"Do the thing, whatever it is," he said. He flung out two fistfuls of the iron and sand in broad arcs, creating a semicircle in front of them

More Tyn screamed as it burned them. The diminutive horde came to a thundering stop only a few feet away.

"Now?"

"I don't think we're going to have much time to consider the best moment. Now, or never, and we can join these poor buggers littering the ground."

Madelyne drew in a deep breath and shouted as loud as she could. "By dint of pen and pint of gin, open gates, and let me in."

The Tyn snickered evilly.

"That's it?" said Harafan. "That's it? That piece of doggerel will get us into the palace of the gods? You're fucking joking! We're going to fucking die!" His laconic manner vanished. Genuine panic surfaced.

"Yes! Yes! The duke told me so."

Harafan's eyebrows rose high up his forehead. He shrugged.

"I don't know what I should have expected. He is the god of booze and shit poetry. I never liked him. That's really it? We've been duped."

The Tyn stormed around the arcs of sand, tumbling over one another in their eagerness to be at the humans, jabbing with their puny spears and hissing through pointed teeth. They were growing braver, coming closer, picking their way between the haphazard barriers Harafan had cast out. Madelyne looked up at the wall of the fallen Godhome. It remained impervious, shut.

"Nothing's happening," she moaned. "I... I'm sorry. I guess he took me for a fool."

"We're finished," said Harafan. "I knew this was too good to be true. I wonder if I can stab them? Can you even kill a Tyn?" He dusted off his hands in the direction of the Tyn, making them shrink back, and drew out his daggers.

"It has been nice knowing you. You know that, right? I take the piss a lot. Life hasn't been kind to us. You've been the one good thing in it. We've no parent in common but you're my sister, you always were, in all the ways that matter."

Touched, she reached up her hand and stroked his shoulder. "I know." She drew her own weapon.

"Come on you little bastards!" shouted Harafan. "Let's have you then!"

The Tyn laughed. A couple played a hideous ditty on tiny instruments. Madelyne's stomach rolled at the sense of magic about to be unleashed.

And then the Tyn stopped. As one, the whole lot of them looked up and shrank back, blinking fearfully at something behind the thieves. The groan of tortured metal screeched over the cemetery, and Madelyne turned.

Nothing had changed.

"What the hells is goin—" began Harafan.

Madelyne and Harafan blinked out of existence.

Screeching, the Tyn turned on their tails and fled into the brush. Bushes quivered into stillness. The Tyn's screams faded, leaving nothing around the Godhome but bones and fallen stone.

CHAPTER FORTY-FOUR
Remnants of the Past

FEEBLE LIGHT BROKE the dark, not enough to truly see by, but enough to grant pale outlines to the walls, Garten's arms, and the debris on the ground. Water glinted around a small box lying on its side.

"Get me up, you oaf, before I drown!"

"Issy?"

Garten groped his way toward her, his feet plashing in standing water and kicking aside half-glimpsed obstacles. Their textures were almost as mysterious as their shapes through the souls of his boots—soft, hard, brittle, unyielding. Glass broke under his heel.

He picked up the box and looked inside. The light was coming from Tyn Issy. Screwing his eyes up he opened the door. The inside of the box was wet with dirty water, and she was not happy about it.

"Morfaan! Brutes where magic is concerned, no fine control over will or form. They should never have been brought into the world." She sniffed. "It is a wonder they lasted as long as they did."

After a few moments Garten's eye adjusted to the gleam of the Tyn and he played the box's light about. "Where are we?"

"Hey! You are not to use me as a lantern!" she snapped.

"How long can you keep this up?"

"A while," she said. "Didn't you hear what I just said?"

"Fine, stop shining, save your dignity. We can both starve to death down here in the dark."

She blew a raspberry, her standard response to sentiments she did not like, but maintained her effulgence, choosing to temper it with a scowl.

They were in a tunnel of some kind, masterfully wrought of well fitted stone patterned with tiny, precise chisel marks. Trash dotted the floor, old bottles, rags, bones and the like, scattered mostly, but heaped up into piles every forty paces. Whoever had stacked it had done it a long time ago; it was old, a uniform mud grey, and smelled only of damp, not fresh rot. Water dripped everywhere, running down the walls into puddles. Small stalactites of dissolved mortar hung from the apex of an arched ceiling. The water around their feet was odourless, muddy but not foul. Garten walked to the wall and touched it. The chill of deep caves penetrated his fencing glove. He panned the light around a little further. A large rat bared its broad teeth at him in a show of aggression, making him stumble backwards in surprise, and bounded off into the dark, its feet sending out tiny, echoing splashes long after it had disappeared. After that, Garten went to retrieve his sword.

"Garten Kressind."

Garten turned back toward the Lady Morfaan's voice, heading down the tunnel in the direction the rat had run.

"Don't go," said Issy. "Let us go in the opposite direction. It is the sensible course. Hey! Are you listening to me? These Morfaan are bad news for everyone. Garten!"

He would not listen. He went some hundred yards down the tunnel, treading carefully where the layer of rubbish thickened into a carpet. Soon the white shapes of the Morfaan leapt out of the dark in Issy's witch glow. Josan bent over her brother, cradling his head in the crook of one arm.

"You will escort us," she said.

"I will gladly take you back to your quarters in the Palace, Lady Morfaan," said Garten, "if you would but show me the way. Where are we?"

"We cannot go back. Not yet. I must see to my love, my brother."

"He is dead," said Garten. "I am sorry."

"He is dead and he will remain so if we are not hasty!"

She did something with her hands that Garten could not understand; it was as if he wasn't seeing them or that they would not be seen. Josanad flattened out, faded, became a representation of himself. She rolled this up, folded it twice until Josanad was the size and shape of a large letter, and secreted him inside her dress. Unconsciously, Garten retreated a step back.

"See," said Issy. "They are not like you. Turn back, my friend, before it is too late."

"Do not listen to her," said Josan. "The Y Dvar who chose the wild were never fond of us."

"Absolutely correct," said Issy. "You are things that never should have been."

"Whereas you squandered the gifts bestowed upon you," retorted Josan. "You will escort us," she repeated to Garten.

"But to where?" said Garten.

"To the Castle of Mists. There we shall restore my brother, and return to the World of Will, whereupon I shall exact my revenge."

"You cannot, Lady Morfaan. The duel was fairly fought and won."

Josan turned from him, and set off further along the tunnel.

"The woman Asteria shall pay, nevertheless."

"You did not think she would win," said Garten.

"She should not. She would not if Josanad had been complete."

"So there is something ails him," said Garten.

"He is a prince among my people, and an emperor to your kind!" she said.

"He was not well. You lied to me."

She continued along the tunnel which went dead straight as far as Issy's light fetched. "We are not immortal as your people believe," she said after a space. "Between our visits to your world we sleep, watched over by others of our kind who have made a great sacrifice. Our vigil has lasted too long. Every time we awake, a little less of our spirit remains. My brother is worse affected than I."

"I understand," said Garten. "My father—"

"Your father and your sympathy is of no interest to me," she said. "Guard me, do your work, and we shall return to resolve this matter of the new High Legate, then I and my brother shall remain to help you prepare for the coming of the World of Form."

"The Twin, the Dark World?"

"Yes. The Twin," she said. She looked in disgust at the rubbish on the floor. "This tunnel was built by my kind thousands of years ago. It brought water to the lower districts of this city, the capital of the eastern province. Now it is choked with your refuse. You have used it, and moved on, ignorant of what it could do for you if used correctly. You disgust me, humanity, you are verminous, beggars, snatch thieves plundering our past."

"Then why guide us?"

"How else are we to rule our subjects?" she said bitterly.

The tunnel took on a curve, and began to head upwards, bringing them out into a complex of large rooms and grand corridors, where the chiselled stone was covered in broken facings of marble. Rubble filled many of the rooms, and the walls between them had been brought down. Light fittings of the Morfaan steel hung from the wall. Puddles of water gathered, still as sheets of ice, on mosaic floors of marvellous intricacy. Everything was damaged, most of it devastated. Some corridors were wide enough to be roads but these were blocked by boulders come down from the ceiling. There were signs of miserable human life in the wreckage, fresher rubbish, a discarded blanket, scorch marks of a fire in a drier room, and, in the middle of a half-collapsed great hall, a huge midden covered in a dense fur of mold.

"You soil the palaces of your betters. Ignorant," said Josan. Worse came. They passed a gurgling waterfall of effluent running from a crack overhead. It steamed and stank in the chill, underground air. Heaps of clay-like faeces spattered the marble. The sewage ran for fifty feet in a revolting stream, before finding its way through a chasm in the floor. Issy's light showed the contents all too clearly, scattering rats from their feast.

"We are under Perus," said Garten. "In the ancient Morfaan city."

"Obviously," said Josan. "This was once a district of fine palaces and galleries. Now it is buried and you have made it your cesspit."

"There was war here," said Garten. "I can see it."

"There is always war," said Josan.

"Where exactly are we in relation to the new city?"

"If we were to walk in that direction," Josan pointed. "We would come to one of the places your kind call the cavernas."

"Let us go there, we might fetch help."

"Not yet. This way."

She led him from the main way and into a building half-crushed by a vast slab of stone dislocated from the cavern roof. The way on appeared impassable, but Josan headed down an obscure path evidently used by others—there were the nubs of tallow sticks stuck to rocks, and the floor had been cleared of loose debris. He realised that he could see all this without Issy, for there daylight seeped into the underworld. When they reached the back of the building, he bade her extinguish her light. She was only too happy to comply.

They were in what had been a windowed gallery. All but one of the columns had been shattered by a massive slippage of stone. A fragment of arch remained, unseated from the column top but jammed in place by rubble. A crack wide enough for a man to squeeze through opened in the wall. At the far end, Garten saw bright day, and heard the faint sounds of city life. A sliver of cliff, built upon with precarious houses, was visible through hazy air.

"So you see," said Josan. "The Caverna of the District of Ravens. In our time this building belonged to a rich merchant, and this gallery looked out across a forest park full of the most beautiful creatures. All that has gone, the creatures are dead, and you are in its place."

"I cannot help what I am," Garten said. "Do not blame me for the way the world has changed."

"It is not you I feel anger for, but for my own kind," she said. "We can help what we are, and we chose badly. This is all our own doing."

She took him along the gallery and through a tiny gap into a wide place that might once have been a plaza open to the outside world, but which was now buried by another gigantic slab of rock that brushed their heads as they walked toward the back. At the rear where natural rock walled the plaza in, there was twenty feet or more of clear space, but at the far side, toward the surface beyond the rock, there were bare inches between the shattered paving and its stony lid. Fragments of statues lay by broken pedestals.

"Here," Josan said stopping. "The swiftest way home."

They stopped by a circle carved into the living stone walling the back of the collapsed plaza. A fine script was carved around the circle's circumference, but it was marred by a crack down the middle, dividing the circle in two and putting its halves out of true.

"You have more magic," said Garten. "You must. This looks like solid rock."

She nodded. "It is solid enough, but there is a layer to the world beyond that which you see. There are many layers, in fact. And many worlds. Here is a weakness in the substance of creation, the underpinning which makes Form, Form and Will, Will. A crack in time and in space. This is a world gate."

"This is how you come from your land to ours?"

"This is how we come home from exile," she corrected. "This realm that you call your own is our land. And once, the gates led to many other places. There were hundreds of such gates in this city alone. Now most are destroyed, the rest hidden or sealed, and it is dangerous to open them. But we must, or Josanad is lost. This one is damaged, but functions still." She bowed her head, and said something soft in her own language. The gate responded immediately, the carved lines shining with a blue light. The crack in the circle hampered the gate's operation, and light sparked and spat in the gap. Josan said something more, and the light stabilised. The stone of the earth's bones vanished. In its place was a tunnel of vapours, just like the one Garten had witnessed in the Meadow.

He stepped forward.

"Wait!" she said, grasping his arm in an iron grip. "It must open at the far end. If you entered now, and it closed at this end before opening onto our destination, you would be lost forever in the Place of Mists."

A distant clap of thunder sounded. A flash marked the opening of the other end.

"Now we may enter. Quickly. I must take my brother to our home. The longer we delay, the less of him there will be to save."

"Stay here," sang Issy.

Garten steeled himself. "No man has done this in history," he said. "Why on Earth would I stay?"

Taking a deep breath, Garten stepped between worlds.

ADAMANKA SHRANE'S BREATH rattled in her chest. She was rotting from the inside out, used up by her magic, but she felt no fear of death. All progressed according to her masters' plans. Should she succeed;

she had no doubt her she would be rewarded, and if she were not, the honour of returning the masters to the Earth would suffice. She was the fulcrum upon which the fate of two worlds hinged. So few could make such a claim.

Her joints hurt. Her hair was greying. Her skin sagged around the neck. Holding her posture in meditation had become painful, but her mind remained sharp. She ignored the agony to commune with her other self, thousands of leagues away at the bottom of the world. Their minds touched, becoming one. She was in her rooms in Perus, hidden in a fold in the world. She was on a plain of snow, from whose front reared the black teeth of buried mountains.

The other half of Adamanka Shrane was occupied calling up a storm, and so Shrane-in-Perus waited and watched. Snow rose to her bidding, dancing in a wind she demanded of the elements. Blue skies covered themselves hurriedly in shrouds of white as a blizzard leapt up from nothing. Shrane-in-Ice remained in a clear space. Winds armed with knives of snow whirled around it. The expedition of the pompous Persin huddled near her, afraid of the fury of the storm she had called, and what else she might do, although their space was still, and above the sky was clear and bright with the midnight sun.

When Shrane-in-Ice had done, the two halves exchanged knowledge, happy to be one again, melancholic at their parting. Shrane-in-Perus retreated a little into the sky after the sharing was over, to watch her other self lead Persin's parade of greedy fools to their doom.

The pain became too much. She let the contact drift. Sending, even between two halves of the same soul, was exhausting for a mage. The pain of it however, was nothing compared to the splitting. Splitting had been an agony to exceed all others.

The Morfaan must be dealt with, and it was that she waited upon. She drifted into a watchful half-sleep, the eyes of her divided soul on the currents of the otherworld while her body slept.

Days passed.

Her eyes flew open. The pulse of an opening way between the worlds rolled out across the city. With swift mage-sight she found the gate, buried deep in the ground below the Gentilla District. The gate was a small one, damaged, but dangerous for its user to reveal.

A triumphant smile spread across her face. The Morfaan had shown her the way to their home. She rose to prepare for the arduous task of contacting the iron gods.

Once the Morfaan were finally extinct, nothing would stop her masters retaking what was rightfully theirs.

CHAPTER FORTY-FIVE
Ambition Foiled

ADAMANKA SHRANE WALKED ahead of Persin's men, her staff punching small, neat holes into the snow's crust. Above them the sun shone in a dazzlingly blue sky, but on every side a gale blew, propelling fat flakes of snow hard as bullets before it.

"We are nearly there," she said. The eye of her magical storm was eerily still, but the noise from the gale could not be silenced, and the men must walk with it blasting their ears. The harnessed dogs had become aggressive with its noise.

"Give me the word, goodmage, and I shall arrange my men," said Persin.

"I have seen the city in my mind. The entrance is akin to a cave, a gate behind. Five hundred yards separates it from the *Prince Alfra*, which lies at anchor in the Morfaan docks. If we are stealthy, we can pass between city and ship without detection. Half your men must surround the ship, the other half go within."

"What about Kressind's mage?"

"I will deal with him. Once he is defeated, no one can oppose us, and inside we shall find the treasures of the ancients."

Persin's avarice was all consuming, drowning his misgivings in imagined gold and glory. The fool was practically rubbing his hands together at the thought of his prize. Shrane would see he got what he deserved.

Sustaining the storm was a crippling drain on her mental resources. Were she whole, it would have been easier, but she were not. She felt herself fading, her essence consumed to feed the maelstrom. Such elemental magic was hard for her to conjure, for her powers were not in alignment with this world, and her staff of iron sent shooting pains up her arm because of it. She was being sucked dry, but there was not long now. The pull of the gate strengthened, she sensed the eagerness of her masters on the other side to make the crossing.

Soon all this would be done, and she could rest.

TRASSAN'S EXPEDITION STRIPPED the rooms around the gate chamber methodically. Complex devices that could have been works of art or machines, or both, were removed, catalogued, bound up in cloth and rope and carted down the tunnel, out of the city to the camp around the iron ship. The larger pieces—the vehicles and other machines of unguessable purpose—were dragged directly by the dogs down the ice road on makeshift sleds. The *Prince Alfra*'s steam winch worked all day, lifting the priceless devices into the aft hold where they were stowed for the journey home.

With the aid of Tyn Gelven, Ullfider catalogued the devices. Trassan bridled at the delay it caused, wanting to get everything out and the expedition away, as much as he understood the need for Ullfider's diligence. He occupied himself by roaming from room to room, irritating his crew by checking on their progress. Most of the machines he could not understand, and he was eager to get it all back to Karsa so he might spend his time unlocking their secrets. Naturally, he would conduct preliminary examinations aboard the ship. There was not a chance Trassan was giving all the devices over to Vand before he had his time alone with them.

In quieter moments he hid himself away in the main body of the city and took out the device from the silver room. The first time he inserted a silver bead into its cavity he held his breath for a full minute. Nothing happened. He tried again, and again. Still the machine did not function as he expected, the light playing on the wires took on no form. He should have let it be, but he could not stop thinking about it and had several more surreptitious attempts. On the fifth failure, he went to the doorway of a building and waited for Tyn Gelven to come out from the tunnel. He called him over.

Gelven was puzzled by Trassan's secrecy but came into the room nonetheless.

"Tyn Gelven, check this for me."

Trassan took the device from its sack as nonchalantly as he could, but was not successful in hiding its importance.

"Goodfellow?" said Gelven. He looked uncertainly to Trassan. A group of sailors came out of the tunnel carrying crates, singing a droning Ishmalani shanty to speed their loading of the sleds. Ullfider trailed them with a clipboard in hand. Trassan shrank back into the doorway. The movement only attracted Ullfider's attention.

"Goodfellow!" said Ullfider noticing him. "I was meaning to find you and... Why... What do we have here?" He took the device from Trassan, who could think of no reasonable objection to him examining it, and turned it over in his hands. "This cavity seems the right size to take a bead of Morfaan silver." His excitement was evident. "Where did you find it? Goodman Vand will be ecstatic! Is it catalogued? Why did you not bring it to me?" Trassan took it back gently from him. If there was one device he did not wish Vand to have, it was this.

"I did not wish the crew to see," he said quietly, and cursed his ill fortune and own impatience while he did so. "Vand has to have this machine, if it is lost, then..." He let the sentence hang. It was lost to Trassan now, worse luck.

"Indeed. I shall note it in the catalogue."

"I would rather you did not," said Trassan, regaining his wits. "We three know of its existence. That is sufficient. We must be wary." He looked at the laughing sailors meaningfully. "Persin might yet have spies in our crew."

"Of course," said Ullfider, glancing suspiciously at the Ishmalani. "Of course. Does it work?" he whispered.

"I'm trying to find that out. When touched by bare flesh, it sings and lights up. I have inserted a silver into the cavity. Nothing more happened." He held it out to Tyn Gelven. "Is it still whole?" he asked.

The Tyn shrugged. He placed a leathery hand upon the deck. "I detect a charge inside, pure and lively as that in a glimmer lamp."

"I hope it's enough."

"We should put in the hold. Keep it safe," said Ullfider, his suspicions roused. Trassan liked the old man, but he was Vand's creature to the core.

"Leave it with me. I'll take charge of this myself and will hand it to Vand personally. You and I can work on unlocking its secrets on the return voyage, Ullfider. See to the loading of the sleds. I'm going back into the chamber."

He carefully placed the device back in the sack, and wended his way through the stream of men coming and going down the tunnel, furious that he had revealed his prize to Ullfider. There was nothing he could do. He would have to inform Vand of its discovery. The best he could hope for would be to get it working before they returned. Such a miscalculation!

The tunnel light had become erratic, and it flickered as Trassan entered. Everyone paused in the gloom, looking expectantly to the ceiling and walls. The light ignited again, and they returned to their tasks.

"Goodfellow Trassan! Goodfellow Trassan!" One of the ship's Tyn hurried toward him from out of the city. Rulsy, she was called, a strange looking creature of childlike proportions, and all the uglier for it. She was assistant to the ship's physic, but spent most of her time with Ilona. "There's big storm coming. I feel it in my bones. Much snow, heavy wind."

"See to it the glimmer lamps on the rope way are lit," said Trassan. She nodded, and hurried off. He went into the treasure rooms. They were almost bare. He saw there was nothing more useful he could do there that did not put him under his men's feet, so went back the way he had come, reemerging from the tunnel into the city's wide avenue, and headed back towards the city entrance. Perhaps on the ship he would have more success activating the device.

He intended to go straight back to the *Prince Alfra*, but was drawn aside a while by one of the scouting groups he had combing the city. They had found an anomaly in the construction, a something that proved to be nothing. By the time Trassan had trudged into the twisted thicket of the buildings to look and back out again, the daylight twinkling in the city dome had dimmed to grey and the rainbows the ice cast had gone out. The storm was upon them.

He left the scouts and continued on his long walk toward the city gates. The sleds had returned moments before from the ship, ready for a new load. Nearly everyone was occupied around the gate cavern and the docks, and he found himself alone as he approached the exit.

Cold wind blasted through the open gates, hooting as it encountered the convoluted architecture of the buildings under the dome. Trassan slowed when he saw that the guard was not at his post.

"Redan!" he shouted. He waited for a reply. Getting none he walked slowly outside. Buffeted by gusts of wind that blew at him first from one direction, then the other, he checked around the entrance cavern.

Piles of crates and rope lay about, as if abandoned, loose tarpaulins cracking like cannon shots. The entryway was devoid of men or dogs. The wind blasted him hard, needling him with snowflakes. Glimmer lamps danced on their poles on the roped path marking out the route to the ship—another trick he had gleaned from Raik's writings, and he was glad of it. Although the lamps were set no further than thirty yards apart, he could see only the first clearly. The second was a smudge on the glaring, flat whiteness of the storm. If he walked into the storm without the lights, he would be lost.

"Redan!" he shouted into the wind, which promptly shoved the words back down his throat. He went further, out to the edge, where the city canopy joined with the ground. Before he had even left its shelter he was subjected to the raw power of the blizzard. His eyes ached from the cold, his lips tightened, threatening to split. He held out his hand to shield his face and stepped out twenty paces. Almost immediately he lost his bearings. Carefully he stepped backwards, using his rapidly filling footprints as a guide to retrace his steps.

"Trassan!" A hand grabbed him and yanked him back toward the city canopy.

Vols Iapetus had him by the shoulder—ruddy in the face, out of breath, snowflakes clogging his eyelashes and beard.

"Vols? What by the hells are you doing out in this?"

"Trying to send this storm away," he panted. "I can't."

"I'm not surprised. Look at it! You could lose the Isle of Karsa itself in this."

"Trassan, since we came here, my facility with my gift has improved.

The things I can do here, away from all the souls of Ruthnia... The weather, it has been good so far, yes?"

"That was you?"

Vols nodded, still gasping for air. Snowflakes melted on his face. "I've been steering storms away from us, but with this I can do nothing. Something is behind it. Someone is behind it, I mean. I can't sense them, I can't see them. They're hiding themselves, masking the magic that made the storm. But the absence that leaves tells me someone with great power is coming."

"Who?" Trassan turned to look out into the white, as if he might see the malevolent wizard behind the storm. By chance, he caught sight of a shape in the snow, just on the other side of the canopy.

"A body!" he said. The pair of them fought their way to it through the storm, ten yards feeling like ten miles.

Trassan rolled the corpse over.

"Redan!" A neat bullet hole punctured Redan's parka over his heart, the fur soaked with blood.

"They're here!" said Vols. "We must get into shelter and fetch Ardovani, I shall need his help."

"Right," said Trassan. "The ship, or the..."

A shot cracked out, almost inaudible against the howl of the wind. Trassan felt punched in the gut. A patch of blood spread across his stomach.

"Vols?" he said, grabbing for the mage's arm. Agony welled up after the blood. He felt like his insides had been scooped out and replaced with hot lead, pain so harsh it bit into his soul. "I've been shot..." he said, and fell to ground.

The storm dropped. Blue sky slid overhead. Men approached, fifty of them, all armed.

Their leader dropped his hood. "Well, well, well," said Vardeuche Persin. "Vand's puppy! Caught outside, how unfortunate."

"Get back!" Vols punched his hand forward. Persin was hurled away, head over heels, and crashed into three of his men. The others opened fire. Vols leaned toward them, eyes blazing. The bullets shuddered to a stop and dropped hissing into the snow.

"Is that how it is?" said Persin angrily, picking himself up from the ground. "Shrane!"

Persin's mage came out from the middle of his men; a woman, staff upraised and crackling with bright blue light. Vols threw a sheet of flame at her. She rendered it into smoke.

"Surrender," she said. "You cannot defeat me."

Vols leaned further forward, arms out behind him, face straining with effort. She raised her hand, palm up, and advanced.

Reality warped across a broad front as Vols attempted to remove the other mage from existence. Her will countered his, their opposing commands to reality butting against each other like solid objects. The fabric of existence was the casualty of this struggle, tortured shrieks and dazzling flashes torn from the air as its very structure was annihilated.

"An Iron Mage, an Iron Mage!" said Vols through clenched teeth. "You are a myth!"

"Vols...!" said Trassan. His eyesight blurred. Every beat of his heart plunged a dagger into his stomach. Cold seeped into his limbs of a kind that would never be warmed.

Adamanka Shrane came to a halt before Vols Iapetus, a rippling sheet of energy between them where their wills interfaced.

"I am no myth," said Shrane. Her staff head swept down to point at Trassan's face. He blinked in confusion, trying to make sense of what he saw. The world was losing its meaning, turning into a jumble of sensations that confounded understanding. "He is dying. You can fight me, or you can save your friend, but you cannot do both, scion of the Goddriver." She planted her staff in the snow. The space between the mages buzzed and rippled. "Your choice."

CHAPTER FORTY-SIX
The Godhome

SHEET LIGHTNING ILLUMINATED a wrecked hall. Madelyne and Harafan dropped from a crack in the air that closed above them with a clap. They fell, half blind, onto a steeply tilted floor, skidding out of control until a pile of wrecked furniture against a wall stopped them finally, and painfully.

Harafan kicked himself out of a tangle of wood. "Are you alright. Madelyne? Mads?" He hunted for his friend, finding her sitting dazed on an upended sofa of gigantic size.

"I think so," she said.

Harafan looked around and whistled. The room would have been vast when the Godhome was level, its falling had turned it into a slanted corridor with an absurdly high ceiling. Light shone from patterns carved into the walls and ceilings, but very dimly, and large stretches were dark.

"We're in the Godhome, but where?" she asked.

"Beats me," said Harafan cheerfully. He toed the debris by his feet. "Look at this!" he said, plucking a dented gold jug from the mess. "It must be worth a fortune." He hugged it to his chest, casting it aside when he spied a pile of diamonds caught in a crease of tapestry. "Oh by the gods! Diamonds?" He scrambled to them and ran them through his fingers. "Diamonds, heaped like sand!" He began filling his pockets, then stopped. "Hang on a moment now, this is a good idea." He picked up the jug again, and filled it hurriedly with double handfuls of the stones until it brimmed. "There's enough here, right in the this jug, to set us up as goodfellows with our own castles, for life. For longer than life!" His eyes shone in the gloom with an almost innocent, boyish avarice. "We've done it!"

"Harafan," she said.

"We can do anything, anything!" His laughter bounced from the walls, hurrying off into the depths of the Godhome. Madelyne peered nervously into dark corners.

"Shhhh!" she said.

"Why? There's nothing here! We're rich, stupidly, massively, madly rich!"

"Rich... ich... ich," said his echo.

"And how are we going to get it out?" she said levelly.

He frowned. "You got us in, did you not find out how to get out?"

She shook her head. "We never should have done this."

"Didn't you think to ask how to get out again?"

"For the sake of all the hells, Harafan! I expected a door, not, not, this! Poof! From outside to in."

"Shit," he said. He hugged the jug to his chest. He thought a moment. An idea lit up his face. "Right. I know. We go to the centre, to the top. There are buildings there, and that broken dome right in the centre where the Yotan was. You can see it right across the city."

"The edge is smooth for hundreds of feet," she said. "We can't climb the metal, it's impossible. It's been tried."

"Yeah," he replied. "That's stopped people getting in, alright, and I'll wager climbing up is impossible, but we can make a rope or something, just lower ourselves down. Easy! Look." He kicked at the tangle of curtains, hangings and drapes on the floor. "This place must be full of rich tapestries and all sorts. None of it's rotted, see?" He held up a section of cloth and tugged it. There wasn't so much as a speck of dust on. "Good as the day the gods were driven away. We can knot it together. It'd make a fine rope."

"If we did, how do we get past the Tyn?"

"We'll wait for when the sun is full on the top side of the Godhome, that'll keep the Tyn away."

"Says who?"

"People. People say. People said the Tyn were really in the park, and they really were. I'm beginning to trust what people say."

"Why didn't we try coming in that way then?" she said accusingly.

Harafan looked at his treasure abashedly. "Too risky, we might have been seen. Can't trust folk not to follow us."

"We could have died coming the other way! Harafan, why they hells do I do anything you say?"

"Because I'm really clever and smart?" he grinned ingratiatingly.

"Fantastic. Your brains," she said. she looked around. "I'd say the Yotan is above us, not below. I suppose we better go up. It's going to be hard. Shall we take some of this cloth?" she said doubtfully. It was shot through with gold and copper thread. "It must weigh a lot."

"Nah, there'll be loads more, I'm sure. Let's find a way out first. We can come back for this if we really need it, and I'm prepared," he said. He fished out a coil of rope for Madelyne from his pack. About fifty yards of it, she thought. To get out, they'd need a rope half a mile long.

He was less concerned by their predicament, and whistled as he stuffed the diamond filled jug into a sack, tied it carefully with string and put it into his backpack. "Oof!" he said. "That's heavy! But *good* heavy. Shame we can't take it all." He looked regretfully at the broken riches. "I bet this is small change to the gods. The really good stuff will be further in, closer to the Yotan."

They worked their way across the room to a huge doorway that led a into corridor that looked to be a giant ring. Its tilted walls curved gently upward, and there was an identical gate on the far side of the room.

"That makes things easier," Harafan said. "There must be a corridor off it somewhere that cuts inwards. If we're lucky the Godhome will have fallen so that we can just walk along it right to the middle. No more climbing!" He patted her shoulder. "That'd be grand, eh Mads?" he said. "We'll go up, have a look around on the way. Once we've got your sack filled up, we won't dawdle, I promise. Then it's bye bye duke, bye bye poverty and the easy life for us!"

But they did dawdle. The going was hard enough without Harafan stopping to examine every room they passed. It seemed that each new chamber contained more spectacular riches than the last.

There were weapons, glass, statues, artworks, strange objects of the Morfaan steel, precious metals and stones of every sort—gold, silver, platinum, rubies, sapphires, diamonds, all attracted his attention. One room contained so many stones piled up against its canted wall that it looked like a pool of water. Madelyne had to haul Harafan back from the door before he could dive in. He emptied his bags and refilled them several times with ever more precious artefacts, a pained expression at how much he had to leave behind always on his face.

"I never knew, I mean, who did, how much wealth there is here!" he said. Their sacks and their packs were full, and they staggered along the tilted coign of ceiling and walls, burdened by wealth, more riches ready to snag their feet. The floors of the Godhome had become cliffs that resisted climbing. Vast chambers present insurmountable obstacles. Traversing the debris taxed their legs. They fought their way across each huge hall, always taking the corridor. The curve of the walls they were walking on increased in steepness. In this remarkable variation on mountaineering they were forced to clamber up what had been the walls, using tumbled statues as staircases, and broken walls and fittings as handholds. Harafan would go up first, and haul their loot after. Madelyne followed behind.

"We're just going in a circle," she said, as they perched in the gaping door of a chamber, the corridor dropping below their feet. "We're not getting any closer to the middle."

"There'll be a way, you'll see," said Harafan.

He handed her a canteen of water. She sipped it gratefully. A chill permeated the Godhome, but the climbing was hot work. There wasn't much water left in her canteen. *We could easily die of thirst in here*, she thought.

Harafan's prediction was realised. Not long after the corridor had become vertical, they came to a crossway in the corridor cut through theirs, running toward the centre of the Godhome in one direction, the rim in the other. They hauled themselves up the lip of the wall and sat with their legs dangling over the junction, grateful for the rest.

"Told you!" he said cheerfully. Sometimes, Harafan's relentless good humour made her want to throttle him.

They were, however, on the wrong side. They had climbed the outer wall for it was less sheer, a decision that, in hindsight, seemed stupid.

"How do we get across?"

"We'll be all right," he said. Harafan took off his pack and dropped his heavy sacks. "You rest, I'll be right back," he said, and headed off down the corridor.

She hunkered down into a crouch, her arms wrapped around her legs.

The corridor was wider than the circular one they had clambered out of, mounded with broken statuary along the earthward side. From the walls the same white light shone, illuminating the wreck of the place. Despite the dimness there were no shadows, no shading. All was exposed like a naked corpse on a dissector's slab.

There was a strange smell to the Godhome, not rot or mould or putrefaction of any sort, but an aseptic nothing that accentuated the coldness of the environs. A silence that crushed all noise reigned supreme. Harafan was rooting about behind her somewhere. He was only a hundred feet away, but sounded much further. The light was as chill as the metal and air, unfriendly and accusing. She shivered. A few minutes inactivity and the sweat chilled her skin. The duke's collar was uncomfortably cold on her neck. To distract herself she tried to picture what Godhome had been like before Res Iapetus, imagining it full of life and warmth. But she could not. The images she conjured showed her a different reality, a cold place always, inhabited by beings uninterested in the lot of humanity, detached from themselves and their worshippers, living in stillness, surrounded by riches they neither needed nor cared for. Living beings transformed into puppets of myth, playing roles they did not want. The Godhome was not a palace, but a gaol of the soul.

Res Iapetus had done the gods a favour.

Harafan thumped back down beside her. She started

"Don't scare me like that!" she said.

"Sorry!" he grinned. From somewhere he had procured three brass candelabras with two tiers of serpentine arms. He knotted a rope about the loop at the top of one.

"Grappling hook, see?" he said. He hefted and threw. His first cast was good. The candelabra clanged off a statue lying atop a second, and disappeared behind. A single yank secured it. Harafan tossed over the sacks, wincing in anticipation of them bursting and scattering his plunder. But they held. He tossed over the other two candelabras, then knotted the rope about the leg of a toppled statue on their side. Half the length remained, and he tied that about his waist.

"When you're over, untie this knot, loop the rope round and I'll secure it at the other side. That way, we can keep all the rope."

He tested it, then lowered himself onto the line, legs crossed over it and gripping with his hands.

When Harafan had clambered across and they had tied the ropes, it was Madelyne's turn. The shaft of the circular corridor yawned beneath her. She went quickly.

"Easy, huh?" he said as he helped her up. He undid the rope, tugging their bridge back across the gap and pulling it back up. "Come on, we're nearly out."

They leapt doorways opening into deep vaults become pits, all of them filled with untold treasures. Objects of stupendous value were scattered everywhere.

"If I'd have been Res Iapetus," said Harafan, "I would have cleaned this place out."

"It wasn't about money," said Madelyne.

"The duke told you?"

She nodded.

"What happened, really?"

Revealing that felt like one betrayal too many, and she did not reply.

A cool wind blew, bringing the scents of Perus into the house of the gods; the smell of soot and shit dirtied the air. Shortly thereafter, they came to the approach to the Yotan. The corridor opened out into a long arcade with a roof of wide crystal panes to keep out the sky. At the end the gates of the great hall hung splintered from their titanic hinges. It was much brighter there, sunlight streamed through the open door. Signs of Res's invasion became apparent. The damage was obvious and direct, affecting the very structure of the city. Such power had been unleashed that the Morfaan metal was dented and discoloured beneath shattered marble. The lights in the wall were out. All the statues were broken, but some had clearly been destroyed before the tilting of the Godhome had sent them tumbling. These were blackened and part-melted.

To get to the gates they had to climb. Enormous statues, urns, obelisks, and other sculptural works made a scree as daunting as that on any mountain. They struggled over the rubble, pausing to marvel at objects thousands of years old, fashioned by inhuman hands before history began. They crested one last hummock of shattered art, and the way out was clear. Through the gates they saw the broken dome, most of its many frames empty of glass.

"The Yotan," she breathed. "The throneroom of the gods. We must be the first people to see this in two hundred years."

Glory had fled. The thrones were broken in their settings. Water streaked the walls. Plants had taken root in windblown soil. Brilliant green moss highlighted every crack in the marble fascia. "How sad," she said.

"Never mind that, see, a way out!" said Harafan. "We can climb out of the bottom there," he pointed to where the dome met the top of the lowermost wall. "It'll be easier than we thought. We should start gathering up cloth to make a longer rope."

"We'll need a lot, it's a quarter of a mile from the buildings on the upside to the ground over the rim. Twice as far from the centre all the way to the edge."

"We'll be able to climb down the building like we climbed up the corridors. It's just the last, smooth section we have to worry about."

"We'll still need about three hundred yards of rope."

"Best get looking then, eh Mads?" he said, and slapped her on the shoulder. He was smiling, close to laughing, she smiled back. "See?" he said. "I told you I wouldn't let you down."

They split up. Ranging along the arcade, Madelyne quickly gathered a bundle of long hangings, tapestries, flags and pennants. She found a room full of clothes of human size. A god could not have worn them, yet there were racks of fine dresses and goodfellow's clothes of an antique style. She put her collection aside and lowered herself into the chamber to gather them up, using hanging rails fixed into the walls to slide down.

"Harafan!" she shouted.

There was no reply.

"Harafan!"

A crow cawed loudly outside the Godhome, its cries brought in by the wind. "Fine, I'll do it myself," she grumbled. She hunted out all the belts and cords she could, thinking to plait them into a sturdy line. After that she chose the most robust looking garments. She couldn't toss them out of the room, the door was too far, so she bundled as many together as she could and tied it up with a loop of rope. Her intention was to shimmy up the pole with the rope between her teeth, and haul the clothes back into the arcade. On the cusp of leaving, she paused.

Something glinted enticingly, resting in a fold of a rich gold doublet like a jewel in a presentation box. She bent to pick it up, thinking it to be a sapphire—she already had dozens, but there was always space for one more—but it turned out to be a fragment of deep blue glass. The edges were razor sharp, so she held it carefully as she examined it. It didn't look like the crystal glass from the roof, too blue. There was something moving inside it.

She held it to the light. A screaming woman's face rushed toward her, sweeping a sword out. The glass's edge bit into her finger and she dropped it. Red dripped from her hand.

"Damn it!" she said, sucking the cut. "Harafan!"

The glass jiggled, agitated as a wasp. She snatched her head aside as it shot off the clothes pile and past her face. Any closer, and it would have sliced into her cheek. The Godhome shook. Madelyne staggered. The clothes heaped in the room writhed with movement. More glass pieces shot up, ripping through the garments. She dodged back, but one skimmed her arm, cutting through cloth and skin. A bass rumbling shuddered through the structure. She clutched at the clothes rails, making herself as small as possible as glass sped upwards all around, sharp and deadly.

The rumbling subsided. The glass ceased to streak upward.

"Mads! Mads!" shouted Harafan. Out in the arcade, glass tinkled on glass.

She began to climb the pole. "Harafan!" she shouted. "In here!" Her blood greased the metal, slowing her, her torn arm stung.

Harafan's head appeared through the doorway, looking down at her with wide eyes.

"We have got to get out of here, right now," she snapped.

He reached for her, she climbed and slipped, he leaned in further. The tinkle of glass grew louder, like an avalanche of smashing bottles. Harafan grabbed her injured arm, and hauled her up. She bit back a cry at the pain as her cut opened further.

"Come on!" he said, dragging her up a pile of masonry.

Madelyne looked back.

There, toward the gates of the Yotan, a figure took shape. Glass shards burrowed their way up out of the rubble, shot across the arcade in blurs, adding themselves to a tall and monstrous being that formed in shifting mosaic—a woman's torso upon a serpent's body, a crown on her head and a sword in each hand.

"Andrade!" said Madelyne.

Glass lips rasped and clicked. "Trespassers!" they said. The voice was hollow, air blown across the top of a bottle. "Trespassers!"

Fragments still flying to join themselves to her mass, Andrade, tutelary spirit of the Earth and warrior champion of the gods, threw herself forward. Her sinuous tail propelled her at the thieves, glass pieces rattling against one another.

Harafan and Madelyne stumbled back and fell down a pile of statue's limbs and toppled pediments. Andrade was on them already, swinging her swords. Harafan shoved against Madelyne, and she banged into a broken-faced head. The sword slashed down between she and Harafan to explode into a thousand pieces of blue glass on the stone, but the goddess drew back her arm and the fragments flew back into place, a swarm of cruelly edged pieces remaking the weapon.

"Trespassers!" she hissed.

Madelyne screamed, and flung herself forward. Andrade was swift as lightning, slamming Madelyne from her feet into rocks that lacerated her ribs.

Harafan scrambled a few yards ahead.

"Help me!" screamed Madelyne.

Harafan looked from her to the towering goddess of broken glass. He paused for a moment. At least he did that before he mouthed "Sorry," and ran.

"Harafan!" she screamed. "Harafan!"

The clicking of glass pieces played behind her. She rolled onto her back. Andrade reared high, triumph on her broken face. Madelyne prepared to die.

A sunburst whited out the arcade. Hot wind blasted out in every direction. Madelyne blinked tears and grit from her eyes. Between after images, she saw the duke, fire wreathing his naked, crimson body.

"Back Andrade! Back!" he boomed. He held up his hand. Fire roared from it.

"Trespassers..." hissed Andrade.

"You failed the last time. Go back to your rest. Back to death. You are no more. You are dead. Sleep now."

"Trespassers!" she said. She raised her sword. The duke punched forward his fist, and a column of fire blasted from it, connecting with the sword and Andrade's arm. The fragments glowed red, then white, the glass running and the pieces fusing together. Andrade screamed. Madelyne scrambled to her feet, urgency blocking the pain from her thousand cuts.

Andrade swung her cooling arm at Madelyne. It bent before shattering into pieces glowing cherry red with heat. These did not return to the goddess, but went black and scattered themselves across the ruins of the hall.

The duke strode forward. "You are dead. Your powers are weak. You cannot stand before me. Leave this woman and this man. They are mine."

Andrade brandished her unharmed arm and sword. The duke took another step forward. Andrade slithered backwards, mouth gaping, becoming more snakelike in her defeat.

"Go back!" commanded the duke.

Andrade screeched, turned, and with the rattle of glass on rock, sped away toward the Yotan.

Madelyne wept in terror and shame. The duke looked down on her through burning eyes. When possessed by wrath he was so much bigger than his Earthly aspect. Fire wreathed his head and limbs.

"You... you came after me?"

"While you wear my collar, no harm will come to you," he boomed. "I take care of my property, Madelyne."

A rush of heat conveyed her from that place. A wall of fire rolled away, and she was in the park, in the shadow of the Godhome near the bench where she had met Harafan. Upon the overgrown road the duke's carriage waited. Markos sat in the driving seat. The drays sniffed curiously at the breeze.

The duke stood before her, his mortal body cloaking his true nature once more. Harafan cowered at his feet in a ball.

"This one would have left you," he pointed imperiously at Harafan. "So fickle mortals are. A lifetime of friendship, and he betrayed you. Shall I destroy him for you?"

"I had no choice!" screamed Harafan. He looked at Madelyne, pathetic in his fear. "Please Madelyne, please, your grace."

For a second, Madelyne would have killed him. Only a second. She could not be sure she would have not done the same as him in his place. Maybe she would have fled too.

"Don't harm him. Please, your grace. Do not."

The duke glared down at Harafan, as if he was going to stamp his skull into pieces under one heavy boot. Madelyne held her breath.

The duke prodded Harafan with the toe of his shoe. When Harafan looked up, the duke raised his finger and pointed down the road toward the safer precincts of the park. "Go," he said. "If I ever see you again, I shall devour your soul."

"Thank you, your grace, thank you!" Harafan scrambled up onto his hands and feet and ran away, his torn pack dribbling riches into the weeds.

"Harafan!" she called.

He did not look back. Something delicate in Madelyne's heart broke.

"You," said the duke. "Come with me."

Numbly, Madelyne reached up her hand to take the duke's.

He helped her up into his carriage.

CHAPTER FORTY-SEVEN

An Offer of Slavery

GARTEN AND JOSAN emerged through a stone door in a long corridor full of hundreds of others. All except theirs was shut. The doors were thin as shell, light visible behind, and joined seamlessly to the stone of the gateways as if all of one piece. As they walked away from their gate, its light dimmed, the edges blurred together, and it became like all the others.

"This is your abode?" he said.

"You expected a palace?" Josan laughed. "This is the Castle of Mists, and here we do not live, only survive."

She led him through a series of vast halls that opened themselves to him in solemn procession. Typical Morfaan craftsmanship greeted his eyes wherever he looked: flawlessly made, artful in form and symmetry, yet all of it lifeless, and of proportions disturbing to the human eye. There was a feeling of great age, but also of impermanence, giving the sense that the building teetered on the brink of dissolution, and that if he put his hands to the jointless marble it would crumble at his touch and show itself to be nothing more than rotted plaster over wood. How chilly, how damp, how drear, Garten thought. A mausoleum. Where there were windows, he saw only mist outside.

"Do not delay!" she chided as he slowed to take in a high hall whose pointed vault was murky with shadow. "Every second Josanad stays without life, I risk losing him forever."

They went into a corridor encircling some other space. A number of doors of differing precious stones pierced the wall. She stopped before one made of emerald.

"I must go into the courtyard beyond. So must you, but you cannot use the emerald door, that is for Morfaan. Go around the corridor. You will find a door made of agate, made for men. Go through that. Do not use the others or you will perish. When you are inside, do not reveal your small friend, for both our sakes."

Garten said he would do as asked, and she went through the emerald door. Josan's urgency had affected him, so he rushed past the other doors looking for his own. Opposite each, matching portals led back into the castle. He came to a door made of a single sheet of blue agate, rippled with lighter blue curves, and the centre a blotched white starburst. It was so thin he could see shadows through it.

He grasped the handle, and his mind was filled with a clamour of voices.

"Someone attempts the door of man!" a male said.

"A new development, finally," said a female. "Perhaps he comes to end us, and this will all be—"

Garten snatched his fingers back, alarmed at the intrusion into his mind. Taking a deep breath, he grabbed the handle again, twisted it sharply, and stepped through into a courtyard of middling size. Five heroic statues ringed a tree of green stone. Chill mist scudded overhead, hiding the castle's upper reaches. The voices began speaking again, questioning him all at once. Garten collapsed to the floor in agony. He heard Josan shouting, quieting the others, and she came to help him to his feet.

"You waste my time!" she hissed.

"Where am I?" he said.

A single voice spoke inside his head. Every word was a nail in his skull, but one voice he could bear.

"We are the Marble Council. I am Mathanad, its leader. Welcome to the heart of the Morfaan empire in exile."

A female voice laughed wildly. "So mighty in our pomp! Fear us!"

"Silence Lorinan!" said the first.

Another voice muttered incomprehensible nonsense.

"Why have you brought him here, Lady Josan?" asked another female, her voice reasoned yet cold. "Is your mission to the world of Will done? Does the enemy come? Is there a new High Legate? Bring us news!"

"No, no, no!" said Josan, full of grief. "Lords, Ladies, please, Josanad is dead, slain in a duel."

"Impossible!" said Mathanad.

"The world of Will has changed much in only thirty years," said Josan. "Events there have outpaced us. Its heart grows weak."

"They use too much. But that might be in our favour. Might they then be ready?" said a second female hopefully. "Can they defy the Draathis?"

"I don't know!" Josan said. "I beg you, let us talk of this later. You must release to me the machineries of revivification, so that Lord Josanad can return. Then I will answer all your questions gladly."

"Where is he now?" asked the second women.

"I have folded him into the two-width dimension. He is in the null state."

"Then hurry," said the female. "I release the machines."

"There must be a vote to release the machines, Helesin!" shouted Mathanad.

Lorinan laughed nastily. "All hail our mighty lord!"

"As you acted before unilaterally, now do I. It is done!" said Helesin. "There is no time for debate. Go Josan, save him!"

Josan ran out, leaving Garten behind. He did not know if he should stay or go.

"What is this?" said Garten. "Where are the other Morfaan Josan told me of?"

Lorinan laughed loudly, and Garten reeled as the sound pounded at his mind. "We *are* the others, foolish little thing," said Lorinan. Her voice hurt more than the others, prickly as it was with incipient madness. "Five of us took ourselves into these statues. Two remained as flesh as ambassadors to your primitive kind. Now we are four, and the flesh may soon be one. Our vigil was never supposed to last so long."

"You tell him too much," warned Mathanad.

"And you will let him leave, I suppose?" said Lorinan. "His bones will lie with the others in the Court of Death soon enough. Let me talk to him, I am bored with your company, you tedious wretch."

There was a short silence, interrupted by the fourth Morfaan's senile mumblings. When they spoke next, it was Helesin's voice that addressed him.

"We five gave up our bodies to watch over this castle and the two ambassadors to the World of Will until such time as we could return."

"Return? The seven of you?"

"Five now. Qurunad fled thousands of years ago, Josanad is probably gone for good, and Solophonad doesn't count anymore, because he's gone mad," said Lorinan. "Isn't that right, Solophonad?" she bawled.

"What? Eh?" said the fourth voice.

"Mad!" she said.

"More than seven," said Helesin. "The others are safe. One day, the enemy will be gone, and we shall come home and recall our brothers and sisters."

"What enemy? The Twin? The perigee of the Twin coincided with the fall of the Morfaan and the end of the age of Maceriyan Resplendency, so say our empiricists. Are they right?"

"See!" said Mathanad. "Science! Rationalism! They begin to work it out for themselves. Perhaps they are strong enough to resist the Draathis after all."

"In all things, two is best," said Helesin. "As with the World of Form, and the World of Will, so were we and the Draathis we created together, we to be of greater will, they to be of greater form. We coexisted for thousands of years, until..."

"Until they turned on us!" snarled Lorinan. "We fought. We drove them away, off to the World of Form they went! We thought it done, and we masters of the World of Will for evermore."

"They returned," Garten said, he examined the statues more closely. He thought he could match their voices with their marble faces.

"The first time they returned they destroyed our homeland, and we dwindled," said Lorinan. "We shut our gates, and turned our attention to the creatures we had collected to serve us. Four millennia passed. We grew complacent. The second time they fell from the sky in burning ships of iron, and attempted to force the gates from our side. It was but a raid, and yet they still cast down the civilisation of men we had so carefully raised up, and poisoned the sun so that its rays burned us. We fled." Her statue was of a laughing maiden, holding aloft a double pipe as she danced. Her expression was at odds with the bitter tone of her voice. The statue was carved wearing a diaphanous gown, revealing her anatomy beneath in every detail. But there was no sign of the lesser arms he had seen on the ambassadors.

"The lesser arms are vulgar," said Helesin, reading his mind. Garten winced at her soul touching his. "Weak. They remind us of the beasts of the Earth."

"The dracons, dracon birds, dragons and so on. All of them have six limbs. We men do not," said Garten.

"You are of another Earth, of another creation," said Mathanad. "You were our servants, conveyed here to aid us in the first war, along with the beasts you husband to sustain you."

"What?" said Garten. This was too much.

"It's true!" said Lorinan. "You were our slaves. We freed you, thinking you might prosper. Have you? I do not think so. Best you die now."

"You must prepare for another war," said Mathanad. "The World of Form, the world you dub the Twin, comes close. At this time, it is easiest to traverse the space between the worlds. And now the Gates of the World will open for them, you will be sorely tested."

"The gates were sealed," said Helesin. "They were our greatest achievement. Once we ranged far and wide across all the many layers of existence, stepping from one reality to the next as easily as you might walk from one room to another. We were forced to shut the gates when the Draathis learned their use."

"And now, now!" gloated Lorinan. "You put yourselves at great peril! You use too much magic, you disrupt the spirit of the world."

"The glimmer you steal from the desert of the Black Sands may seem infinite to you," said Mathanad. "But what it draws upon is not."

"The locks we placed upon our gates are wrought of powerful spells that require much magic. They are failing because you are greedy," said Helesin. "You deplete the world spirit, and the magic that sustains the Earth."

"Should the Draathis still exist, they will fall upon your people in great number, and slaughter you all!" said Lorinan exultantly.

"And if not, then you will return, to resume your overlordship of our Earth," said Garten.

"Just so," said Mathanad. "We would aid you in this war if we could, but Josanad's mind is failing whether he survives or not. Josan has forgotten much of what she knew. We of the council cannot leave this place."

"Death or slavery? That is our choice?"

"Extinction or peace," said Mathanad. "You were our slaves, you are no longer."

"But you will be our masters again."

"Are you not the masters of your dogs? We are as high above you as you above they. It is the way of things," said Mathanad. "Do not resent it."

"But we thought you our friends, our advisors!"

"No doubt the dogs and goats and other creatures you brought into our world with you feel you are their friends," said Mathanad, "until they are led to the butcher's block, or have their children snatched away. We are kinder masters than you. Without us, the era of Maceriya's Resplendency would never have occurred. Science, magic, art, healing, power! All these things we gave to you. If you submit you shall be raised up to untold heights again, and worlds unnumbered will be yours. This would have occurred before, were it not for the Draathis. You will be safer as our subjects than on your own, you cannot be trusted to manage your own affairs. We see that now."

"The Hundred will never acquiesce to that," said Garten. He turned, uncomfortable that he could not keep all the statues in view, as if they might step down from their pedestals and run him through while his back was to them. "I understand why you will not permit me to leave," said Garten. "Very well. But who shall stop me? You?"

"We have servants."

"Which he shall evade. You always were dimwitted," said Tyn Issy, breaking her silence. She opened the door of her case from the inside and threw it wide.

"An Y Dvar!" shrieked Lorinan. "Here, in the Castle of Mists, in the Court of Marble!"

"Hello," Issy said. Pressing up against the bars of her travelling case she pulled faces at the statues.

"We are betrayed, undone!" shouted Mathanad.

Garten reeled. The panic of the Morfaan council ground at his mind with a millstone's power. He staggered to the agate door and tumbled through it, slamming it against the psychic racket so hard the delicate mineral pane cracked. Peace returned. Head swimming, he leaned, panting, against the wall.

"You should not have done that," said Garten.

"I don't like them. I don't care."

"The feeling appears to be mutual," he gasped. He shook his head to clear it and could swear he felt his brain moving inside his skull.

A wailing cry filled the castle with sorrow. Garten looked up. "Josan?"

"Most likely," said Issy. "She does not sound very happy."

THEY FOUND HER sobbing in a hall full of quiet devices. Her brother sat in a coffin-shaped, stone machine alive with red and yellow light. He was whole in body, but not in mind. Lips twitched over nonsense sounds, and he dribbled freely. He reached for his sister with all four of his arms, the fingers moving feebly to stroke her dress. They smeared gelatinous liquid on her clothes. Josanad let out a moan, dumb as a dracon-cow's lowing, when she moved away.

"Lady Morfaan!"

Josan looked up accusingly at Garten, then went back to weeping without restraint.

Garten approached her awkwardly, unsure as what to do. He placed his hands on her shoulders. Her bone structure was odd under his hands. She leaned into him hesitantly, then completely, clawing at his back and squeezing him mightily in her grief.

After a time she took in three trembling breaths and gasped out, "His mind is gone. It did not work. Josanad, my love and hero of the Morfaan, is dead."

In his stone coffin, Josanad blinked stupidly. Josan's tears returned. Garten held her awkwardly, taken aback at her display of raw emotion. When she calmed, she pushed Garten away.

"Will you return with me, to Ruthnia?" he asked.

"I must. Matters there hang in the balance. The chance of war between the Hundred Kingdoms increases if I am not there to ratify the election of the High Legate."

"You sound as if you care for the fate of mankind," he said.

"I do. Who wishes to see suffering that can be prevented?"

"And not only for your own people? Your plan is to supplant us, and rule the Earth again."

Her inner eyelids blinked sideways. "They told you. Who we were, what we are."

"They told me my people were brought to the Earth to be your slaves."

"That was so, in the beginning. Our relationship changed. In the last era of the Morfaan our kinds worked together. The remaining few of my people dwelt in the Parrui, the sky city over Perus that you call the Godhome. We remained as advisors and teachers, no matter what grandiose claims Mathanad might make. Before the Draathis returned and destroyed everything, there was harmony, and you prospered under our guidance."

"And now, they could come back? All of them?" said Garten.

She was occupied with her brother's slack expression, and had seemingly lost interest in Garten.

"Tell me!" he demanded.

"The Draathis? All of them. Yes."

"I was told I was to be killed for the privilege of receiving this information."

"Impossible. I will protect you. I cannot do this alone. Josanad is gone. You are an asset that cannot be squandered. We must go back to the World of Will. If your people are to stand any chance, they must be united and prepared. The Council wished to wait out the return of the World of Form and see if the Draathis yet lived, but I believe they do. All that has happened in Perus this last week has been intended to drive you apart and make your defeat all the easier. The Draathis have their agents still on Earth. The mage Shrane is one. The Draathis will return."

"And Josanad?"

Josan went to her brother, and eased him back into the coffin. Its glass lid slid down and clicked shut. He panicked and scratched at the glass, until the device robbed his breath and he fell into an unnatural sleep. "This machine will sustain him. Perhaps, if the Draathis can be overcome, and we might return, then we shall recover enough of our lost arts to save him. His soul is still within the bounds of his flesh, though it is weak. Maybe it can be healed and his mind made whole. But we must triumph first."

"We can fight," said Garten. "If we fought before at your side and aided you in driving these Draathis out, then we can do it again."

Josan favoured him with a sad smile. "It is not so simple. Now come, we must be away."

She led him up stairs to the second level, through a huge arch too big for the material confines of the Castle of Mists. From there she took him through a door back into the Corridor of the Gates.

"Come," she said. "We shall return the way we came. Only the main gate, the one we drove our carriage down, is open ordinarily. I took a risk using the one beneath the city. I behaved rashly. We must go back through it in order to properly shut it. Then I will destroy it to prevent others following us."

They went down the corridor. Josan slowed. Light blazed from a gate.

"No!" she said. "It is open! I am too late!"

The corridor shook. A massive hand of black, smoking iron groped around the door frame. It patted the wall, as if ensuring it was real, then seized it, and heaved. A head and shoulder emerged and withdrew. The gateway was too small to admit it, so it slammed its shoulder into the other side. The jointless stonework cracked, the fragments bulged. The gate's light shone blindingly. It winked out, and the wall collapsed into rubble.

Placing its hand either side of the smoking hole, the Draathis pulled itself out into the Castle of Mists. It was huge, far taller than a man, bigger than a Torosan godling. Its body was cast with an impressionistic interpretation of muscles and armour. Its blockish head was crude by comparison, a simple rectangle, wider than it was tall, with brutal features for a face—a jutting brow over glowering red eyes, and a heavy, protruding lower jaw. The sound of heat-softened metal parting accompanied its movements. It pointed a finger at them.

With a spine-tingling roar, the Draathis charged.

CHAPTER FORTY-EIGHT
A Gate is Opened

Trassan's captors had taken him back into the city. He came to to find himself up against a crate in the gate room, a fur spread under him by Persin's men, a kindness that baffled him, for the members of Persin's expedition were a hard-looking lot. Olberlander mercenaries for the most part, stiffened by Maceriyan veterans, none of whom looked to have a care for anyone but themselves. A half dozen had their guns trained on the Karsans, the rest went about the chamber ransacking the carefully packed artefacts not yet taken to the ship. His own men regarded him worriedly—Bannord, Ardovani and Antoninan among them. Vols was at one side, his hands splayed wide over the wound in his stomach. Ilona knelt at the other, gripping his bloody hand. His fingers were icicles in her warm grip, and he shivered from the very core. Cold sweat beaded his face, trickling onto lips that were whiter than his skin. One of Bannord's marines, that idiot Darrasind, pressed on the wound hard to staunch the bleeding. Well meant, perhaps. It felt like the man were trying to insert his entire fist into his chest cavity.

"To think it has to come to this," he said.

"Silence!" hissed Vols. His teeth were clenched and face knotted in effort. His magic was palpable. Trassan felt the struggle between the actuality of his wrecked body and the intention of Vols to make it whole. The mage's mind pushed past blood, and bone and mind, deep in his soul and beyond the veils of the material world. He appreciated the effort, but it felt wrong. He was restless. His spirit was gripped by an urgent need to leave mortality's cage, and kept rising up, only to be pushed back in by Vols' will. The mage was as powerful as a locomotive. He fidgeted against it. Trassan was dying, and his soul was eager to seize its freedom.

"You are such a little man," said Trassan woozily. "But you are mighty. You crush me, a steam press of a person! I'll never doubt you again. And you, you Bannord? You owe him an apology."

"You must not think on your condition!" hissed Vols. He grunted as his concentration slipped. The stain of dark blood under Darrasind's hands widened. "You set your will against mine, it interferes with my magic."

Trassan chuckled. Muscles he had never really noticed before scolded him with agony.

"I am sorry. It hurts quite a lot."

"Why is he like this?" said Ilona.

Ardovani squeezed her shoulder. "Shock, blood loss. An inbred bloody mindedness."

She smiled at the last, and patted his hand. Bannord looked sidelong at that.

"Do not joke! You are accepting your death with every smile. Do not give in! Deny death!" said Vols, surprising Trassan with his forcefulness. "Aid me Ardovani, please!"

The magister withdrew his hand from Ilona's guiltily, and looked helplessly on. "I know no healing spells, and my will is not so strong as yours. I... I cannot help you, not in the way that you require."

"Then distract Trassan! He is in danger of slipping free! I cannot heal him until his soul is seated again."

Ardovani braved the glowers of Persin's men and knelt by Trassan's head next to Ilona.

"Goodfellow..." began Ardovani uncertainly.

"Trassan, please. We have shared too much." Trassan sighed. His breath burned his lungs. When it issued from his mouth, it tasted of copper. "Such a marvellous machine the human body is, so much more refined than my own efforts of brass and iron. Only now I realise it. How I wish I knew more of its working. Tell me," he clasped Ardovani's forearm feebly. "Have I wasted my life? Should I have been a physic?" In his giddiness Trassan found the notion

immensely funny, and tried not to laugh. More for appearance's sake
than the pain. Did no one else find death so amusing? Life was a big
joke, at the end of it, death the punchline.

. "Do not let him think on the condition of mortality!" said Vols.
Sinews quivered on his neck and hands. "Keep him focused on the
now, on the immediate, on the future!"

"Then speak to me of my killer," said Trassan. He lifted his head
weakly in the direction of Adamanka Shrane. She stood on the gate
platform facing the sealed portal, studying it closely. "Who is this
mage?"

Ardovani looked at Vols, but received no response. He leaned
closer in to Trassan's ear and whispered.

"She is an Iron Mage. An order long dead, or so it was thought.
They were secretive, never numerous even in the days when mages
numbered in the hundreds and the gods still ruled the heavens.
Their magic is unlike any other. Legend has it that they take into
themselves the essence of iron, dangerous, because iron is the death
of magic and the antithesis of the working of will. They wield it in
their hands—see, she has an iron staff—and that the excitation of
the magic via the medium of the metal makes them deadly powerful,
though the stories say it takes a terrible toll on their bodies and their
souls. Others have tried this method. They tried it in my college.
Beyond the mindless alchemical reaction of iron and magic, wilful
magic through iron has never worked, and so the Iron Mages were
thought to be a myth."

"Evidently not," said Trassan. "And I thought I was being original
with my combination of iron and magic. I never will be now, original,
not a mage." He giggled.

"Do not speak of your deeds as done, goodfellow, please!" said
Ardovani.

"Pfff," said Trassan.

Persin noticed Trassan staring over at the gate, and chose to leave
Shrane to her task. Perhaps he meant to gloat, but upon seeing
Trassan lying upon the blood-soaked fur, the ice coloured crimson
by his ebbing life, his face fell, and he tugged at his lip apologetically.

"I am sorry goodfellow," he said in Karsarin. "It was never my
intention to injure you."

"Only humiliate me," said Trassan. "And kill my employees by sabotage."

"A few unimportant lives are lost in any great venture," said Persin, "but to kill a man of your rank and talent? What do you take me for?"

"A Maceriyan cock," said Trassan amiably.

Persin shook his head dolefully. "Such language," he said. "A pity. I hoped you would be more refined. Have I not given you comfort with this fur? Do I not let your mage tend to you? I would have him save your life, if he can."

"Did your man not shoot me, right in the liver? Did you not drag me all the way back here rather than treating my wound where I fell?" said Trassan, mocking Persin's accent. "Why do you bother with your apologies? Envy of Vand motivates you. Envy is a cruel master. It takes away everything you already have while you are fixated on that which you do not. From plagiarist, to saboteur to murderer, you lose your honour when you could have remained a simple Maceriyan cock."

Persin shrugged. "Business and war are the same. I had hoped you would understand."

Trassan propped himself up a little further on his elbow, bringing forth a bark of disapproval from Vols. "I do understand. What do you expect? A noble handshake and a quip as I die? Fuck you, you Maceriyan windbag. You pompous, fat, envious prick. Fuck you to death."

The effort of this invective was exhausting. Trassan sank back. His eyes were so heavy. "I should sleep," he said.

"Do not!" Ilona urged. "Trassan, wake, please!"

"I am very tired."

Persin was not done with him yet. He attempted to gloat now, but it was half-hearted, and he looked nervously back at Shrane. With some satisfaction, Trassan realised Persin was out of his depth and could not control his mage.

"You do not deserve to win. The baubles you have taken here are nothing! The greatest store of knowledge is locked behind that door, out of sight of this world. My mage will open it, and you will see the prize that I have rightfully won!"

Vols' eyes opened wide. Ardovani stood. Persin's men backed away and brought up their ironlocks, ready to fire.

"She must not open that gate!" said Vols. "She must not!"

Vols' attention slipped from Trassan. The effect was immediate. Black dots swarmed his vision. Blood bubbled up in his throat. He coughed, the convulsions hammering spikes of pain into his chest. Blood splashed down his front as he gasped for air.

"Naturally, you would say that. And it is too late." Persin smiled widely and gestured behind him.

"Stop her!" shouted Vols at Persin's men. "There is something on the other side, something malevolent!" The mercenaries wavered, their guns dropped a fraction.

"He's a mage," one said doubtfully.

"He's more than that," said another. "He's the God-Driver's kin." Too many glances were cast in Shrane's direction for Persin's comfort.

"Another word, and you die," said Persin, pointing to Vols. "Return your attention to your master and heal him."

Vols, conflicted, looked to Trassan for direction.

"Stop her," Trassan said. "Stop her. I'm done. I've made a terrible mess of it all. And to think I was worried about the bloody whistles."

Shrane slammed down her staff, and the ice burned. The floor around the platform cracked. Jets of steam blasted upwards. A beam of ruby flame, twisting in on itself, lanced out from the crystal at the tip of her staff, slamming into the untarnished covering on the gate. The centre glowed.

"You really should make her stop," said Vols.

"Too late," said Persin with a smile.

The cap shattered, falling away in black pieces that went to dust.

Vols threw up his hand. An invisible shield arced over the Karsans, the handful of mercenaries standing guard and Persin, just as a deadly radiance blasted from the gate, incinerating men, crates, tarpaulins, ropes, artefacts—everything in the room that was not either Shrane or the gate. The jets of steam exploded into geysers that bored through the ceiling. Chunks of ice fell down around the edges of the hole, splashing to slush on Vols' shield. The chamber convulsed, shrinking in on itself as the world underwent a fundamental shift.

The corridor leading back to the city shattered with a great cracking roar, compressed in an instant as whatever magic that stretched out that part of reality beyond its natural dimensions spectacularly failed.

The light died back. The gate opened wide, the circle spreading out into a broad ellipse that touched the melting walls of the gate room. Streams of water pouring down from the city, were lit red by fire on the far side, for there was a plain of black rock, volcanoes fountaining lava into skies of smoke that glowed from within.

Upon the plain was an army. A million metal monsters ready to invade the Earth. Shimmering ripples skated over the surface of the image, lessening by the second.

"By the driven gods," said Persin. "What have I done?"

Vols' shield dropped. Ice creaked dangerously all around them. A huge crack ran up the wall where the corridor had been, choked with lumps of ice. On the other side came the rattling, tinkling rumble of structures collapsing. The City of Ice groaned. Its final minutes began.

Trassan laughed. Pain attempted to defeat his mirth, but he overcame it. "Persin, Persin, see what envy brings you?"

"The gate is stabilising, they will come through in seconds," said Vols, staring at the rift. "I am sorry," said Vols to Trassan, and leapt at Adamanka Shrane.

SHRANE MET VOLS in flight with a sound like two immense steel drums colliding. They stopped, instantly, halted by the collision of their wills. Hovering beneath the hole in the ceiling, a corona of lightning flashing around them, they commenced battle.

"The duel of mages!" said Ardovani. Trassan never ceased to be amazed by the magister's ability to find wonder in the most dire situation. With Vols gone, he had but a few minutes left.

"Well Persin, now what?" croaked Trassan.

Persin and his few remaining men looked around uneasily. One ran for the crack in the wall.

"I..." said Persin.

"Do you want to live or die?"

"What do you think Kressind?"

"You!" said Trassan as loudly as he could manage to one of the mercenaries. "Give my men their weapons. If you want to live, we have to work together. We can take you on the *Prince Alfra*, although I will see your master in court for this."

"My dogs, they are still outside," said Antoninan. "We can get to the ship."

"We could just take them," said a mercenary to Persin. "The others guard the vessel."

"For how long?" said Trassan. "How do you know our men have not overpowered yours?"

"If we kill them we must fight those metal giants on our own," Persin looked back warily to where the creatures waited patiently for the gate to open, rank upon rank of them. Hunched, iron things with coals for eyes and fists the size of barrels. "The shimmer on the skin separating this Earth from that other is almost done. They will come through soon." Persin looked to Ardovani for confirmation.

"The science of the Morfaan's world gates is beyond me, but that would seem logical."

"Vols may yet get the gate closed," said Trassan. "But we cannot rely on it. Go!"

Reluctantly at first, then with great haste, Persin's survivors handed over the Karsans' weapons. Persin had twelve men remaining, Trassan sixteen. Most of the Karsan ironlocks had been stacked on the far side of the room. But seven held by the mercenaries had survived, as had Ardovani's strange gun.

The chamber was a wreck. Everything modern made had been reduced to ash. Greasy smears on the discoloured, melting ice marked the deaths of Persin's other men. Precious artefacts of Morfaan steel were twisted skeletons, no more use than the ancient wrecks Arkadian Vand had pulled from the soils of Ruthnia. Pools of water gathered on the deformed floor. Lumps of ice tumbled down from the crumbling ceiling, while the ground groaned painfully, tortured to breaking point.

Four men linked hands under Trassan to lift him. He grunted at the pain as they bore him up, gripping Ilona's hand so hard she whimpered. He pulled her in close.

"Persin, he has my satchel. If nothing else survives from this trip, see that it gets to Katriona. Do you understand?"

"Yes cousin," she said. "Trassan, I am sorry."

He squeezed her hand a final time before letting go. "Not nearly so sorry as I."

With a terrifying crackle and boom the two mages intensified their efforts to annihilate one another. Bursts of lightning and less natural energies slammed into gouts of unearthly flame as the joined parties ran for the crack in the wall and clambered its shifting, dripping barrier of ice. They spilled out on the far side. The two mercenaries guarding Antoninan's sleds backed up, guns raised.

"Stop! Stop!" said Persin, huffing down the mound. "We are going together. All is lost. Shrane betrayed us."

About lay ruination. The city shook. The delicate, fluted web of the buildings was breaking apart. A musical tinkling of destruction rang out from across the convoluted streets and suspended pathways. Cracks spidered the dome, and as they watched a enormous expanse of it sagged inward and collapsed across the avenue with a resounding roar, barring their way back to the ship.

"We'll have to get out through the side of the dome," said Antoninan, running between his dogs and slashing at the hobbles the Maceriyans had placed on their feet. Others joined him, and soon the dogs were free. Antoninan waved his arm frantically. "Everyone on the sleds."

"There are too many!" shouted Persin, shoving at his own men in his panic. One hit him in the gut with a rifle butt, folding him in half.

His assailant looked Antoninan dead in the eye. "The dogs will manage," he said.

"On board, all of you!" commanded Antoninan.

The party scrambled onto the sleds as the city shook violently. Ice burst in sprays of crystal and water, sending fist sized chunks toward them. Several men were pelted, one fatally. They waited, desperate to go as Trassan was brought painfully over the mounded rubble of the wall and laid onto the lead sled as gently as possible. Trassan's contorted face suggested it was not gently enough. When he was aboard and tied down, Antoninan leapt onto the driver's perch behind him.

"Out! Out!" said Antoninan. "That way!"

He cracked his whip over the dog's heads.

Valatrice refused to move, but lifted his head high, nose twitching. A flick of Antoninan's whip across his flank drew a quiver from his leg, but he still did not set out.

"Move damn you, move!" bellowed Antoninan. A triangular lump of ice as big as a temple steeple fell from the dome less than a hundred yards away. Its point speared the ground and the whole toppled sideways, smashing artful tracery that had stood for aeons into nothing.

Antoninan whipped Valatrice again, and again. The other dogs whined and hunkered down, tails curling between their legs.

"Why... does... he... not... go?" said Trassan, his breaths were a saw dipping in and out of his ribcage.

A final time Antoninan whipped his lead dog. The mighty dray gave him a penetrating stare and showed his teeth. "Not that way, fool. This way."

With that he reared onto his hind legs, forelimbs pawing as he took the strain of the sled. He howled, and his teammates and the drays on the second sled responded, standing themselves, or leaning into their harness to tug the sleds into motion. The sleds rasped into motion, crushed ice complaining under their runners, then picked up speed. The dogs pulled hard, claws scrabbling at the ground until they were going fast enough to jog, then run. Valatrice barked loudly and added in perfect Karsarin.

"Hold fast, this will not be easy."

He plunged down a dark street that seemed to go nowhere. The second sled followed. No sooner had it left the avenue and sped into the deeper city than the buildings behind them collapsed into a millions shards, and the dome was quick to follow.

VOLS IAPETUS GLORIED in his might. No longer did his ability slink from him like a fox in the night, but rushed into the embrace of his mind to be directed as he saw fit.

The Iron Mage sent a wave of magic that burned him, impossibly infused with the spiritual essence of iron, the magic-killer. He swung out his arm, imagining a fountain of sparks to stay the wave, and so it was. His will imposed upon mundane reality the form and effect he desired. From somewhere beneath the realm of matter and being he took the power, and he felt it give as the world was rewritten to his design. As they fought, they rose higher. This was her desire, but he gave into it, reinforcing it with his own talent, so that they flew on the air as surely as if it held them up in its hands. Up they went, up through the hole in the roof into the cold. His eyes shone with magic, and he imagined Shrane slipping from the wind to be dashed to pieces on the hard ice below them. She fell, then checked herself, and flung a spear made of blue light towards his heart.

"The scion of the god-driver!" she mocked, and she spoke into his heart. "Let us see what makes you!" Reality became plastic under the opposing efforts of their will, screaming strange atomic screams. Their beings bled out into the fractures and thus into one another. Her thoughts were his, and his hers.

He saw a childhood spent with a dying hag. Snatches of a long, lonely life spent treading back and forth across red sands. A life spent in hiding, alone, cleaving to a creed she no longer believed in. One aim was ever in her mind, never thought to be realised, but embraced fully now it had arrived. Diligence rewarded by fate, she was destined, or believed herself to be. Such people were the most dangerous of all.

In her turn, this is what she saw of him: a life of missed potential, a boy that disappointed all, and when his ability failed to grow, ridiculed. A red fox named rabbit by his tormentors, a dreamer frightened of his dreams. Children mocking him in their fear and disdain. No friends, no lover, no confidence. Threaded through every memory that shamed him was the magic that would not obey his call.

Viciously, she tapped into these insecurities and threw them into his face.

"You are nothing!" she half sung, a croon of despair. "See how little you are, child of heroes. You shame your ancestor with your weakness," and her voice merged with a memory of his mentor, his face sunken with disappointment and his words, though spoken in anger, taken to heart. Vols remembered his tears.

Vols shrank back as his past attacked him. *I cannot do this, I cannot do this*, he thought. *I cannot do anything. I am not Res Iapetus. I cannot. I am not Res Iapetus. I cannot do this.*

So many times he had said, *I cannot do this.* To every farmer with a failing crop, to every government minister facing a crisis, to every parent with a sick child, to every mother with a missing daughter.

He fell, the gravity of failure clawing him from the sky. Shrane saw his weakness, and streamers of blue and gold fire roared past his ears, barely dispelled. The ground rushed up at him. Through the glare of the gate he saw the things from beyond. They stood motionless, awaiting the opening of an entrance barred against them for eight thousand years. They were patient. He felt determination more pervasive than the cold. An elemental patience, solid as the rock and as indomitable as the sea.

"I have waited for them. I, Adamanka Shrane, last priestess of the Iron Church, and they chose me! Who are you to defy me, failure? Disappointment. Weakling."

She tossed him upward. The city dwindled to the size of a model. He tumbled helplessly as straw doll. Hurricane winds snatched at him, rolling him around the sky.

"They come into this world to reclaim what was stolen. This is their Earth, not the Morfaan's, nor man's. They are the children set to inherit, and they will be denied their birthright no longer!"

He shared the pain as Shrane's soul burned—the toll of her toxic magic. Her gift was impure, not like his. Not innate but placed into her by foul means. The source of her ability was a canker in her soul. While her body revelled in triumph, her ghost shrieked as it was consumed. There was so little of her left, the cries were whispers.

Shrane let the winds drop, and he fell again. He was so intimately connected to her, more so than the most ardent of lovers, he knew she would not snatch him from death again. She was done with toying with him. He would die, and then the world would burn.

I cannot do this, he thought again, *but I must.*

Somehow, thinking of others made it right. The cause of his failure had always been about his own failings. He saw that now. This was something that had to be done, no matter how he felt.

Selflessness loosed his will.

Magic bloomed in him with the glory of a thousand dawns.

He stopped four feet from the ground. For a second he spun slowly around, feet pointing skywards, then he righted himself, and flew upwards. He pulled moisture from the clouds, moulding it into daggers of hard water that spewed from his outstretched hands in multitudes.

"I am not Res Iapetus," he thundered. "I can never be Res Iapetus!" The daggers streamed from his fingers with murderous speed. "I am Vols Iapetus, and you shall find me mighty enough."

With her iron stave Shrane batted his daggers to spray, but they were too many to all be destroyed. One pierced her shoulder, another her thigh. She dropped, recovered, then fell steeply as Vols smote her with a blast of power that stripped flesh from her body, neck to hip, exposing glistening muscle and creamy bone. Screaming, she plummeted down, crashing into the wreckage of the dome around the gate.

Vols alighted next to her, his body thrumming with potential. She lifted her strange, semi-human face, stranger now for its mutilation. "So you find your strength at last," she said. "It will not be enough. I am but a half. When you face the whole, you will fail." She smiled with elation at something behind him.

Vols was too late. The spirit of the Earth retched as something repugnant pierced the membranes of space and time. A spear of light roared into the heavens, blasting apart the blue of the sky until the dark of night was revealed. The light shut off, air rushed back in on itself with a sonorous peal. A dome of light bloomed from the gate, racing across the ground toward him. For a second before he was torn to pieces, Vols stood upon the soil of a black world of fire and fume, surrounded by an army of iron things radiating heat enough to cook him. A corresponding hole opened in the pall of smoke shrouding the sky, and he found himself looking up at the Earth.

The Twin, he thought, as he choked on unbreathable air. I'm on the Twin.

Vols' body was atomised. The space between the Earth and the Twin was compressed to nothing. To the sounding of brazen trumpets, the Draathis began their march.

The Gates of the World were open.

CHAPTER FORTY-NINE
The Heart of Mists

METAL LIMBS SCREECHING, the Draathis advanced, preceded by a wall of withering heat. Hot breath shimmered. Its mouth and eyes shone with the searing glare of molten metal. It punched at the walls as it came, shattering marble and exotic minerals. The floor cracked and blackened under its feet. Garten could not comprehend how it could move. It looked like nothing more than a crude statue given life, a half-finished work executed by a mediocre artist. But move it did, and fluidly, accelerating into a hunched, clanging jog that shook the castle.

"Run!" Josan screamed. "Run!"

She grabbed his arm, and they sprinted away from the creature, but they were fowl before the dracon; it would catch them in five long strides. Garten's fear threatened to kill him. His legs wobbled beneath his body, refusing to bear his weight.

Josan stopped by a smooth door of mother of pearl; he skidded into her, knocking her hand away from the doorhandle. She looked behind them as she groped to open it. Inner eyelids nictated rapidly over her eyes. Garten saw she was as terrified as he was. The Draathis was upon them, and swung back its fist to strike. The door banged open. Josan yanked him through, slamming it behind. The roar of the Draathis cut off.

They were by a window, high up a tower. The room seemed to serve no practical purpose, being very small. There was barely enough room for he and Josan to stand side by side. A small window looked out onto the seething mist. A narrow stair led downward.

Garten expected a smoking iron fist to smash through the delicate door, but there was no sign of the Draathis.

"We can evade it, if we are stealthy," said Josan. "You must follow me. Do not open any door. The ways of the castle are not straight. Only I can take them. You will be lost."

"Why did you take me from the hall of the gates? We need to leave!" he said.

"Yes, we do," she replied. "There is nothing here that can stand against it. Our cause is lost, but there is something I cannot abandon."

"Then what? Back to the hall?"

"First we have to lure it away from the gates. It should be easy, the Draathis hate my kind and it will pursue me until I am dead. Its hatred will be our salvation. We might escape because of it," she said.

"Are there more? What if one stands guard and waits for us?"

"If there were more, we would have seen them." She leaned out of the window and looked around. It had no glazing, and the sill was slick with moisture. Garten could see nothing past her shoulder but vaporous blankness. "The gate was damaged. To get through it like that from the World of Form, it must have had help from the World of Will." She pulled her head back into the room. "The mage. She was waiting. It was a trap. She must have known I would do anything to save Josanad. I revealed the location of a gate to her. Once, one of the Draathis would have posed little threat to me, but now? I have no weapons, I am alone."

"Do not despair," said Garten. "Or we will die." He took her hand. It was curiously dry and rough.

"Despair is all that is left. Today I am witness to the last hopes of my people burning in the flames of the Draathis. We must get away, or the Morfaan will die and your people will follow."

She pulled herself free of Garten's grip and headed for the stairway without another word. Garten could only run behind, Tyn Issy's lantern-like box jounced in his hand as he went round and round the stairs.

"You cannot trust her," said the Tyn.

"We do not have much choice," said Garten.

"This place is a lie, Garten. The Morfaan bend things to forms more pleasing to them. They use everything they encounter, be it magic, worlds, or people. These stairs will go on and on far longer than you might think, or stop suddenly, depositing you far away—and I mean very, very far away—for reasons no other than caprice, and damn the cost. Nothing they do is straightforward. They were created to be perverse; creativity is their function. They are intentionally unbalanced, but without check they have wrought untold harm on so many places. This world they have made is an abomination. To create this refuge, they stole land from another place, and another time. Such things can kill stars and all their children if done without care, and the Morfaan are rarely careful."

"What do you expect me to do?" said Garten. Issy was right, the stairs went on, growing darker.

"Be careful," said Issy.

"My dear Goodlady Tyn," said Garten. "I really do not know how much use that advice will be."

Light engulfed them. The stairs ended. Garten ran after Josan into a huge hall full of golden radiance. Enormous gems, each fashioned into a teardrop shape, hovered over the flagged floor, nailed in place by rays of light. Josan headed for the centre of the room where the biggest gemstone floated. An opal, alive with inner, kaleidoscopic fire.

"Oh no," said Tyn Issy. "Oh no oh no."

Josan ran to the gem. It hovered trapped within a beam of gold just above head height. She reached up and plucked it from its surrounding ray of light. As soon as the gem left the beam the light was extinguished. Gems plummeted from their stations, cracking into the marble. The hall plunged into darkness a moment, until a glow kindled itself in the gemstone, lighting Josan's hands pink and softening the dark.

"This is the Heart of Mists, the last hope of all Morfaan," she said, holding it out to show him. "Now we can leave."

"Garten, don't let her take that back into the world," said Issy.

"Why?"

Issy made a frustrated noise. "I can't say!"

They ran toward a tall portal that hissed open as they neared. Screaming violated their minds. Four voices calling out in terror floored them both. The Heart of Mists bounced across the floor as Josan fell. Garten regained his feet, clutching his head. Josan was worst affected, and writhed on the ground.

"Lady Morfaan?" he said.

"It... It is killing the Council!"

Garten staggered as a violent agony stabbed him in the temple. She screamed.

"Lord Mathanad! He is dead!" moaned Josan.

The castle shook. Garten heard beasts roaring in the distance outside.

He grabbed Josan under the elbow and pulled her to her feet, dragged her to where the Heart of Mists lay on the floor.

"Don't let her take it!" said Issy.

"No!" said Josan. With trembling hands she plucked it up, and they stumbled from the hallway into another corridor, through yet another door, and down a short flight of steps. Garten could make no sense of the castle's architecture. Now they were in a gallery, looking down on the courtyard. The tree was felled, its creamy stone branches shattered. Lord Mathanad's statue was a smoking ruin. The Draathis was pounding at another, that of the insane Lord Solophonad. The stone cracked. Another bone-curdling shriek blasted Josan and Garten as the statue exploded. A green ghost shot skywards, blasting aside the mist and sending it into violent turmoil, but there it stopped. Solophonad's essence had nowhere to go, no way out of the bubble world, and it rushed from one side of the limited sky to the other, taking brief form at the end of each traverse, before finally it dissipated with a cry more horrible than all the rest, staining the mists an eerie green and sending flickers of queasy light throughout the whiteness.

The Draathis went to assault the statue of Helisin. It grabbed the head. The Draathis was so lumpen looking Garten expected unthinking violence, but the Draathis took its time, shifting its grip, searching the statue for the weakest point, all while Helisin screamed and screamed.

"Stop!" screamed Josan. "Stop!"

The Draathis looked up at them with its soulless eyes. With a grinding of stone, it shoved the statue sideways from its plinth leaving it jammed against the wall. Evidently a living Morfaan was a greater prize, for it strode from the courtyard, kicking one of its precious doors to flinders and dragging its massive bulk through.

A terrible roar echoed up a staircase entering the long gallery. The glow of blacksmith's fires tinged the walls with orange.

"What now?"

Josan turned about in a panic. "I... I don't know."

"Think!" shouted Garten.

She swallowed, her head bobbed in that odd, dracon-like way. "This way," she said.

She ran for another door that slid up into the wall as she neared. The Draathis hauled itself up the staircase, iron hide scraping on the sides, fingers biting into stone and melting them with their heat.

They went into a long corridor covered floor to ceiling by delicate jade cameos set into the marble. Hundreds of thousands of faces looked out of the rock, all Morfaan.

"The Path of the Commemoration of the Beloved Dead," she said. "We should not go this way, but we have no choice," said Josan.

The Draathis followed, bursting through the doorway. It ran its hands along the cameos in the wall, shattering them and leaving their sockets smoking.

Josan moaned to see her ancestors' images defiled. Garten snatched her hand and tugged her along. The corridor was broken into shorter lengths by numerous low arches, each too small to admit the Draathis, but though they bought precious moments for the fugitives, the arches only slowed the Draathis for as long as it took to smash its way through. The racket of demolition harried them up the corridor.

"Are there not more of your magic doors?" he said.

"No. Only the straight way now," she said breathlessly. Her face was lined with pain. She clutched the Heart of Mists to her chest like an infant. "But we are nearly there."

The corridor curved, then straightened. The door at the end was so far away it look no bigger than Garten's thumbnail. "We'll never reach it," he said, slowing. His words came out between heaving gasps.

"Let me out," said Tyn Issy. "I will face it. But you must be away.

Once I have dealt with the Draathis, I will be a far more terrible enemy to you than it is."

"Do not free her!" said Josan.

"Let me out. Break my collar," said Issy heavily.

Garten stopped. The Draathis was stuck in an archway a hundred yards behind, pounding away at the stone. Marble shattered under the assault. In moments it would be through.

"Quickly! It will be through soon," urged Issy.

"I thought I could not."

"You can, if I allow it. You see, my friend. We do not go into slavery unwillingly. Do it!"

He placed the case on the floor and opened the outer door, then unsnapped the catch holding the inner cage door closed. Issy gave him an unsettling grin. Garten paused.

"Your geas," he said.

"I can contain myself long enough for you to be away. Technically, we are not on the Earth any longer, and so technically the geas do not hold so strongly."

"Technically?"

"Technically. Your choice. Your chance."

"She will kill us both!" said Josan. "These Y Dvar are sworn enemies of my kind."

"Your people have a lot of enemies," said Garten. He opened the door. Issy extended her neck with her head on its side. Delicately, Garten undid the tiny clasp holding her collar shut. His fingers brushed her skin, sending a pleasurable tingle up his arm. He feared to harm her she was so small, but no sooner was the collar undone—a little bit of wire, that was all it was—then Issy drew in a deep breath, and swelled in size.

"That's better," she said, her voice deepening. "That's better!" She stepped from the cage, growing as she did, miraculously emerging as large as human woman. Now she was as big as he, Garten was struck even more by her beauty. She could indeed have passed for a goodlady, and one any man would have been glad to accompany her. Then her eyes shone, and she opened her mouth, displaying her sharp teeth, and the illusion was gone.

"Away with you Garten Kressind," she said. "I quite like you and your funny little family. I really don't want to eat you." She continued to grow, her human form melting away. Her limbs stretched, her head thinned, and she transformed into a shining creature made of sparkling light.

"Hello little Draathis," she said. The iron monster smashed its fist through the apex of the arch, bringing down a shower of stone on its broad shoulders. It pushed through the rubble, and stood tall. "Come to auntie." The shape of Issy's new body was lost in its own radiance. Garten had the impression of wings spreading, or perhaps long arms clad in shining raiment, then Issy blazed like the sun, and he was forced to turn away.

"What have you done?" said Josan. "You have set it free!"

"I did what I had to," said Garten. He took her arm and dragged her into a reluctant jog.

"You do not know what they are," she said.

"Then perhaps you should have told me," said Garten.

They reached the door and fell through it as Issy struck the Draathis with calamitous impact.

They found themselves back in the Corridor of Gates. The acrid stink of hot metal polluted the air. Some of gates that had not been smashed by the Draathis were active, their edges defined by light seeping around them, but the ones Josan wanted were dark. When she opened them there was only bare marble behind. She swore in her own tongue.

"This one will have to suffice," she said, pointing at a door that was lit. "It leads back to the World of Will, at least." The castle shook, and a tremendous blaring came from the Path of the Dead. The lights of the gates blinked and flared. "The magic of the castle is fading. The locks are breaking. I only hope that the gates left on the Earth will remain closed a while yet."

"The Draathis could be coming through now," Garten said, imagining an army of those things let loose in Ruthnia.

"Not yet. We have time." She yanked open the door. More dazzling light was behind. Garten resolved then and there to spend some time in a dark room once he got home. "Go through. I will meet you. Find somewhere safe to wait for me. Stay an hour, no more. If I do not come by then, then I will not be coming."

"Leave with me," he urged. "Staying here is suicide."

"I have to save Josánad, what is left of him. Do not attempt to convince me against this course of action. He is my love, and I will not listen. Do not come back through the gate."

"Wait!" he said. But she pushed the Heart of Mists into his arms, and shoved him hard through the door. Unlike before, there was no sense of a tunnel here. Nothing met his feet, and he fell through a void of light. He caught one final glimpse of Josan peering down at him from the door, high above, and heard the roaring of the Draathis. Then she shut him out of her world.

He fell for an age, until suddenly he found himself trying to breathe water. A storm of bubbles bore him upward, he turned over and over, clutching at the Heart of Mists like his life depended on it, but still there was no air. His vision swam, became patchy, and went black.

Garten came to on a beach walled by cliffs. Hot sun beat down upon him. The sea shushed on the shore. Taking the great opal under one arm he fled the sand, not halting until he found a vantage point up on the cliffs.

From the clifftop he watched the beach for far longer than an hour, until the sun plunged its fiery orb into the bosom of the sea.

Josan did not emerge.

CHAPTER FIFTY
A Very Fine Vessel

THE DOGS RAN hard, the sled slewing behind Valatrice and his team. Ice shattered on every side of them, tumbling down in glinting, deadly falls. The narrow streets of the city echoed with the tumult of destruction. The passengers were silent, grimly holding on, snow-stung eyes fixed forward. Ice growled and screamed as it fell to pieces, the sonorous noise of the city's collapse a carillon of destruction. Antoninan held helplessly to the rail of the driver's perch as Valatrice led the dogs without his direction.

"Halt, Valatrice! Valatrice! You will kill us all!"

The giant dray paid him no attention, intent on his own course, left, right, left again, the sled tipping onto one runner and slamming into walls as Valatrice switched course again and again, taking them down a seemingly random route, the second sled following his lead.

But random it was not.

"The sun!" shouted Ilona. A broad sweep of daylight sliced the dome wall, shining in through a tall crack to illuminate the jagged fragments of buildings. Rainbows rose from the destruction, hanging on the sprays of ice crystals filling the air but the catastrophe was not yet done. At the sight of daylight Valatrice pulled harder, the dogs panting explosively as they put all their efforts into the harness. The dome overhead trembled, ice snapped apart musically. The crack ran crookedly up the wall, opening up the roof. Great chunks fell from the sundering, and slowly, the dome there began to collapse.

Valatrice let out a bark. The dogs heaved harder. The sled flew up a ramp of crushed ice and snow, out through the dome wall and into the sunlight. The second followed half a second later as the dome fell inward. Once indestructible, now it seemed as fragile as fine porcelain. From the rear of the city, a column of light stretched into the sky, piercing the blue and disappearing beyond it.

"Run! Run! Run!" shouted Valatrice. His dogs obeyed, though it taxed them hard, and their pink tongues lolled long.

"To the ship, get us to the ship!" shouted Persin. Valatrice had already turned toward the docks, running parallel to the massive dome as it cascaded into final ruin, crushing everything inside. They came round the front of the city, unable to see the ship at first beyond the heaped ice of the ruined entrance cavern and the clouds of ice particles billowing from the city. Ice had spread itself across the flat ground between city and docks, and Valatrice was forced to take them around it, nigh to the edge of the water. Shouts of dismay went up from the passengers, Maceriyan and Karsan alike.

There was Haik's ice-bound schooner, but of the iron ship, there was no sign. The camp was wrecked, much left behind. Bodies were scattered around the dockside, Ishamalani sailors, Maceriyan bravos, Olberlander mercenaries.

Valatrice plunged on, skirting the water's edge.

"There she is!" shouted Darrasind. Bannord leapt from the still moving sled, along with others. Antoninan called to his dogs to stop. Finally, they obeyed.

The *Prince Alfra* had descended the slope of water, and was making at full speed toward the channel that led out under the wall of ice.

"They're escaping. I cannot say that I blame them," said Bannord. He spat into the snow. "I suppose they'll hide out down there until the next low tide, then sail away.

"The caverns do not completely fill with water?" said Persin.

"Not that it's any of your business you murdering bastard, but I suppose not," said Bannord. "We're going to have to look to our own survival." He addressed the mixed group on sleds. "Men, get these supplies gathered up. Anything that might be useful. Quickly now, I've a feeling we'll not be alone for long."

"What are you doing?" said Persin. "Who are you to command these men?"

"I'm an officer in the Karsan Maritime Regiment, that's who, and you're an inch away from being shot," Bannord said. Persin's hired guns halted, torn between moving at Bannord's command and heeding their employer.

"He's right," said Antoninan, switching to his native Maceriyan to win over his countrymen. "We'll need everything we can find to survive."

"We could descend the ice, wait for them to come out," said Darrasind.

"We'll be caught and killed before that happens," said Ardovani. "We have to flee."

Antoninan looked at the mixed band of men, so recently thrown together. Despite him sharing nationality with some, their mistrust of him was all too obvious. "This is no longer about pride or nation," said Antoninan, "but simple survival. You're either with us, or you can stay here to die. There is no other option."

One of them pointed his gun at Antoninan. "We could kill you all, and take your sleds. We could catch the ship, or wait for our comrades aboard the other two vessels of our expedition."

Antoninan strode up to him aggressively, arms out, and pressed his chest against the gun's barrel. "What is your name?"

"Mazarine," said the man, eyes narrowed.

"Go on then, Mazarine. Kill me. Do you know the way north? It looks like your fellows are dead, and in all likelihood the *Prince Alfra*'s crew will kill you too. If you cannot rendezvous with the *Prince Alfra* or your fellows, what will you do then? Only I know the way to the Sorskian passage. Without me, you are doomed. Without me, Ruthnia is doomed. I am the greatest polar explorer ever to have lived, and you would kill me? Kill me, you kill your mothers and your fathers, your sweethearts and your children. For if we do not return, then the knowledge of this threat will remain unknown until it is too late. Can you imagine what those things will do to Ruthnia?"

The man was unconvinced. The iron ship was nearing the channel. He kept his ironlock on Antoninan. Valatrice growled. The other dogs lay on the ice, chests heaving from their sprint, but he stood, fur bristling.

"I offer a simpler choice," the great dog said. "Kill him, and I will kill you."

His dogs stirred, yellow eyes fixing on the mercenaries.

Valatrice's words cowed Persin's men, and the rifle was lowered.

"Do you have your own dog sleds?" asked Antoninan.

Mazarine nodded. "We concealed them to the east. Three."

"Then fetch them, and be back here swiftly. Take the supplies, the crates, everything!" said Antoninan. Hesitantly at first, the men obeyed, working with greater speed when Bannord pointed to the north. A high column of steam rose into the still sky there, filling the sky with a menacing rumble.

"They are coming," Bannord said. "Mazarine, be quick."

The Maceriyan nodded, and set off at a jog with a handful of his fellows.

Trassan watched all this with disinterest. The arguments of men no longer applied to him, he had his own journey to make.

"Ilona," he said, faintly surprised at how weak his voice had become.

His cousin came to his side, solemn faced, and he groped for her hand, gripping it feebly.

"Tell Veridy I truly loved her. You will do that for me?"

Ilona nodded, her eyes filling with tears.

Trassan turned from her, and with the last of his strength lifted his head so he could watch the *Prince Alfra* enter the stone channel, and pass from sight under the crust of snow. A banner of glimmer-polluted steam trailed behind it for a moment after it had gone, and then spread apart and vanished.

"She was such a very fine vessel. Father always warned me against overreaching myself." He smiled ruefully. "I suppose I did in the end. But it was a fine ship. Make sure you tell the world that I, Trassan Kressind, made it, and not my arse of a master, Vand."

Ilona nodded, biting her lip.

A look of contentment suffused Trassan's features. His eyes closed, and he never spoke again. Trassan continued to breathe while the sleds were stacked and their loads tied down. Mazarine returned, Trassan was lifted gently and placed atop Valatrice's sled, but none could rouse him. The Draathis were coming from the gate, black on the snow, the immense heat of their iron bodies vapourising the ice into a spreading fog. He saw this, though not with mortal eyes.

"Can we survive?" he heard someone say.

Not I, he thought.

"First, we must outrun them," said Antoninan. "We best pray they are slow. Valatrice, to the east, then north. If we can get onto the pack ice, we should be safe."

I will not, he thought. The pain had gone. The sled hissed over the snow and the skies opened to Trassan. He saw the way clearly, he needed no Guider to help him on. What was revealed elated and scared him, but he had no choice but to leave.

Trassan needed no ship for his next voyage.

His ghost streaked heavenward as the sleds picked up speed, the dogs labouring under the weight of men and goods. They would suffer for their exertions in the days to come. Trassan understood that, as he understood so many things he had not while he still lived. Terrible things would happen. He saw that, for the future was open to him now. But nothing of the Earth seemed particularly important any more.

Only one other saw the architect of the *Prince Alfra* depart. Tullian Ardovani followed Trassan leaving this world, a faint outline heading up into the sky and onward into a place his vision could not penetrate. On top of the pile of lashed boxes, Trassan's breathing stilled.

Ardovani closed his eyes and silently wished Trassan's ghost well.

Ardovani would tell Ilona later that her cousin was dead. For now, he stared resolutely at the northern horizon, away from the approaching army of Draathis and the end of the world.

CHAPTER FIFTY-ONE
Madelyne Transformed

MADELYNE AWAITED HER fate with her head hung. The duke seemed in no hurry to deliver it. He looked at the blind on the window of the carriage as if he could see through it, listening to the bells ringing all over the city.

"There will have been lights in the Godhome from my confrontation with Andrade's ghost," he said. "They will think the gods are returning." The duke stared at Madelyne. She felt the heat of his gaze on the top of her head. She dared not meet it. "What balance have you tipped, I wonder, with your little adventure?"

Madelyne shook. Blood from her wounded arm soaked through her tattered clothes and into the upholstery of the seat. Fibres of cloth stuck in her wound and pulled painfully whenever she moved it.

"Are they wrong? Andrade is back already," she said.

"That was not Andrade, not in full, only a remainder. Even gods have ghosts, Madelyne. If you had encountered the living Andrade, you would be on your way to one of the many hells by now. You met a wraith, a glimmer of her power, that is all."

"I would have perished anyway. I am lucky," she said. "You saved me." She met his eyes, though it took all her courage.

"I did," said the duke, his expression stony. "Maybe I should not have. You lied to me. Women come to me to be loved! To be safe and cared for. They come for the chance of an eternity of bliss and companionship. They do not come to me to steal."

"Some do. Some come only for the money. They use you."

"No more than you have," he said.

"I am sorry. I promise I shall be good. Please." She slipped from the seat to floor where she knelt and rested her forehead on his thigh, her wounded arm stiff at her side. "I only did it because I promised Harafan. I almost did not. I never expected to... I... My feelings... I don't know what is happening to me."

The duke rested a heavy hand upon her neck, and stroked the base of her skull, toying with the links of her collar with a long fingernail.

"I know what is happening to you. You cannot help yourself."

She nodded miserably.

"Raise your head."

She looked up at him, hope in her red eyes.

"Do you think I was unaware of what you were about, Madelyne?"

She blinked, her lips parted, but she could muster no words. "I..."

"I knew you were lying from the start. Why do you think I chose you? Your scheme's brazenness fascinated me. Here, I thought, is a strong woman, one that is willing to endure torment for her own gain. Such will! I thought. She might have it in her to be my equal. What kind of woman puts herself into this situation?" He sighed and lifted the edge of the carriage blind with his finger and peered out. "There are women who greatly enjoy what I offer, and have come to me for that alone. Others seek my wealth and my position. Others yearn for deathless life—although curiously few. But you, you wanted to cheat me, I admit not directly, but you were dishonest nonetheless. Cheat a god! You did not want anything of mine, you had a goal of your own. I respected that. And still we have found affection for one another despite it." He dropped the blind back in place and looked down at her.

"Yes, yes we have!" she said. "I have."

"I know," he said. "I know."

She forced her hurt arm to bend so she could clasp her hands together under her chin. She bowed her head. "I know you. You are kind, and wise, and merciful. You could have left Harafan to die, but you saved him." The crust on her wound broke, and blood dripped into the carpet.

The duke watched the blood flow disinterestedly. "I considered it, he abandoned you. I would have burned his soul in front of him for that. But how would that have made you feel, if I had occasioned your foster brother's death?"

"I'm sorry," she began to sob. "I am hiding nothing else, please do not let this be my last test. Please."

He was silent. When he spoke next, his words were measured and portentous.

"Why do you wish to remain with me?" he asked.

"Because I love you."

"Another lie?"

"No! I swear!"

"It is not the acts of physical love? Not the money? Not immortality?"

"No, no. Those things I could find for myself elsewhere. It is you. You are why I wish to stay. You are no demon as they say, but a caring soul. I can see that you hurt. Let me stay with you, let me help you. I hurt also, in here." She put her hand on her heart. "I have never had anyone, not like you. Now Harafan has gone, we are both alone."

He nodded, and growled affirmatively. "Very well. And you promise me no more lies?"

"Never. Not one," she said earnestly. "For everything else I have told in all our discussions has been the truth."

"And will you take me as your only one, and remain true to me for all time?"

"There is no other like you. There is nobody that could tempt me. Take me back, and I will love only you."

He lifted her chin.

"And do you submit yourself to me completely, body, heart and soul, to be my companion and my plaything, to obey me in all things, and to follow me without question, come what may? To give yourself to me no matter what pain I may mete out to your body, or the discomfort I might put you to. That I might brand and whip you, and push you into the heights of exquisite agony?"

"I already agreed, at the beginning. I have not refused or departed."

"This is a new start, and it may last a long time, and there are many other tests yet to come. Do you submit yourself to me entirely?" he demanded.

"Yes," she said, sobbing. "Yes I will. I think I can. I am yours."

"And do you place me above yourself?"

"I am nothing. You are everything."

"And you do not speak only from terror of what I might do?"

"No. Not only."

The duke searched her eyes a long time and let out a sorrowful sigh. He let go of her face and looked away to hide his disappointment.

"You are telling the truth. That is unfortunate."

With a single, swift movement, he grabbed the top of Madelyne's head and twisted it with great force, shattering her neck. Her head lolled to the side, her final expression one of incomprehension.

The duke drew in a sharp breath through his teeth and shut his eyes. He was not without compassion, and her death hurt him.

Corpselight stirred around Madelyne's head. A being of green light rose from her body. Her soul's face was sad, full of questions she could not voice. The veils of life and death parted. A light shone from above, and the duke looked into the realm beyond with her. The next life beckoned. He looked into this place forever denied him, with its wonders and continuations, cruel extinctions and miraculous turns of fate. Madelyne rose toward it, but the duke grasped her ghost, digging his fingers deep into the stuff of her spirit. She looked down at him plaintively, eyes pleading, begging to be set free.

"I do not want someone to be mine entirely," the Infernal Duke told the ghost. "I seek someone who can take pleasure from all that life has to offer, pure and abominable. I wish to bend them, to see how far their spirit will go without breaking. You broke, Madelyne. You seemed so spirited. I will have not someone who will subsume their will to mine. I want a companion, not a slave. Gods need worship to live, my love, but I crave equality. You had to be tested. I am sorry that you failed. I would have given you the world in return for a further spark of defiance, but that was not to be."

The ethereal light shone where the carriage ceiling should be. A chorus of free spirits called to Madelyne from the other side of death's veil. She raised her arms toward them in a silent plea for help.

The duke would not release her. He stuffed a scrap of her being between his lips, and drew in a mighty breath. Madelyne's shade struggled as it was drawn degree by tortuous degree into the duke's mouth. His eyes glowed with her stolen soul's light. She could not speak but she keened quietly as she was consumed, her body and her limbs slipping down his throat. Then her head, ballooning as it was forced into his maw. His jaws distended as he sucked her down. The top of her head vanished, and the screaming stopped.

The light above went out, closing with the finality of a slammed door.

When the duke was done, he had an eighth skull on the chain at his neck. He parted his shirt to admire it. Ghostly eyes rolled madly within its empty sockets a moment, then faded away, and it became a glass bead. The duke tucked his new necklace into his shirt and looked at Madelyne's broken body in distaste, at her hands still clasped together in a final plea. After a moment's thought he opened the door and rolled her from the carriage with his foot. She flopped into the overgrown road. The bushes twitched with sinister movement. Red eyes blinked hungrily in their depths.

"Feast well," the duke said.

He looked up. Flickering witchlight still played over the underside of the Godhome. All over the city bells rang as Perus raised its voice in praise of the returning gods.

The duke pulled the door shut and hammered his cane's head into the ceiling of the carriage. "Markos! Home!" he shouted. "I have business in Karsa," he added to himself. The drays bayed loudly and the coach raced away into the night.

From the brush around Madelyne's corpse, the Wild Tyn emerged.

CHAPTER FIFTY-TWO
The Black Sands

FAR OUT IN the black sands, beyond any place trodden by human feet, a lone dracon rider rode up to the edge of a bluff of sandy rock. He pulled back on the reins, bringing his mount to a halt. It stamped from foot to foot and croaked, irritated that its run had been interrupted. Shushing and patting his mount into stillness, the rider lifted a battered brass telescope to his right eye and focused it upon the desert below.

Hundreds of leagues of glittering black sand rolled away into the east and west. Behind him were the broken nubs of ancient hills, worn down by relentless winds. North was where his attention went, toward a grey-green blur that walled the desert from horizon to horizon. Great mountains, huge and imposing, still hundreds of miles away, but so lofty their presence dominated all.

Heat haze wavered on the crests of dunes. Shining silver pools of false water collected in the troughs. It was hot in the far north. Beyond the mountains was more desert, and then more still, albeit of a less uncanny kind. Past that, the strange and mysterious lands of Ocerzerkiya, and the emperor there.

But there was no way through the mountains. No pass breached the High Spine.

The rider swept the glass back and forth, caught something, and panned back. He leaned forward in his saddle, causing his dracon to shift and chir. Movement in the desert. Through his glass, he spied a caravan of dozens of carts flanked by modalmen riding their great beasts. He ran the glass up the line, to where it faded into a spreading cloud of dust. He snapped the glass shut.

Rel Kressind unwound the scarf from his face. His skin was dark from the desert sun, a browner stripe across his eyes where his skin had tanned more deeply. Black sand stained the lines in his face, lending him years he had not yet experienced.

He cupped his hands about his mouth. "I see them!" he shouted. His voice spread out upon the hot breeze, smeared to silence by the immensity of the desert.

With a honking low, Shkarauthir's mount huffed its way up the steep slope to the ridge. Garau, the beasts of the modalmen were called. They were fast, but their odd arrangement of six legs did not suit steep hills and it complained all the way to the top.

"They're heading dead north, toward the High Spine. There." Shkarauthir shaded his eyes with two of his hands and looked where Rel pointed.

Among the many things Rel had learned of the modalmen was that their eyesight was weaker than a man's in daylight, and it took Shkarauthir a while to find the caravan.

"We shall go closer. We shall see."

"They are there. I have seen them."

"I see dust and smears."

Rel wheeled Aramaz about. "Can you not see your way to trusting me yet?"

"What is trust?" said Shkarauthir philosophically.

"You could look through my telescope, that would settle it."

"A modalman trusts no device," said Shkarauthir. "We shall see, when we go there."

"You just said, 'what is trust?'."

"Indeed," said Shkarauthir gnomically.

"Fine," said Rel. "But there they are, and they are going north, as we will presently see when we've wasted a day getting closer to look. You can head off my seething resentment by telling me what's up that way. Where are they headed? There are no passes through the High Spine to Ocerzerkiya, not that I know of."

"You do not know everything." Shkarauthir turned his mount around, and they descended the hill together. Aramaz darted around the garau's feet. It snorted in annoyance at the smaller beast. Aramaz croaked happily back.

"So you keep telling me," said Rel, giving up on his attempts to stop his dracon baiting the garau.

"They do not go to the far lands. They are headed to the fallen citadel."

Rel waited for more. "Yes? Is that it?" he prompted. "Fallen citadel? A bit more information please," said Rel, frustrated at Shkarauthir's unforthcoming nature.

"Like your fort of glass. A castle of our masters, broken."

"And, and?" said Rel. "What is there for them?"

Shkarauthir considered his answer a long time, or maybe he was making Rel wait for his own amusement. After a few months with the modalmen, he was beginning to suspect they might have a sense of humour.

"That is simple, small one," Shkarauthir said eventually. "They are on their way to the temple of the Brass God. And now, so are we."

Shkarauthir let out a whoop. His garau responded and broke into a lumbering gallop. Rel reined Aramaz in and let Shkarauthir get ahead to join up with his two clanmates at the foot of the hill. He pulled his scarf up over his face.

"Bloody modalmen. Bloody desert. I never should have screwed Goodfellow Dorion's wife," Rel muttered to himself, and sent Aramaz running after.

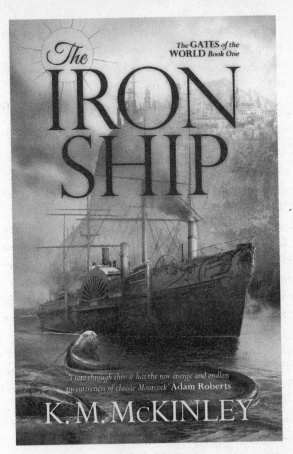

The GATES of the WORLD Book One

The IRON SHIP

'I tore through this: it has the raw energy and endless inventiveness of classic Moorcock' **Adam Roberts**

K. M. McKINLEY

ISBN: 978-1-78108-333-8

Merchant, industrialist and explorer Trassan Kressind has an audacious plan – combining the might of magic and iron in the heart of a great ship to navigate an uncrossed ocean, seeking the city of the extinct Morfaan to uncover the secrets of their lost sciences.

Ambition runs strongly in the Kressind family, and for each of Trassan's siblings fate beckons. Soldier Rel is banished to a vital frontier, bureaucrat Garten balances responsibility with family loyalty, sister Katriona is determined to carve herself a place in a world of men, outcast Guis struggles to contain the energies of his soul, while priest Aarin dabbles in forbidden sorcery.

The world is in turmoil as new money brings new power, and the old social order crumbles. And as mankind's arts grow stronger, a terror from the ancient past awakens...

This highly original fantasy depicts a unique world, where tired gods walk industrial streets and the tide's rise and fall is extreme enough to swamp continents. Magic collides with science to create a rich backdrop for intrigue and adventure in the opening book of this epic saga.

 WWW.SOLARISBOOKS.COM

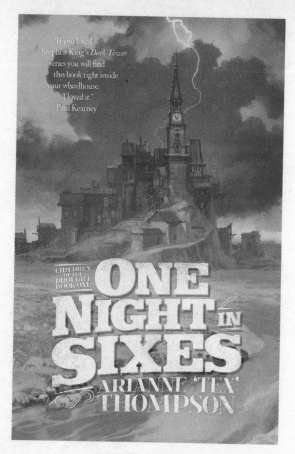

CHILDREN OF THE DROUGHT BOOK ONE

ONE NIGHT IN SIXES

ARIANNE 'TEX' THOMPSON

ISBN: 978-1-78108-237-9

Appaloosa Elim is a man who knows his place. On a good day, he's content with it. Today is not a good day. Today, his so-called "partner" – that lily-white lordling Sil Halfwick – has ridden off west for the border, hell-bent on making a name for himself in native territory. And Elim, whose place is written in the bastard browns and whites of his cow-spotted face, doesn't dare show up home again without him.

The border town called Sixes is quiet in the heat of the day, but Elim's heard the stories about what wakes at sunset: gunslingers and shapeshifters and ancient animal gods whose human faces never outlast the daylight. If he ever wants to go home again, he'd better find his missing partner fast. But if he's caught out after dark, Elim risks succumbing to the old and sinister truth in his own flesh - and discovering just how far he'll go to survive the night.

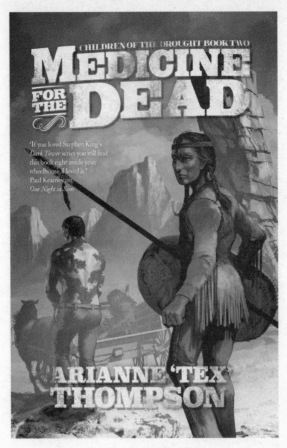

CHILDREN OF THE DROUGHT BOOK TWO

MEDICINE
FOR THE DEAD

'If you loved Stephen King's
Dark Tower series you will find
this book right inside your
wheelhouse. I loved it.'
Paul Kearney on
One Night in Sixes

ARIANNE 'TEX' THOMPSON

ISBN: 978-1-78108-306-2

Two years ago, the crow-god Marhuk sent his grandson to Sixes. Two nights ago, a stranger picked up his gun and shot him. Two hours ago, the funeral party set out, braving the wastelands to bring home the body of Dulei Marhuk. Out in the wastes, one more corpse should hardly make a difference. But the blighted landscape has been ravaged by drought, twisted by violence, warped by magic – no-one is immune. Vuchak struggles to keep the party safe from monsters, marauders, and his own troubled mind. Weisei is being eaten alive by a strange illness. And fearful, guilt-wracked Elim hopes he's only imagining the sounds coming from Dulei's coffin. As supplies dwindle and tensions mount, the desert exacts a terrible price from its pilgrims – one that will be paid with the blood of the living, and the peace of the dead.

 WWW.SOLARISBOOKS.COM

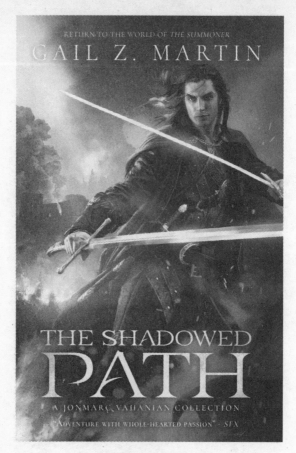

RETURN TO THE WORLD OF *THE SUMMONER*

GAIL Z. MARTIN

THE SHADOWED PATH

A JONMARC VAHANIAN COLLECTION

"ADVENTURE WITH WHOLE-HEARTED PASSION" - *SFX*

ISBN: 978-1-78108-438-0

Soldier. Fight slave. Smuggler. Warrior. Brigand Lord. You may have encountered Jonmarc Vahanian in the Chronicles of the Necromancer but you don't really know him until you walk in his footsteps. This is the start of his epic journey. A blacksmith's son in a small fishing village before raiders killed his family, Jonmarc was wounded and left for dead in the attack. He tried to rebuild his life, but when a dangerous bargain with a shadowy stranger went wrong, he found himself on the run.

Gail Z. Martin returns to the world of her internationally best-selling books with these thrilling tales of adventure and high fantasy, collected together here for the very first time.

 WWW.SOLARISBOOKS.COM

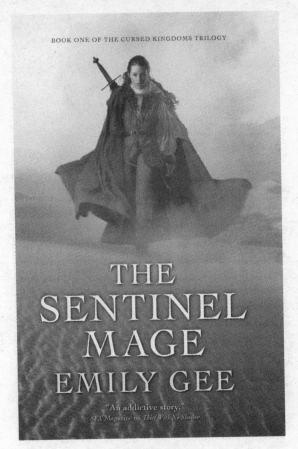

BOOK ONE OF THE CURSED KINGDOMS TRILOGY

THE SENTINEL MAGE

EMILY GEE

"An addictive story."
SFX Magazine on Thief With No Shadow

ISBN: 978-1-907519-49-9

In a distant corner of the Seven Kingdoms, an ancient curse festers and grows, consuming everything in its path. Only one man can break it: Harkeld of Osgaard, a prince with mage's blood in his veins. But Prince Harkeld has a bounty on his head - and assassins at his heels.

Innis is a gifted shapeshifter. Now she must do the forbidden: become a man. She must stand at Prince Harkeld's side as his armsman, protecting and deceiving him. But the deserts of Masse are more dangerous than the assassins hunting the prince. The curse has woken deadly creatures, and the magic Prince Harkeld loathes may be the only thing standing between him and death.

 WWW.SOLARISBOOKS.COM